Five interesting things about Rekha Waheed:

1. Born and raised in West London, Rekha graduated from SOAS, University of London, with a BSc. and Masters in Economics. She brings the intricacies of cosmopoitan, city-savvy, Brit-Asian Muslim experiences to the mainstream.

2. My family and friends used to call me the Ice Princess, a reputation that I busted with the release of my first chick lit book, *The A–Z Guide to Arranged Marriage*.

3. I'm driven by a hundred different dreams and find it impossible to relax.

4. I'm a planning freak who loves every type of food in the world, travelling and Chanel No. 5 perfume, and would make one brilliant E! News presenter.

5. I wish I could cook intuitively, without burning, over/under cooking or forgetting what ingredients, spices and herbs make for a good meal. Until then, I'm happy to continue to extend my encyclopaedic knowledge of the best restaurants in London.

By Rekha Waheed

The A–Z Guide of Arranged Marriage
Saris and the City

My Bollywood Wedding

Rekha Waheed

little
black
dress

Copyright © 2010 Rekha Waheed

The right of Rekha Waheed to be identified as the Author of
the Work has been asserted by her in accordance with the
Copyright, Designs and Patents Act 1988.

First published in Great Britain in 2010 by
LITTLE BLACK DRESS
An imprint of HEADLINE PUBLISHING GROUP

A LITTLE BLACK DRESS paperback

1

Apart from any use permitted under UK copyright law,
this publication may only be reproduced, stored, or transmitted,
in any form, or by any means, with prior permission in writing
of the publishers or, in the case of reprographic production,
in accordance with the terms of licences issued by the
Copyright Licensing Agency.

All characters in this publication are fictitious and any resemblance
to real persons, living or dead, is purely coincidental.

Cataloguing in Publication Data is available from the British Library

ISBN 978 0 7553 5614 0

Typeset in Transit511BT by Avon DataSet Ltd,
Bidford-on-Avon, Warwickshire

Printed and bound in Great Britain by
Clays Ltd, St Ives plc

Headline's policy is to use papers that are natural, renewable and
recyclable products and made from wood grown in sustainable forests.
The logging and manufacturing processes are expected to conform to the
environmental regulations of the country of origin.

HEADLINE PUBLISHING GROUP
An Hachette UK Company
338 Euston Road
London NW1 3BH

www.littleblackdressbooks.com
www.headline.co.uk
www.hachette.co.uk

'It takes half your faith to get married, and then the other half to stay married!' So said my mom in one of her many life lessons.

Mom and Dad – those life lessons are my constant source of strength, motivation and inspiration; thank you. My gratitude also extends to the Waheeds for your unwavering support, the Parvezs for your endless encouragement, and the Rahmans for the many laughs.

Specifically, I want to say a big thank you to Laura at MBA and Claire at Headline. Your advice and guidance are invaluable and always much appreciated.

Finally, 'My Bollywood Wedding' wouldn't have been possible without Nazim. Thank you for being my rock and making it a pleasure to keep the faith.

Translations

AsSalaamAlaikum	Muslim greeting
Azhan	Call to prayer
Bhabhi	Sister in law
Bhai	Older brother
Bhaji	Fried Indian fritter
Bhenjhi	Sister
Bheta	Son
Bhouna	Dry curry
Biriyanis	Meat mixed pilau rice
Chachi/Chachijhi	Paternal aunty
Chai	Tea
Chooris	Bangles
Dholki	Indian drummer
Dua	Prayers
Dupatta	Long chiffon scarf
Foopi	Paternal aunt
Haldi	Tumeric
Henna	Hen party
Hijab	Headscarf worn by Muslim women
Holud	Bachelor party
Jilbab	Long gown worn by Muslim women
Kaku	Paternal uncle
Kalaa	Maternal aunty
Kandaan	Entire family
Kara	Wide gold bangles
Khoothi	Dog
Lengha	Female Indian outfit: long ornate skirt and blouse
Mahr	Dowry
Mahram	Guardian
Masaala	Indian spices
Mendhi	Henna painting
Mitai	Indian sweet
Nikab	Face veil worn by Muslim women
Paancini	Engagement
Pagul	Crazy
Qawaali	Indian folk spiritual music
Ristai/Alaaps	Wedding proposal
Saya	Protective shadow
Shalwaar kameez	Indian female outfit, tunic over trousers
Sharwaani	Indian male outfit
Sylhethi	Of the Sylhet; Bangladesh city
Walimah	Wedding party thrown by the groom's family

Storyboard Chapters

There is no such thing as an absolute alaap; agree and arrange the wedding asap

My name's Maya Malik, and I'm a thirty-year-old ex-SLAAG. My peers have banished me from the single, lonely, ageing Asian girl's club to the promised land of the married because I now have the Absolute *Alaap*. This is the marriage proposal taken by a hopeful couple to their respective families to obtain the blessings from both sets of elders. For those of us who know better, singletons know that there is no such thing as an absolute *alaap*. Whilst I no longer have to hide from my mother's groom-searching methods, or search for the perfect man from the diminishing stock of eligible bachelors that consists of mummy's boys, closet gays and the emotionally disturbed, I still have to turn Jhanghir Khan, the man I love, into my *husband*. For there is no guarantee that the blessing will be given without conditions. You see, my biggest fear isn't my impending loss of female independence; it's the realisation that I have to navigate in-law expectations, dowry discussions and wedding communications not as a successful accomplished Brit-Bengali woman, but as a shy, modest, demure bride-to-be. Which, in all honesty, is quite a challenge. And whilst

I may no longer be a single or lonely or ageing Asian girl, I live in the stomach-churning, self-doubting, paranoid state of uncertainty, knowing I am still a long way from being married.

Naturally, my prayers will increase manifold to impress the good lord that I'm worthy of getting access to the promised land of the married. The traditional way, with the blood-red *lengha*, antique gold jewellery and a feast to rival all feasts. I just have to hold on to Jhanghir Khan long enough to have my perfect wedding dress, diamond and day that I have long waited for. Until then, I will invest heavily in Patience to reward me with the wisdom and grace to know when to keep my mouth shut and to remember that finding the right man does not naturally translate into happy ever after. For now the fact remains that I, Maya Malik, am getting married.

Everyone knows that Asian weddings are mired with protocols that are otherwise known as pitfalls. Traditionally, this is how it happens. The prospective groom gets his family to give an alaap to a prospective bride's family. An introduction is arranged, they meet, fall in love and both families manage the wedding discussions, which, when fast forwarded, result in happy ever after – or something close to that. In my case, I took a detour on the said protocol. I proposed to Jhanghir, in public, on stage in front of every possible elder in my family. Whilst it seemed like a great idea at the time, I dropped myself into a pit so deep I've yet to reach the bottom. The good news is that I've provided gainful employment for our Bengali community gossipmongers who have never been busier. The bad news is that the gossip is about me, or, rather, my 'desperate bid' to get married due to a) being pregnant, b) forcing Jhanghir's hand in marriage, or c) being pregnant and forcing Jhanghir's hand in marriage. Given that Chachijhi Fauzia, Baba's sister, gossips amongst the best, we hear the worst and each time we hear a new version of the truth, Amma fears the worst. The worst being Jhanghir's family retracting the *alaap*. That would be *the alaap* that's meant to be absolute.

'They're coming around,' Amma stated as she popped the cordless phone back on to its terminal. 'Officially.'

'Who's coming around?' I asked, catching the worried glance she exchanged with Chachijhi. 'Amma, who's coming . . . ?'

'Why couldn't you wait?' Amma asked as she sat at the breakfast table. 'I mean, Jhanghir is a good, decent boy; he would've proposed to you after the award ceremony, he would have done it the right way.' The mere mention of the award ceremony bought flashbacks of the year that had brought me to this point. Jhanghir and I met at uni and had that friendship that just stopped short of being anything more. Fear, doubt, stubbornness, pride – they stopped us from taking that step. He was the super-rich American Bengali studying medicine and I, the unsophisticated girl from the modest family. Yet, in spite of living in two continents, the years that passed did little to diminish our closeness. When reality slapped me into the realisation that I was going to lose him to another woman, I did the unthinkable. I jet-setted across the Atlantic to New York to stop his wedding. As if that wasn't humiliation enough, I chased after him until I broke with convention and asked him to marry me at a big art competition in front of family, friends and colleagues. When Jhanghir joined me on stage to agree, I knew we had something worthy of being a classic romcom. Only my family never ceased to remind me why breaking with convention had ramifications beyond the wildest of imaginations.

'This is true. So much of this rumour and gossip could've been avoided if you were patient, Maya.' Chachijhi, who happens to be one of the biggest gossipers in England, left me incredulous with disbelief. 'They all ask why rush? Why not wait for the boy to ask for your hand?'

'If most people knew the truth, actually, what I did was quite special.'

'You think this is a Bollywood film?'

I smiled at the idea that my onstage impromptu proposal would make for a stunning Bollywood epic. Only the mental image jarred to a stop when I caught Amma's glare.

'Oh, you think you're in some love-story Bollywood movie like *Ashwariya and Abishek*, and the rest of us will dance in the background to your songs like this?'

My jaw dropped at the sight of Chachijhi shaking her bootie. In plain English, and every other language known to mankind, what she was attempting to do was wrong. Not only did Chachijhi have the misfortune of being short and overly voluptuous, but she also lacked the grace and rhythm to pull off the bootie shake. Amma and I waited in disturbed silence for Chachijhi to finish.

'Jhanghir's family want to bring round a formal *alaap*,' Amma explained as Chachijhi parked herself on a stool and panted to get her breath back. 'His parents want to bring other elders in the family to reassure them that we're a good family and that there is no basis to the gossip.'

'But Jhanghir hasn't mentioned anything to me.' My heart plummeted at the realisation that my impulsive actions could very possibly cost me my marital bliss.

'He hasn't?' Chachijhi asked between deep, long breathes.

'Well, that's because he's a specialist children's

surgeon and he's busy finishing off his research paper before he flies back to New York,' Amma threw in, refusing to give Chachijhi ammunition to fuel the gossip surrounding me.

'They were here the day after Maya's Art Awards night where she proposed to Jhanghir, so why the need to visit again?' Chachijhi pushed. She leaned forward to ask me, 'He didn't tell you?' I shook my head and caught Amma's glance.

'It's not Jhanghir's job to defend us,' Amma stated, containing the situation. With Jhanghir's lapse in communication, she was giving me courage in the face of potentially losing an absolute *alaap*. But the fact remained that Jhanghir had failed to inform me of this development. 'If Jhanghir's family want to visit, then we welcome them with open arms. We have nothing to hide, nor do we have anything to be ashamed of. So, let the family know that we're hosting an *alaap* for Maya. In fact, let the community know, because this is an absolute *alaap*.'

Two days later and almost a year since the last *alaap* that I'd had at home, I found myself at the bay window in my parents' bedroom waiting for Jhanghir's family to arrive. My parents, along with my stunning twin sisters Jana and Hanna, our oldest sister Ayesha, and brothers Tariq and Taj, all waited anxiously in the living room. I, on the other hand, felt totally calm and prepared. This time, Hanna and Jana didn't have to school me on the appropriate outfit to wear. I chose the chiffon nude-tone *chooridar shalwaar kameez*, straightened my hair into a silken black blanket and applied the best of Bobbi Brown to leave me glowing with pure happiness. Nor did they have to prep me on the *ristai*'s bio data; I knew Jhanghir inside out. This time I was fully prepared. Pent-up nerves and cheeky rebelliousness fought at the thought of proving Jhanghir's family wrong and impressing them with our winning ways.

'That smile looks too naughty to be good.'

I laughed at Ayesha's comment and watched her enter the room. Younger than Tariq, Ayesha, at thirty-six, never failed as my trusted adviser. 'They're two minutes away.'

My heart and smile dropped at the announcement. This was it. Suddenly, the importance of the day dawned on me and I couldn't breathe. I held my sides and forced myself to take deep, long, slow breaths.

'I can't do this,' I whispered as the flutter of nerves in the pit of my stomach turned into a mass of butterflies on acid. 'They're going to watch me, judge me, and size me up and I care. I never cared before, but I care now because it's Jhanghir, and I care that they give their blessing,' I babbled as I paced the length of the bay. 'What if they change their minds?' There, I'd said it. The question that had plagued the entire family. The question that no one dared ask. And then, my courage failed me. I couldn't face rejection. I wasn't prepared for it. So I looked at Ayesha, and frowned. 'I can't do this,' I repeated, grabbing the edge of my parents' bed as the light-headed giddy feeling consumed me before I fell on to it.

'Maya!' Ayesha called out, rushing across to me. 'Amma! Hanna! Jana! Maya's fainted. She's fainted, oh my God, Maya's fainted.'

'I haven't,' I mumbled as I rolled on to my back and stared at the ceiling. Only the mumble wasn't loud enough. Within seconds the room was filled with every member of my family.

'Push her head down between her legs.' In an instant, I was flipped into a sitting position and forced to sit with my head between my legs as everyone shouted at once.

'Get some cold water.'

'Grab some raw garlic for her to chew herself back to her senses.'

'No, not garlic, mustard does the trick.'

'Throw ice over her, that'll bring her around.'

'She hasn't eaten ever since they called—'

'It's the stress, the tension,' Chachijhi finished, using her flimsy *dupatta* to circulate some air.

'Everyone move out of the room, she needs air, she needs to get herself together,' Jana shouted as she waddled into the room.

'I'm fine,' I muttered from the undignified position that I was forced to remain in.

'Yes, of course you are . . . look at you, you're wasting away,' Amma cried, using a small A5 diary to blow cold air in my direction. Her penchant for melodrama knew no bounds at the worst of times. 'How is she going to get married at this rate?'

'Maybe it's an omen . . .'

'Chachijhi, it's not an omen!'

'Your mother only sent Ayesha up so that Maya wouldn't stumble down the stairs on her bum like last year, and looked what happened. It's an omen . . .'

'It's not an omen,' I muttered, struggling to get myself free.

'What are we going to do with her? What are people going to say?' Chachijhi continued.

'Let go of me, I didn't faint and I'm fine!' I bellowed, bringing everyone to a sudden silence. I pushed the hand away from the back of my head so that I could sit upright and face the silence. I pushed my hair back from my face and breathed deeply before straightening up my clothes. The silence extended into an unforgiving quietness. 'I'm fine,' I repeated in a more reasoned, quieter tone.

'She's fine,' Hanna stated in a hesitant, disbelieving tone.

'She's fine,' Baba repeated, touching my forehead before pulling back at my glare.

'They're here,' Little Hamza added as he trundled into the bedroom.

'Who're here?' Amma asked.

My five-year-old nephew clambered up on to my lap and cupped my face to make me look at him. When I gave Tariq's son my full attention, he said, 'The people downstairs. I letted them in.' The silence that followed Hamza's answer felt unbearable. 'I letted them in, Foopi. I showed them to sit down and they asked for you, Foopi. I tell them everyone screamed, you fainted and everyone was making you better.'

'Hai Allah!' Amma cried falling on to the bed beside me. 'What are they going to think? The rumours about rushing to get married, and now they hear she's fainting!'

Chachijhi fell on to the bed beside Amma to fan her with her *dupatta*.

'Foopi, Nani's fainted too!' Hamza chuckled as he threw himself on to the bed beside Amma and proceeded to fan himself with her *sari*.

'Can somebody go downstairs please?' I asked calmly as my family became paralysed with uncertainty. 'Anyone?' I added.

'I go downstairs,' Hamza offered, shuffling off the bed. 'I'll tell the people Nani's fainted too.' Hamza had barely left the room when we all shot out after him. In the rush, I bumped into Tariq, who knocked into the twins, who collided with Ayesha, who pushed Baba on to Jhanghir's dad, Mr Khan.

'No!' I cried out, closing my eyes shut as I prepared to hear Mr Khan tumble down the stairs. Seconds passed in silence. Slowly I opened one eye to find Baba and

Taj holding Mr Khan firmly on the landing.

'I came up to check if everything was OK,' Mr Khan said whilst clearing his throat.

'Yes! Yes! Everything's fine, thank you!' Baba shouted, feeling the need to clap Taj on the back before drawing Mr Khan into a bear hug. Everyone laughed nervously and greeted Jhanghir's father.

'Foopi, fainting is fun, let's do it again!' Hamza called out as he took my hand and smiled up at me. I wanted to disappear and wake up in a normal land where there were normal families and with normal children living normal lives. Instead I simply smiled back at my nephew.

'Good, good, that's very good,' Baba said as he clapped Mr Khan on the back again.

'Yes, very good. Let's all go downstairs for some masaala chai.'

'Everything's going well. They've been talking about the families and now they're talking about the wedding. That's good, Maya, that's very good,' Jana said, after the commotion had passed. She sat down heavily on the bed and massaged her bulging belly. 'They've finished eating, thank God, because the aromas were making me nauseous. By the way, I've been sent up to bring you down.'

'You shouldn't be climbing the stairs when you're pregnant!' I chided, taking a final look in the mirror before placing the *dupatta* loosely around my head. 'Who's who downstairs?'

'Well, Jhanghir's parents are here; his mother's lovely, but the dad's a little off . . .'

'Off?' I pursued, knowing that Jhanghir's father still disapproved of our union.

'He wants a rich pretty socialite for his boy,' Jana

shrugged off. 'The one you need to watch out for is his sister-in-law, aka pretentious label-wearing perfectionist, and her parents, and there are no words to describe them. So, be careful what you say.' With this bit of advice, Jana and I walked downstairs. As hard as I tried not to think about the entrance, I felt my knees weaken and my heart race. In a few moments, I would walk into a room full of strangers, put myself on display, smile shyly, chat discreetly and do all the things that were alien to me but expected of me. And all I wanted to do was see Jhanghir and watch him smile before telling me that everything would be OK. That this *alaap* was, indeed, absolute.

'And here she is!' The shrieking announcement made me jerk back against Jana. I looked at the four-foot-ten man with the ungodly orange hairpiece on his head and smiled nervously. 'Here she is, here she is!'

'Here I ammmm.' I smiled as I felt Jana's painful pinch warning me to behave. Jana stood at the entrance to allow me to walk into the room in front of everyone.

'*AsSalaamAlaikum.*' It was barely a whisper, but I felt every pair of eyes on me, some smiling, some assessing, and some judging. I dared not look at Jhanghir directly as I sought out an empty chair and sat down quickly before my knees buckled beneath me.

'Foopi's better!' Hamza laughed as he raced into the room and jumped on to my lap. I kept smiling as I secured him on my lap.

'How are you, Maya?' I recognised the calm, sober tones of Jhanghir's mother.

'I'm fine, thank you . . .'

'She fainted, I fainted, we gots to all faint!' Hamza interrupted, gurgling with laughter.

'That game's finished, Hamza!' I teased as he twisted to look up at me.

'Is everything OK, Maya?' I heard Jhanghir's words and felt instantly warmed. I nodded before looking at him briefly. It was the briefest of looks, but it was enough to remind myself that he was handsome beyond words.

'Everything's perfect, thank you.' I wanted to dispel with protocols, so that I could talk to him, laugh with him and feel at ease with him. And yet, I dared not take another glance in case I was deemed to be forward.

'We heard you fainted.' The cut-glass public school accent patronised and mocked in equal measures. 'I must say, you do look a little peaky. How are you feeling now?'

I looked at the lady and knew the striking, carb-emaciated, perfectly groomed, designer-wearing woman was Jhanghir's sister-in-law, Seema.

'I'm fine, thank you.' I was polite. And I hated myself for it.

'Even if you feel nauseous, you must eat.' She was after my blood.

'Thank you for sharing your experience, but actually I love my food . . .'

'So Bhai, how long are you here for?' Amma cut in as she passed me a small bowl of mitai with a warning stare. I took the bowl and fed Hamza as the conversation took off around me. Quietly, I watched my parents build the bridge that would afford them an absolute *alaap*. In turn I looked at each of Jhanghir's family and noted the wealth they came from. I wondered if I would fit in, if I would be accepted, or whether I'd be patronised and looked down on for coming from humble roots. I looked at Jhanghir, who sat in a form-fitting charcoal grey suit and crisp white shirt talking with his *Kalaas* and being questioned as to what kind of a husband he would make. I had known him long enough to know that he was a good man, but I wondered whether he'd be affectionate or tactile or whether we would retain that childlike sarcastic banter that seemed so lightweight in the face of marriage.

'He's a good boy.'

I jerked around to see Seema's father. He'd caught me staring at Jhanghir and now all I could do was stare at the matted orange-coloured monstrosity that was his hairpiece.

'That's why my parents approved of him.' He laughed at my comment and leaned forward towards me. I leaned back, intent on keeping some distance between myself and the rug.

'When my Seema married Jhanghir's brother, I cried with joy.' I nodded at his exaggerated declaration. 'Now Seema's so happy. She wants for nothing. Nothiiiinnnnnggggggggg. She is so lucky and you will be so lucky too.'

'If God wills . . .'

'Of course God wills. I run garment factories in Dhaka, thirty together. When Seema married Shah, I gave her ten factories as her dowry. She runs them and she's doing a brilliant job. Maybe you can get into family business once you stop with all this painting nonsense.' Suddenly, I felt like an unaccomplished failure compared to the perfectly composed but cold woman. I continued smiling at the flippant comment.

'Maya's won an internship at Brown's; she's very good at painting,' Jhanghir interjected. 'Maya's talent was recognised at the Khan-Ali Art Awards—'

'Isn't that where Maya dramatically proposed to you?' Seema cut in with a condescending laugh that lacked any warmth.

'That's the night I won the internship to study in New York,' I redirected as Baba leaned forward, bristling with pride. 'It'll be the perfect start to a new career, one I've dreamed about for—'

'Yes, but does it pay? How many penniless artists are there in the world? Come on, Jhanghir, just because you're a hot-shot surgeon earning big bucks, you can't let Maya get lazy,' Seema's father suggested, with a raised brow.

'Foopi, what's that?' I ignored Hamza's question as he pointed at the hairpiece.

'I have no intention of becoming lazy or of being carried through life,' I stated, struggling to keep Hamza steady as he twisted away from me to go to the orange-haired uncle.

'That's the attitude!' He laughed as he took Hamza from me. 'Use your consultancy skills and knowledge of fashion to help build the family business, correct?'

'That's not what I want to do—'

'What do you want to be a painter for? When Jhanghir's father told me Jhanghir is ready to get married, I said to him the girl must be lovely, she must be educated and she must be ambitious. Maya, you must be ambitious—'

'We're very happy with Maya,' Mrs Khan interrupted calmly. I nodded and smiled at the support she had given me in front of Rugman. At the corner of my eye I saw Hamza twisting round in front of Rugman.

'Can you cook? You know we say the way to a man's heart is through his belly, eh?' Amma choked at the question. 'Seema's a talented cook. She has a professional chef at home and even then she insists on making the most wonderful curries a husband could dream of.'

'Oh Pappa, you exaggerate!' Seema laughed a little too readily. I forced myself to smile, praying for the conversation to move on, but deep down inside of me, I knew it wouldn't.

'Maya, what's your best dish?'

I stared at Seema. She stared right back. Seema knew I was no domestic goddess.

'Chicken korma! The dish for royals!!' Amma answered to fill my silence. 'Maya makes the best chicken korma, I don't know where she learned it, but it really is the best.' I knew my mother was digging my grave so I wasn't the least bit surprised when Seema asked the inevitable.

'So, Maya, how do you make your korma so good?'

I cleared my throat and hesitated. 'Uh, it's not that . . .' I couldn't lie. I just couldn't. 'Ah, it's really not that amazing, it's just a regular—'

'Nonsense! Your korma is amazing!' Amma insisted, glaring at me momentarily before she smiled at Seema. 'That's not her only great dish . . .'

'Oh really?' Seema asked with unbridled glee.

'Oh no,' I whispered as my mother leaned forward to go into detail.

'Lamb bhouna, chicken broast, shaag ghoost, chingri bhouna, dhal, pilau, biriyani, akhni—'

'OK, Amma, we don't want to boast!' I laughed nervously, trying to stop her.

'And then there are her kebabs . . . lamb kebab, shish kebab, shami kebab. Maya is very talented in the kitchen, very very talented.' I closed my eyes at my mother's statement and wondered how I would explain my demise from 'masterchef' to kitchen novice after marriage.

'Wonderful, wonderful . . . I can't wait to taste your cooking, Maya!' Rugman laughed as he clapped his hands with delight.

'Neither can I,' Seema added with a short smile and raised brow.

'What's that?' Hamza asked again, looking at Rugman's rug.

'I'll take Hamza,' I offered. Rugman refused, picked up Hamza and continued discussing recipes and dishes with Amma.

'Foopi, what is it?' Hamza asked, peering up at the hairpiece. 'Foopi, is that dead?'

The conversation moved on to the menu for our wedding, but my nephew who scrambled up on to the sofa behind Rugman fixated me.

'I got it! I got it!' Hamza bellowed, as he gripped the hairpiece to rip it off of Uncle's head.

'Get him off, get him off!' Uncle shouted as he gripped his wig to his head. Everyone leapt up, moving around the tea table to stop the chaos.

'Hamza, stop!' I cried out, trying to reach Hamza over Uncle who was braying like a mule in agony.

'Kill it, Foopi, it's an animal!' Hamza continued, pulling it from side to side and taking the yelling Uncle with him.

'Stop him, somebody get him off me!' Uncle cried out, moving sideways and backwards and forwards and every other direction Hamza dragged his hairpiece. Jhanghir leaned around me to grab Hamza's waist, and I watched speechless as Hamza refused to let go of the rug until part of the hairpiece came loose in his hand.

'I got it, I killed it.' Hamza cheered as everyone stood around in silence watching Uncle pat what was left of his hairpiece back into place. Bhabhi rushed in to take Hamza from Jhanghir. 'I killed it on the man's head, Mummy,' Hamza continued as he showed her his prize. I rushed forward and took the chunk of hairpiece from Hamza before his mother removed him from the room. I stared down at the tuft of hair in my hand and closed my eyes to stop the laughter from spilling out. I knew it was that laughter that gets you in the pit of your stomach, the one that leaves you laughing so hard that you can't breathe and, worst of all, you can't stop. I took my time, breathed in deeply. Once I had composed myself, I cleared my throat and turned around to Uncle. I opened my hand and held it out to him. Everyone stared at the bedraggled hairpiece in the palm of my hand.

'I, uh, would you . . . do you want to stick it back?' I stopped and saw how the rug on his head sat battered and skewed on the side on his head. 'It's falling . . .' I couldn't speak without laughing. 'Your hair . . .' I said, pointing to his head as tears blurred my vision. 'Your hair, it's falling offffff.'

'Maya!' Amma's shout had me racing out of the room before I was overtaken by fits of laughter.

That's how I left my absolute *alaap*, unmindful of protocol, uninhibited in emotions and full of heartfelt laughter. For that's who I, Maya Malik, am. After the Khans departed, Amma screamed blue murder, Bhabhi took to telling Hamza off, and Chachijhi made a quick escape to spread the news to the community. I, on the other hand, pulled out Baba's old recipe manual because I realised that I wanted to learn how to cook for my husband-to-be. Because I still believed in this *alaap*. Yes, fate conspired against me; she refused to allow me to progress as some shy, witless airhead pretending to be a goddess in the kitchen. She reminded me that I am as far away from being the perfect cook as George Clooney is ready to walk down the aisle with me, and I knew that the talks for the *alaap* were far from being fully resolved. But Jhanghir made a promise to marry me in good faith. As long as that promise remains blessed by the good lord above, it's as close to an absolute *alaap* as it can be.

Biriyanis, bhounas and bhajis –
it's a boy's world

So, from the moment we understand the difference between man and woman, we're told that this is a man's world. A world that has been built on men's terms, using men's rules, by male hands. But weddings, and everything related to weddings . . . now that's a world where we women reign supreme. Well, at least we're meant to. You would think that decisions about stunning dresses, over-the-top bling, and that *big* day inspired from your scrapbook of tips, styles and designs torn from years of back catalogues of *Asian Bride* and *Asiana Weddings* normally fell into the realm of the female. Not in the Asian world. Somehow, the man still reigns supreme here too. Discussions of dowries, dates and dresses are led by the groom's family, and whilst the bride's family work hard to broker the best deal, often they acquiesce to the groom's family to avoid derailing the overall wedding. So, I was thankful that Jhanghir was a modern man who would collaborate with me to give me the beautiful, Bollywoodtastic wedding I wanted. It didn't worry me that the discussions that night weren't concluded, or that Jhanghir's family had left in a rush; I decided that Jhanghir and I would make the necessary decisions to take this wedding forward.

That was my plan until I entered the kitchen the following morning to find my parents, Tariq *bhai* and my sisters locked in a serious conversation. They stopped at my arrival and clocked the heavy pile of bridal magazines I was clutching against me. Pushing my glasses up, I looked at Baba, who avoided my eyes.

'What's going on?' Short, sharp glances were exchanged until Amma started.

'Come! Sit down, join us for breakfast, we were all talking about the wedding,' she said, laughing uncomfortably amidst the silence of my family.

'They set your wedding date, Foopi,' Hamza informed me.

I dropped the magazines on the counter, digesting the information that my nephew shared. Leaning back against the counter, I folded my arms across myself and looked at him for any further updates on my wedding. 'And they want the wedding in New York . . .' Struggling to finish the word, he took a deep breath and looked up at his father. 'It's America, isn't it, Daddy?'

'When did this happen?' I forced myself to smile, trying to ignore the fact that someone had made decisions about the biggest day of my life without involving me.

'It's no matter, all that matters is that you're finally getting married!' Amma tried to be positive, but the continuing silence around the table belied her enthusiasm. 'You just need to learn how to cook for that boy and feed him well with many different dishes.'

'Really?' I waited for someone to tell me, but everyone seemed preoccupied with staying quiet. 'Shall I call Jhanghir to find out—'

'You don't need to call . . .'

'It's no big deal . . .'

'Don't call him . . .'

The sudden burst of comments told me that something wasn't right, so I waited until Baba spoke.

'Jhanghir's mother called late last night. She's an honest woman, I give her that much,' he said, before looking straight at me. 'Apparently, they weren't impressed by our hospitality; they think you're very immature and they were deeply offended by what happened to Seema's father—'

'That wasn't my fault, Daddy,' Hamza clarified with total sincerity, sensing he might be in trouble.

Immature! Immature, I couldn't believe they thought I was immature. I continued smiling even though indignation mixed with a heady cocktail of shock and humiliation coursed through me.

'. . . And so she said no further discussions need happen as Jhanghir's father would like the wedding on the first of August in New York, and their guest list extends to seven hundred people,' Baba finished, then folded his arms and sat back.

'I can't fly, then, I'm due in mid-August,' Jana added as she helped herself to another pancake. 'Actually, most of our side won't be able to attend . . .'

'As long as we, her parents, attend, no one else needs to be there. All we want is to see Maya married,' Amma pointed out, ever committed to the cause of getting me married.

'Yes, we'll go as guests of the very high fly Mr Khan, not as the parents of the bride!' Baba threw back.

'We're her sisters, of course we want to see Maya marry . . .'

'She's thirty; if we lose this *alaap*, we may never find another man for her . . .'

'Jhanghir's father thinks we're not good enough,' Baba muttered. 'This is his way of keeping my family away . . .'

'Jhanghir's father should've at least spoken to Baba, and not got his wife to pass on his message. How rude is that?' Hanna continued, pouring Baba a fresh cup of tea. Before I could get a word in edgeways, they were caught up in a conversation about boycotting the wedding. They didn't notice when I slipped away to my bedroom. There I pulled my hair into a bun, tempered my anger and cleared my throat before calling Jhanghir.

'You want to tell me what's going on?' I asked when he answered.

'Your timing sucks, Maya, you couldn't have caught me at a worse moment,' he told me, making me frown. I knew him well enough to know he was close to losing his temper, and he sounded pretty close. 'Meet me for lunch at Pizza Express at St Christopher's Square; we need to put a few things right. See you there at one p.m.'

Before I could speak, Jhanghir hung up. I wasn't sure how to react to the short, curt instruction, so I smiled tentatively. He was intent on putting things right, or at least that's what I told myself. But then the niggling doubt forced me to pick up my phone again.

'I'm getting married on the first of August, in New York, in front of seven hundred strangers,' I announced to my best friend Tanya. *Hijab*-wearing, ultra-sharp, extra-cosmpolitan and still-single Tanya was the one friend I trusted to cut through the crap and tell it how it was.

'Great, so you want to tell me which idiot thinks you can arrange a wedding in less than six months in the Big Apple where you know nothing about venues, decorators and wedding suppliers?' Tanya's caustic question made me smile. 'Let me guess, the mother-in-law?'

'Guess again.'

Tanya took a moment, and then she tutted at her mistake. 'Oh I get it, it's the big man, isn't it? Jhanghir's father. Well, that's no surprise, he wanted his son to marry his equally wealthy best friend's daughter; instead, his son chooses an unemployed, aspiring artist he knew from uni. Of course he's going to be pissed off.'

'Thanks, Tanya,' I muttered, wondering why I'd called Tanya when I knew her crystal-clear breakdown of the situation at times left me feeling worse.

'Well, have you told them what you want?' Tanya asked. 'You know what you want, don't you?' At her question, I paused. I was getting married to Jhanghir; how, where and when shouldn't matter, but it did. 'Maya!'

'Here, I want to get married here, in London,' I told her quickly. 'I'm meeting him for lunch to figure out what's going on.'

'You know what you've got to do,' she said, as if her train of thought was the easiest to read. When I stayed quiet, she groaned in despair. 'Cry.'

'What?' I asked shocked by the suggestion that I needed to resort to the age-old female trick to get my way.

'Cry. Trust me, it does the job.'

'That's just low!' I breathed out, unable to fathom doing it.

'It does the job. Listen to me, guys don't get girls' logic; they're not programmed to, especially when it comes to family politics. So just cry to get what you want. Don't rationalise, just cry,' Tanya insisted. 'I do it all the time, and Javed's giving me the wedding I've always wanted.'

'Jhanghir's different, I've known him for ever, he's going to fight my corner,' I explained, pulling out several tops, trousers and dresses to try on.

'You'll end up resorting to tears . . .'

'I'll explain that as we are the bride's side, we can decide to have the wedding here in London. He'll understand that all my family are upset by how this has been managed.'

'Mark my words, you must cry,' Tanya continued.

'I won't need to. I know he'll see it from my perspective, he's Jhanghir, he gets me.' Despite Tanya's amused reaction, I was confident that rationality underpinned the ability to get any outcome. I mean, how could Jhanghir not give me the wedding that I had dreamed of?

'When all else fails, you will cry,' Tanya reminded. Laughing at her words, I wrapped up the call to get ready to meet Jhanghir.

As agreed, we met at Pizza Express behind Bond Street at one p.m. Jhanghir had already got us a table and he stood up at my arrival. Then we engaged in the most awkward exchange of hugs that ended with polite pats on the back that reflected zero level of intimacy. The move from best friends to a couple on the verge of getting married wasn't happening as smoothly as I had expected. But, at that moment, we chose to ignore that uncomfortable exchange.

'So, what happened last night?' Jhanghir asked before we had even sat down. I had spent the morning shifting through my cupboard until I decided on a black pair of cosmopolitan capri pants and crisp, white, long-line shirt, finished with a neat side-bun hairdo. All of it was lost on the man who was to be my husband.

'Orange juice,' I told the waiter, giving myself time to deal with his blunt question.

'My dad was mad as hell, he wasn't impressed at all

by you, your family . . . and, and . . . poor Uncle, he was attacked by your nephew and all you did was laugh.'

'OK, are you telling me that that hairpiece didn't deserve to be destroyed?' My attempt to lighten the mood didn't go down too well, so I stopped smiling.

'He was humiliated . . .'

'After he spent the evening judging me . . .'

'He merely made the point that we have skilled cooks in our family and he expects the same of you.'

'By comparing me to your perfect sister-in-law who, by the way, needs to eat a couple of burgers – seriously, the Posh Becks look isn't healthy.' Jhanghir stared at me, unimpressed by my observation. 'Two burgers, that's all. Tell her she'll feel much happier.'

'That's what I mean, everything is a joke to you.'

'A joke?' I repeated in confusion.

'Yes, a joke; the hairpiece episode left a grown man humiliated.'

'I tell you what's a joke, setting a wedding date for seven hundred people on the other side of the Atlantic in less than six months without talking to the bride's family. Now that's a joke!' And with that bombshell out in the open, we sat in silence staring at each other both fully aware that this could get nasty. I refused to look away from his direct stare, telling myself not to get distracted by how attractive he looked, how absolutely, indescribably handsome he was. Neither of us was going to step down.

'Are you ready to order?' The waiter asked, placing my drink before me, looking at the two of us uncertainly.

'No,' we answered together before we turned to our menus. The waiter disappeared. Peeking over the top of my menu, I watched Jhanghir focus on his. When he refused to look up, I put mine down and leaned forward.

'Do you know how insulted Baba felt that your dad

didn't even have the courtesy to call him to discuss the wedding date?'

'My mum called—'

'Exactly. To tell everyone that your dad had dictated the date, location and guest list!' I finished, punctuating each point. 'Do you know how much it will cost my family just to fly out to America, let alone pay for seven hundred people to eat?'

'You're worried about money?' Jhanghir asked as if it was the least of his worries. 'Pops will take care of that. He doesn't expect you to—'

'Oh, yes I forgot, because we're obviously not able to pay for a good wedding.'

'Listen, he expects the best for me because he's used to the best. He's not going to accept a feeding-the-masses from your dad's restaurant served out on disposable plates in some run-down community centre for his son's wedding!'

Shocked at Jhanghir's judgement, I narrowed my eyes. Such was the impact of the insult that I couldn't even think of an equally wilting remark to return. So I tried a different tact, a quieter, less feistier and a deeply hurt tact.

'It's our tradition for the bride's family to host the wedding and for the groom's family to do the walimah reception to receive the new bride. Can't we stick to tradition for our wedding?' I whispered, looking down sadly and quietly shaking my head.

'My dad wants as many of his associates and family to attend a sophisticated celebration, not a third-rate cheesy wedding.' The softly, softly act obviously died in the face of Jhanghir's judgement, so I stared at him, determined to get him to understand.

'But half my family won't be able to fly out, my friends won't even get a look-in, and I'll be celebrating with strangers.' Still nothing I said made any difference to Jhanghir's decision.

We went several rounds of defending and criticising and then covered the same ground again before Jhanghir, out of pure frustration, confessed: 'My dad doesn't even want to be at the wedding!'

'Are you ready to order?' The waiter had returned without either of us noticing. We glared at him until he disappeared again. In that moment, I realised that it was futile to try and get Jhanghir to see my perspective. He was intent on putting the considerations of his family before mine.

'My dad wants to host our wedding to give me away, but he's being denied that right. Your dad wants nothing to do with the wedding, and yet he insists on hosting it.' I whispered. Then, I did something that I thought I would never do. I burst into tears. I covered my face with both my hands and sobbed. Not quietly, not discreetly, but in plain noisy view for all those around us to see. Peeking through my fingers, I caught Jhanghir's stunned look. He had never seen me behave like this before. Unsure of himself, he leaned forward and patted my arm, but I swotted his hand away and continued crying.

'Maya . . . stop crying,' Jhanghir whispered, embarrassed. I cried harder. 'Why are you crying?' Frowning at his question, I paused and lowered my hands.

'I always dreamed that my dad would give me away, here in London, in front of all my family and friends,' I whispered, as tears spilled down my cheeks. 'I'm going to be moving to New York with you, and it means so much to me that Baba can give me away . . . so much that I can't—' Before I could finish, I burst into tears again. Diners around us gave Jhanghir dirty, unforgiving glances. Through my tears, whilst waving the napkin around to make my point, I explained loudly how much I was leaving behind to start a new life with him and how it hurt me to think Baba couldn't give me away properly. Diners around me nodded in understanding. One even handed me a new tissue, which I thanked her for, before continuing my woeful story of never having the wedding that I had always dreamed of. In the middle of it, Jhanghir pulled up a chair next to me to lean in close.

'Stop crying, it doesn't suit you.' Taken aback by his attitude, I looked at him and piped down. 'You really are something, aren't you?' he said.

'I really, really, *really* want to get married in London,' I said. He curbed a grin and nodded.

'You'll have your wedding in London,' he stated, wiping away my tears. 'But the date sticks and we'll have three hundred guests on my side.'

'A London wedding, the first of August, six hundred guests in total,' I confirmed, smiling softly. 'I'm getting married in London!' I told the diners around me, who smiled at my announcement. Turning back to Jhanghir, I stopped smiling at his serious look.

'I like biriyanis, lamb bhounas and bhajis,' Jhanghir informed me.

'I'll learn how to make them before we get married,' I promised, loving the way his eyes creased in the corners when he tried to stop smiling.

'I don't expect a housewife who cleans and cooks all day long . . .'

'Good, coz I'm really really bad at cooking and cleaning all day.' I bit my lip, realising that I needed to let him finish.

'I need you to get on with my family,' he added.

'I want that too,' I assured him. 'But I don't want to join your father's corporation like your sister-in-law.'

'You don't have to. Listen, my dad's set in his ways, he

just needs time to get used to you, Maya . . . Hell, it took me years to get used to you!'

I laughed at his comment and hit his arm playfully. We were back to being old friends, in safe territory and at ease with each other. That was OK for now. You see, I was happy with the outcome. Yes, it was driven by the age-old female ability to cry on impulse and, yes, I did feel guilty resorting to it. This, however, was a case of the means justifying the ends. You see, we operate in a man's world, where male logic and reason reign supreme. And if women are to get anywhere in this world, throwing out the male rule book and using female wiles is sometimes the only way for us women to get what we want. Who said that was a bad thing?

Curb your tongue or compromise your commitment

Cooking, cleaning and childbearing. Not too long ago that was the definition of a housewife. Now, without a doubt, it is the inability to curb your tongue and to challenge every expectation. With the wedding relocated back to London, Amma had me in the kitchen with the intent of turning me into the British Bengali's answer to Delia Smith. Amma was intent on teaching me seven dishes, believing that that was the route to happiness. Seven dishes; one for each day. She had laid out all the ingredients, spices and herbs and held out an apron to me.

'Put it on,' Amma instructed.

'Amma, there's a wedding to plan . . .'

'Listen, I won't have anyone tell me my daughter can't cook for her husband,' she told me, putting the apron on me before tying it around me. 'And Jhanghir has the type of family who have no problems openly criticising anyone.'

'Listen, I just need to know how to cook a good biriyani, a lamb bhouna and one vegetable bhaji—' I stopped at the swift smack to the back of my head.

'What happens when the in-laws come to visit? You think they'll be impressed with your three dishes?' she asked as we walked over to the kitchen counter.

'I'll get a takeaway and present it as my own—' I stopped as Amma's glare evaporated the courage I thought I had. 'How about I go to Dad's takeaway and learn from the chefs there?'

'Your brother's banned you because you keep insulting the customers,' she dismissed, picking up her tray of spices to hold before me.

'I promise not to insult the—'

'OK, Miss Know-it-all, tell me, what are the seven most important Bengali dishes to impress your guests with?'

Clearing my throat, I looked at my waiting mother and thought about my favourite dishes.

'Lamb bhouna, chicken curry, aloo muttan . . .'

'Hai Allah!' Amma burst out, looking upwards for God's help. She took a deep, patient breath before giving me a notebook and pen. 'Write this down, because you will need to remember this when I'm not there in New York to help you and . . . and . . . you'll be alone, not knowing what spice to mix and—' Tearing up at the thought of my departure, Amma paused and dabbed at her eyes with her shawl.

'Amma, teach me the seven best dishes,' I said softly, distracting her back to her duties before I started crying too. She smiled and patted my cheek softly.

'OK, chicken broast and chicken korma are dishes made for kings; they're stately, rich and meant to be served on grand bowls.'

I wrote down everything Amma said because it was Amma's way of preparing me for life as a married woman. She cited the importance of lamb chops, Illishya fish, butternut squash vegetable bhaji, and rich, fragrant dhal to be served with pilau rice. Once I'd finished my notes, Amma held out her tray of brightly coloured spices and seeds, pods and broken sticks of bark.

'These you use for your garaam masaala curry base: bay leafs, cardamom pods, cumin and cinnamon sticks,' she told me, pointing to each as I made animated notes. 'Now, tell me which spice is which.'

Looking at the range of coloured spices, I bit my lip, determined not to live up to my mother's expectation of being useless in the kitchen.

'Haldi!' I announced proudly, pointing to the yellow turmeric powder. Amma wasn't impressed. 'The brown one's curry powder and that red one . . . that's . . . that's . . .' I leaned in close and smelled the powder, only I sniffed too hard and started coughing uncontrollably.

'That's hot chilli powder!' Amma said with despair as I raced to the sink to clear my nose. The burning sensation made my eyes well with tears. 'Why did you snort it? What am I going to do with this child?' Amma asked, pulling my hair back into a ponytail before forcing me to face her. Through tear-filled eyes and running nose, I saw her hold out a tissue. 'Blow,' she instructed. And, like a child, I did just that. 'Again!' For the next five minutes, Amma and I spent more time cleaning my nose than learning about cooking. By the time we finished, I looked like Rudolph the red-nosed reindeer's human relative.

'Ready?' she asked, holding up the offensive tray of spices with a wide smile.

Just as I nodded, ready to face the multicoloured spice tray, the doorbell buzzed to life. Amma's smile dropped. I had the perfect escape route and I didn't think twice about taking it.

'Don't take your time, hurry back, there's much to learn!' Smiling at Amma's orders, I walked down the corridor to peer through the glass of the front door. I forced myself to keep smiling when I saw Jhanghir, Victoria Beckham-wannabee Seema, and a man I could only describe to have the blessed looks of George Clooney and the body of John Abraham standing on the doorstep. In contrast, I was dressed in my bright-red plaid pyjamas with a flowery apron that was finished off with a scraggly ponytail and a red nose to match. In short, I couldn't feel any less glamorous.

'Maya, don't think you're getting away from cooking today! Your father was too soft on you!'

I didn't think it was possible to feel any more embarrassed, but it was. 'Excuse me.' I smiled before racing back to the kitchen, pulling my apron off and neatening up my ponytail.

'Jhanghir's here!' I told Amma, who froze. 'With superbitch Seema and this other guy . . .'

'Which other guy?'

'I don't know, I've never seen him before!' We both stared at each other with shock.

'The older brother!' Amma breathed out in surprise, pulling her apron off, before rushing to put everything away. 'Give me your word that you'll curb your tongue today?'

'Amma . . .'

'I want your word,' she insisted, holding my arm until I met her stare. She needed my reassurance that I would be on my best behaviour, so I grinned and nodded. Gratefully and almost nervously, Amma nodded too. And then she whacked my arm. 'Don't just stand there, go and open the door!' Racing back to the front door, I sneaked a peek into the living room and thanked God Hamza hadn't left his destructive mess of toys and teddies everywhere.

'Sorry, I just . . . had to . . . you know . . .' With

nothing intelligent to say, I stopped talking and opened the front door.

'We should have called ahead,' Seema said, curbing a smile.

'That's OK, we always have people coming and going. I mean, visiting us . . . we always have family popping in and—'

'What are you doing on the doorstep?' Amma demanded, pushing me out of the way to pull Jhanghir in. 'Come in, come in!' she invited, leading them into the living room.

They filed in after Amma, and I froze when the mysterious man paused to smile at me. He was as close to George Clooney as you could get without being George himself.

'Maya!' Starting at Amma's call, I looked away and turned to her. 'Drinks!' she whispered from the living-room door before mouthing, *'In our expensive crystal glasses.'*

Rushing across to the kitchen, I pulled out Amma's expensive collection and silver tray to pour the cold drinks complete with crunching ice. Pausing, I held a cold glass against my cheek, distracted inexplicably by the stranger. Taking a few deep breaths, I shook my head clear and carried the tray through.

'We're not going to stop, Maya, we're going to see venues today. Seema *bhabhi* and Zain have given up their day to help us.' At Jhanghir's words, I kept smiling. Seema replicated my smile, the type that never reached your eyes because it was the last thing you wanted to be doing.

'Today?' I asked as Jhanghir nodded.

'I've got to get back to the States for my rotations soon, so I need to cram in as much as I can before then.'

'Very practical. I've been telling Maya to get

organised for the wedding as there's not much time,'
Amma fabricated, handing the glasses to the guests. 'This
is Jhanghir's cousin, Maya, his younger uncle's only son.'
I smiled stupidly at George look-a-like Clooney, until
Jhanghir frowned at me. Clearing my throat, I looked
away before removing the stupid grin from my face.

'I take it you're not in the middle of some arty thing
today and can spend time with us?' Seema asked, looking
at her carbonated drink with distaste.

'Of course she can!' Amma burst out. 'Go change, go
get ready, they have a schedule of venues to visit.'

'You've booked meetings already?' I asked Jhanghir
who nodded at Seema.

'It's the least I could do for my little brother,' she
brushed off, looking at Jhanghir with a tinkering laugh.
'I've told him that in his absence, I will manage
everything.' The words resonated in my brain like the
revelation that Ricky Martin was indeed gay. I clocked
the familiar glance between the two. I didn't like it.

'We're lucky to have Seema *bhabhi*,' Jhanghir stated,
failing to comprehend that *I* wanted to manage my
wedding and that *I* wanted to make the necessary
arrangements given that *I* was the bride. Of course I
didn't say that when I looked at the grinning Seema who
knew exactly what she was doing. She was going to be
my nemesis and it was going to take some smart moves
to stay one step ahead of her.

'Are you OK, Maya?' Seema asked, knowing full well
that I was on her level. 'You seem a little off and your
nose . . . are you coming down with something?'

'I'm fine, thank you,' I returned, refusing the instinct
to touch my nose. 'I should go get ready,' I said, leaving
the living room. Walking up to my room, I closed the
door, held the pillow over my head and screamed.

*

Thirty minutes later, I sat in the back of Seema's tinted black BMW X6, clutching my pile of wedding magazines next to the scrummy man I couldn't even look at. Jhanghir sat in the front next to Seema, who drove like a maniac whilst shouting out curt instructions to her PA on speakerphone. There was no room for conversation until Seema finished her call.

'So, we've got four viewings today. My favourite's the Landmark; it just has that wow factor. So does the Mayfair Millennium. I've booked the Hilton in Holland Park, there's no wow factor, but we can get wedding decorators to jazz it up. The only Asian venue worth checking out is the Decorium; it's the only one that can hold six hundred people without turning the venue into a tuna can. The downside is that everyone and their dog has booked the venue for their wedding.'

'A venue's a venue.'

I jerked my head round to look at Jhanghir; eyes wide open at his response. I bit my lip to stop myself from correcting him, knowing full well that Seema was watching my every reaction with sharp, shrewd eyes.

'There are a couple of other venues that would be worth looking at . . .'

'I don't think we'll have time to fit any more in today,' Seema dismissed as she raced through a red light at Queensway.

'If the Hilton on Holland Park is just a back-up idea, why don't we cancel that and go see one of the venues I think are—'

'Because the Hilton isn't a back-up idea. As I said, with the best decorators, it can really be quite impressive,' Seema clarified.

'Come on, Bhabhi, it's worth looking at the ones Maya likes,' Zain said. I focused on looking through my magazines as my heart raced at the cousin's support.

'We've got the entire day, I'm sure we can fit them in.'
I was acting like a schoolgirl with her first crush and I
had to put a stop to it. Ignoring his support, I folded a
magazine at the page I had earmarked and leaned
forward.

'Bayliss House, we should go and see this venue,' I
said, handing the magazine over to Jhanghir who looked
at the picture of the grand country manor.

'Oh please! It's in the middle of nowhere!' Seema
laughed, pulling on to Baker Street.

'I've been to a wedding there, it's impressive,' Zain
offered as he leaned forward to take the magazine from
Jhanghir. I shifted aside, and he registered the reaction.
'It's definitely worth seeing,' he told Jhanghir before
frowning in my direction.

'Make an appointment,' Jhanghir told me. I pulled
my mobile out and leaned back until I could catch
Seema's eyes in the rear-view mirror. With a slow smile,
I arranged the viewing. She wasn't happy to be
overruled. She wasn't happy at all.

The entrance to the Landmark was grand. Once you
entered through the double doors, the huge winter
garden that was the lobby stole your breath away with its
tall palm trees, Venetian-inspired double stairways and
light-filled atrium. Before I could take it all in, the events
organiser rushed across to meet us and headed straight
for Seema.

'Congratulations! You must the beautiful bride and
groom-to-be!' he assumed in a strong Italian accent,
making Seema blush as he shook Jhanghir's hands.

'Actually, that would be—'

'My name's Marco Panetella. Please, come with me,
we don't have a single minute to waste!' the camp
organiser cut me off, beckoning us all to follow him.

Jhanghir smiled at me apologetically as Seema wound a slim arm through his to lead him forward. 'You're very lucky we had a cancellation on the day you're after. Normally, we're booked eighteen months in advance for summer weddings; to get a booking six months before the wedding . . . Puff! It's never heard of!'

'She likes being in control.' Starting at Zain's quiet comment, I curbed a grin and followed Marco. 'It takes a little getting used to,' he said, walking beside me.

'No kidding,' I muttered, trying hard to keep up with the organiser who spoke a word to the dozen without stopping to take a breath.

'So tell me, how many guests will be at the wedding?' The wedding planner asked as we walked through the hotel. 'I can just imagine the stunning Indian wedding, full of vibrant colours . . .'

'Oh, it's not going to be a typical Indian wedding, this one's going to be understated, elegant and extremely modern Asian fusion-inspired,' Seema corrected as I bit my lip, reminding myself of the promise I had made to Amma.

'Of course, madam. I love the Indian culture, it is very classy, and I spent eleven months backpacking across India—'

'We're not Indian and we're not interested,' Seema told him before walking into an opulent ballroom. 'Tell me the facts about your wedding package – costs, contractors, and execution.' She was good. I didn't like her, but Seema was a woman who got what she wanted and she didn't care who got hurt in the process. As Marco stuttered through his speech, I wandered off, walking around the grand ballroom and staring up at its stunning chandelier. It would be a lavish affair; with a beautiful three-course meal full of Nuevo cuisine treats. And yet, as breathtaking as it was, I couldn't imagine my wedding here. Shaking my head, I headed back to the group.

'. . . so our packages range from a hundred and twenty-two pounds per person upwards.' I caught the end of Marco's words and froze at the price tag. Biting my bottom lip, I did the maths. At £122 per person, our wedding for six hundred would cost nearly seventy grand without any of the finishing touches to factor in.

'How much?' I repeated, questioning the outcome of my mental arithmetic.

'And you are?' Marco asked with a raised brow and patronising tone.

'I'm the bride, and I'd like to know the cost per person to have a wedding here.' My dry tone wasn't missed on Marco. He looked confused and hesitantly turned to Seema. She coughed discreetly to hide her embarrassment, indicating to Jhanghir to quieten me.

'A hundred and twenty-two pounds per person . . .'

'I thought that's what you said.' Laughing nervously, I rubbed the back of my neck, wondering how on earth I would manage the expectations of the Khan family.

'Excuse me,' I said to Marco, before taking Jhanghir aside.

'Are you insane?' I whispered, turning to face Jhanghir when we were out of earshot. 'How is Baba meant to pay for this?'

'He's the father of the bride, he's meant to pay—'

'Close to a hundred grand? Are you kidding me?' Jhanghir shook his head and I realised he was absolutely serious. 'He'd have to sell the takeaway to get that kind of money!'

'I'll ask Dad to pick up the tab . . .'

'No,' I stopped Jhanghir, bowing to my pride. 'It's Baba's responsibility as the father of the bride.'

'Is there a problem?' I jerked round to find Seema

watching us with a raised brow.

'No, no problem,' Jhanghir answered, walking off to join her. 'We've reservations about this venue.' He left me in the middle of the hall, and went to round up discussions with Marco. Zain caught me watching the two of them and, at that moment, I knew we both thought the same thing: why was Jhanghir spending more time with Seema than with me, his wife-to-be?

'We're leaving,' Jhanghir called from the double-door entrance. He didn't wait for me to join them, so I rushed to catch up with them.

No more was said of our brief conversation. We went to the Mayfair and then on to the Hilton at Holland Park. At both locations, Seema ran the show with Jhanghir, talking themes, menus and costs as if she was planning her own wedding. Several times I tried to join in on the discussions but Jhanghir brushed off my comments, preferring rather to pander to the needs of his sister-in-law. Each time this happened, it brought me closer to telling them both what I really thought. To keep my promise to Amma, I curbed my tongue, turned round and left them to it. Heading for the bar, I ordered a strong coffee and sat fuming at the way my wedding was being hijacked.

'I take it that this isn't the one either?' Zain said, joining me and ordering a cold drink.

'Hotel ballrooms are all the same, right?' I returned, thanking the waiter for my coffee.

'But these are some classy joints.' Raising a brow at his reply, I shrugged. 'You're still not impressed!' he said with a slow, rumbling laugh. It was infectious and I finally smiled. 'Stand up.'

Looking at Zain, I frowned as he got up and held his hands out.

'What are you—'

'Come on,' he insisted, grinning as he leaned down to take my hands.

'What are you doing?'

'Susshhhh.' Stopping at his instruction, I watched as he placed a hand on my hip and took my hand. 'Now, if you want, you can hear music anywhere and you can dance anywhere,' he told me. I swayed with him, unable to stop myself from grinning up at him. 'Can you hear it?'

Looking up at him, I stopped and pulled back. 'This is so stupid,' I told him, seeing guests around us smiling at Zain's antics.

'Yes, it is.' He didn't give up. Pulling me back, he took my hand, held my back and started swaying. 'Anywhere you want, you can stop, sway and smile.'

'That's so cheesy!' I laughed and he joined me, chuckling in agreement. Yet we stood there, dancing and laughing in self-conscious embarrassment. Moments passed, and I looked up at him. He looked at me and we stopped.

'Are we interrupting?' Seema's crisp, curt question felt far worse than being doused with ice-cold water. Spinning round, I found Jhanghir staring at us.

'I was trying to convince Maya to have a first dance.'

'I'm not sure that that's the kind of help Jhanghir expected from you when we asked you along today,' Seema said with a slow smile.

Clearing my throat, I pushed my hair back and gathered enough courage to meet Jhanghir's piercing stare. More than feeling guilt or embarrassment, I was glad he'd seen us. I wanted him to be jealous, I wanted him to be angry. I wanted to push him into an argument so that I could demand why he didn't put me first.

'We have one more venue to see.' And with that, Jhanghir turned on his heel to leave. That was it. There was no argument. Jhanghir simply showed no emotion, gave no reaction. I wanted to scream at him to get some attention, to get my Jhanghir back. And yet, one look at smug Seema, and I stayed silent. She gave me a disapproving look before tottering after him. I stared after them, trying desperately hard to silence the unnerving voices within me. Jhanghir and I had lived continents apart. After university, he relocated back to New York and set his sights on becoming a surgeon whilst I built a career in London. Still across different time zones we remained close and interdependent. He was that one constant throughout my singleton years to whom no one came close, and yet, at this moment, I had never felt more distant from him.

'Next time, you're going to have to be more discreet!' Zain told me, holding my bag out to me. Dragging my glance back to him, I wondered what insanity had caused me to behave so recklessly.

'There isn't going to be a next time,' I told him as Zain grinned and shook his head.

'There's always a next time,' he told me before heading for the exit.

Frowning at what sounded like a promise, I shook my head to stop myself from smiling at his cockiness before rushing forward to join them.

In the afternoon, we viewed the Clay Oven and Ruislip Country Club; to both, Seema afforded five minutes of her time before stating that 'every man and his dog had their weddings at these venues and Jhanghir's father would rather miss his son's wedding than attend a typically kitsch bog-standard Indian wedding'. Still, I refrained from speaking my mind. Preoccupied with Jhanghir's quiet demeanour, I accepted her decisions and we sat silent in the BMW, making our way to Iver House, the last venue we were booked to see. From the moment we entered through the huge iron gates to drive along its rolling green grounds, to pull up in the front of the impressive traditional manor house, I was captivated.

'Welcome to Iver House.' I smiled at the elderly gentleman who met us at the entrance. 'I'm Jas, I'm here to explain why you should have your wedding here.'

Laughing at the confident introduction, Jhanghir introduced us before we followed him into the manor. Walking along a corridor, Jas parted a set of double doors to let us into a sprawling modern atrium flooded by the natural light from the glass ceiling.

'This is where your guests mingle and enjoy a few appetisers with entertainment in the background, and down there, well, that's where the magic happens.' At Jas's direction, we rushed to the edge of the atrium and stared in stunned surprise as we looked down at the grand ballroom below. It was surrounded by floor-to-ceiling glass walls so that the views of the rolling manicured grounds surrounded the ballroom. 'We open up the doors to allow guests to wander at the end of the event.' I spun round to look at Jhanghir. This was it. This was the place where we were meant to be married. He held my eyes as I smiled. Without a word he nodded.

'Really, is this it?' Seema breathed out, taking the large marble stairs down to the ballroom. My smile faltered as I jerked round to glare at Seema. She was trampling over my wishes and it was getting harder to control my feelings.

'Of course, you will have decorators to customise it to your wishes,' Jas advised.

'And the date . . . you still have the first of August free?' I asked, quickly walking down the stairs with him with a wide smile to keep him sweet.

'Yes, it's the only summer date we have free, but we expect to fill it very quickly.'

'Do you provide decorators and catering?' Seema asked, traipsing up and down the ballroom, inspecting every angle and crevice of the space.

'Yes we do. Two months before the wedding, we ask the bride, groom and six members of the family to come in to taste our dishes to set their own menu . . .'

'I assume that it's the run-of-the-mill Asian menu?' Seema derided. 'Chicken tikka, naan, lamb bhouna . . . oh, it's so dull and so done!'

'There's nothing wrong with Asian meals,' I reassured Jas who frowned at Seema.

'We have over twenty starters, thirty main dishes, and ten desserts for you to build a menu with. I can assure you, it's rarely a dull or done menu here at Iver House.'

Smiling at the event organiser, I walked to the glass wall and stared out at the green. Seema and Zain grilled Jas behind me. It didn't matter, because I knew this was the venue.

'This is the venue,' Jhanghir agreed, coming to stand beside me.

'With six hundred guests, we can't afford to pay more than thirty-five pounds per head,' I stated. 'My family has a twenty-five-thousand-pound budget. That's all I have to make this wedding work,' I confessed unable to meet his eyes.

'This is a joint event, Maya, we're splitting costs down the centre.' At Jhanghir's words, I turned to him with wide-eyed surprise. We normally had two events, the big reception thrown by the bride's family and a follow-up event hosted by the groom's family. Jhanghir was offering to join the events into one big bash to help me manage the financial burden.

'Are you sure?' I asked and he nodded. Looking back at the rolling grounds, I smiled.

'This is it,' Jhanghir stated just as Seema beckoned him back to the discussions.

'So, this is it,' I breathed. 'This is where we're getting married.' Even as I said the words, it felt unreal. Butterflies coursed through me and I couldn't stop grinning. A million and one ideas rushed through my mind about what to do and how to set up the venue, and yet the only thought that stuck was the realisation that I had found my dream location. Surprisingly, we had accomplished what we had set out to do. We had a wedding venue. This would be the point from where Jhanghir and I would start our married life. And then it dawned on me. I had had umpteen opportunities to derail the focus by ranting at Seema's controlling ways and Jhanghir's apparent indifference. But I hadn't. I had kept my promise to Amma, and the pearls of her wisdom suddenly made sense. You see, just because we have the ability to voice our opinions, our wants and needs, it doesn't mean we have to assert them at every given opportunity. Speaking alone doesn't get you what you want; speaking at the right time when it matters most, does. Sure enough, curbing my tongue had paid dividends.

Diamonds and dowries are a girl's best friend

Doubts damage expectations of diamonds and dowries. Jhanghir had secured Iver House for 1 August with a neat deposit before promptly dropping me off with total indifference. Nothing. He gave me nothing. Yes, we were getting married, but beyond the act of getting married, there was meant to be more. So, like any girl with instincts telling her something wasn't right, I picked up the phone to my best friend, Tanya.

'Is it me, or is Jhanghir gay?' I asked, back in my room and looking at myself in the mirror. I was attractive – at least, I thought I was. With long black hair, wide brown eyes and full lips, I couldn't be mistaken for being ugly. 'I'm far from looking like a dog's dinner, aren't I?' I had to ask.

'Have you been smoking something funny!' Tanya asked dryly. I sucked in my cheeks and stomach to see whether it made any difference. 'Jhanghir's not gay and you're not ugly.'

'Well, why . . . umm, why won't he . . .' I didn't know how I could tell her that Jhanghir didn't try it on with me without sounding like a dog on heat.

'My psychic abilities are defunct today, what's wrong?' Tanya encouraged.

'Are you and Javed ... well, you know, do you guys ...' Pausing, I checked that my bedroom door was firmly closed before falling on to my bed. 'Do you and Javed ...' Still I couldn't say it.

'You're asking if Javed and I do the dirty mambo or get close to it?' Tanya finished.

'No! Well, yes ...' Clearing my throat, I turned on my stomach and whispered. 'Are you intimate with—'

'Is Jhanghir pressuring you? A swift kick to the nuts will sort that out for you,' she offered. Closing my eyes, I groaned at the irony of her words. She couldn't be further from the truth if she tried.

'That's the thing, Tanya, he's not interested,' I confessed with a frown.

'What do you mean?' Breathing out in frustration, I waited for the penny to drop. 'No, wait, are you telling me he doesn't fancy you? Maya, you're talking about Jhanghir, you're *soulmate*, your uni mate, the guy who—'

'I don't think he knows how to be anything other than my mate,' I explained. We waited in awkward silence but I felt embarrassed at the truth of our relationship.

'He hasn't tried to hold your hand?' Tanya finally asked.

'No.'

'Jhanghir hasn't kissed you?' she continued.

'No.'

'He hasn't groped you?'

'Tanya!' I chastised, smiling when she chuckled at my reaction.

'Do you think he's a virgin and he's just shy in that department?' Tanya suggested.

'We spent uni days together and I know too many of

his secrets, including the fact that he's not a virgin.' The clarification left us both at a loss. 'We're not even as close as we used to be. We don't talk like we used to and all he's interested in is making all the decisions with his bitch for a sister-in-law!' I told her before explaining the frustrations of the day that had been made worse by Jhanghir's indifference.

'He *doesn't* fancy you,' Tanya breathed out as if she'd been hit with a revelation. I sat in unimpressed silence. 'What I mean is, he hasn't seen you as a woman . . .'

'I'm a woman, Tanya, there's no mistaking the fact that he's marrying a woman.'

'What I'm trying to say is that he's in that no man's land right now. He's seen you as a buddy who's suddenly going to become his wife. You guys haven't had that normal courting, flirting, messing around transition, so you've got to give him the green light.'

'To do what!' I asked with indignation.

'I thought you wanted him to come on to you . . .'

'I do, well, obviously not like an animal in heat, but yes – yes, a little forthcoming . . .'

'Maya! No wonder the bloke's indifferent. He can't read the confused signals you're giving him,' Tanya surmised. 'Tell me honestly, what's bugging you?'

'We're getting married, Tanya, and you'd think we were strangers. We have no moments. You know, those moments when you know that a guy's into you, he looks at you, really looks at you . . .'

'Sweetie, you're worrying for nothing. Jhanghir is crazy about you,' Tanya told me. 'You want him to look at you? Give him something to look at. You're both going wedding outfit shopping tomorrow – well, get him to help you in or out of the outfits . . .'

'What do you mean?'

'Girl, he's going to see you naked after you marry, so

give him something to look forward to. Remember, sexy lingerie may make you feel sexy, but it'll make him want to get sexy too.' By the time I hung up, I was going through my lingerie drawer, smiling naughtily courtesy of Tanya's very, *very* honest advice.

The following morning, I waited at Green Street station dressed in a nude silk tunic with chiffon sleeves worn over jeans, with my hair pulled back in a low, loose side bun. It was only eleven a.m., and Green Street was bustling with activity. Packed shalwaar kameez stores, Indian gold jewellery shops, Asian accessories and wedding boutiques, as well as halal butchers and discount grocery stores, had shoppers shopping competitively to get the best outfit at the best price. Rifling through my wedding book of cut-outs, I looked at the pictures of stunning wedding dresses that had captured my imagination. Jhanghir texted me, saying that he was about to exit the station. Taking a deep breath, I looked at my reflection in the shop window, smiling at the barely-there make-up I wore, to match my barely-there lingerie.

'Hey.' Turning at the greeting, I smiled up at him. Taking his aviators off, Jhanghir looked at me. 'How you doing?'

'Good,' I told him, forcing myself to meet his eyes and hold them. 'And you?'

'Good,' he returned, muting a grin.

'Good.' We were having a moment and when he reached out, I caught my breath. The seconds ticked by agonisingly slowly, so that when he took my wedding notebook from me, I frowned, having been left wanting.

'Seema *bhabhi* gave me the names of a couple of designer boutiques to visit.'

'I'm sure she did,' I said, bristling at the mention at

Ms Perfect and still smarting from his lack of interest.

'She says the others are a waste of time, so why don't we keep it short and wrap this up?' Jhanghir added, shaking his head at some of the picture cut-outs in my notebook. 'Actually, why didn't you agree to letting her have your wedding trousseau custom-made in India?'

'Because this is our wedding and I want to choose my wedding outfits,' I explained, wondering why he didn't comprehend that.

'She also said to stay away from typical Indian styles by avoiding the whole red and gold Christmas-tree look, like this one,' Jhanghir said, pointing to one of the cut-out images which only happened to be one of my favourites. So, without a word, I started walking.

'Maya?' Taking my arm, he pulled me to a stop to face him.

'This is my wedding dress, I get one chance to get it right,' I reminded him. 'So I'm going to take my time visiting as many boutiques as I need to, to find the perfect dress.'

'Good, let's hit those designer boutiques to find a good dress—'

'A *good* dress?' I breathed out indignantly. 'This is my wedding dress and it has to be *perfect*.'

'What I'm saying is, you can find it in one of the three boutiques Seema *bhabhi*—'

'I appreciate the suggestions, but you should know that I'm prepared to visit every wedding boutique twice or three times over until I find the perfect outfit,' I told him, watching him until my words firmly sunk in.

'You're going to turn into a bridezilla, aren't you?'

Crying out in frustration, I pulled my arm away and walked on ahead. A few minutes later, we walked into swanky Dhamini's and headed for the third floor. A super-skinny *hijab*-wearing sales assistant with heavy eye make-up clocked Jhanghir and made a beeline for us.

'Can I help you?' she said, passing me by to stop before Jhanghir.

'Sure,' he told the impressionable girl with a disarming grin. She returned his smile.

'I believe my sister-in-law Seema Khan phoned ahead this morning, asking you to put aside a number of your latest range. Would you go and find out who dealt with that?'

Two things struck me at that moment. First, without the slightest hesitation, the sales assistant couldn't move any faster to serve Jhanghir and second, without being present, Seema was still pulling the strings to my wedding, even determining which wedding dresses were best suited to me.

'She's actually on her way.'

I froze at the returning sales assistant's comment, realising that my plan to tempt Jhanghir was about to disappear. 'Here . . . she's coming here?' I asked, remembering to smile to cover the obvious disdain in my tone. The sales assistant nodded.

'It'll be good to have her input, no?' Jhanghir asked.

I looked at him and narrowed my eyes, wondering if he was pushing me on purpose or whether he was serious. Nodding quickly, I turned away before he could read my real thoughts.

'We need to find Maya a wedding dress, so do you think you could give us a hand picking out some really classy outfits – subtle in colour, elegant and understated? Rule out any over-the-top Christmas lights blingtastic-looking outfits, OK?'

Once again, the sales assistant all too eagerly disappeared to do his bidding. Jhanghir followed her as she walked between large glass display units to pull out outfits that matched his brief. I, on the other hand looked around, watching other couples shopping for the perfect wedding dress. There was the corporate couple, where the guy instructed the assistant to get the best of the best for his fiancée. I spotted a mixed-race couple, where the Indian girl pulled out a fine-tailored *sharwaani* for her besotted English husband, and then there was the couple that were so into each other that finding a dress appeared to be the last thing on their minds. I looked over at Jhanghir and realised that we were different. That unsettled me. Spotting the red outfit zone, I wandered over and touched the stunning traditional ruby-gold wedding outfits. Stroking the soft, sensuous material, I wished we were looking at this range rather than Seema's Westernised alternatives.

'Maya.' Turning at Jhanghir's call, I spotted him standing by the assistant who held up a few outfits. 'You wanna try these on.' Realising that Seema hadn't yet arrived, I spotted my opportunity to flirt with him. Smiling, I nodded and followed them as they headed for the large, well-lit changing rooms. Jhanghir sat down on the cream lounger and took the refreshment another assistant rushed to give him. Leaving my bag with him, I stepped into the changing room, where the assistant arranged the wedding outfit. The stunning creamy Japanese silk *lengha* was a fitted mermaid skirt that had a long, long train ornately embroidered with tiny antique gold beads.

'Give me a shout when you need the bodice fitted at the back,' she told me, eager to get back to chatting up Jhanghir.

'Uh, I've seen one just like this in scarlet red, would you be kind enough to go and pick that up for me?' I asked, smiling when she looked at me with narrowed eyes. She was reluctant to go and I wondered why women had a problem listening to other women.

'Size ten?' The comment was smart and caustic, somehow implying a size ten was the equivalent to being obese.

'Size eight.'

She looked me over before giving me that sympathetic but false smile before disappearing. Shutting the door behind her, I rushed to get out of my tunic and jeans. Gently I pulled on the heavy *lengha* skirt, struggling to get it up over my thighs. Sucking my stomach in tight, I twisted and turned and hoiked it up until it slid over my hips where it clung to every flabby curve like a second skin. Needing to make my move on Jhanghir, I pulled the bodice on, and held the front of it close to me, before calling out to him.

'Could you give me a hand, doing the back up?' I looked down demurely and waited with contained excitement. The door swung open and I turned with half a smile.

'Oh no, that look is just not working!' Seema declared, sizing me up and down before making me turn. Paralysed with humiliation, I let her twist me and turn me to fasten the back before she led me out into the lobby area. I could barely walk in the super-fitted skirt, and tried to grab the shawl whilst hobbling to keep my balance. But it was too late, Seema had me standing in front of Jhanghir like a pea with too many large pods. He stared at me silently. I spotted the smallest of frowns before he coughed to clear his throat and forced a smile.

'That's very . . . well, uhh, I'm not sure about the colour . . .'

'Colour?' Seema cried out, wrapping her arms from behind me to grasp my untoned tummy. 'Sweetie, you need to get rid of this, and this, and this . . . and what is this?' she demanded, pointing out every flabby part of my body before holding up my arms to show off my batwings.

'That's my arm,' I answered, refusing to look at Jhanghir as humiliation coursed through me in waves of a growing scale.

'That's not an arm, that's called unnecessary baggage!' Seema corrected. 'You need to get out of that because, honey, that does nothing for your body.' Without another word, I half hobbled, half hopped back to the dressing room. Once in there, I leaned against the wall. I didn't think it was possible to feel any more shame. Shaking my head, I refused to dwell on it. Standing straight, I unzipped the *lengha*, cursing when it snagged. No matter what I did, the zip wouldn't give, so I tried to pull the *lengha* skirt down. Only I couldn't bend over because the fitted bodice wouldn't allow me to. Reaching behind me, I found it impossible to unclip the bodice. Dreading the thought of having to call anyone for assistance, I twisted and turned over and over again until I leaned against the wall, panting for breath. There was no hope, it was impossible to get out of the outfit alone without ripping it to pieces.

The skinny assistant peered into the changing room. She looked at the *lengha* stretched to its limits at my hips and the half-opened bodice. And yet we stood there. She knew that I needed help and I knew I needed her help. But she waited for me to ask with half a smile. And surely enough, I broke.

'Will you unclip me?' I asked, turning round. She stepped forward to help until I was free of the bodice.

'The skirt . . .'

'I can manage the skirt. Thank you,' I told her as she closed the door. At that point, I tried to ease the skirt over my hips. Only, it didn't slide down, no matter how much I tugged and pulled at it. It simply refused to go down. Frowning, I looked at my hips, measuring them and wondering whether it was possible for air to add on enough weight to get stuck in a dress. Taking a deep breath, I hoisted up the entire skirt in the attempt to pull it up and over my head. Only the skirt refused to go beyond my boobs. I twisted, stretched and sucked in the deepest breath possible and nearly passed out with the effort. Defeated, I gave up and let the *lengha* fall about my hips. Jhanghir waited outside and I refused to let the world know that I was too fat to wear this gorgeous wedding outfit.

'Uh, is everything OK?' At the knock, I wrenched on my tunic and paced inside the changing room.

'Just a moment,' I yelled back and then, with a deep breath, once again tried to force the top of the *lengha* over my hips. Crying out in frustration when it stubbornly refused to move, I resolved to live in the changing room for the rest of my life, because anything other than that would be a fate worse than death.

'Maya, are you OK?' Jhanghir's worried question made me freeze. Was it worse to seek help from Jhanghir, knowing he would see me at my worst, or to seek help from Seema, who would never let me live this moment down? 'Maya?' Flashes of images of her recalling this moment at any and all major family events made the decision for me. Opening the door, I grabbed Jhanghir and pulled him in.

'I can't get out of the *lengha*,' I told him as he stared at me.

'What do you mean, you can't get out of the skirt? Pull it down . . .'

'I've snagged the zip, I can't get it free and it doesn't go down!' I explained before demonstrating the fact. 'See, it's stuck, I'm going to have to be cut out of it . . .'

'Listen, you got into it, you can get out of it,' he told

me, stepping forward to grip the edge of the skirt. I bit my lower lip, savouring the fleeting touch of his hands. He started to slide it down, but it went down only so far. 'Maya, breathe in . . . Maya!' Snapping out of my thoughts, I looked up at him. 'Breathe in.' Doing as I was told, I watched as he kneeled down before me, continuing to ease the material over my behind. 'Hold my shoulders and bend over me.' Just as I did what he said, the door was jerked open.

'Is everything OK?' We froze as Seema found us in the compromising position. 'I'm sorry, I . . .' Unable to finish, she slammed the door closed.

'Bhabhi!' Leaving me stranded, Jhanghir raced after her to explain it was perfectly innocent. In fact, I wished he'd let her believe what she thought she saw, for that was better than her knowing the truth. I stood back against the wall and looked up to find the sales assistant smiling at me from the entrance of the changing room. Using one finger, I beckoned her.

'Call your manager down. You need to cut me out of this.' And with that, I folded my arms and waited. I'd been wrong. In that moment I realised that shame actually had no limits.

We left Dhamini's after Jhanghir had settled the matter with the manager. Neither Jhanghir nor Seema mentioned the incident again. In fact, they didn't know what to talk about after the commotion, so, awkwardly, we moved on to the next boutique. And then the next and the next. We visited more than a dozen boutiques, and at each boutique, Seema strode in to order assistants to pick out this outfit and that designer dress, followed by curt instructions for me to wear and display umpteen outfits. Only nothing she chose was right for my body shape, height or size of figure. Seema seemed to forget that, unlike her, I wasn't a size zero, neither was I an impressive five feet seven inches tall, and I certainly didn't have the figure to carry off the designs she hand-picked. So whilst every other bride-to-be came out of changing rooms close to tears and gushing at having found the *perfect* outfit, I came out close to tears knowing that everything I wore turned me into a dumpy midget. Worse still, at each boutique, Jhanghir looked more and more like he was losing the will to live. When he finally called for time out, I couldn't agree fast enough to end the series of humiliating experiences I was being forced to endure. Stopping for a quick snack at Lahori Karahi, I sat quietly as they discussed the wedding over mouth-watering sizzling grilled kebabs. Longingly, I looked at the lamb chops Jhanghir devoured, refusing to give Seema another opportunity to criticise me.

'We should call it a day,' Seema announced as Jhanghir finished up. 'We've seen every boutique worth seeing.'

'What about Suraya's? Their range is in every bridal magazine,' I pointed out as we left the popular kebab house. Tanya had raved about it, and if there was one boutique I was determined to visit, it was Suraya's.

'That's it after this,' Jhanghir said, leading us down Green Street.

'I haven't heard of it, is it one of those massive warehouse-style discount retailers?' Seema asked as we weaved through busy crowds. I didn't bother justifying my decision, instead we stopped in front of the small boutique and went downstairs. Three of the walls were draped with no more than fifteen wedding outfits and immediately a blood-red, antique gem-encrusted *lengha* suit in the far corner of the boutique struck me. Jhanghir dropped on to the large sofa in the middle of the floor and Seema worked around the displays, inspecting each of the outfits.

'I'd like to try this,' I instructed the assistant who took the heavy ornate outfit to a fitting room.

'I've found the perfect one,' Seema called out, picking out an outfit that looked exactly like the half dozen I had tried on that morning. 'This will look amazing,' she said, handing it to the assistant to hook up in the dressing room. 'Try this one first.' Nodding, I headed for the changing room. Looking at the cream outfit Seema *bhabhi* had picked out, I shook my head, lacking the energy to entertain her whims. Turning to the opposite wall, I looked at the outfit I had chosen and couldn't help smiling. Pulling my hair into a topknot, I slipped off my pumps and changed quickly. Slipping on the four-inch heels the boutique supplied, I pulled on the fitted *lengha* skirt. I refused to look in the mirror, worried it looked as bad as the others I had tried on. Without another moment to lose, I pulled on the ornate blouse and called the assistant in to zip me up. Once done, I waited with bated breath until she placed the heavy embroidered veil around my shoulders and over my head. Slowly, I looked into the mirror. It was perfect. The Maharajasthan-inspired *lengha* fitted like a glove, making the most of my curves and complimenting my sun-kissed complexion. It looked understatedly breathtaking, so, with a nervous smile, I stepped out. I turned to Jhanghir and waited for him to look up from his phone.

'Jhanghir!' I called out when he failed to look up. At the sound of my voice, he looked up and then paused. Seema spun round to look at me and froze.

'Well, it's classically traditional, and, well . . .' Seema trailed off as Jhanghir stood up and came to stand before me with a wry grin.

'I take it you ignored everything I said about keeping it subtle in simple understated colours with as little bling as possible,' he stated. I frowned at his words, disappointed at his reaction to what I thought was the *perfect* dress.

'You don't like it,' I accepted finally, meeting his eyes. I read his mischievous look and saw that he was testing me.

'Who'd have thought you would scrub up so well?' Jhanghir said as I raised a challenging eyebrow.

'Nothing less than a one-carat diamond ring will match this dress,' I told him, seeing him contemplate my suggestion without an ounce of sincerity.

'Just a carat?' Jhanghir checked with me.

'Anything more would be a little too bling, don't you think?'

'Umm, you may have a point,' he agreed thoughtfully. The smile in his eyes seemed to disappear. 'This is a new you I have to get used to,' he confessed, and for the first time I realised that he found our transition from best friends to a newly engaged couple as difficult as I did. His candour warmed me.

'It'll only get better, Jhanghir,' I promised.

'Really?' he asked, the mischief in his eyes belying his deadly serious tone.

'Really.' With that guarantee, I passed him by to walk along the floor to look into the floor-to-ceiling mirror. The woman staring back at me looked like the bride I wanted to be. The dress was stunning and original. Jhanghir came to stand behind me and I looked at him in the mirror. We stood in silence, watching each other until the manager came to talk to us. Then Jhanghir stood aside and let me discuss the customisation of the outfit, much to Seema's annoyance. The outfit would be built for me, to my exact measurements, with every detail the best suited to my body shape. Every so often, I looked up and found Jhanghir watching me. And each time it made me smile. Getting married wasn't easy, and yet small things like a fleeting smile or one shared glance made it feel real.

Jhanghir and I parted company when my friend Sakina texted me asking me to join her at Caffé Nero when she finished up at work. I spotted her with Tanya with our customary devil's chocolate cake as I entered the café. Heading for the counter, I waved at her and signed, asking if either of them wanted a top-up. When they refused, I ordered a machiatto before joining them on the sofas.

'I've found the perfect dress!' I announced, bubbling over with excitement. 'It's beyond anything I could ever have imagined and I've found it, but, oh my gosh, you're not going to believe what happened at Dhamini's! I can never go there again, ever – oh yeah, let's not forget that Seema *bhabhi*, aka "Posh wannabee", literally told me I was obese. Seriously, she pointed out all my wobbly bits in front of Jhanghir . . .' I trailed off as I noticed an unnaturally quiet Tanya. Looking to Sakina, I knew something was wrong when she indicated towards Tanya's hand. I looked at Tanya's hand and it took me a moment before it dawned on me. Her engagement ring was missing. I couldn't take my eyes off the place her ring was meant to be, for fear that my fiercely independent friend had pushed the man who had been besotted with her beyond the point of no return. Javed had bent over backwards to convince Tanya he was the man for her, and now my friend refused to look at me.

'Tanya?' I asked and waited until she turned to face me.

'Javed and I broke up,' she explained with a short smile. 'He met someone else . . .'

'What?' My shocked outburst attracted disapproving looks from other coffee-loving patrons. Ignoring them, I looked at Tanya, noticing her pale, drawn complexion. Composing my thoughts, I leaned forward and looked straight at Tanya. 'There's been a mistake. Javed is besotted with you, he's the most besotted man I know, you've made a mistake.'

'Are you really that bloody naïve about men?' Tanya asked without a shred of emotion. 'They think with their pencils and the rest be damned.' Jesus, it's times like this that I wish I could drink,' the *hijabi* breathed out, before sitting cross-legged on the sofa and resting her head in the palms of her hands. Sakina and I exchanged glances, both knowing that Tanya was hurt deep, very deep.

'What happened?'

Tanya paused at my question, and I wished I hadn't asked. She was close to tears – well, as close to tears as I had ever seen her, but she refused to cry. And then she spoke about how they had been having rows for weeks about dowries, with Javed claiming that she had driven him away with her demands. He then went on to confess that he'd fallen for a girl at work, someone who loved him like Tanya never had. She spoke clearly, rarely faltering, as if it had happened to another person. 'So I returned his ring,' Tanya finished quietly. 'He can give it to his new fiancée.' Sakina and I sat in silence, too shocked to speak and struggling to find the words to comfort Tanya.

'You know the stupid thing?' Tanya asked, and we both shook our heads. 'I really loved Javed.' The simple admission brought tears to my eyes and I scooted across next to her.

'Let me talk to him . . .'

'No, Maya . . .'

'Let me find out what he's thinking . . .'

'He's thinking about how to get into that bitch's panties . . .'

'Stop,' I told Tanya, making her look at me. 'Is he worth fighting for?'

'Are you kidding? He's an arsehole who two-timed me just before we were meant to get married . . .'

'We're talking about Javed. He chased you until he convinced you that he truly loved you and that doesn't just disappear,' Sakina interjected, frowning with concern.

'Well, apparently it does,' said Tanya, fighting to stay composed and then she looked up at me with wide tear-filled eyes. 'What am I going to do?' she whispered before giving in to her tears. I pulled her into a hug, and rubbed her back, shocked by the revelation. Javed was the most sensible, principled guy we knew, and he had fought for years to win Tanya. If he was prone to cheating, then what hope did the rest of us have? As I held my sobbing friend, my thoughts turned to Jhanghir. My dowry had yet to be agreed and I knew that this age-old tradition of arranging a prenuptial agreement would test our commitment. With our families barely talking to each other, and our relationship taking the scenic route to intimacy, doubts about our compatibility multiplied exponentially in the face of Javed's behaviour. Diamonds and dowries may be a girl's best friend, but sometimes, just sometimes, we forget that they come a distant second place to the man in our life.

Eliminate egos and estimate everything

If Tanya's devastation taught me anything, it was to be in control of my life. It wasn't that I didn't trust Jhanghir, but I knew there were no guarantees, and with the obstacles we faced, it'd be nothing less than a miracle if we made it to the wedding day. So I decided that I would take the reins back from Seema to arrange a wedding that was becoming of the grand Bollywoodtasic dream I had. Of course, I would use every single one of my diplomacy skills and charm to get control, because this was my wedding and I was the bride. At least, that's what I told myself when I joined Jhanghir and Seema for lunch the following day. I found them at Busaba's tucking into Thai dishes that made your mouth water. Handing my mac to the waiter, I watched them talk over a document Seema referred to. I greeted them and sat next to Seema. I caught Jhanghir's eyes and smiled.

'Your timing's perfect! Take a look at this,' Seema said, handing me the document they had been looking at. My smile faltered as I stared down at a project map for my wedding, complete with colour charts and timelines.

'You don't have to worry about a thing! I've got it all under control. Go ahead and order,' she added, beckoning a waiter over with a subtle nod of the head. I ignored the waiter, staring down at my wedding plan.

'Maya, do you want to put your order in?' Jhanghir asked. I couldn't even look at him because he would read the outraged indignation written all over my face.

'I'm not really hungry,' I told the waiter before looking back down at the plan.

'It's great that you're watching your weight, Maya; I didn't want to say anything but I'm so relieved that you've realised what you need to do.'

I wasn't offended by Seema's words because it was then that I noticed the wedding cost estimates that ended with the grand sum total of £210,000. Baulking at the figure, I shook my head and looked up at her.

'You need to back off.' OK, so diplomacy wasn't a strong skill of mine. Both Seema and Jhanghir frowned at my comment.

'Are you OK?'

'Have you seen this?' I asked Jhanghir, who nodded as if I'd asked the dumbest question in the world. 'Have you really seen it?'

'I've just said yes, Maya; it's a wedding plan. Seema *bhabhi*'s taken care of all the arrangements,' Jhanghir told me as if I needed the explanation. Taking a deep breath, I paused before looking at them both.

'This is my wedding,' I told them, but they stared at me as if that fact made not a jot of difference. 'I'm the bride.' I waited again, and still they looked at me with that blank, confused look.

'Yes, and Jhanghir's the groom, and I'm your *bhabhi* who's more than happy to take care of everything,' Seema pointed out as if I was slow.

'I would like to make the plans for my wedding . . .'

'But I've done that for you,' Seema said, tapping the paper with a smile.

'These aren't the plans I made.'

'Take a closer look, I've got the best caterers, the best decorators, the colour scheme mapped . . .'

'Maya, what Bhabhi's trying to tell you is that everything's been taken care of . . .'

'But I don't want it to be! Look at this,' I burst out, pointing to Seema's plans. 'We're having a string quartet playing classical music to which we're meant to have our first dance.'

'Don't tell me you don't do dancing in your Sylheti community!' Seema laughed.

'We don't, and we don't hold weddings in ballrooms decorated Arctic-white with the minimalist sterile look of a nuclear laboratory. I don't want a modern, contemporary, Arctic-white wedding!'

'Anything else?' Seema asked, sitting back to fold her arms.

'We don't serve alcohol at our weddings, so there's not going to be a bar, and I don't want a full English menu when the majority of our guests are going to be Asian.'

'There's a quality called gratitude. I'd advise you to look it up,' Seema suggested as she collected her purse.

'Ungrateful?' I breathed out in disbelief.

'Maya,' Jhanghir warned, but I chose to ignore him.

'I've spent the past week following you around, being ignored, invalidated and sidelined. You have looked down on every single suggestion I have made as if it's not good enough.'

'You're stepping up in the world through this marriage, you need to adjust your standards accordingly . . .'

'My standards are fine where they are, you just need to remember this isn't your wedding and you need to back off.' By the time I'd finished, Seema was storming out of the restaurant.

'Do you know what you've done?' Jhanghir said as he threw some notes down to cover the cost of the meal.

'Don't go after her . . .'

'You've alienated my father, humiliated my uncle and now insulted my sister-in-law . . .'

'Don't go.'

Jhanghir chose to leave. He followed after Seema, leaving me at the busy Bond Street restaurant alone. Grabbing my bag, I raced after him. 'Why her?' I demanded, pulling him round to face me just before the Selfridges entrance.

'What?' Jhanghir asked in confusion.

'Why do you put her first? Why do you always put her needs ahead of mine?'

'Maya, what are you talking about?' Jhanghir shouted.

'Seema *bhabhi*, you always put her first!' I shouted back. 'You're marrying me, I'm going to be your wife, and you never consult with me. There are no calls, no emails. We don't even talk and we're meant to be getting married . . .'

'I can't do this now,' Jhanghir told me through clenched jaw as he leaned forward.

'Don't walk away from me.'

'Do you know how close my family are to boycotting my marriage?' I shook my head at his question, and he rubbed his jaw to calm himself down. 'I have been spending all my time trying to bring my dad round, you have just alienated the only person who seems to be able to bring him round,' Jhanghir explained.

'He doesn't approve of me . . .'

'Can you blame him? I'm about to lose my family, I neglected my job so that I can give you the wedding you want and you still complain that I'm not romancing you or whispering sweet nothings to you.'

'You always back her.'

'Really? So which venue did you get? Who chose your outfit?' His point hit home and I wanted to kick myself for my outburst. 'Get your ego in check, Maya, and grow up.' And with those words Jhanghir stormed off. I stood there watching him, feeling like the most selfish, spoilt brat in the world.

Things went from bad to worse that evening when, unannounced, Jhanghir arrived with his mother, asking to speak with Baba. Immediately Amma started fretting that the wedding was being called off. I hadn't told anyone of our fall-out earlier that day, so, paralysed by fear, I waited with Amma in the kitchen.

'Maya, they're asking for you,' my sister-in-law Shireen *bhabhi* said as she entered the kitchen after having served the refreshments. Pulling my shawl around me, I walked into the tense living room to take a seat by Baba.

'Maya, Jhanghir and his mother think it's important that you are here during these talks,' Baba started. Jhanghir's despondent expression worried me. 'Jhanghir's father is unhappy with this wedding; he's not given his blessing and it's unlikely that he'll change his mind.' As Baba spoke, my heart raced with the fear that Jhanghir had changed his mind. I had no doubt that the posh wannabee had raced back to Jhanghir's family to exaggerate the events at Busaba's, and now, well, now there seemed to be no going back. 'As a result, it's unlikely that his brother, Bhabhi and respected elderly members of the family will attend either.'

'I'm really sorry. My husband's family and friends form a small community and they tend to marry amongst each other. Anyone who's an outsider, well, they aren't welcomed as they should be,' Mrs Khan explained. 'It's not right and it's not fair, but it's what it is and we have to deal with it in the best possible way.' I glanced at Jhanghir and it was the first time I noticed how exhausted he looked. 'Jhanghir's hospital have called him back so he's flying to the States tomorrow . . .'

'So you're leaving?' I whispered through my dry, parched throat, assuming that he was giving up. 'Just like that, you're going?'

'My hands are tied, Maya. Belleveue Paeds gave me discretionary leave and they need me back in surgery.'

'So the wedding's off?' Everyone looked confused by my question.

'No, that's why I'm here tonight; so that we can get everything straight before I head back to New York,' Jhanghir cleared up, annoyed by my assumption.

'He has no choice, Jhanghir needs to get back to work,' Baba explained. I stared at Jhanghir until he met my eyes.

'It's unlikely I can get any time off before the wedding.' My heart dropped at his words. 'Which means that you're going to have to make most of the decisions, do you understand?' I nodded and realised that he had chosen me over his father and his wealth. It hadn't been an easy decision and it showed on his face.

'That's not a problem, I have my wedding plans,' I assured him.

'And everything's gotta to be down-sized, OK? Dad's decision to disown me means my cards have been cancelled and access to my trust fund has been blocked. I'll figure out if I still have the flat to go back to, as it's my dad's . . .'

'Don't worry, we'll cover the wedding,' Baba offered, but Jhanghir shook his head.

'I didn't expect this, so I need a little time to get on top of my finances and then I'll transfer you funds to pay for the wedding.' The speed and severity of the disownment spoke volumes of the depth of Jhanghir's father's disapproval. It also exposed Jhanghir to the realities of managing on a salary, a concept he had never had to worry about because of his family wealth.. Baba called Amma to join us and she came in and sat down

'They've come to discuss Maya's dowry. Now, traditionally we need elder members of both families to witness the agreement but, given the exceptional circumstances, Jhanghir's asked me to consider what he can give Maya . . .'

'This is very unusual, surely we can ask Maya's uncle and aunt to come over . . .'

'Jhanghir and his mother have asked me in good faith to act swiftly and I've agreed. They have suggested a dowry consisting of twenty thousand dollars cash plus thirty tolas of gold for your wedding jewellery, as well as fifty per cent of any shared savings you both come to accumulate, God willing,' Baba summarised.

'I would have given you more, my daughter, celebrated it, even, but my hands are tied with the decision my husband has made,' Mrs Khan said sadly.

'Hanna and Jana got more cash—'

'Are you happy with your dowry?' Baba cut off Amma to ask me directly. I had no way of gauging whether the size was fair or not, what I did know was that Jhanghir was committed to me. Putting aside my feelings and being totally pragmatic, I asked myself whether, in the event of a divorce, I should expect more from Jhanghir, who, after all, was a surgeon going places very fast. And then Tanya's heartache came to mind, and I knew there were serious consequences to requesting more than the groom could manage. So I looked at my father for guidance and he smiled gently before saying, 'Accept it, Maya.'

'I accept,' I whispered happily.

'Good,' Jhanghir breathed out with a nod of his head. 'We shouldn't hold you up any longer, I've got to go and pack to catch the early morning flight.'

'Nonsense, you'll eat with us before you go . . .'

'No, really, I have a lot to sort out tonight,' Jhanghir said, suggesting that he had more than packing to deal with. Baba didn't protest any further. Jhanghir remained tense and preoccupied when we saw them off, so we knew relations with his family were at their worst. After they left, Baba and Amma called Tariq *bhai*, Ayesha, Hanna, Jana and Taj to a family meeting. They arrived one by one, and filed into the living room to have a heated discussion about the actions of Jhanghir's father. Taj and the twins demanded that we pull out, outraged that Mr Khan considered us to be an unworthy family to join with, whilst Ayesha and Tariq *bhai* advised everyone to support Jhanghir, who had acted honourably. Nobody noticed when I slipped out of the room. At a personal level, I was offended at the treatment and judgement of my family, but I couldn't be more proud of Jhanghir's actions. So we weren't industrialist with five generations of merchant wealth to lift us up into the uber-rich world. But we were a good, decent and honourable family – something that Mr Khan failed to acknowledge. And yet, I couldn't get angry at him because Jhanghir's predicament and subsequent actions would weigh heavily on him and there was no getting away from the fact that I was the cause. I thought about Tanya and I thought about the sacrifice Jhanghir had made for me and I knew I couldn't give up on him. I called him and left a message, but my phone never rung. I tried not to feel anxious and focused on trusting Jhanghir to do the right thing. Looking through Seema's very comprehensive and almost impressive wedding plan, I started scaling back my Bollywoodtastic wedding. Egos, estimates and expectations aside, this was my moment to support him.

Flirting compromises your faith and faithfulness

Heathrow Airport first thing on a Monday morning was never a great place to find someone. In fact, you couldn't choose a busier time if you tried. Still, I filed past the Virgin Atlantic check-in queues searching for Jhanghir, determined to see him alone before he left. Passengers for his flight were being called to go to the boarding gate so I raced up to the first floor and waited at the security entrance where family and friends waved their loved ones off. I chewed my bottom lip, hoping he hadn't already gone through the gates. Taking my phone out, I searched my messages but there were none. Then, from the corner of my eye, I spotted Jhanghir. Turning around, I froze when, by his side, stood Preeya, his stunning and recently married ex-fiancée. The girl Mr Khan had hand-picked for Jhanghir was now with Jhanghir, my fiancé. Slipping across to Tie Rack, I hid amongst the rails and watched with narrowed eyes as they walked arm in arm through to the security zone. They seemed deep in conversation and at one point Preeya put an arm around Jhanghir's shoulder to hug him as they waited in the slow queue. My eyes nearly popped out when Jhanghir pulled her into a hug and wrapped his arms around her. Ignoring the rising rage within me, I quickly sent Jhanghir a text: *'Have a safe flight, miss you already, x'*

Frowning at the corny message that I would never otherwise have sent, I looked back at the beautiful couple. Jhanghir pulled back from Preeya to look down at his message, which Preeya all too happily read. They chuckled at it before Jhanghir pocketed his phone. He didn't bother replying. I waited until they walked through the security zone before leaving Heathrow Airport. A million questions raced through my mind, none more worrying than the thought that Jhanghir had turned to Preeya, my old nemesis, for support. I refused to call him and demand a million and one answers. I stopped myself from speed-dialling Sakina to super-analyse what this all meant. Instead, I chose to wait; wait for answers he would voluntarily give me, to explain what I had seen. He had asked me to trust him, to believe in him, to have faith in him. And yet, as women, we're programmed to suspect BS at the first sign. But I held myself back. Too much had happened in the past forty-eight hours, and right now my female intuition was bruised. So, I gave myself time to have faith in fate to reveal the truth.

Jhanghir didn't contact me when he landed. Neither did he call, Facebook, email or do anything close to resembling communicating over the following days. So I stayed quiet and focused on our wedding. By the end of the week, I walked into the living room to find Amma with Chachijhi Fauzia discussing my wedding with all my cousins: Leila, Meena, Pana, Mana, Kara, Zarah and Farah.

'Here she is!' Leila called out, getting up to envelop me in a warm hug and, more to the point, a cloud of

Chanel No. 5. 'OK, bride-to-be, why is Chachi organising us for your wedding? And what are we going to do for your *henna*? Because I'm now married and wiser, I can say that I've forgiven you for not dancing at my *henna*, so I'm happy to share my wedding wisdom with you.' Marriage hadn't eased my cousin's penchant for wanting to be the centre of attention, so I looked to my mother.

'What's going on?' I asked, sitting on the floor between Pana and Mana.

'There're five and a half months to your wedding, and everything's still to be organised,' Amma explained with a warm smile.

'And we know you are stressed and worrying over Jhanghir's family, and we want you to know that we are a hundred and fifty per cent supporting you,' Chachijhi added. 'I thank God I have been blessed with Leila's husband. Her mother-in-law is a mental case, but the rest of the family are wonderful, but I know not everybody can be as lucky as Leila. Still, don't you worry about anything, we will take care of everything.' I didn't know what was worse, being seconded to my cousin again or the thought that Chachijhi Fauzia was taking care of my wedding plans.

'Have you booked a make-up artist?'

I shook my head at Pana's question.

'Who's doing your *henna*?'

I shrugged and bit my lip.

'Have you got your song list for the wedding and *henna*?'

Again I shook my head.

'Have you chosen your cake?'

'What about the look for your bridesmaids?'

I kept shaking my head as the girls reeled off questions nineteen to the dozen about details for the wedding that I hadn't even contemplated.

'What have you done?' Amma finally asked, looking nervously to Chachijhi, who smiled smugly at my lack of preparation.

'I've decided on the theme of the wedding . . .'

'You're having a themed wedding? Like a fancy dress wedding?' Leila derided, snorting at the suggestion.

'Fancy dress? You mean dress up like Wonder Woman and Catwoman?' Chachijhi Fauzia gasped in disbelief. The thought of my short, overly endowed aunty dressed up as Wonder Woman made me shiver with horror. And before I could stop it, my family fell into a heated debate.

'Who would go as what?' Zarah asked.

'We could go as the Pussy Cat Dolls!' Farah suggested, causing Chachijhi to touch both her cheeks in a sign of asking God for forgiveness.

'I bagsy Catwoman,' Leila demanded.

'But I want to go as Catwoman,' Pana countered as Leila shook her head.

'Seriously, you've got to admit, I've got the figure to pull it off . . .'

'Who's going where as Catwoman?' Taj asked, walking into the room to fall on to the sofa between Amma and Chachijhi Fauzia.

'I am, at Maya's wedding,' Leila and Pana both answered.

'Why don't you both dress up and I'll decide?' Taj suggested, laughing when everyone threw cushions at him. 'OK, OK. Maya, you decide!' he said, causing everyone to turn to me to determine which one of my cousins would get the honour.

'Is this another cultural sell-out idea from your in-laws?' Taj asked dryly.

Unimpressed, I looked from him to my cousins.

'There is no fancy dress wedding.'

'But you said—'

'I said themed wedding, as in having a unique wedding style.'

'But it's a Bengali wedding, you don't need to create a style,' Taj pointed out.

'I don't want a bog-standard Bengali wedding with a pretty backdrop, flowers and head table where the three-course meal is the only event.'

'But that's how every Bengali wedding is,' Taj said in confusion.

'That's why I want mine to be different . . .'

'Different?' Amma and Chachijhi said, shaking their heads. 'Why can't we just have a normal wedding, like everyone else?'

'Yeah, Maya, just keep it simple. The groom arrives first, the bride arrives two hours late. Food is served. Pictures are taken and everyone goes home with a full belly happy,' Taj said. I turned to him and was sure I caught a quick wink thrown in Pana's direction. Following his line of sight, I spotted Pana looking down with half a smile. Narrowing my eyes, I looked back at Taj, who realised that I had caught the interaction. 'Actually, unique sounds good. What's your idea?' he asked with a sudden change of mind.

'The colour theme is mint-green, antique gold and cream,' I started before explaining how I wanted a mogul-inspired wedding, with big, bold Islamic calligraphy lining the walls, bronze lamps forming a warm glow and billowing silk veils turning the hall into a mogul's court. By the time I finished, they stared at me in silence.

'We're still going to have Bengali food, aren't we?' Chachijhi asked hesitantly. Realising that no one understood my vision, I changed tact.

'Shall we decide what you girls will wear?'

Immediately my cousins jumped to action, grabbing at wedding magazines to pick out the latest trends. We spent the afternoon reviewing films, playing songs, talking about how we were going to do what, where and when. Sometimes, the girls broke out into an impromptu dance, copying the Indian dance routine playing on the screen, other times, Amma tried to convince the girls to sing age-old wedding songs. It caused everyone to fall into fits of laughter when she was joined only by Chachijhi in painfully out-of-tune renditions of some of the classics. Slipping into the kitchen, I spent the rest of the afternoon calling up make-up artists to discover two undeniable facts. One, Asian bridal make-up artists charged a fortune to turn you into the most beautiful you possible. And two, they got booked up a year in advance, which left me with a long list of crossed-out names and no make-up artist.

'I can't find a make-up artist,' I announced as I burst into the living room. 'I've called every single one listed in the Asian bridal magazines and they're all booked, every single one.'

'I've got a friend,' Leila shouted out, pulling me down to sit next to her. 'She's changed careers and has been training for the past six months. She's really good, I can call a favour.'

I tried not to doubt Leila's offer. We had a competitive past, and Leila always had to do more, speak more and dramatise more. But now I had no choice and I had to have faith that she meant well, so I smiled and handed her the phone to make the booking.

That evening I looked down at all my wedding notes and to-do lists and ripped out pictures that my cousins and I had pulled together. Smiling, I recalled the dancing, singing and jesting from the day. Opening up my wedding book, I looked down at my sketches for my wedding and I knew that I needed to paint. It only felt like yesterday that I gave up the secure monotonous world of corporate consultancy to enter the uncertain, non-paying world of artistry. Despite the horror of my family about 'going into the arts', somehow, in a short time, I had made an impact. I had a Khan-Ali bursary to Brown's, so not only would I be living a dream of being with Jhanghir, but I would also finally be fulfilling my dream to become a serious artist. All the change of becoming a married woman hundreds of miles away from my family would be tempered by my passion to paint. Not from afar would I stare at Rothko, frown at Monet or look with wonder at Azizza Essa's master-pieces. I would be creating art. Me, Maya Malik. With a short smile, I felt that tingling feeling deep within me at the thought of painting. In a flurry of activity, I grabbed my notebook and headed down to the garage where I had set up a small corner to paint. Setting up a new canvas, oils and my brushes, I sat down on a stool. Looking down at my notes, I smiled. It was time to paint my wedding to life.

'Maya!' Turning at Amma's call, I found her stepping into the garage. 'Oh my . . .' she breathed out, looking at the large painting in striking gold and cream. I had worked through the night, testing colour combinations before painting the calligraphy perfect.

'What do you think?' I asked smiling and stepping back to give her a full view. Pushing my hair out of my eyes, I stared at her until she clapped with delight.

'This is . . . this is beautiful.' Amma laughed before turning to the garage entry. 'You have a guest, Jhanghir's cousin.'

I froze when gorgeous Zain walked in. Dressed in

chinos, white T-shirt and navy cardigan, he looked like he had just stepped out of an Abercrombie and Fitch ad. Nervously, I touched my messy hair, cringing at the thought of being found make-up free and caked in paint.

'You're good,' he stated, assessing the painting before looking at me.

'Thanks,' I muttered, using a rag to clean my paint-smeared hands.

'I see why you earned that Khan-Ali bursary. You're very good.'

Turning to Zain, I folded my arms self-consciously and then leaned back against the counter. Taking a deep breath, I forced myself to think of Jhanghir to help pull myself together.

'Have you come to talk about my paintings, or is there something I can help you with?' I asked, causing him to chuckle.

'She has many more,' Amma said, pointing to the canvases that I had stacked up against the wall. 'She's very talented; my daughter the painter.'

I looked at Amma with a frown. Eighteen months ago she was crying blue murder because I had chucked in a 'decent office job' as an analyst to paint, and now . . . now she was parading my work like mother hen.

'Yes, she is.' The tone in Zain's voice caught my attention, and I curbed a smile, realising that it wasn't just the painting he was appreciating. Amma caught the interaction and coughed disapprovingly.

'So what can we do for you?' she asked directly.

'Jhanghir *bhai* asked me to ask Maya if she needs a hand with the wedding preparation.'

'We're fine, thank you.' Amma didn't trust him and she wasn't going to let him think otherwise. 'Maya has all the family she needs to arrange a wonderful wedding.'

'Jhanghir's been in touch?'

Zain looked surprised at my question. 'He didn't tell you I was popping in today?' He frowned, when I shook my head. 'Have you guys spoken?'

'Of course they have!' Amma laughed, covering my hesitation. 'I can barely get a moment with my daughter any more, it's wedding this and wedding that, just wedding, wedding, wedding!' She laughed, taking his arm to lead him out of the garage. 'Why don't you finish up, Maya, and join us in the living room.'

Turning round, I frowned at Jhanghir's silence. I had been patient, I had waited for some indication of what Jhanghir was thinking, but this . . . sending his cousin to check up on me when he could just as easily call . . . this was unacceptable. Quickly, I put away my paints, hung my painting to dry and then took my brushes into the kitchen to wash them and leave them out to dry. Catching my image in the small mirror, I groaned, wiping at the paint smears on my forehead and cheek. Accepting that Zain had already seen me at my worst, I gave up and walked to the living room where Amma was busy matchmaking Zain by singing the virtues of my cousin Man-eater Meena.

'There you are!' she trilled as I leaned against the door and looked at them. 'I was just telling Zain about our wonderful Meena. Isn't she the loveliest girl to see?'

'Very lovely,' I agreed, smiling at Zain with a raised brow.

'And she's a godly person. My goodness, I've never seen such a turnaround in character; really, one day she woke and bang, *hijab*, *jilbab*, *nikab* all in one. Isn't she a very good girl?' Amma said, looking to me for confirmation.

'Very good,' I confirmed, holding Zain's eyes. 'Weren't you telling me that you were thinking of settling down?'

'Really?' Amma gasped with a wide smile. 'Well, Maya, why don't you introduce Meena to Zain? In fact, let me see if I can dig out a picture of Meena, I'm sure I have a few from Leila's wedding last year,' she muttered, leaving the room to hunt out a suitable picture.

'Thanks,' he acknowledged with a muted grin.

'No problem,' I returned, unable to contain a smile as he finally chuckled. Unsure of what to say, we looked at each other until our smiles faltered.

'The wedding—'

'Yes,' I said quickly, digging my hands into my pocket.

'The plans going well?'

'Yes . . . yes, they are.' I didn't know what he was doing, but whatever it was, I knew it was wrong. The vibe we had, it was most definitely wrong. 'I'm having a mogul-inspired wedding; you know, lots of silk drapery, lots of lamps and calligraphy . . .'

'The painting . . .'

'Yeah, that's for the wedding,' I finished, reading his thoughts.

'That's great, let me know if I can help with the decorators. I've a facilities manager who overlooks my software businesses. I could put you in touch with him.' Not only was this sculpted George Clooney lookalike a sight to behold, he was also a successful entrepreneur.

'Sure,' I accepted, more than content to work with him.

'Wednesday.'

'What about it?' I asked as he frowned and cleared his throat. 'I'm busy,' I blurted out, shocked that he seemed to be asking me out.

'Wednesday?' Zain checked as I nodded and folded my arms. 'In the afternoon?'

'All day.' There was no way I would compromise my

future with Jhanghir by being so close to temptation. Because that's what Zain was. Temptation. Albeit one hot, smoking, irrefutably attractive temptation.

'That's a shame. Jhanghir asked me to take you shopping for your wedding jewellery . . .'

'Oh! Right!' I breathed out, having totally misread his signal. 'Yeah, that's fine!'

'So you can make Wednesday?' he asked, confused. I nodded when he realised my assumption and shook his head. 'Pre-Jhanghir, there would've been no doubt about it,' Zain confirmed.

'There's only ever been Jhanghir,' I told him.

'That was before we met.'

I refused to smile at the cheeky reply.

'There will only ever be Jhanghir.'

He contemplated my answer and then smiled. 'You sure?'

I hesitated at his question and we watched each other, flirting.

'Yes,' I answered in spite of my thoughts.

'Everything fine?' Amma asked, walking in on our silence whilst clutching a bundle of photos.

'We're going to go gold shopping,' I told her, causing her to look at Zain with a frown.

'With him?' Amma forced herself to smile after her abrupt question. 'Good, I'll ask your *chachijhi* and Meena to join us. This is my niece,' she continued showing him the fifty or so photos of my cousin. Shaking my head at Amma's behaviour, I caught Zain's glance.

'Maya, do you want to start preparing dinner?' Amma didn't miss a thing.

'I should get going too,' Zain said, rising to leave.

'But you haven't seen all of Meena's photos,' Amma pointed out, making Zain sit down again. Curbing a smile, I gave him a nod before leaving them to it.

Standing outside the door, I smiled at the thought of shopping for wedding jewellery with Zain. Jhanghir came to mind, and I stopped smiling. Frowning, I headed up to my room to shower and change, telling myself that Zain was a bit of eye candy, a bit of male totty, that I could appreciate from afar. There was nothing wrong with that. Nothing at all. And yet, I couldn't look at myself in the mirror, I couldn't shake the guilty feeling. The shared humour, the passing comments, and the looks . . . it all felt too natural, too instinctive. Leaning against the cold glass mirror, I bit my lip, cursing sod's law. Before Jhanghir, I had spent months, no, years, waiting to bump into a Zain, a man who made my George Clooney dreams a real possibility. And he turned up now. Now, when I was engaged. Ready to marry the man of my dreams, who also only happened to be the man who had disappeared from my life a week ago, with his stunning ex-fiancée. Preeya was the Ivy-league educated, ultra sophisticated, stunning family friend who had been hand-picked by Jhanghir's father to be his future wife when they were mere teenagers. She was the one I had hotfooted across to New York to stop Jhanghir marrying. Despite now being married to Jhanghir's cousin with a lovely baby boy, Preeya had remained close friends with Jhanghir. She was the one woman who brought out the green-eyed monster in me because I knew something Jhanghir didn't know, and that was that she was still in love with him. Though that was not my secret to share with Jhanghir, her appearance in Jhanghir's life when things between us were at an all-time low was worrying. More than worrying. It was deeply concerning. In that moment, I switched on my laptop and logged into my email.

To: JKhan@NYMedics.com
From: MayaM@Instantmail.com

OK, so this is how it works when two people want to get married. They speak, they talk, they share their dreams, they share secrets and special moments, and they work together to have the best start to their married life with the most amazing wedding day possible.

And then I look at us, and we are so far from that. Yes, we have some exceptional challenges and family pressures, but surely they should bring us closer? Yes, we're separated by an ocean, but that's never been a problem in the past. And yes, we're trying to figure out how we move from being good friends to becoming husband and wife, but surely it's not meant to be this awkward, this impossibly hard?

The fact is this: I've never felt more distant from you than when you were here beside me, talking about getting married to me. I saw you speak the words, but I know you didn't feel them, so if you spoke out of obligation to me because you raised my hopes about getting married, tell me. Tell me, because we shouldn't marry out of obligation. Tell me, because five years down the line I don't want you to blame me for the rift with your family. Most importantly, tell me, because I need to know this is going to make you happy.

I read the message and then reread it half a dozen times, hesitating to press the send icon. I knew I was risking a wedding, the wedding I had dreamed of for what felt like an eternity. Escaping singledom had been the goal for so long that marriage alone felt like the promised land. Right now that felt like the biggest con ever. Surely being locked in an unfulfilling union was a fate worse than singledom? I fought to find the faith and courage to do the right thing. I had to be honest with Jhanghir because only that could strengthen my faith in him, in us, and in our future. If fate was to test my faithfulness, I needed more than a mere promise to get married. Closing my eyes, I whispered a quick prayer and hit send.

Glamonomics — a girl's guide to gold and glamour

There was only one thing a girl could do when things were tough, and that was to spend a day in the company of her best friends, being pampered. With an AWOL fiancé, a wedding going nowhere fast, and the very real possibility that I could give in to temptation, I called Sakina and Tanya and convinced them to pull a sickie to spend a day at the Sanctuary spa centre. We met at Covent Garden and looked at each other. There was no denying that we had arrived, each with our own demons weighing heavily on us. Without a moment to lose, we headed for Floral Street, where we walked through the deceptively small cosmetics store to the back to take the stairs up to the spa sanctuary. After we had registered ourselves, booked various treatments and massages, we took our dressing gowns and walked through to the bright, spacious dressing rooms.

'He hasn't been in touch,' Tanya offered as we walked in flip-flops down to the calm exercise pool. 'I thought Javed would be in touch by now.'

'He's such a disappointment,' Sakina muttered, leading the way through the corridors that connected heat rooms, spa rooms and the breathtaking Koi Carp Lounge.

'And your family? Are they OK?'

'My parents flipped, I thought my dad and brothers were going to kick the crap out of Javed,' Tanya said as we passed the hammam and spa to get to the pool. 'I wanted to kick the crap out of him.'

'Would you consider contacting him?'

Tanya's hesitation told me that she had.

'No, she can't give him that satisfaction,' Sakina protested. It was a weekday, and as such, the all-female spa centre was very quiet. We took off our gowns and eased ourselves into the long, low-lit pool.

'Hear me out,' I told them as we swam side by side. 'When Jhanghir was about to get married, we were not talking about him fancying another girl, marrying another girl, you guys convinced me to get on a plane and get to Manhattan to stop him.'

'That was different . . .'

'Na, ah,' I corrected Sakina. 'What if Javed's waiting for you to fight for him?'

Tanya faltered at my question, lost her stroke and went under water. Stopping, we treaded water until Tanya emerged and pushed her hair back from her face.

'You serious?' she asked as if the thought had never entered her mind.

'Deadly,' I returned, seeing her wipe the water from her face as if to clear her thoughts.

'Why would he . . . why would he do that?' Tanya asked.

'Who knows why men do anything?' Sakina returned, making Tanya and I both look to her with a frown. And yet she couldn't have said anything truer as I thought of Jhanghir's lack of response to my email. Putting Jhanghir to the back of my mind, I looked at Tanya.

'What if Javed is waiting for you to fight for him, Tanya?'

'He wouldn't put our future at risk with a made-up story to test me . . .'

'I'm not saying he didn't fall for another girl, but just ask yourself this, what if he needed you to convince him you are his future? Are you willing to lose him because of your pride?' And with that, we started swimming again. Only this time we swam alone, at our own pace, and lost in our very own troubles.

'Shah's gone cold on me,' Sakina admitted as we left the pool to head for the hammam. Entering the dark steam room, we found our own spot and lay down on the wooden slabs. Within moments, the steam eased the tension from our bodies. A patron poured more water to raise the steam levels, and I stretched in the overly warm relaxing room. 'He wants time out.'

'Give him all the time he needs by telling him goodbye,' Tanya muttered as she wiped herself down with a towel.

'I think time out is healthy,' Sakina defended as she leaned on her arm to look across at us. 'It gives me the chance to see if Shah's the one.'

'You mean it gives Shah the chance to play the field whilst keeping you on standby.'

Ignoring Tanya's curt assessment, I lay back and looked at the starlit ceiling.

'Cut him loose, Sakina,' I told her. 'But do it after a good night out so that his last memory of you is giving him the push with a wide smile.'

'Why would I smile?' Sakina asked, and I knew she feared a future without a man at her side. She still thought that that was a fate worse than being with someone who made her feel replaceable.

'No man likes to be given the push, no man likes to think he's replaceable,' Tanya explained.

'You should meet Zain . . .'

'Who's Zain?' Both of them asked together as we decided to leave the steam room to relax in the large, circular Jacuzzi. Smiling, I looked at them as we settled in.

'Oh my, I haven't seen you smile like that since . . . well, since Jhanghir agreed to marry you.'

I stopped smiling the instant Tanya made the comparison. 'He's Jhanghir's cousin . . .' I trailed off, seeing the glances exchanged by Sakina and Tanya. 'It's not like that,' I challenged before they thought the obvious.

'Of course not,' Tanya accepted too quickly.

'Why would it be?' Sakina added, with half a smile.

'It's not!' I assured them. They both laughed and, before I knew it, Tanya had grabbed my leg and pulled me under. Then we started dunking each other and gasping for breath all at once until we leaned back against the edges laughing.

'Are you going to fess up about this Zain man?' Tanya asked, trying to get her breath back.

'OK, he's the spitting image of George Clooney, and each time he walks into the room, I feel like a sixteen-year-old girl with her first crush.'

Once again Tanya and Sakina exchanged knowing glances.

'You're getting married, Maya, remember? To that guy you flew across the Atlantic for . . .'

'I know, I know!' I cried out. Taking a deep breath, I cleared my thoughts and looked to Sakina. 'That's why I think you should meet him; he's Jhanghir's cousin on his dad's side. His mother's Italian, which explains his smouldering good looks. Oh, and he's an entrepreneur;

he runs a series of software businesses . . .'

'And he's single?' Tanya asked in disbelief. 'You sure he's not gay?'

Remembering how he looked at me in the garage, I shook my head.

'Definitely not,' I breathed naughtily, laughing when Tanya splashed me with water.

'Will you meet him?' I asked Sakina, who hesitated at the opportunity, because of her current predicament with Shah. 'OK, I'm going gold shopping with him . . .'

'You're shopping for your wedding gold with a man you fancy who doesn't happen to be your fiancé?' Tanya asked.

'Jhanghir asked him to look after me in his absence . . .'

'It sounds like Jhanghir needs to be careful what he asks for.'

Ignoring Tanya's loaded comment, I looked at Sakina.

'Come shopping with us. Lord knows, I'll need someone sane, given my mum, Chachijhi and cousin are coming along,' I invited. 'Shah wants time out, so why not test what's out there? You have no ties to anyone, right?'

'But you fancy him . . .'

'When you see him, you'll know that it's impossible not to fancy this man,' I clarified. 'Just say yes!' I beseeched Sakina, whooping when she finally agreed. With mission accomplished, we grabbed our gowns and headed up to the restaurant where we chatted and laughed over a light salad lunch. We talked about everything that had nothing to do with our confused, complicated lives and we laughed so much that other patrons tutted at us with disapproval. After lunch, we headed for the luxurious Koi Carp Lounge where we reclined back with cool long drinks.

'So you want to give us the heads up on your wedding?' Tanya asked as I shook my head. 'C'mon, we know something's up.'

'Jhanghir's entire family is boycotting the wedding.'

'What!' Tanya and Sakina cried out, shooting up to stare at me.

'Except for his mother and cute cousin. The rest of them, well, they're all listening to Jhanghir's father.' I turned on my side and looked at my friends.

'So . . .' Tanya trailed off, wanting to know everything.

'So, Jhanghir's going ahead with the wedding,' I completed with a shrug. Tanya and Sakina copied my shrug until I giggled.

'Stop!' I laughed when they came to sit on my lounge chair to look down at me.

'I saw him fly back to NY with Preeya.'

'*The* Precya?' Tanya gasped in disbelief.

'She's the one his dad hand-picked for Jhanghir, right? The one who married his cousin?'

I nodded at both of Sakina's questions.

'He hasn't been in touch since last week. I've heard nothing from him. Yet he talks to his cousin Zain, telling him to make sure the wedding plans are on schedule.' I looked at both of them. 'That's not normal, is it?' They stayed quiet and I shook my head.

'He's got a lot on his plate, Maya. He probably doesn't realise how he's coming across . . .'

'I emailed him yesterday, telling him this isn't normal.' They both looked at me with wide, expectant eyes. 'And I've heard nothing.'

'Wait a minute,' Sakina said before disappearing for five minutes. Tanya and I talked about the reappearance of Preeya in Jhanghir's life and stopped when Sakina returned with her iPad.

'No, that's not allowed!' I said when she sat between

us and switched it on. 'We're having an unplugged, disconnected day with no emails, calls or texts . . .'

'We're going to hack into Jhanghir's email account.'

'Of course we are,' I threw back as if it was the most natural thing to do. 'Forget it being illegal.'

'Try his Facebook account, Sakina, he'll have pictures up,' Tanya advised, seeing nothing wrong with Sakina's actions.

'Jhanghir's a friend of mine on Facebook, we don't need to hack . . .'

'Do you have full access?' Sakina asked, while Tanya looked at me pointedly.

'Yes.'

'To all his Facebook emails?' Tanya followed up.

'No, why would I have that?'

'Because that's where the interesting stuff lies. Who he's meeting with, what's happening, what his thoughts, his real thoughts, are about marrying you.'

Staring at my friends, I tried to fight my curiosity. I said I tried, because in truth the urge to know all those answers beat my points of principle hands down.

'How do we do this?' I asked as we all turned to face the screen.

'Tell me his favourite film, sport and pin-up star.'

I turned to Sakina with a raised brow.

'Hey, it's a scientific fact, single red-blooded straight males make up their passwords from those three things,' she defended with half a smile. 'I'm a computer engineer, I know these things.'

'*Godfather 2*, Grand Prix and Angelina Jolie,' I admitted, watching Sakina type in varying permutations of words, letters and words related to those three facts.

'TombF1Horse. Nope. Hamilton2Tomb. Nah. Marlon 2TombRedBull. Nope,' she muttered. 'GodFerrari2Jolie.'

'Maya, why don't you log in and let's see what Mr

Khan has been up to in the past week.'

I did as I was asked and we hunched around the screen while I navigated through Facebook to Jhanghir's page. Seeing the many conversations between Preeya and Jhanghir about meeting up, words of support and encouragement, we sat back in silence. I logged out and Sakina shut down her iPad.

'It's nice that he has someone he can rely on,' Sakina said to try and break the silence.

'That someone should be me,' I muttered, picking up my cold drink to take a long sip.

'Great! This is just great!' Tanya burst out, throwing her hands in the air. 'She's been dumped, I've been dumped and you're being ignored for an ex-fiancée. We really do know how to pick them. Let's celebrate!'

I burst out laughing at Tanya's audacious summary.

'Let's raise a glass!' she persisted. We couldn't help but follow suit.

'To idiots who want space,' Sakina stated.

'To fools who change their minds for the office bicycle,' Tanya threw out.

'To misguided fiancés who think they won't pay for playing with an ex,' I added as we clinked glasses and laughed at our carefree attitudes. It didn't matter that the lives we wanted to build seemed further from our reach than we wanted; what mattered was that we were together, sharing our worries and, most of all, still laughing. We spent the rest of the afternoon getting massages, manicures and pedicures. We visited the sleep tank several times until we were chucked out for laughing uncontrollably, we took turns on the high swing over the large atrium pool, and then relaxed in the Thai chill-out room. And when we couldn't laugh any more and were ready to leave, we left the Sanctuary glowing.

*

I returned home to find my sisters sitting round the dining table in the kitchen arguing about whether or not to wear matching *saris* whilst making wedding favour boxes.

'You like?' Hana asked, holding up the cream wedding favour bags that were to hold all kinds of sweet treats.

'You've got quite a factory line going here!' I laughed as Jana placed the first sweets in the middle of the sheer gold wrap. She then passed it to Ayesha, who added hard-boiled wrapped treats, who then gave it to Shireen *bhabhi*, who put the last of the nuts and raisins in before handing it to Hanna, who tied up the little basket with a mint-green ribbon.

'You had a good day?' Ayesha asked with a broad smile.

'It's about to get better!' I laughed as I heard my nephew racing down the stairs before running into my open arms.

'Where have you been? I've been waiting and waiting for you before my afternoon nap!' Hamza told me before wrapping his arms round my neck to give me the biggest hug he could muster. My sisters all laughed at his antics and I smiled as I took him up to my room. I tucked Hamza into my bed, picked up my laptop and then slipped in beside him. Hamza drifted off as soon as his head hit the pillow. Switching on my laptop, I logged into my email and spotted the message from Jhanghir.

To: MayaM@Instantmail.com
From: JKhan@NYMedics.com

Maya, I'm just going to accept that your timing's defunct at the best of times, and impossible and infuriating at the worst of times.

I returned to NY to find that I'd been locked out of Dad's apartment with all my belongings packed up in boxes and fifteen-hour shifts for four weeks straight. And then, of course, there's your email. Trust me, I've had better welcome-home messages.

So, tell me, why now? Why would you now decide to get all insecure and needy on me after everything I've done in the past few weeks to stand by you?

The message left me unsatisfied. There was no mention of Preeya, his constant companion and supporter, and it failed to address any of my questions. So, I responded with:

To: JKhan@NYMedics.com
From: MayaM@Instantmail.com

Needy? Insecure? Are you kidding me? More like confused and worried. Confused as to why you think it's normal to not talk to your fiancée in over a week. Worried because I don't want that to become normal for us.

What you seem to forget is that I saw how disappointed you were with your father's decision. But, rather than talk to me, you shut me out. Yes, you've chosen to stand by me, but what about allowing me to stand by you?

I hit the sent icon and moments later, when the house phone rang, I knew it was Jhanghir. When Amma walked into my room talking posh Bengali, I definitely knew it was him. However, there seemed to be no end to her questions and when she showed no sign of handing the phone over, I walked over to her and took the cordless receiver from her.

'Kids these days, no respect!' I heard her mutter before she left my room. Sliding on to my lounge chair, I huddled my knees against my chest and smiled into the phone.

'So, you finally decided to break cover?' I asked, warmed by the sound of his dry chuckle. I had missed the sound of his laughter and I cherished it now.

'And which part of wanting to marry you fails to tell you that I want to spend the rest of my life with you and have you stand by me?' This was the Jhanghir I knew, the one who cut to the chase with that dry humour that made me smile from within. He sounded more relaxed, happier.

'The part where you seem to forget to call me but can find the time to Facebook friends and call your cousin to pass on messages to me,' I returned.

'If you needed to talk to me, why didn't you just call?' He had missed the point; he was meant to call me because he missed me, but I was damned if I was going to tell him that. 'You never had an issue calling before at all hours of day and night.'

'I thought you were going to call, that's all,' I brushed off, raising a brow when I heard him chuckle.

'Oh, I see, you want to do the romcom thing. Have me call you to say I miss you, is that it?'

'No!' I cut in despite myself. The silence that followed told me that he knew that I did want to do the romcom thing.

'Maya, we have a good thing, so why would you want to swap that for the luvvy-duvvy chocolate and flowers crap you see in the movies?' Jhanghir's logic made sense. 'I can't believe you're turning into such a softie—'

'I'm not!' I defended again too quickly, so I stopped being so defensive. 'I just need to hear your voice, to hear that you're OK.'

'I'm a phone call away, Maya.' His reminder was gentle. 'If you get stressed with all the wedding arrangements, just call me. Now tell me where you're at with everything.'

And so I spent for ever telling him about my plans for a mogul-inspired wedding, glad that I had the chance to field his questions and get his input as well as laugh at his quips. Then I told him about my paintings, and about my spa day with the girls, and just when I had begun to tell him about the style of jewellery I was going to look for, he said, 'You should get Preeya's input on that, she has great taste in jewellery.'

Just the mere mention of this ex-fiancée's name made me freeze. 'Really? I might ask her to come with me—'

'She's in New York right now, I can ask her to email you over some ideas.'

I took a deep breath at his offer and, trying not to sound at all insecure, I asked, 'Have you seen her lately?' The still silence that followed my question answered the question.

'Hey, did I mention to you earlier that Preeya's been a star for letting me crash at her's until I find a place for us?' He knew full well that he hadn't told me but the admission threw me.

'That's . . . very kind of her,' I forced myself to say.

'And she's been great, honestly, she understands the mentality of my family and she's made the past week bearable. She's working on bringing my family round to accepting our marriage.'

'Lovely,' I muttered, wondering how much of Jhanghir's relaxed and happy demeanour was down to being with Preeya.

'Mo is in London at the moment, so you should try and do lunch with him one day.'

Learning that Preeya's husband was in London

leaving Preeya alone with Jhanghir made me feel a hundred times worse. But then nothing prepared for me Jhanghir's next comment. 'And by the way, Preeya's convinced Seema *bhabhi* to join Zain gold shopping tomorrow. She knows that going through Bhabhi may be the only way to get Dad's blessing; isn't that great?'

I could barely bring myself to speak and, in spite of every cell rebelling within me, to make Jhanghir happy, I forced myself to agree.

Asians shopped for wedding jewellery like no other nationality I knew. It had to be gold; glamorous, unmissable, stunning gold. The sets comprised of a stunning necklace with matching earrings, bangles and hair ornament. They varied from the slim and discreet sets to those that often got mistaken for chainmail body armour. There were no limits to how much gold a bride wore. Unfortunately, there was no comprehension that sometimes big did not mean better and that sometimes all it meant was poor taste. And yet there was no getting away from the fact that the weight of the wedding jewellery defined how wealthy the groom was. So when we met Zain and Seema outside Ram Prakash, everyone was notably tense. Seema *bhabhi* looked at me with disdain.

'You're looking well,' she stated with a muted smile. 'I see you've chosen to stick to the cuddly cute look.'

The dig at my size hit home, and before I could reply she turned to smile at Amma. They spoke openly, even though I knew Amma hadn't forgotten how Seema had looked down at us. Chachijhi was less forgiving, choosing instead to introduce Meena to a bemused Zain. And when Meena showed more interest in her mobile phone than in Zain, I all too happily stepped in to introduce Sakina to him. Judging by the way she stared at him, I knew that his George Clooney-esque gorgeousness left her stunned.

'Let's go in!' Chachijhi muttered, hurrying Meena into the famous jeweller's. We followed her in and watched as Seema *bhabhi* spoke to the owner's son whom she seemed to be on first-name basis with. Immediately, he started pulling out a number of sets.

'I've given him Jhanghir's budget and he's pulling out all the jewellery sets he has in that price zone. But be prepared, it doesn't stretch far in a shop like this.'

'Is that it?' Chachijhi muttered when she had assessed the five sets put out on to the glass counter. 'Leila had triple this amount for her wedding.'

Before Seema could storm again at the insult, I stepped forward and said, 'I prefer discreet but ornate sets, Chachijhi.' Defending Jhanghir appeared to calm Seema's reaction. Even so, I read the disappointment in Amma's expression as she looked at the sets. The sets were beautiful, but they weren't the big and beautiful sets that stood out at weddings. Then I spotted the fifth set and smiled. The necklace was a delicate golden lace chainmail that fell in a V. Zain saw my reaction and reached out to pick it up. Holding my hair back with one hand, I moved in front of a mirror before Zain put it around my neck. It wasn't gaudy, or loud, it was just perfect. Catching Zain's eyes in the mirror, my heart skipped a beat at his expression.

'It's beautiful on you,' he told me before stepping back. Ignoring the chaos he caused within me, I turned to Amma and Chachijhi and smiled. They smiled too and I knew it was the one. We spent the rest of the afternoon choosing the matching *karas* and *chooris*, and earrings. And when the entire set was pulled together, Chachijhi, in spite of Seema's embarrassed protest, began bartering. You see, we're taught from a young age that there is no fixed price in gold shops because we know the way gold prices are set. Discounting the base rate of gold and labour charge, we haggled over the remaining margin until buyer and seller came to a happy medium. But Chachijhi refused to compromise. She continued bartering and sweetening the assistant, before bartering again until she wore him down. Such was the success of her negotiating skills that, with the saving she made, she managed to buy me an additional half a dozen slim, golden *chooris*.

We left Ram Prakash with four slim, square velvet-covered boxes with enough gold to buy a new car. As custom dictated, the gold stayed with the groom's family until the wedding day so we watched Seema and Zain leave with it. They were looking at each other with wide, white smiles. And then, without a single word, we hit the shops of Southall. Bangles, *bindis*, clutch bags, shawls and all kinds of glitzy, sequined, gem-encrusted accessories needed for weddings were bought as if they were going out of fashion. We shopped until we physically couldn't carry any more. We walked to the car, talking over each other about what was needed, when and how it would be used. We weren't in any rush to get home, so when we arrived at the car and shoved everything into the boot, we stopped and looked at each other. Once again, without another word, we headed back to the high street. You see, the trick to glamonomics is simple, ladies; treat yourselves well, spoil yourselves occasionally and, when needs must, shop, shop, shop!

Hunger strikes, hooker make-up and hidden secrets

*C*uddly. She had called me *cuddly*. And, by that, she
meant fat. That evening I stood in front of my long
mirror, dressed just in a vest and pants to judge whether
I was *cuddly*. I was a long way from being fat, but ever
since Jhanghir and I had agreed to get married, I had
slowly given up using the gym. OK, it's wrong to assume
that having a man meant you had the right to let yourself
go, but you did. *Cute*. She had also called me *cute*. So I
lacked the sharp, angular features and salon-defined
hairstyles that carb-emaciated models had, but I had the
sculpted cheekbones, wide angel eyes and natural
pouting lips that took me out of the *cute* category. That
didn't put me in the sexy category, either, and I was
determined to be sexy the next time Jhanghir saw me. In
that instant, I committed to daily jogs, a harsh diet (type
still to be confirmed) and a sexy new haircut. Taking to
the Internet, I browsed through the million-and-one
different diets to choose from that best suited my appetite
style. The no-carb diet was a no-no diet for me since
caffeine was my only vice in life. Others to be negated
included the cayenne pepper and lemonade two-week

detox, the cabbage soup two-week diet, followed by the new baby food-fad diet. I read up on the blood-type diet, the California sushi diet, as well as the Zone diet, macrobiotic diet and South Beach diet. I kept reading until I came across the liquid diet, which allowed soups, milkshakes, porridge, and fruit juices. Writing down everything I needed to know about it, I stuck a current all-too-honest picture of the flabby me on my wall calendar next to the picture of Halle Berry stepping out of the sea in James Bond. That was the body I wanted. That was the body I was going to bust a gut to get.

By midday, I was starving. The tomato and basil soup I had had for lunch had failed to satisfy a single taste bud, let alone feed my appetite. Topping up with several mugs of coffee, I waited for Leila to turn up to take me to my make-up trial. At fifty pounds a session, the trial was essential for brides to determine the hairstyle and look for the wedding day. Now this is an area brides have got wrong with tragic results. I'd seen one too many brides painted in the wrong-colour foundation, with the delusion that being painted white was the same as being white. Often caked in make-up, brides-to-be all too easily forgot that less can be more when finishing off the look with gigantic false spider lashes that left the bride looking more like the groom in drag. With those horror stories in mind, we turned up at Saira's, Leila's make-up artist friend, for my trial. She led us through her home into the room she used as a studio.

'Take a seat,' Saira said as I took off my jacket. 'So, tell me what you want.'

Which I did. I said, 'No heavy foundation trying to whiten me up. No cake-on make-up where the eyes, cheeks and mouth all clash. And finally, no huge tarantula-sized eyelashes,' I listed, making her laugh. 'I just want an elegant, understated look with strong lips and strong eyes.'

'And how do you want your hair?' Saira asked, touching my long black hair.

'Classically pulled back into a high bun. Maybe something like Julia Roberts's double-high-bun style when she won the Oscar?'

She nodded and smiled. 'I'm going to cover the mirror, OK? It's for your benefit,' Saira told me, pulling a white sheet over the mirror. 'It makes for more of a surprise at the end.'

Smiling at her logic, I watched her open up her large make-up toolbox to lay out her numerous brushes, foundations, cream pots, and all sorts of make-up. Saira was easy-going and down to earth. We chatted throughout the first hour as she moisturised my face to prepare it for the foundation she applied using her brushes. Once applied, she went to make tea and I looked at Leila, who gave me the thumbs up. Smiling, I felt a million dollars, albeit a hungry million dollars. Before long Saira returned to the room, handed us our coffees and then resumed her work. This time, she worked for what seemed like for ever on my eyes. There was shadowing, shading, lining and then more shading. I kept my eyes closed as she promised to attach tasteful lashes on to accentuate my eyes. Once done, she used another hour to finish shading my cheeks and painting my lips. Then she started on my hair. It actually felt good to have someone brush my hair, so I closed my eyes and enjoyed the feeling of being pampered. It took her a while to get me into the style that I wanted but when she managed it, she faced me with a beaming smile.

'You're naturally pretty as it is, but this, my God you look like a supermodel!'

Grinning at her words, I waited with bated breath as

she pulled the sheet off the mirror. Looking at the woman staring back, I froze. I was looking at Priscilla Queen of the Desert.

'You're speechless!' Saira breathed out tearfully. 'Oh my God, you love it, don't you?'

I kept on smiling, scared of what would happen if I stopped smiling.

'She's speechless!' Saira told Leila who came to stand beside me. I couldn't meet her eyes, because I was horrified. In just under three hours, Saira had managed to transform me from a pretty Asian woman into a white ugly man in drag. I'd never thought that was possible, but somehow Saira had achieved it. Desperately, I tried to find one redeeming point to talk about. But nothing from the caked-on foundation, multi-coloured eye-shadow, tarantula eyelashes, garish blusher and crimson-red lipstick looked good.

'Your hair looks great!' Leila said with a false laugh. I nodded with a hesitant smile as I looked at the well-done hairdo. Still, I couldn't speak. When the doorbell rang, marking the arrival of her next client, Saira disappeared to answer the door.

'It's not that bad,' Leila whispered quickly before I could start.

'It's worse than bad!' I whispered back. 'It's a tragedy!'

'Don't exaggerate, you look good . . .'

'You're lying!' I snapped, bursting out into a beaming smile when Saira walked back into the room.

'I'm so pleased you love it!' she gushed as she tidied up her make-up chest. 'When Leila asked me, I was nervous! She's my friend, so I've really pushed myself to give you the look you want for your wedding.'

I held on to my smile, wondering what she would have done had Leila not been here.

'We love it! You're so talented!' Leila told Saira before giving her a hug. I listened to their excited banter whilst reaching for my bag. Reluctantly, I pulled out my purse to hand fifty pounds to Saira.

'I'm so glad you like it. I'll do exactly the same style on your wedding day, OK? So that's three hundred pounds to be paid on the first of August, yes?'

I couldn't answer, so I looked to Leila.

'Sure, put her down. I'll come by next week with all the details,' Leila laughed, following Saira who showed us out. I walked to Leila's car and stayed in stunned silence all the way home, mortified by the thought that I looked like a man who wanted to look like a woman. Taj stopped talking on the phone when we walked in to stare at me.

'That's a crime. Whoever did that to you, you need to report them to the police . . .'

'Shut up, Taj!' Leila breathed as she glared at him to leave me alone.

'Maya, we need to talk,' Amma called out from the kitchen. I headed there and kept a dignified silence as everyone stared at me, speechless. They were in the process of decimating a very rich-looking cheesecake, but even that failed to distract them from my face.

'Doesn't she look great?' Leila asked, waltzing into the kitchen.

'Like a great guy,' Jana muttered, leaning forward to scrutinise me. 'Correction, like a great female-looking man.'

'More like a Vegas showgirl working the streets,' Hanna suggested.

'Stop being silly, it just seems unnatural in this setting. Imagine her on stage, under the lights . . .'

'She's not performing at G.A.Y. Astoria, Leila, she's meant to be getting married,' Ayesha pointed out.

Without a word, I left the kitchen, walked up to the

bathroom and scrubbed three hours-worth of war paint from my face. Thirty minutes later, I rejoined my sisters with a glowing face that was a little red and raw from over cleansing.

'You owe me a make-up artist,' I told a sheepish Leila and it was at that point that I spotted Chachijhi sobbing into Amma's arms in the garden.

'What's happened?' My sisters looked to Leila who shook her head. 'Why's Chachijhi crying? What's going on?' Still they stayed quiet. 'Fine, I'll go and ask Amma . . .'

'No! Let Chachijhi be, she's very upset.'

'When Meena found God, she also found a man,' Leila told me finally. I looked to the window, and shook my head. Chachijhi didn't look like she was crying out of joy. So I looked back at Leila for an explanation. 'He's a black Muslim.'

'Right,' I whispered, looking to my sisters who all avoided my eyes. 'He's a—'

'You heard me, he's a Trinidadian Muslim,' Leila stated. 'They met at some seminar, he asked her to marry him and she agreed.'

'What . . . what does . . .' Looking back out into the garden, I frowned when Chachijhi beat her chest whilst sobbing. 'Is he educated?'

'Yes, he's a director at a private equity firm.'

'Why is Chachijhi crying!' I asked in disbelief. 'He's frickin' rich, he's a catch—'

'He's not Bengali,' Ayesha finished, unimpressed by my outburst.

'Why is everyone sad? Meena's caught a big fish, do you know that these guys make billion-dollar deals, they buy companies and—'

'He's not Bengali,' Hanna repeated, as if I had missed this fact.

'He's educated, he's got a fantastic career and he's a Muslim, what's the problem?'

'He's not Bengali!' Jana told me. I shook my head and stared at everyone.

'And?' I asked, seeing everyone stare at me in confusion.

'And she's marrying out of the community, Maya, you know that that's a problem . . .'

'I don't see a problem. Meena's met a guy who is doing the decent thing, why are you all turning this into a problem?'

'Really?' Freezing at Chachijhi's question, I turned to find her walking into the kitchen from the garden.

'She's marrying an unknown to us, but you don't see that as a problem?'

'Chachijhi, he is an educated Muslim who is a professional.'

'He is to be kept a secret until he is nothing to this family. Understand?' she shouted. 'Understand?'

Nodding at her demand, I waited until she stormed out of the kitchen.

'Do Dad or Uncle Khalu know?' I asked, turning and seeing my sisters look to each other.

'Khalu left for Bangladesh as soon as Meena told them,' Ayesha explained. 'Dad's trying to get him to come back to deal with this.'

'This is such a mess!' Leila breathed out, grabbing her bag to leave.

'You still owe me a make-up artist, Leila!' I shouted behind her, only to stop when I saw my sisters staring at me. 'I'm not going to pretend Meena's announcement is a disaster.'

'You know how the community is . . .'

'Well, I proved the community wrong by getting married. Meena can prove them wrong about marrying outside the community.' With that said, I caved in to the cheesecake staring at me. The shock of seeing myself converted into a man trying to be a woman, followed by the biggest scandal to hit this Bengali family, was enough to make me reach for a spoon to take the biggest slice of cheesecake possible. Hunger strike over, it was time to hit the calories.

Identity is idealistic, but it's not set in stone

Whoever invented the Internet unknowingly managed to save my wedding. Following my make-up disaster, I scoured the Internet to find Aisha, the make-up artist who had trained in Hollywood before settling in Surrey to build a big portfolio of happy stunningly beautiful brides. Without any hesitation, I booked a trial quickly, unwilling to lose her to another bride arranging her wedding at the last minute. It was then that I stumbled over an Asian calligraphy website. It was a poorly designed website, almost putting off the user with its tedious links and poor graphics. I googled artists in the same field one after the other, and was surprised by the quality and range of offerings. In an instant, I felt inspired. I knew I had to put my work on the Internet to reach out to the second and third generation of multi-cultured, professional jet-setters who would pay for my unique, heritage-inspired art. Without a moment's hesitation, I pulled my hair back into a neat ponytail, donned my tracksuit and hooded top, and then raced down the stairs, where I put on my trainers and switched on my iPod. I spent the next hour jogging . . . or, at least, trying to. At first I ran in thirty-second sprints and then spent the next few minutes doubled over gasping for breath. I did that a few times before realising why the tortoise beat the hare. So I slowed down, slowed right down until I found a rhythm. It didn't matter that women twice my age sprinted past me and disappeared into the distance. Nor did it matter when the elderly on their morning walks passed me by; what mattered was that I was jogging myself into shape so that when Jhanghir saw me next, he would see a sexy, smart successful businesswoman running her own Internet gallery.

'You'd better sit down,' Baba advised when my jog had left me fighting for breath in the kitchen. He didn't look up from the morning newspaper, but I refused, even though my legs felt like jelly ready to give. Leaning against the wall, I focused on breathing, whilst pretending to stretch my arms.

'You need this,' Amma said, handing me a cold can of coke. Instead of opening it, I held it gratefully against my hot cheeks until I knew I wouldn't explode into a mass of untoned jelly.

'I hope you're not on a mission to be an anorexic bride,' Jana muttered as she strolled into the kitchen, dressed in loose pyjamas and Amma's dressing gown.

'You're not at work today?'

She shook her head at my question and massaged her ever-growing belly.

'Your brother-in-law's investing in a surgery in Dubai, so I've taken the week off to spend it here.'

'Don't you think you need to save your leave for the wedding?'

Jana looked at me, unimpressed. 'You'll be lucky if I can waddle ten feet by the time we get to your wedding, so use me now while you can!'

I laughed at her predicament and reached over to hug her. 'In that case, let's hit the boutiques of Wembley High Street this afternoon, we can get Mum, Dad and you sorted for the wedding,' I suggested as Dad dropped his paper to look at me.

'I have a *sharwanni* from the twins' wedding that fits me fine.'

'Baba, you can't wear the same outfit again . . .'

'It is a perfectly decent, very expensive *sharwanni* the twins had custom-made for me. I am not forking out another three hundred pounds for an outfit that I will wear for one day.'

Turning to Amma, I pointed at Baba who had returned to reading the paper.

'Tell Baba he can't wear an outfit he bought three years ago—' Stopping, I looked back at Baba to stare at his rotund belly and smiled slowly. My silence irritated him enough for him to drop his paper again. 'In fact, I don't think it will fit Baba any more.'

'These kids, what do they know about the value of money!' he muttered. 'In my day, we wore a vest and a *longi* to a wedding and that was it!' The mere suggestion that Baba had gained weight made him wag his finger at me, before setting off to prove me wrong.

'So when did this Dubai idea come about?' I asked, turning back to Jana. Amma handed me a plate of breakfast that I passed on to Jana who gorged on it as though food had just been invented. I watched until half her plate had disappeared in what reminded me of a raucous scene from *The Gremlins*. Once her appetite was satisfied, Jana turned to Amma and asked for a second serving to be prepared.

'That's where the money is, the population's growing exponentially and so is the need for doctors. Hanna's husband went too. In fact, Tariq *bhai*, Taj and Ayesha are all investing in it. We're opening up an Indian family business,' she finished with an Indian accent, laughing as she took a second helping of eggs and beans gratefully. I didn't laugh. Instead, I sat down with a frown.

'Why haven't I been told about this?'

Jana didn't slow down in finishing off the second portion, only when she saw my expression did she pause.

'Because you have a lot on your plate, you have a wedding to organise, you're moving out to New York . . .'

'That's doesn't mean I'm not part of the family or that I'll never see you all again.'

'*Pagul*!' Amma said, tapping the back of my head. 'Your life is going to change when you're a married woman; your focus for the first few years will be on Jhanghir and building a home with him. It's a big change for women, but you have the added pressures of moving to a whole new continent,' Amma finished tearfully.

'Don't forget your in-laws, dealing with them sounds like a full-time job,' Jana added, sitting back with a big mug of peppermint tea. 'Jhanghir will, and should be, your first priority until you settle into being a married couple, and that takes time, Maya.'

'But all that has nothing to do with the fact that you guys are leaving me out of family decisions.'

Jana looked to Amma nervously before meeting my eyes.

'Maya, we're thinking of moving out there—'

'What? You mean everyone? Amma, Baba, Tariq *bhai*—'

'Calm down, it's not going to happen overnight,' Jana told me. 'Career wise, apart from China, there isn't another place in the world that is as financially rewarding for doctors than Dubai. It has a great family culture, and it'll be great for Amma and Baba—'

'Even Taj? What's he going to do there?'

'He's negotiating all the deals right now. He's going to drive business development so that we can grow quickly.'

'But you know Dubai's economy has collapsed and people are leaving in droves . . .'

'That's why the guys have gone out there. This is a good time to buy property and set up a business because all the rates are discounted.'

'But this is our home, this is where we grew up. This is who I am.'

Jana smiled and nodded. 'And you're going to go on to become Jhanghir's wife. Everything changes with time, Maya, we just need to adjust and accept that that's life,' Jana said softly.

'This is who we are, this is where our identity starts and you're all going to pack it up and take it out to Dubai.' The lump in my throat got bigger as I fought to keep my tears at bay. 'It's a nine-hour flight from New York to London; it'll be even longer once you all move to Dubai.'

My quiet words were enough to push Amma over the edge. Covering her face with her *dupatta*, she burst into tears, and cried. 'My baby's going to New York, she's leaving us, she's going far, far away.' Jana looked like she was tearing up too. I confronted the realisation that life as I knew and loved it was changing beyond my control.

'Maybe . . . maybe I could convince Jhanghir to join the business,' I whispered, my eyes welling up. 'He's a surgeon, maybe . . . we could join you out there . . .' Before I could finish, we all burst into tears. I was getting married. We were all happy about that, but that meant leaving the family nest and up until that moment, I had not grasped what that actually meant. It was then that Baba strutted into the kitchen, stomach pulled in to stop the tightly fitted *sharwanni* from tearing at the seams. We cried even harder as he paraded himself around the kitchen, convincing no one that it was a good look. At the sight of us crying, he threw his hands up in despair. 'OK, OK, I give in. It's shrunk and it doesn't fit as well as it used to. Fine! I'll buy a new one,' he shouted. 'There, are you happy!' But the crying didn't stop, so he backed out of the kitchen muttering, 'Women! There's no pleasing them!'

The realisation that my family were in the process of uprooting and relocating out to Dubai weighed heavily on my mind. Clad in jeans and cream silk tulip dress with flat pumps and my large Michael Kors Fulton bag, I headed for Mayfair's Café d'Lebanon at Seema's invitation. Having closed a big manufacturing deal with a high-street retailer, she decided to throw a celebratory party at the last minute. I was late as usual, and rushing towards the famous bar. Asian girls never went anywhere alone, at least not without one or four best friends to give moral support, but that wasn't the case here. This was my journey to make. Having said this, knowing that Zain was going to be there made me feel somewhat better; in him I felt like I had a friend. Stepping into the dimly lit bar, I took the marble stairs down and pushed through large doors to enter an ornate bar filled with the vibe of the Middle East.

'Can I help you?' Turning to the stunning model maître d', I nodded.

'Seema Khan's party.'

She led me through the busy bar along the cobbled water stream splitting the bar from the dark dance area. 'I see them,' I told her before heading towards the group. They were all dressed to kill, stunning, cosmopolitan and all very confident at having a great time.

'Maya!' Seema called out, beckoning me. 'Hey, guys, this is Maya, Jhanghir's fiancée,' she introduced, shouting above the pounding music. Noting the many bottles of wine, champagne and spirits on their table, I knew I would be the outsider.

'I'm sorry I'm late . . .'

'What's your poison?' Turning at the question, I looked at a grinning gorilla of a man, dressed in red corduroy trousers and a see-through black jersey.

'I don't drink . . .'

'Come on, Maya, we're celebrating!' Seema encouraged as she raised a glass of champagne. 'Make an exception,' she added with a cheeky wink. Gorilla Man held a glass out to me.

'No thank you, I'll have an orange juice . . .' I trailed off as smirks registered around me. Seema felt at odds holding her flute and put it down with a raised eyebrow.

'Where are we going to have dinner?' I asked.

'We're celebrating here, darling!' she told me.

'You know what they say, "take a bite, trousers get tight; kill the calories, look like a *Posh wannabee*"!' a bitchy looking model told me without an inflection of a smile.

'So have you been here before?' I asked, trying to break the awkward silence. Gorilla Man took back the flute of champagne and murmured something to the girl next to him who giggled in my direction.

'Orange juice,' Zain said, stepping forward with my drink. 'You look great.' I raised an eyebrow at his compliment and smiled when he gave me a cheeky wink. In comparison to the ultra-svelte bodies draped in what could pass as butt-skimming, low-hung chiffon handker-chiefs, I could only be described as dowdy in the company of the uber-elite Asian world. I looked at Seema's short, backless dress; she couldn't be any more Western in contrast to the traditional girl who attended *alaap* discussions at my house.

'Something funny?' Zain asked, noting my curbed grin.

'My dad would have a heart attack if he thought I'd wear something like that.' Realising how square I sounded, I regretted my comment instantly.

'So you're the quintessential good girl, I take it?' Zain asked, leaning on the table.

'Of course,' I returned.

'Really?'

Nodding at his question, I held his eyes, refusing to smile even though they creased at the corners. Another loud beat started and I jumped as Seema's friends rushed past me to join the heaving dance floor.

'You coming?' Seema stopped to ask. Shaking my head, she shrugged indifferently before rushing over to join her friends.

'Go ahead,' I told Zain, but he shook his head as I perched on a stool. 'Don't feel you have to babysit me . . .' Before I could finish, one of the girls returned to drag Zain off behind her. Sitting alone, I held my bag on my lap and watched like the ugly girl who was never asked to dance. There were dance poles in various corners, and those brave enough used them to give punters free views of things that they would otherwise have to pay to watch. That, the drinking, the cavorting, all of it was at odds with my faith, and, with everything changing around me, I didn't want to compromise that. In fact, I didn't fit in, so I swayed to the music knowing that this was a different world and one that I didn't want to be a part of. I spoke to those who returned briefly to empty out successive flutes of champagnes, but they rushed back to the dance floor. When I had had enough,

I checked my watch and got ready to head for the exit.

'Thinking of making tracks?' Turning at Gorilla Man's question, I smiled guiltily. 'I should wait for Seema *bhabhi*,' I said as he helped himself to a fresh flute of champagne.

'Would you be offended?' he asked, pausing to check. But I wasn't, so I shrugged, indifferent. 'Sure you are,' he said, putting his glass down.

'You think I'm square because I choose not to wear butt-skimming boob-tube dresses . . .'

'You don't have to apologise,' he told me, forcing a smile that failed to reach his eyes.

'I'm not,' I corrected. 'So, you carry on.'

'I wasn't asking for permission,' he pointed out.

'Yes you were,' I told him, jumping when police sirens screeched through the bar causing everyone to jump on to tables and race on to the dance floor cheering wildly. Gorilla Man hoisted himself on to our table and held his hand out to me. I loved this track and, when my curiosity got the better of me, I dropped my bag, and took his hand to join him on the table. Standing in front of him, I hollered when the DJ brought the bar to life with Black-Eyed Peas' 'I gotta feeling'. Everyone without exception was on their feet moving to the music. Before I could stop myself, I was dancing and singing along to the anthem. Looking back at Gorilla Man over my shoulder, I laughed at his surprised expression. Then I felt his hand on my hips.

'I knew you were a tease,' he breathed into my ear, sliding his hand down. The instant he groped me, I jerked around and gave him a short, hard slap. When he dropped his hands, I slipped off the table, grabbed my bag and headed for the exit.

Seema appeared from nowhere with a wide smile.

'You're leaving already?' she asked, standing in my path.

'I . . . it's getting late,' I told her, looking back at Gorilla Man who had jumped off the table whilst cupping his cheek. 'I should get going.'

'You guys looked like you were having a good time! I got a great snap, look,' she said, holding her iPhone out to me. The photo captured what looked like Gorilla Man whispering into my ear with his hand hard on my hip; it looked private and intimate. Looking up at Seema, I watched her smile disappear. 'I wonder what Jhanghir would think if he were to see that picture?'

'You know nothing happened,' I told her as she snatched her phone back.

'Oh, but the picture tells you something else, doesn't it?' Seema laughed. Pushing past her, I stormed out of the bar and raced up the stairs.

'Hey . . .' Being spun round, I stopped and stared at Zain. 'What's going on?'

'Nothing,' I bit out, refusing to divulge what had just happened.

'Something happened, what did Seema say?'

'Nothing . . . she didn't say anything.'

Zain held my shoulders to look me in the eye. He didn't believe me and I couldn't hold his stare.

'Let me take you home.'

'No, I'm fine . . . you should go and join your friends.'

Zain shook his head and tipped my chin up until I looked up at him.

'This isn't my world. You guys live a different life. Tonight you guys spent more on drinks than the monthly salary my older brother brings home.'

'Did she say anything about you being poor?'

'Poor?!' I laughed, moving his hand away. Pushing my hair back from my face, I shook my head before looking at him. 'We're normal, Zain . . .'

'That's not what I meant . . .'

'It's exactly what you meant!' I shouted. I didn't know why I was so angry with Zain. He wasn't responsible for Seema's threat. I desperately needed to talk to Jhanghir, I wanted to hear his voice, I wanted to hear him tell me everything would be OK, I wanted to tell him about the relocation plans my family had and to talk to him about how out of place I felt amongst his people.

'I don't know what happened with Seema, but for what it's worth I'm sorry you feel so bad.' Tears welled up at his quiet words, and I shook my head. Before I could control myself, I burst into tears.

'Hey, what's wrong?' he asked, wrapping his arms around me. I covered my face and tried to stem the tears. It was too much change, I didn't know where or what I was meant to be, and worse still, Seema had those pictures that could ruin everything. Zain didn't speak, he simply let me get it out of my system.

It felt good to be held. When I had no more tears to cry, I wiped my face and looked up at him. He smiled and wiped away the strands of hair from my eyes.

'You OK?' Nodding at his quiet question, I held his eyes for what felt like an eternity.

'Why aren't you with someone?' The question came out before I could think twice, but with it said, I waited for him to answer.

'I don't know,' he answered. And then, with a bemused grin, he asked, 'Why are you with someone?' We were stuck in a moment. For the life of me, I couldn't think, let alone give him a reason. So I looked away and smiled. Hearing the discreet cough beside us, we both looked up to find Seema.

'I wondered where you'd got to.' Both of us jerked apart at her comment, it was then I noticed her camera phone had a red pulse, telling me she had recorded our moment.

'What did you say to Maya?' Zain asked.

Seema giggled with delight and pointed at the two of us.

'Poor Jhanghir, first Preeya cops off with his cousin and now you . . .'

'I'm not copping off with Zain!' I clarified, feeling so guilty that I couldn't look at Zain.

'Sure you're not,' Seema laughed, throwing Zain's jacket at him. 'If you're finished, we're going on to Mahiki, unless . . .' She looked at me and raised a suggestive brow.

'What's wrong with you, Seema?'

'Zain, don't,' I said, watching Seema delight at his comment.

'Oh, better listen to the secret girlfriend!' she trilled as Zain stormed off. Standing there I stared at Seema and watched her stare after Zain.

'Jhanghir . . .'

'Jhanghir won't know a thing about tonight – *if* you work with me,' Seema told me with half a smile. 'I like things my way. As long as we both understand that, nothing happened tonight.'

'But nothing did happen,' I told her and she looked back at me with narrowed eyes.

'Good, so we have an understanding.'

'I'll explain to Jhanghir . . .'

'Go ahead, Maya. Who do you think he'll believe?' Seema asked as if there was no doubt. 'Look at us and look at you, do you honestly believe you'll fit in? Play nice, Maya, otherwise the fairytale happy-ever-after you're planning with Jhanghir may just turn into a never-ever-after.'

And with that, she spun round on her heels and sauntered back into the club. I made my way home, reeling from the fear of the havoc she was intent on causing. I switched off my mobile, fearing that call from Jhanghir demanding answers to Seema's pictures. All the way back, I was a breath away from breaking down. I slipped into the house unnoticed and stepped into the living room. Normally, a dose of George Clooney put the world to rights for me, but as I crouched by the flat screen, I looked down at the DVD cover of *Out of Sight*. It was as if Zain starred back. Closing my eyes, I shook my head, wondering if my only source of refuge was now gone for ever. Dropping the DVD, I raced upstairs and closed my bedroom door behind me. Dropping on my bed, I looked at my mobile and contemplated switching it back on to confide in Jhanghir. He was one phone call away and yet I couldn't make the call. I was lost. I wanted to call Tanya, and get her clinical, confident advice, but she was living her own nightmare. Holding my head, I stared up at the ceiling. Life at home was changing. The world I was about to join was alien to me. The man I was about to marry wasn't the man who had held me or stood by me this evening. That fact shook me to the core. And the only truth was that I had a wedding to organise and if change was coming, I wanted to be as prepared for it as possible. I was becoming a new me, with a new identity, and I realised that I couldn't hide from it or be intimidated by it. I had to do it on my own terms.

Just get physical

I spent the night tossing and turning. If it wasn't the fear of waking up to Jhanghir's angry calls, it was the guilt of being held by Zain that kept me up. Either way, I barely slept. If sly Seema didn't ruin my chances of getting married, I had to look radiant for my wedding; and losing sleep wasn't something I could afford to do. Asian weddings are about two things: big food and the stunning, elaborately staged pictures. Screwing up either would cost you your family's reputation. So when sleep continued to evade me at sunrise, Seema's cold analysis of me had me in front of the mirror inspecting every part of my body. At some point in between being single and being engaged I had stopped going to the gym. And it showed. I carried what Seema called 'unnecessary baggage'. My tummy was soft, OK, flabby, my arms were the opposite of taut, and my thighs . . . there was no describing them. Cringing, this was not the body I wanted Jhanghir to see on our wedding night. Images of Priyanka Chopra, Bipasha Basu, Nicole Scherzinger and Angelina Jolie and their perfectly lithe and curvaceous bodies came to mind. I wanted to have the perfect body and the body I had was far from perfect.

'*Unnecessary baggage*,' I whispered as I reached out for my phone.

'Why are you calling me at this ridiculous hour?' Leila muttered, answering her phone.

'What time's your zumba class?' I asked, rifling through my drawers for my sweats.

'What?'

'Zumba . . . you know, that Latin American dance-exercise-craze-thing you religiously attend?' I heard her mumble something. 'What?'

'Eight a.m,' she repeated before ending the call and hanging up on me before I could agree to meet her. With a wry smile, I left for the bathroom to do my morning prayer ablution.

Two hours later, amongst the group of early morning exercise enthusiasts, I waited for Leila in my track bottoms and fitted T-shirt. I stretched my arms and legs gently to warm up, pleased to see that I wasn't the biggest one in the gym studio. No one could miss the portly red-haired lady who wore the yellow headband and orange body leotard that left nothing to the imagination and who appeared to be perkier than a cheerleader before a high-school football match. She laughed excitedly before doing star jumps as part of her warm-up routine.

'Hey you, you're going to love this!'

Turning at Leila's equally perky call, I stopped. She was toned to perfection and dressed in bright pink leggings, with a hot-pink tank top. She looked like an extra on Madonna's *Like a Virgin* video and I felt like the dumpy sidekick who never made it to the final cut. Leila started stretching next to me, folding into positions that shouldn't have been possible. 'This is high impact, it's bang, bang, bang! You think you can keep up?' Leila asked, showing off some salsa moves, fully aware of the eyes on her.

'Sure,' I answered, taking a couple of steps behind her so that I stood amongst the back row.

'When did you last work out?'

I straightened at the question, tugging at my T-shirt and conscious of my flubber blubber.

'Are we ready!'

Starting at the bellowed question, I stretched up on to my toes to see the instructor step into the dance studio with a small mike to yell into. 'Are we ready?'

'Yeah!' the class shouted as the studio came to life to the sound of Shakira. And then it began. An hour of intensive, non-stop, unforgiving dance routines that changed tempos from salsa, mambo, chachacha, samba, belly dancing, hip hop and bhangra that left me gasping for breath. On several occasions I stopped, unable to keep up with the pace of the group. Leila moved step perfect with a bright smile and extra enthusiasm, and then Miss Orange bumped into me whilst performing a wild form of animal dancing. I stared at her, open mouthed, but nothing abated her enthusiasm. Only when she stopped in front of me to wind herself low did I recoil.

'You, in the red T-shirt, do you want to stay fat for ever?' Turning at the instructor's demand, I froze. Humiliated, I shook my head. 'Get moving.'

I jumped at the instruction and joined in again. Before long, I was panting and gasping for breath. Grabbing my sides, I winched at the painful stitch.

'Dance, damn it!'

I looked up at the instructor who moved like a mercenary. 'I can't, I have a stitch.' The entire room kept dancing as she clapped her way to the studio door.

'Out, there's no room for slackers here!'

Walking out as instructed, I headed for the changing rooms, fully conceding that my first attempt at getting skinny had failed miserably.

I wasn't about to give up so quickly. That week I attended Ashtanga Yoga with Tanya and Sakina. We were kicked out for breaking into hysterical laughter when the male instructor decided to fold me into positions I couldn't get out of. Of course, we all paid the following day when every single muscle God designed made itself known to us. Hot baths and several paracetemols later, we tried Legs, Bums, Tums, followed by spinning classes and then aerobics, where we all turned up in acid-coloured leotards. I made a diary of everything that I ate, before finally turning to a liquid diet. By the end of the week, I was exhausted, and no closer to losing the ten pounds that would get me close to my perfectly toned body. Lying in my bed deflated, I logged on to my email and smiled when I spotted an email from Jhanghir.

From: JKhan@NYMedics.com
To: MayaM@Instantmail.com

So, wife-to-be, if I didn't know you so well, I'd say you were avoiding me. But I figure you're turning this wedding into 'the' event of the year and in the midst of it have forgotten that it takes two to get married. You're forgiven, but don't let this turn into a habit. On this side of the Atlantic, I've secured us a neat apartment, two blocks from the hospital and one block from Central Park, it's smaller than I'm used to but Preeya's helping me do it up. I'm working all the hours possible, and it's ridiculous that this is the first time I've had to try to make ends meet. Sure makes me glad that Seema *bhabhi* and

Zain are there to make sure you have everything you
need. Touch base sometime, I'm only your fiancé.

I had no right to feel jealous at Preeya's involvement in
shaping my future home when I had stared longingly
into Zain's eyes, but I did. The fact was, I didn't want her
around Jhanghir, I didn't want her to be there waiting
when he returned to *our home* after a long shift with
dinner ready. That was my job. And yet, I had no right to
suspect him. I started an email, and then aborted many
attempts to write him a response. How could I tell him
that I didn't want Preeya to be decorating our future
home, how could I tell him that I wasn't working with
Zain or Seema, and, most importantly, how could I tell
him that I was no longer in charge of the wedding? So
instead I wrote:

To: JKhan@NYMedics.com
From: MayaM@Instantmail.com

Fiancé, whilst you're busy picking out the colour
schemes and soft furnishings for our apartment, I'm busy
getting our wedding arranged. I need you to help me
decide on the wedding-card designs. I've attached
images of the ones I like, let me know your thoughts.

I hit the send icon and knew instantly he would know
that something was wrong. Not waiting for a response, I
grabbed my bag and went to join Tanya. We had decided
to jog three times a week to get me into shape for my
wedding. Yet when we met, we spent the first half hour
talking about Tanya's unsuccessful attempts to reach
Javed. He was ignoring all her calls and emails. When we
started jogging, I suggested that she stop by his

workplace and when Tanya stayed quiet, I realised that had already been tried and tested unsuccessfully. We discussed the possibility of turning up at his house and ruled it out on the basis that she would be branded a stalker.

Instead, she said, 'So Sakina keeps asking about Zain.' It was my turn to go quiet and it wasn't missed on Tanya. 'I told her that you'd be happy to set them up since you are her best friend who is no longer single and committed to the love of her life, to one Jhanghir Khan, cousin to said Zain Khan—'

'OK, OK, stop!' I told her, coming to a halt and staring at her.

'You going to tell me what happened?' Tanya asked, as she adjusted her headscarf neatly around her slim shoulders. She didn't stop jogging although I stood still and contemplated telling her about Seema. Taking a deep breath, I shook my head and jogged to catch up with her.

'Nothing happened,' I said as I joined her. 'I'll set them up.' She turned to look at me and I stared straight ahead.

'Sakina told me he's hot, proper hot, so you can admit you fancy him.'

'I don't fancy him . . .'

'But you said you did, cuz he looks like George Clooney . . .'

'But he's not George Clooney,' I pointed out and we stopped to stare at each other.

'Just the two of them,' Tanya said, watching for every sign of reluctance.

'Sure.' My response made her grin and I started jogging again.

'Good,' Tanya said as she caught up with me.

'Good,' I returned.

'How's Jhanghir?' Tanya probed, looking at me with a wide smile.

'He's good.'

'I take it that you guys haven't had phone sex yet?' She burst out laughing at her audacious remark and raced for her life when I bolted after her.

To: MayaM@Instantmail.com
From: JKhan@NYMedics.com

Cards? Wedding cards? That's all you have to say to me after a week's worth of silence? Now I am intrigued, because I know more happens in the life of Maya Malik than a dilemma over wedding-card designs. So spill.

Jhanghir's email was waiting for me when I got back from my jog. I remembered the way he teased without smiling, but one look at him and I'd know exactly what he was up to. I smiled at the memory and held on to it when I started writing.

To: JKhan@NYMedics.com
From: MayaM@Instantmail.com

I want you here with me, by my side, for each decision to make for this wedding of ours. But you're not. You're on the other side of the Atlantic, with your ex-fiancée, furnishing what is meant to be our home, whilst I organise our wedding with another man. My friends are throwing a surprise lingerie party and we have our *paancini* where we're to be formally engaged in a week's time, and I'll sit through those alone. So, when I ask you about card designs, tell me what you want so that I can think one piece of this wedding reflects some part of you too.

By the time I had showered and changed into a *shalwaar kameez*, Jhanghir had responded. And, despite myself, I couldn't stop myself smiling at his cocky reply.

To: MayaM@Instantmail.com
From: JKhan@NYMedics.com

Well, it's nice to know you're not only missing me, but that you're also as jealous as hell. So, Maya Malik, what's running through your mind? Whilst we're on the topic of indiscretions, how come I wasn't invited to this surprise lingerie party? As the groom, I have a vested interest in making sure only the sheerest and silkiest pieces are chosen. And for the record, keep your *chachijhi* from going over the top on the ten-pack cotton granny pants from Primark's budget range; they won't be needed until our seventh child is born, at which point I'll look for a fitter, firmer and slimmer wife no. 2!

And you know that the groom doesn't attend the *paancini*, because, culturally, my mother will accept your engagement on my behalf. And I know you want me tied to your side as all wives want of their husbands. But right now I'm still a free man and I'm quite content to remain a bachelor with all its virtues because when we take our vows, life as I cherish it right now will never be the same.

With a cheeky smile, I bit my lower lip and typed.

To: JKhan@NYMedics.com
From: MayaM@Instantmail.com

OK, carry on enjoying the virtues, or lack of, of your bachelorhood – I won't ruin it with any further talk of lingerie parties.

With that thought, I hit the send button. I knew that bachelorhood for Jhanghir was as appealing as another liquidised broccoli and carrot meal was for me. He didn't reply because he would have to show his cards. This made me smile for days because silence itself spoke volumes. At the end of the week, I joined a belly dancing class. It was time to up my game. I had a long way to go to get fully toned, but I was going to get there. I watched the instructor sway her hips, heave her bosoms and wind her way seductively around the studio.

'You think you're at an aerobics class?' The Egyptian instructor asked, stopping in front of me. Shaking my head, I looked around frowning at Tanya and Sakina in confusion. And before I could speak, she yanked my T-shirt up to knot it beneath my bust and looped a chiffon belly-dancing scarf around my hips. She placed a hand on the softest part of my belly and jiggled it. 'Could be a bit bigger, but remember, it's not what you have, it's what you do with it that counts,' she told me with a smile, before swaying off. I turned to my friends and pointed to my not-so-flat belly.

'Perfect,' I mouthed as they jerked up their T-shirts likewise. For once, being super skinny wasn't the goal; being able to use what you had with confidence was. I looked around the dance group and realised that there wasn't a super-skinny carb-hydrated girl in sight, only women who wanted to be super sexy with a cheeky smile.

'Follow me,' the instructor called out, starting with the basic hip weave in the shape of the number eight. And slowly we began to copy her. At first, we were unco-ordinated, laughing at each other when wrong parts of the body moved in the wrong direction. However, the disjointed, almost unnaturally exaggerated movements slowly became smoother and, soon enough, my attention was caught when I looked in the mirror. Then I understood the beguiling attraction of belly dancing. It was a physical dance, a very seductive, intentional dance. Each move was aimed to draw the eye and the imagination. With that influence, you were the one in control. With Jhanghir in mind, I smiled. There were many times where a woman could use a skill like belly dancing. I, for one, was fully committed to learning that skill. It really was time to just get physical.

Know your menstrual cycle well

There are certain conversations that aren't had in Asian families. This isn't necessarily a bad thing because there are conversation points that should never be had. One of these is the topic of conception: what, when and how. Mums and *auntijhis* still feel that single Asian women live in total ignorance about the horizontal tango and the mysterious art of conception. And worse still, they feel that somehow they have to equip you with *the knowledge* before marriage.

I realised this was my time when I walked into the living room to find a pensive Amma and Chachijhi. As soon as I entered, they looked up and forced smiles before patting an empty space between them for me to sit down.

'Come sit.' Amma's steely request stopped me from backing out of the room.

'We're going to go shopping, all of us, wedding shopping . . .'

'Your sisters have been told to wait half an hour,' Amma cut in. Reluctantly, I sat down, squeezing between Chachijhi's generously proportioned body and Amma's tall, lean figure.

'So, Maya, how are you?' Chachijhi's nervous question made me frown.

'Fine,' I answered, looking straight ahead and dreading the next thirty minutes of my life. I had thrown back two ibuprofens to cope with the onset of my period, and my mood, to say the least, was just foul. This wasn't a good time to have *that* talk.

'Good, good. Well done,' Chachijhi chuckled before clearing her voice. 'And your friend?'

'Jhanghir?' Chachijhi laughed as if I had said the funniest thing. 'Tanya?' Still she laughed and shook her head. 'Sakina . . . oww!' I cried out when she smacked my knee and sat smiling at me, without a glimmer in her eyes.

'You know, your *monthly friend* who comes to stay for maybe five days, maybe seven days . . . how is your friend?'

It dawned on me that she was referring to my period. My smiled dropped.

'Fine,' I managed to get out, wishing that I had thrown back enough pills to dull out what was to come.

'Regular?'

'Y . . . yes.' I hesitated, having to think back a few months.

'So you're not taking the pill? I have to ask,' Chachijhi said as I turned to her with wide eyes. 'We have to talk about these matters . . .'

'No; no, we don't, I have a doctor . . .'

'You can't talk to Jhanghir about these matters, these are women's matters.'

'No, *my* doctor!' I corrected as Chachijhi shook her head.

'He is your doctor husband . . .'

'Stop her,' I said to Amma, turning to hold her hand.

'This is for your own good, Maya,' she told me. 'You must be prepared for your married life.' Turning away from the melodramatic comment, I cringed as Chachijhi took my free hand. There was no way to escape this, so I sat defeated as both women held one of my hands and stared at me knowingly.

'When Leila got married, I told her no babies in year one of her marriage. And I explained to her how not to have babies. You may be my brother's daughter, but I see you as my own and I must give you the same advice.'

'Honestly, you really, genuinely don't have to,' I said to her with the last bit of hope that it would make some difference. It didn't. Instead, she chuckled and patted my cheek.

'You'll thank me after you're married,' Chachijhi told me before leaning down close to me. 'OK, Maya, when you get married, you and Jhanghir will have relations, not like blood relations or friend relations, but relations where you . . .' And with that I looked straight ahead and listened to twenty-five minutes worth of cringe-worthy conception advice. She covered the duties of sharing a bed, the virtues of fulfilling a man's 'needs', understanding the different types of contraception and, the importance of knowing your cycle. I turned every shade of pink known to the human eye, and then sat mortified when she talked about her wedding-night surprise. By the time she'd finished, I wanted to stay celibate for the rest of my life.

'I know, I know,' she whispered, pulling me into a bear hug. 'Don't worry, my child, we all have to come face to face with the snake one time in our life.' At that point I bit my lip, closed my eyes and dreamed that I was somewhere far, far away from the Malik household.

'Ha ha, look at her, she's still in shock from the menstrual-cycle talk!' Hanna laughed as she drove us to Ealing Road in Wembley. It was indeed my time of the month, and even though I had taken two ibuprofens, nothing dulled the sound of Chachijhi's advice ringing in my ears. 'You know we all had the snake conversation with Chachijhi—'

'Please don't mention the snake!' I said, turning to my sisters. They stared at me before we all burst out laughing.

'We're going to Sakoni's first,' Jana said as Hanna parked up her X6.

'We've only just arrived,' I pointed out and winced when Ayesha tapped the back of my head.

'I'm eating for two, and I don't get to decide when to eat! But the bump is telling me now's the time to eat,' Jana told me as she eased herself out of the front seat and neatened her tunic over her growing bump.

'The bump is telling you it wants Sakonis?' I asked as she looked at me and nodded without any hesitation.

'Bump wants pani puris followed by a long cold glass of mango lassi,' she clarified. I frowned at Ayesha, who shrugged.

'But, we've only got four hours to find you all outfits before I go to see the wedding decorators . . .'

'Actually, you can rule me out. By the time you get married, all I'll be able to wear is a sack,' Jana threw back at me, shuffling towards Sakoni's as if it was going to shut down before she got there.

'Sack . . . she's going to wear a sack . . .'

'It'll be a nice sack with a few sequins and Swarovski crystals on it . . .'

'Ignore her,' Ayesha advised. 'Shireen *bhabhi* and Jana can go and eat at Sakoni's while Hana and I choose our outfits.'

'But the outfits have to match . . .'

'No they don't.' They all spoke at once so I stopped walking.

'You're wearing matching outfits – like my brides-maids; they're all wearing the same colour and style,' I told them, pulling out my wedding book to rifle through the pages until I got to the outfits section. Holding up the relevant pages, I showed them the glued-on pictures of *shalwaar kameezes*, colour swabs and material patches. 'I've got it planned: the sisters, aka you guys, wear emerald, ruby and gold similar to the outfit Ashwariya Rai's wore in *Umrao Jaan*. Skinny-legged *shalwaar*, with fitted ornate *kameezes* with full skirts—' I stopped as Jana walked back and stared at the pictures.

'Brainbox, how do you think an eight-month pregnant woman is going to fit into a fitted *kameez*?'

'It can be customised to—'

'To fit around my bump like I'm ready to do a bud bud bling wearing Demi Moore bump-flashing front-page exposé, right?' Jana asked.

'I knew it!' I burst out, slamming my book shut. 'I knew that it would be too much to ask to have a wedding Mogul style . . .'

'What the hell is a Mogul-Inspired wedding?' Jana asked, turning to her twin Hanna in confusion. 'Why can't we have a straightforward Bengali wedding?'

'Because I don't want a typical Bengali wedding!' I defended. 'I've gone over this.' I started as I opened up my book again and worked through the pages illustrating the sumptuous courts of the Moguls, citing the opulent lifestyle of Shah Jahan who built the Taj Mahal in memory of his beloved wife Mumtaz. I drew on the colours, the outfits, the grandeur, citing films like *Devdas*, *Mugli Azam* and *Umrao Jaan*. When I stopped, I stared at my silent sisters.

'She wants to rebuild the Taj Mahal to re-enact a love story!' Jana breathed out.

'Not the Taj Mahal!' Ayesha whispered.

'With Jhanghir's family playing the big bad villains!' Hanna laughed.

'You want us to dress up like Rajas and Ranis from the Mogul empire, fine! Just find me something that doesn't make me look like Christmas tree,' Jana told me. 'Now, I'm starving and I'm going to eat.'

We watched her storm off with Shireen *bhabhi* struggling to keep up with her. Ayesha, Hanna and I walked towards Variety Silk House, where we spent the afternoon pulling out ornate, extraordinary outfits in a myriad of rich, luxurious colours and soft, sheer material. Both Ayesha and Hanna tried on outfit after outfit, changing their minds between *saris*, *lenghas* and *shalwaar kameezes*. Every time the assistant brought out a new outfit, we found another reason to delay making a decision. Three hours later Jana and Shireen *bhabhi* found us as we entered Benarus, the world-renowned wedding boutique.

'Amateurs!' Shireen *bhabhi* declared, spotting our empty hands before leading the way in. We followed behind her and worked through the exclusive bespoke pieces that were delicately laid out. Jana, short on patience, sorted through the displayed items as if she was sorting through a rack of bargain-basement seconds.

'Uh, can I help you?' The question wasn't a question; it was more of an order for Jana to stop. And it came from one of the prototype shop assistants – perfectly groomed with a mane of long black silky hair, cake of meticulously applied make-up and long, lithe limbs elegantly draped in a trendy but tasteful *shalwaar kameez*, who had the innate ability to look down on anyone who was not as pretty or groomed as she was.

'Not until I can find something,' Jana returned without even a second glance at the assistant who had stepped in her way.

'Why don't I show you the outfits?'

Jana stepped back and raised an eyebrow, watching the assistant neaten up the displayed items.

'So show me then,' Jana stated as the assistant smiled purposely and took her time before pulling out an audacious acid-pink monstrosity.

'This looks like it would compliment you,' the assistant said as we all rushed forward to hold Jana back. 'Is there a problem?' she asked with an amused expression.

'Do I look like I want to be dressed in a Quality Street wrapper?' Jana demanded of the assistant who shrugged, haughty and indifferent. '*Khoothi*—'

'Let's go,' I stated, escorting Jana from the boutique. The rest of my sisters followed close behind.

'What is it with Asian assistants in clothes shops? Why do they make you feel like a tramp?' Jana snapped. 'She's a shop assistant, barely sixteen, with probably two GCSEs to her name and I'm a doctor . . . an educated, professional, good-looking, faaatttt doctor!'

We stared in silent wonder as Jana burst into tears and blubbered about looking fat and ugly at her baby sister's wedding and how she was going to ruin the wedding I'd dreamed of. Hanna rushed across to reassure her twin that she wasn't ugly or fat and I looked down at my wedding book. With half a smile, I shook my head and walked to my sister.

'Hey, fatty,' I called, forcing Jana to look at me. 'Why don't we look for the *hungama* slash Grecian goddess-style *shalwaar kameez*? That'll hide your bump beautifully . . .'

'But you wanted a Mogul wedding! How's a Grecian dress going to work?'

'Seriously, who's going to guess the difference between a Greek and Indian dress as long as there're sequins and crystals everywhere, right?'

My sister looked at me with tear-filled eyes and when I smiled, she burst out laughing.

'My hormones are everywhere, the bump is taking over everything and I can't . . . I can't stop crying and I don't know why.' Pulling Jana into a warm hug, I smiled and patted her back whilst she promised she didn't know why she was crying. Behind her Hanna scrambled through her bag to find something that Jana could eat. I beckoned her to hurry up. 'Don't get pregnant, seriously; you get fat, you get over-emotional, you want to eat all the time and nothing fits . . .' Jana stopped when Ayesha held out a packet of cheese biscuits to her. None of us looked at each other as Jana peered at us through narrowed eyes.

'You lot are evil!' she stated, taking the snack. 'Don't laugh,' she warned, but it was too late; the rest of us burst out laughing as she opened up the packet to take a big bite.

Not a single item had been bought and the shopping trip turned into a big disaster. Not that any of my sisters looked worried as they headed for Kebabish, where they went to town ordering the most mouth-watering, succulent mixed-grill kebabs available in West London. As far as my family were concerned, an empty-handed shopping trip wasn't a failed trip if the trip ended in Kebabish. I left them to it and raced back to Alperton station to make the meeting with the wedding decorators. It would the first time I'd seen Zain since that incident outside Café d'Lebanon, but I was over that. Jhanghir and I were now in regular contact, and there was no chance of my making panda eyes at Zain again. In fact, so sure of it was I that I had invited Sakina to join us for coffee in Ealing after our meeting. Then I spotted Zain and my conviction deserted me as fast as my will power did when offered a slice of the devil's triple chocolate cake. Taking a deep breath, I approached him.

'Hi,' I greeted, wishing I could sound more confident.

'Hey,' he returned dryly. Avoiding his eyes, I held my wedding book up and pointed to it.

'There's so much to do and we are running out of time.' I started a line of babbling nonsense and he humoured me as we headed towards the wedding decorators. I didn't pause until we entered the office, where I announced, 'We're here.'

'Yes, we are,' Zain agreed. My smiled faltered and I turned away to spot our wedding assistant.

'Are you Sumi?' I asked a professional-looking lady who nodded and beckoned us over.

'Please have a seat,' she invited. 'My, aren't you the gorgeous couple . . .'

'No . . . no, we're not . . .'

'Yes, you are! Don't be so modest! You make a stunning couple and you'll go on to have beautiful, beautiful babies!' she declared with wide-eyed delight. I coughed ungracefully, refusing to look at Zain.

'She's my cousin's fiancée.'

Sumi looked like she'd been slapped at Zain's statement, but she kept smiling. 'Well, if your fiancé is as good-looking as this young man – and, just for the record, I'm single – then you'll most definitely go on to have beautiful babies,' she said, fully recovered and batting her lashes at Zain. The audacious flirting made me turn to Zain, and I curbed a groan when he flashed her a charming grin.

'So, shall we talk about weddings?' I announced when Sumi seemed quite content to smile at Zain for the rest of the afternoon. She cleared her throat, recovering herself, and then tapped busily on the computer, suddenly very busy, before turning to me with a blinding white smile.

'Yes, shoot! Tell me what you'd like.' Her ultra confident act didn't fool me. It was obvious that she was trying to impress Zain. I walked through my idea for a Mogul wedding. When Sumi started to pay attention, she was incredibly helpful and full of suggestions, showing a portfolio of pictures that best suited my requirements. We looked through pictures of palatial stages with luscious swags of embroidered silk backdrops, majestic thrones amidst elegant romantic lighting and exotic flower displays.

'These are beautiful . . .' I breathed, looking at Zain. 'This . . . this Arabian nights theme, with its bronze lamps, low tables, big silken cushions and huge *sheesha* pipes, I want that for my *henna*.'

'Great.'

'There're going to be one hundred guests at my *henna*, and the colour theme is antique gold and sunset-burnt orange,' I outlined as Sumi tapped in all the details about what, when and where.

'How about a DJ?' Sumi asked and I shook my head.

'My brother's friend is going to manage that,' I explained before I discussed the lighting, ornaments and floor that needed a big dance area.

'What about the car for the wedding?' Sumi continued, showing us their luxury car collections. 'What about arriving on a elephant?'

'An elephant sounds cool – you know, one of those ones decorated in garlands of flowers and paint,' Zain said, turning to me with a curbed smile. 'I can see Jhanghir arriving on a prettied-up elephant.'

'He'd use it to trample all over you!' I told him, causing Zain to raise an eyebrow. Sumi was watching our interaction closely, so I shook my head and stated. 'No elephant.'

'A horse?' she offered hesitantly.

'Yeah, how about a horse?' Zain suggested. 'Maybe it'll gallop off into the sunset.'

I looked at Zain pointedly and he tried not to grin.

'Let's stay away from animals,' I advised, turning back to Sumi.

'We're good on the car front,' Zain told Sumi without looking away from me. 'We'll get Jhanghir's father's Bentley—'

'No, we won't.'

Zain stopped at my refusal. 'It's a car, Maya,' he pointed out.

'It's Jhanghir's father's car,' I reminded him, refusing to give way on the matter.

'You're being stubborn.'

I held his gorgeous thickly lashed eyes and shrugged at Zain. He dragged his eyes away from my stare and turned to Sumi. 'We'll come back to you about the car.' Sumi looked at each of us uncertainly, unsure of what to make of our heated exchange, before breaking into a wide smile.

'OK, what about the groom's guy *holud*?' Sumi continued, tapping into the right folder on her large Mac to illustrate the range of bachelor parties that they had hosted.

'We're taking care of that,' Zain announced, causing me to frown.

'What do you mean?' I asked, turning back to face him.

'We're hosting it in New York so that most of his friends and family can attend.'

'Really, when was that decided?'

Zain didn't look pleased at my demand but the fact

remained that the pre-marriage celebrations presented a chance for members of the family to turn up at each other's party to inform the other through song and dance how unworthy they were to marry. All done in good humour, in jest, and aimed to build ties and camaraderie between the two families.

'Seema *bhabhi* suggested it to Jhanghir and he agreed,' Zain said.

'Right,' I muttered, fighting the instinct to face Seema head on. 'Great.'

'So no Guy *Holud* to organise?' Sumi pursued hesitantly.

'No Guy *Holud*,' Zain stated, holding my eyes and stopping me from disagreeing. When I stayed quiet, he leaned forward until he was too close. 'Right?' But I refused to move back.

'Sure,' I accepted. Neither of us backed down, and neither of us was going to give way.

'And the wedding . . .' Hearing Sumi's terse question, we both turned to look at her until she pointed down at my wedding book nervously. I cocked a brow. 'Shall we talk about the wedding?'

I turned back to Zain and smiled. 'Yes, let's talk about my wedding,' I said.

'So talk about your wedding,' he told me, trying to derail my line of thought.

'This is what I want for my wedding,' I told Sumi, looking down at my wedding book at the cut-out images of the courts of Muglee-Azam.

'She knows what she wants,' Zain told Sumi, who no longer smiled at him.

'This?' she asked, pointing down at the picture. Nodding, I smiled, turned to Zain, and, without the slightest hesitation, said, 'I want you to give me this.'

*

Some time later, Zain and I made our way to Kensington's Patisserie Valerie to meet Sakina over a coffee. As we waited for Sakina to turn up, I gave Amma a phone update on the wedding plans and Zain sat opposite me looking through my wedding book.

'You really have a talent,' Zain said, pointing to my Islamic calligraphy sketches when I ended my call. 'You should sell this stuff, I'd commission you—'

'Sure you would!' I jested self-consciously before looking at him with a smile. 'I'm a developing artist, I know I've got a long way to go before—'

'No, seriously, this is good art,' Zain corrected, leaning forward. 'Have you thought of putting it online? Building an online gallery?'

'I thought about it, but I don't know how to,' I admitted reluctantly.

'You're kidding me?' I frowned at his patronising response and shook my head. 'Give Matt a call, he heads up one of my web design and analytics companies. He'll set you up . . .'

'I appreciate your help, but I can't afford a corporate web designer.'

'No charge,' Zain said, putting a business card down in front of me.

'And what do you get out of it?' I asked, knowing that nothing in life was free.

'I get a say in the pricing strategy and take a seven per cent commission on every piece you sell.'

Raising a brow at his offer, I looked down at the card. I weighed up the risks of working with Zain, George lookalike Clooney, against the chances of getting my art recognised by a wider market.

'I can't,' I refused, pushing the card back to him. 'I'm busy with the wedding, the move to the US—'

'Because of what happened at Café d'Lebanon,' Zain

finished. I didn't say anything and when I stayed quiet he reached for the card. I closed my eyes at the disappearing opportunity and before I could stop myself, I prevented him from taking the card.

'Jhanghir's involved from the start with every decision,' I told him, placing my fingers firmly on the business card to retain it.

'Of course,' he acquiesced with half a grin.

'No, not of course,' I corrected, picking up on his amused tone. 'You mean, *of course*.'

'*Of course*,' he mimicked in an English accent. I refused to smile.

'And no more moments, OK?' I told him, using the temporary understanding to clear the tension between us.

'Moments?' he pondered, raising a cheeky brow.

'Moments, as in between you and me, no more moments.' Zain chuckled at my explanation. 'I'm serious, I'm getting married to Jhanghir. I put my reputation on the line by taking on the community and crossing the Atlantic ready to ruin another girl's wedding so that I could spend the rest of my for ever with Jhanghir, so no more moments. He's the one I want.'

'And you need to tell me this because?' Zain asked.

'I'm getting married. Me. Maya Malik. I'm finally getting married. Do you know how long I've waited for this, how long my mum's waited for this?' I stopped when I realised how desperate I sounded in trying to make him believe me. 'There's only ever been Jhanghir,' I finished.

'Well, then, you should get married, right?'

I simply nodded.

'Why aren't you with somebody?' I asked him again.

He shook his head and held up his hand to stop my line of enquiry.

'Would that make you feel any better?' I bit my lower lip and looked up him. Nodding, I held his eyes before smiling. 'Really?'

'Yes, really it would,' I burst out with a grin. 'Why aren't you with somebody, some tall, leggy bombshell?'

'Who says I'm not?'

My smile dropped. 'You're seeing someone!' I breathed out before realising that he was testing me.

'It matters, doesn't it?' Zain asked and I shook my head belying my reaction. I avoided meeting his heavy-lashed grey eyes. 'You don't get to choose, Maya.'

'Tell me your story, Zain Khan.'

'I don't have a story . . .'

'Everyone has a story,' I clarified. My fingers on the edge of his business card were a fraction away from his. I looked up at him directly. 'Tell me.'

'I don't have a story,' Zain said, letting go of the business card to sit back. I picked it up and put it away.

'You haven't dealt with your past and you won't share . . .'

'Share what?' We both turned to find Sakina standing behind us.

'Nothing . . .'

'Our pasts.'

Zain and I gave different answers at the same time and then looked at each other.

'Have I interrupted something?' she asked with a hesitant laugh, before taking off her jacket to sit between us. 'Caramel macchiato,' she breathed at Zain, who frowned at the order. When he looked at me with a frown I mouthed it to him again and watched him leave to do her bidding.

'What was that?' I whispered to Sakina the minute Zain left the table.

'Tanya told me to be sultry . . .'

'Sultry doesn't mean stupid!' I told her as we both looked to Zain. He caught us staring and we smiled guiltily before looking back at each other.

'Did I sound stupid?' Sakina asked, losing her nerve. Calming my own rattled nerves, I shook my head, telling myself not to be hard on her. I looked to Zain and then back at my friend.

'No, no you didn't,' I said. It was time to do the right thing for us all. 'After he gets back, I'll leave . . .'

'You don't have to, that'd be so obvious . . .'

'Sakina, we've done this a hundred times over. Just enjoy the coffee with him and be yourself,' I finished with a supportive smile when Zain headed back to us.

'One caramel macchiato. I got a refill and an OJ for Maya since she's on a crazy health diet,' he stated, sitting down to face the two of us watching him. 'Did I . . . did I forget something?'

'No, not at all,' I laughed, activating the fake call alarm on my phone before taking the bottle of juice from him. 'Sakina has a question to ask you about setting up online businesses.' With that introduction, Sakina took over. When my mobile sprang to life, I stepped away from the table to take the fake call. I took my time speaking to nobody and caught Zain's glance. I knew that he knew what I was doing, but that still didn't explain why I felt alive when he looked at me with those deep dark eyes. I blamed it on my hyper hormones. Every woman knows that being over emotional, extra sensitive and cranky during her cycle is normal. I told myself that I was being normal but, deep down, I knew that I was lying to myself. Jhanghir was to become my world, and maybe, just maybe, the reality of that, given our hot-and-cold relationship of late, made this . . . this thing with Zain feel that much more intense. Either way, guilt now cast a heavy shadow over everything. Ending my fake conversation, I returned to the table to collect my sketchbook and notes.

'I've got to run, Mum's just called me. Something about my wedding dress . . .'

'I thought you'd sorted out your wedding dress?' Zain pointed out.

'Yeah, you've chosen . . . your wedding dress,' Sakina finished, realising too late that she'd not helped my cause in making a smooth exit. Clearing my throat, I grabbed my bag and thought clearly.

'It's my family!' I improvised, holding my bottle of juice and sketchpad. 'They all want to wear coordinated outfits, and they've taken the day off to go shopping and Mum can't explain the colour theme—' Stopping myself from rambling, I stopped and looked at them both. 'I've I got to run.' And with that I left them to it. I stepped out on to the high street and looked back at them through the glass window. I felt bad watching them, and paused when I spotted them laughing. They looked comfortable together and I couldn't explain why I felt deflated. I looked down at my empty wedding finger, knowing it wouldn't be long before it was adorned and pledged with a vow to build a life with Jhanghir. I smiled sadly. Life was all about timing, and sometimes life chose the worst moment to throw in distractions. Zain was a distraction, I told myself and, leaving him to Sakina was exactly the right thing to do at this time. Ignoring the ringing doubt in my head, I headed for the underground back to my world and my wedding.

Lessons in lingerie

Nobody would think that Muslim women knew the first thing about lingerie. Whilst the convention suggests that we live in shrouded oppression, the opposite couldn't be more true. This explained why Tanya took it on herself to throw me a lingerie party. The *hijabi* not only had a wicked mouth to shame the rowdiest of football hooligans, but she had the imagination to match them too. With curt instructions to turn up in nothing less than three-inch heels, hemlines no longer than six inches, and enough make-up to shame Jordan, I dreaded to think what our elders would make of it. Holding the nude-coloured lace shift dress against me, I grinned at the evening ahead.

'Maya, your *baba* wants to have a word . . . do I need to ask what that dress is for?'

Holding the dress behind my back, I looked at Amma and shook my head. She did that thing where every mother can reduce a grown-up woman to a childlike state with one piercing look. So what's the dress for?'

'Amma, it's for my girl's night . . .' Stopping the start of what would be a circular conversation, I dropped the dress on the bed and then led Amma out of my bedroom.

Taking the stairs down to the kitchen, I stopped when I found Baba in quiet conversation with Tariq. They stopped the instant they saw me.

'Sit down,' Baba suggested, pointing to the chair next to him. The solemn face of my brother told me that bad news was about to be shared and the only thing I could think of was the lingerie party that was waiting for me.

'What's happened?'

Baba looked to Tariq to answer my question.

'Baba had a chat with Jhanghir's mother about your dowry,' he began. 'And he's not very happy.'

Turning to Baba, I found him staring down at his clenched hands. 'Why didn't you tell me you were having the chat?'

'The dowry's for the elders to determine, Maya. It's to allow wise, impartial decisions to be made in the interests of the bride and groom,' Tariq explained. Baba refused to look at me.

'I thought we'd agreed the dowry before Jhanghir left for New York?'

Silence followed my comment and finally Baba looked up. Slowly, he shook his head.

'What has changed?'

'Your wedding gold obviously is part of the *mahr*—'

'What does the dowry comprise of?' I asked, frowning when Baba avoided my look.

'Your wedding gold plus ten thousand pounds in the event of a split,' he answered.

'But that's not it, is it?' Deep down I knew that what Baba would say next would change things between Jhanghir and me. And yet, I needed to know. 'Baba?'

'If you sign a prenuptial agreement wanting no part of his father's fortune, his father will attend the wedding and there's twenty thousand pounds more in your dowry.'

The sting of humiliation reddened my cheeks. The insult was beyond comprehension and we sat in silence.

'Can I have the twenty thousand pounds and not have his father at the wedding?' I asked, in a muted attempt at humour. No one saw the funny side and I quietened. The truth was I didn't know what to say to make this better for my saddened parents. Jhanghir must have known about this, I couldn't imagine it being discussed without his consent and yet, the man I knew would never agree to this unless . . . unless he wanted to please his father so much that he was prepared to humiliate me and my family.

'You're not to jeopardise this wedding,' Amma stated, reading my mind.

'Baba,' I asked, turning to my father. Without a word, he pushed his chair back and left the kitchen. He was a proud man and this insult cut deep.

'You're not to risk your wedding and your future. Your father and I will deal with everything else.' Closing my eyes at Amma's words, I fought the rage within me.

'Promise me?' By the time I opened my eyes, Tariq *bhai* had left the kitchen too and Amma was sitting next to me with tears in her eyes.

'Don't make me promise,' I whispered with tears slipping down my cheeks. 'They've insulted Baba, you, our entire family . . . why would you want me to marry—'

'Because this is about you and Jhanghir and your future. Everything else is words, it means nothing.' Amma placed a hand over my heart and smiled through her tears.

'My baby, I brought you up to be a good human being; I know you're not marrying Jhanghir for his father's wealth, so sign the paper, let the stingy old man hold on to his fortune, and know that you will be the bigger person for it.'

'Being the bigger person is about doing the right thing, Amma . . .'

'Yes, and you're doing that by allowing us to manage the dowry. You are not responsible for what is offered but you are responsible for what you accept, and to accept Jhanghir alone is the right thing,' She explained patiently. 'Now promise me you won't jeopardise this wedding.'

I struggled to speak until Amma gripped my chin and forced me to meet her eyes. 'I promise.'

Armed with my reluctant word, she kissed my cheek and left the kitchen to find Baba. But Amma's words did little to settle the rage inside me. I didn't want Jhanghir's father at my wedding, near my family or anywhere near me. I feared speaking my mind, I feared that I would tell his father in no uncertain terms in front of my six hundred guests that I didn't want his fortune, or his properties or anything he owned. And yet, I knew I couldn't. I knew that to speak my mind would jeopardise my wedding, my future and my relationship with Jhanghir. I had given Amma my word and I was, for now, bound by it.

Two and a half hours later, Shireen *bhabhi*, Amma and I arrived at Jana's house all dressed in *jilbabs* and *hijabs*.

'You're here!' the excited squeal alerted us that Leila with Meena and Chachijhi had arrived at the same time. And, much like us, were adorned in the same Arabian get-up. 'Are you ready for a naughty night?' Leila asked laughing.

'What is this dressing-up business? What happened to having simple, easy weddings!' Chachijhi muttered, walking ahead in a foul mood.

'Hey, is it true?' Turning at Leila's question, I frowned. 'That he thinks you're after his daddy's money?'

Staring at my cousin, I wondered how it was that we could be related.

'Yep, he's right. I'm going after every single penny,' I threw back before walking away in my four-and-a-half-inch black stilettos.

'No need to be sarcastic!' Leila shouted as I joined Amma and Chachijhi at the door, where Chachijhi pressed the bell repeatedly.

'Why doesn't anyone answer the door—'

'SURPRISE!!!!'

Before we knew it, a shower of every type of lingerie rained down upon us, courtesy of my group of friends and family who opened the door.

'What the blasted hell is going on here!' Chachijhi shouted, pulling a double-D bra off her head as we all burst out laughing at the greeting.

'Mummy, would you cool it?' Leila muttered, taking her mother in.

'Come in!' Jana said, beckoning us in. Shaking my head, I laughed and hugged everyone around me. Before I could get round to everyone, the sultry sound of Sakina blasted through the house. Hana and Ayesha grabbed my hands and rushed me into the extended living room. All the furniture had been removed with just big bean bags lined up around the huge flat-screen entertainment system.

'What is going on here?' Chachijhi demanded as she took off her *jilbab* to reveal a flowery polyester *shalwaar kameez*. 'I need a tea, I'm getting a headache.' Amma did likewise and followed behind her.

'Strip!' Ayesha announced. And with that instruction, *jilbabs*, *abayas* and *hijabs* went flying off. The room was filled with women with big hair and tall heels dressed in smock dresses, shift dresses, baby-doll camisole dresses. And then as the shrill calls of Bedouin women pierced through the room, my friends parted to let in two women dressed in belly-dancing outfits with veils over their faces. Clapping we all moved to the beat, encouraging them on and then they pulled off their veils. In an instant, everyone started whooping and hollering at the sight of Tanya and Sakina at their finest. They danced round me until I joined right in. Winding my hips, and shimmying my shoulders. I spun round and round until we whooped with happiness.

When the dancing subsided, everyone gathered around on the bean bags, tucking into finger food, ready to give the low-down on marriage, men and the marital afterlife.

'OK, people, don't give Maya a hard time; she's having a hard time with her in-laws,' Leila announced as she took off her five-inch heels to sit down on the floor. I locked glances with Jana and Hanna who knew these matters were kept within the family.

'It's not all bad, Maya,' Hanna told me with a warm smile. 'Early on, marriage is tough, even for dopey-eyed, infatuated lovebirds. Adjusting to a man in your life, every day for the rest of your life, isn't easy.' She sobered up the conversation. 'And sometimes the in-laws make it harder than it ought to be . . .'

'In-law problems . . . Oh please don't get us started on that!' a distant cousin muttered. But that was the only invitation the girls needed.

'My mother-in-law couldn't stand to see me make her son smile. She dragged him away each time . . .'

'That's nothing! My mother-in-law gave me the leftovers that her sons didn't want to eat. I mean, who does that to a new bride?'

'Hold up, my sisters-in-law told me what they wanted cooked for dinner . . .'

'Mine was the worst; for some reason, no matter what

I did, I was never as good as my mother-in-law's daughters. They cooked better, so if I cooked three dishes, her daughters cooked ten blindfolded and with one of their hands tied! But you know the worst thing?' We all shook our heads at the question. 'She gave my kids cheap clothes and toys compared to what she gave her daughters' kids. That's when I stopped caring, that's when I took control and moved out.'

'But surely your husband's put a stop to this?' Pana asked sadly when all the married women in the room fought to share their stories.

'The husband? Huh!' One married friend laughed. 'Nothing the family does is ever wrong, premeditated or malicious. Apparently, it's all in our heads!' The chorus of yeses that followed that statement worried me.

'But you all married these guys of your own choice,' I pointed out. The naïveté of my comment made the married women stare at me as if I was stupid.

'Yeah, but the family comes along with the package. Don't underestimate the power of the family.' Our family friend spoke to me directly and it resonated with me.

'Ignore her,' Jana said, pulling me round so that together with Tanya and Sakina we formed a little circle. But I couldn't. The burden of in-law expectations and judgements is a burden all married Asian women carried. And I didn't know if I had the wisdom or grace to carry that burden well.

'It's a wonder that any of you lot are still married!' Tanya stated, putting an end to all the sad, shared experiences. 'If you're not careful, Maya will never get around to using these!' she added, throwing a pair of suspenders at me. I stared at her as she held out the first of many lingerie boxes. Finally, I laughed along with the girls as my friends unveiled boxes of sheer, saucy lingerie. They pulled me into the centre and countered my embarrassed refusals until I opened up more daintily covered boxes of silky smalls. I covered my face in sheer embarrassment at the see-through negligées, and then looked in confusion as I held up tiny bits of stringy garments – I couldn't figure out what they were for.

'This you wear to get what you want,' Sakina said, holding up an itsy bitsy stringy set made of the sheerest chiffon.

'This you tell him to get lost with,' Jana countered, holding up granny pants worthy of a big mumma with a big girth.

'And this you say "Hello, boy" with!' Pana teased, showing me a ruby-red negligée.

'And this I eat!' I announced when I found a tub of chocolate. 'All right, so whose great idea for a gift was this?' I asked, holding up the jar for everyone to see.

'Well, Jhanghir *bhai* won't mind your chocolate craving when you lick it off him!' Zara pointed out as I looked at the label closely to realise that it was body chocolate.

'I like this present!' I admitted, making the girls whistle and laugh in equal measure.

'We're ruining my baby sister!' Hanna cried out, pulling me into a big hug before taking the chocolate away.

'I want to be ruined!' I laughed, taking the chocolate back from her. 'I've waited a long time to get ruined . . .'

'That's my girl!' Tanya threw in as she returned from the kitchen with a large silver tray full of Häagen-Dazs, hot chocolate drizzle and marshmallows. 'So tell me, what's inches long, expands on need and shrivels up around water?' Everyone stopped at the leading question that nobody dared answer when Tanya placed the tubs amongst us.

'The girl has no shame!' Chachijhi muttered as she

walked in after Tanya with large trays of samosas, spring rolls and onion bhajis. I bit my lip and smiled at Tanya who opened up a tub of cookie dough ice cream.

'Slugs,' she answered, holding back a grin. 'The more interesting question is, who knows the difference between a slug and a—'

'OK, time to choose the best Indian and Western songs for Maya's *henna*,' Ayesha cut in quickly, as I caught Tanya's naughty wink. As the conversation took off about song styles, order and dance routines, I sat back lost in thought. Lingerie of various kinds would keep a marriage going for so long. Beyond that, respect and loyalty would carry it through thick and thin. My in-laws thought it fit to buy my integrity and Jhanghir had allowed it. He had allowed my family and, by default, me to be insulted, in fact, disrespected, with a twenty-thousand-pound price tag. What else he would allow concerned me deeply. By all accounts, family influenced marital success and happiness and I didn't know if my marriage to Jhanghir would last if he continued to put his family's happiness ahead of mine.

Manage marriage, madness and mayhem

I woke up with a heavy head. They say women have a sixth sense and that trusting it is as important as trusting your best friend. Right now, the last thing I wanted to do was trust my instinct. Since the dowry discussion, I hadn't heard from Jhanghir and, deep down, I knew that his silence spoke volumes. Weddings should be small, intimate affairs centred on the two people making vows to each other. Not Asian weddings. These are massive events, filled with family one-upmanship and politics that even the courts at The Hague couldn't unravel. Needing to clear my head, I decided to go for my morning jog. Showering and changing into my joggers, I headed downstairs and stopped when I heard crying from behind the closed kitchen door. Frowning at the thought that something else had happened to upset Amma, I burst in and froze when I found Amma hugging a sobbing Chachijhi. Amma waved me away, but Aunty had spotted me before I could back out of the kitchen.

'Did you know?' Chachijhi asked through tear-swelled eyes. 'Did you?' Shaking my head I looked to Amma for support. 'You must have known!' she stated before bursting into tears again.

'*What's happened?*' I mouthed to Amma, who waved for me to leave.

'She's getting married . . . to that coloured boy!' Chachijhi burst out as if she had read my mind.

'Who is?' I asked quietly.

'Who do you think?'

Looking to Amma, I saw her mouth: '*Meena!*'

'They want to get . . . they want to get married!' she blurted out. 'How am I ever going to show my face to the community again?' said Chachijhi.

And she was right. Whilst the Bengali community had been in England for more than fifty years, it was still fiercely insular and conservative. So when changes like this occurred, word spread fast and the only thing we could do was give support.

'He has a great job, he's wealthy . . .' The silent reception to my words killed my intent to make my point.

'He could be the King of Timbuktu, but as long as he's not a Bengali, he's a nobody.'

I knew that wasn't true. If Meena's man was indeed a king, Chachijhi would accept him regardless of whether he was white, black, Bengali or otherwise. The ability to say '*My daughter is Queen so and so, making me Queen Mother of so and so*' would be too tempting for Chachijhi to reject.

'But he's a Muslim.' Both Amma and Chachijhi stopped to look at me.

'Does it matter?'

'Yes, actually, it does; it makes him acceptable under our religious laws.'

'What does she know!' Chachijhi muttered as she used her crumpled-up tissue to clear her nose noisily.

'I know that Islamically we can marry anyone as long as they're from the same faith . . .'

'So why didn't you bring a coloured boy home?' Chachijhi demanded.

'Because I found Jhanghir.'

'Because you knew your parents would never accept a—'

'No, because I found Jhanghir!' I corrected.

Amma leaned forward to point out: 'Maya has Jhanghir; she doesn't need to look for anyone else.'

Chachijhi and I paused to look at Amma.

'You see, double standards; my own family is judging me already, discriminating against me after all that I've done for them just because my daughter's lost her mind!' she added melodramatically, holding her head in her hands.

'No one's discriminating against you . . .'

'So will you talk to her? Get her away from this mad talk of marrying outside the community?' Chachijhi demanded of me. I shook my head, angry at her attitude, knowing that it would hurt her.

'You should judge him on whether he's a good man, a good Muslim and whether he'll make a good husband . . .'

'He's not part of the community!' Chachijhi shouted. 'They'll have mixed-race children . . .'

'Chachijhi, stop!' I stated, ignoring Amma's warning look. 'God made us, and we're all equal in his eyes on all levels except faith. If Meena has found a good man who makes her a better person, you should be grateful.'

'Talk to her, Maya, she respects you, you can bring her to her senses.'

Shaking my head, I backed out of the kitchen. I heard the sobbing start up again and felt terrible for leaving my aunty in tears. I had to do what was right, and condoning Chachijhi's attitudes wasn't something I could do. My day had started off badly, I just hoped it didn't get any worse.

*

Ayesha joined me on my drive across London to Green Street for my first fitting. We didn't talk about the Khans dowry offer; neither did we talk about Meena's indiscretion. In fact, so superficial was our conversation that we ran out of small talk and sat in near silence until we arrived at Suraya's. Walking down to the boutique floor, I greeted the owner and waited for the assistant to bring out my customised wedding outfit.

'You're going to love it!' I told Ayesha with a wide smile, watching the assistant bring out an orange-red ornate *lengha* suit to hang up on the changing-room wall. Assuming it was for another client, I turned back to Ayesha. 'It really is stunning, the minute I spotted it, I knew it was the one—'

'Maya, it's ready,' the assistant told me, indicating the open changing room where the orange-red outfit hung. I refused to believe they could have screwed up my wedding dress, as my heart stopped and my stomach dropped.

'I think there's been a mistake, that's not my wedding dress,' I told the assistant who frowned and went to check the order books. 'Mistake!' I told Ayesha, who watched the assistant return.

'I think you're mistaken – you see, this is your order.' My smile froze and I walked to the changing room.

'But this isn't the colour that I wanted,' I told her. 'I said that the colour should be a deep red, like velvet-rose-red, and this is orange-red . . . I don't want orange-red, I didn't ask for orange-red,' I told her, trying not to get emotional at the sight of what was meant to be my wedding dress. The assistant disappeared in a hurry and returned with the designer in tow.

'There seems to be a problem?' he asked as he looked at the hanging outfit as if he was in love with it.

'This isn't my wedding dress.'

'Yes, it is.'

'No, it isn't.'

'But you ordered it.'

'In velvet-rose-red and antique gold . . . and you've given me orange-red with Indian shiny yellow bling bold gold, and that's not what I ordered. I've got accessories, shoes, everything for deep velvet-rose-red, not orange-red, I ordered velvet-rose-red!' Tears stung my eyes and I couldn't help the pitch of my voice increasing the more I spoke.

'OK, Ms Maya . . . we'll have to remake it,' the designer conceded, causing Ayesha to come and stand by me. I stopped and looked at him.

'Remake it?' He nodded. 'From scratch?' He nodded again. 'But I've got less than eleven weeks to my wedding . . .'

'But we have no choice,' he told me.

'Great, my wedding's in eleven weeks and you're going to need twelve weeks to get my dress ready . . . that's just bloody great!' I pointed out, shrugging as if that wasn't a problem.

'Maya, please try this on . . .'

'I'm not wearing that to my wedding!' I shouted, making everyone jump.

'Maya!' Ayesha chastised, not one for public outbursts. 'Don't turn into a bridezilla . . .'

'Forget being a bridezilla, I just want to be a bride. When was the last time you saw a bride dressed in neon orange for her wedding?'

'OK, OK . . . if you try it on, I can make the alterations to it so that I can send this to India to have a copy made in the material and colour that you want.'

I stared at the designer long and hard enough for him to read that I wasn't happy or impressed at all. When I thought he had got the message, I entered the changing room and put it on. Nothing about it was right. The colour, the fitting, the shape. It was just horrible and so far from what I had expected that when I walked out in four-inch heels, I was very, very close to tears.

'You've lost weight. This will look much better if we pin here and tuck here,' the designer told me, pinning different parts of the dress around me. 'Bingo! We've got the perfect structure,' he finished with a short clap of his hands. Looking at Ayesha, I felt my lip quiver and sniffed when she smiled.

'It'll be perfect,' she promised. Turning to the designer I looked at him through narrowed eyes, remembering the horror stories about wedding dresses from the lingerie night.

'Listen, I want the dress ready in nine weeks, so that gives me ten days for you to fit it and make it perfect. OK?' The designer was about to protest, but I held my hand up to stop him. 'This is your mistake, it's your responsibility to sort it out and get me my dress in nine weeks.' And with that I walked to the changing room and burst into tears.

Several hours later, I sat in Manju's make-up room for the second make-up trial for my wedding. She was the only make-up artist left who had a free booking in August and that was only because one of her clients had cancelled on her. I couldn't afford to lose her and yet, with eyes swollen from crying one too many tears over my disastrous wedding-dress fitting, I was in no mood to be made up into a trannny. So when she returned to her salon, I held out several of her wedding magazines.

'This is the colour of my wedding dress, I want striking but subtle make-up to complement that,' I began as she rolled a stool before me to start prepping my face.

'Sure,' she answered, using a moist wipe to clean my face of any make-up. Quietly I waited for her to ask me questions about what I wanted, but Manju was content on continuing without a word. When I couldn't wait any longer, I sat back and smiled up at the slim, pretty Indian woman.

'I really don't want too much foundation, you know, I really want it natural-looking with strong eyes and strong cherry lips.' Nodding, Manju leaned round and opened up her make-up boxes to find the best foundation to suit my complexion.

'Don't worry, I'll make you beautiful,' she told me. The short comment meant to reassure me failed to do just that. So I looked at the magazines until I found a sophisticated look that would look good with my outfit.

'Like this: dark, smokey eyes, strong lips, subtle cheeks . . .'

'I understand,' Manju said again with a cursory look at the image, intent on getting back to making me up. Leaning back from the foundation sponge, I looked at her.

'Are you sure you get what I want?' When Manju held my eyes and nodded slowly, I sat back straight again. And then she began. In total silence, she deftly applied the foundation, shaded my eyes, lined my lids, dusted my cheeks and then painted my lips. In less than twenty minutes, she sat back and smiled. Frowning, I peeked my eyes open. I found Manju packing away her cosmetics.

'We're done?' I asked in surprise.

'Yes, you look beautiful.' She smiled, pointing towards to the large mirror behind me. Swivelling round, I looked at my reflection as Manju started brushing my hair. I froze at the sight of barely there make-up with rainbow eyes and dark brown lips. There was nothing elegant or understated about it. In fact, there was nothing classy or subtle about the way I looked.

'Uh, stop,' I said, wincing when she wrenched my hair back into a tight knot. 'No, really, stop.' Moving away from Manju, I turned round to face her. I smiled so that she didn't feel unappreciated, but there was no hiding the fact that I wasn't impressed.

'Sorry, but this really doesn't look like anything I showed you . . .'

'You don't like it?' she asked sadly. Taking a minute, I chose my words carefully.

'It's not what I asked for.'

'You said strong eyes and strong lips, everything else subtle. That's what I've given you.'

'I didn't ask for rainbows to be painted on to my eyelids . . .' Stopping at the sight of Manju tearing up, I looked down at the magazines and opened up on an image that I liked. 'I wanted something like this, that's why I showed you the pictures . . .'

'But you look so pretty, how can you say this isn't pretty?' Manju said as tears dripped on to her cheeks. 'I think you look beautiful . . .' She couldn't finish because she was trying so very hard not to cry. I bit my lip, urging myself not to give in to the tears, not to accept this level of service, and yet the sight of the woman crying quietened me. Without another word, I sat back down on the stool and handed Manju the hairbrush.

'It's not so bad, is it?' she said with a watery smile. I shook my head and closed my eyes. The image of turning up in an ill-fitting neon orange suit with wild make-up was fast becoming a reality and I had to breathe deeply to control the floodgates of tears. I let Manju brush, tease and cajole my hair into the biggest beehive I'd ever seen, but I didn't speak a word. When she had sprayed enough hairspray to make a girl band proud, I knew she had finished. Silently, I handed over forty pounds, made no promise to book her for my wedding, and headed back home. I let myself in, and stopped in front of my family.

'Maya, we're ... we're ...' I stayed quiet as Amma wrinkled her nose at my appearance and leaned in to take a closer look. 'Uh ... yes, well, we're all planning your *cinipaan* at Mehdi's; we need you to come and join us.'

'That looks ...' Jerking round to look at Taj, I speared him with a deadly stare, daring him to finish his thoughts. He thought otherwise and looked away whistling. Without a single word, I walked past my entire family, who stared at me in silence, and up to my room.

To: JKhan@NYMedics.com
From: MayaM@Instantmail.com

Jhanghir, what's wrong? I can't handle your silences right now. Today, I discovered that my wedding dress is neon orange and sized for an obese troll bride. As if that wasn't bad enough, I went for a make-up trial where I paid an emotionally imbalanced make-up artist to turn me into a troll. And I have an entire *kandaan* downstairs planning our *paancini* at Mehdi's when you've disappeared off the face of the earth. So if you've rediscovered your love for Preeya or realised that your father's choice of bride is the way for you, then tell me, because this marriage-to-be is madness right now. I'm the bride, I'm meant to feel fabulous, but if that is never going to happen, have the decency to tell me. I can be fabulous elsewhere.

New fancies favour no one

There are times when you wake up and find that nothing, with no exception, is going your way. Like today, the day of my *paancini*, the formal announcement of my engagement to Jhanghir. So this is what happens at a *paancini*. The groom's family sends the bride a beautifully wrapped *sari* and accessories to wear to the celebratory dinner. The community gossipmongers judge the quality and beauty of the *sari* harshly so that only the best gift survives criticism. Now, given that my groom's family barely acknowledged my existence, the likelihood that I would receive such a gift or have any of Jhanghir's family turning up to witness the formal announcement, was as likely as a Brit winning Wimbledon. So I lay in bed, wearing my teeth-whitening mouthguard, no *sari*, a family running around getting ready for a celebratory dinner twelve hours in advance, and an absent fiancé who had yet to reply to my email.

'C'mon!' Tariq announced as he stepped into my room. 'Stop feeling sorry for yourself, we're celebrating, and that's all that matters.' Pulling my duvet over me, I curled up into a ball and hid away from the world.

Then, taking out the mouthguard, I frowned and said, 'I don't think it's a good day to have a *paancini*.' Intent on staying in bed all day, I stayed put. 'I think we should cancel everything, the *paancini*, the *henna*, the wedding. I'm not interested in getting married any more, I just want to be a painter.'

Tariq pulled the duvet off the bed, and I peered up at him.

'Have I told you how I used to find you hiding at the bottom of the garden playing with ants when anyone got you mad?' I stopped myself smiling when he sat down beside me and pushed the hair back from my face. 'You would swear that you needed no one and that you would make a home with the ants.'

'I don't need anyone, I choose to—'

'You choose to get ready for your *paancini*,' Tariq told me with half a laugh. 'You're not a kid any more, Maya, no matter how much you want to, you can't hide away and not deal with your life.'

'My life? My life?' I asked, sitting up to pull up my sleeves. 'My life sucks, Bhai, my fiancé's been AWOL for the past few weeks, I have my engagement party to go to without any gifts from Jhanghir's family, and I'm meant to face the community as if that's normal.' The anger died within me and I looked at my brother. 'I don't know if I want a future where I'm forever humiliated in front of the community.'

'Do I need to remind you that you asked Jhanghir to marry you in public?'

'But I didn't know that marrying him would mean his family treating my family like dirt.'

'Stop.'

'And Jhanghir allows it – in fact, he doesn't even talk to me; he's like a reclusive fiancé on a permanent bachelorhood sabbatical.'

'There's a package for you downstairs.'

'Like he doesn't even care that he's getting married—' I stopped when Tariq *bhai*'s words slowly registered. Biting my lower lip, I stopped myself from smiling but raised my brow in query. He nodded and moved out of the way when I screamed, scrambled out of bed and raced downstairs. Pushing my mouthguard back into my mouth, I called out, 'Where is it?' I stopped at the bottom, when I found my sisters and cousins standing around Zain and Jhanghir's mother. I was dressed in a full-sleeved white cotton nightie, with bed-head hair, no make-up and unable to hide the protruding mouthguard.

'Here it is,' Zain said, trying not to smile. Looking at the beautifully wrapped gifts, I couldn't stop smiling. And then I realised that everyone was staring awkwardly at the mouthguard. Pretending to cough, I slipped it out and held it behind my back.

'Come through, come through—' Amma stopped when she saw me. 'Maya . . .'

'Come join us,' Mrs Khan suggested kindly, beckoning me to sit down. Pulling my hair down over one shoulder, I walked with them into the living room.

'Get the refreshments,' Amma instructed Pana and her sisters who were spending their summer break with us to help me prepare for my wedding.

'Please, bhenjhi, we really can't stay. I've only just landed and we have so much to get ready for,' Mrs Khan said as Zain put the box on the coffee table. 'We really hope you like it.' I knelt down by the coffee table. Looking up, I smiled as all my family watched me with happy, expectant eyes.

'Open it!' Jana encouraged. Taking a deep breath, I reached out and opened the box slowly. 'Let's see.' Taking the top off, I looked down at a sheer champagne-coloured chiffon *sari*. It looked like the one I wore the night of my art competition when I asked Jhanghir to marry me.

'He looked for it everywhere,' Mrs Khan informed me as I gently caressed it softly.

'He could've saved a bomb and just asked me to wear the one I own.' Everyone laughed at my comment, but I was touched by his consideration.

'There's more,' Leila pointed out, sneaking forward to point towards the unopened boxes. Putting the *sari* down, I pulled out the Swarovski-encrusted bangles, followed by an elegant jewellery set. A chorus of 'ooohhhs' and 'aaahhs' echoed around the room with the revelation of each item until I found a small jewellery box. I knew what it was before I opened it. I unclipped the box and looked down at the diamond pendant necklace Jhanghir had once given me.

'Let me put it on you,' Ayesha said as my twin sisters sniffed back their tears. Holding my hair up, she placed it round my neck and then gave me a warm hug.

'Are you happy?' Looking up at Mrs Khan I nodded. 'Then I'm happy too, but we really must be going.' As she reached out to *salaam* everyone, I caught Zain's eyes and my smile faltered. He nodded and I touched the pendant that sat at the base of my neck. Looking away, I saw that Chachijhi had caught the exchange.

'Isn't Jhanghir wonderful?' Leila breathed out as she hugged me before going through all the gifts. Clearing unwanted thoughts of Zain away, I laughed and agreed. This was no time for new fancies. Not when it was far from welcome.

My house turned into a madhouse in advance of our departure to Mehdi's for my *paancini*. All the men huddled in the living room, uncomfortably dressed in smart cream *punjabi*s, grumbling about why it took women so long to get ready. It was a fact that every room had a sister, aunt or cousin hogging the mirror, or changing and applying make-up. I, on the other hand, locked myself in my room and logged online. There was no email from Jhanghir, but looking up at the box that contained my *paancini* gifts, I refused to give up on him.

To: JKhan@NYMedics.com
From: MayaM@Instantmail.com

Yes. If you were here this evening at our *paancini* about to ask me to publicly accept your offer of marriage, the answer would be yes.
I miss your sarcasm, Jhanghir, it managed to put my world to right no matter how wrong my world felt.

'Maya!' The banging on my door told me my cousins were ready to turn me into a fiancée. 'Maya, let us in, we have to get you ready. We're already running late and your dad's getting impatient. Let us—' Leila stopped when I opened the door and leaned against the framework. I smiled as they bundled in past me, each taking a part in getting me ready. Leila took the *sari* to drape around me. Pana took my make-up case ready to polish me up and Zara got my bangles ready. Looking back at my laptop, I stared at the empty inbox and smiled slowly. Taking a deep breath, I closed the door and stood with my arms stretched out beside me. And as if by magical instruction, my cousins instantly took to converting me into a woman ready to be engaged.

Mehdi's, Baba's favourite Persian restaurant in London,

had been booked to host the dinner. Just outside it, I sat in Taj's car with Tariq *bhai* and Taj waiting to be called in.

'You can relax,' Tariq said as I focused on breathing in and out. My heart was racing, my hands were clammy and I was shaking at the thought that both families were meeting for the first time in public. Holding my arms out, I shook them, trying to get rid of the tension from my body.

'What are you doing?' Taj asked with a frown.

'I'm nervous . . . can we just go and get this over with?'

'No, you can't just waltz in; try and act like a lady!' Taj threw back. I carried on shaking my arms. 'Stop.'

'I can't, I'm nervous . . . I need some tissues, have you got any tissues, I'm sweating . . .'

'You can't say that, you're a girl,' Taj pointed out turning to Tariq. 'Why doesn't she act like a lady?'

'Shut up, Taj! This is my day, and I'm sweating and I need tissues, so go and get me tissues!' I shouted. Taj and Tariq stared at me for a few seconds and then both scrambled to go and get me some tissues. I continued to shake my arms, wondering why the formalities of greeting each other took so long. I mean, why couldn't they just say hi, come and get me, and get the whole ceremony over and done with?

'Hey.' Looking up at Tanya's voice, I nearly cried with relief. 'Look at the pretty you.'

'I'm going to pass out . . .'

'You're not going to pass out,' Sakina said as both of them got into the back of the car on either side of me. 'You look so beautiful!'

'I need some tissues.' Taking the sheets of tissue Tanya held out, I stuck them inside my blouse under my armpits and sat there cross-armed. Both stared at me as if I had gone crazy, but I didn't move. This calmed me and right now I needed to be calm.

'Well, aren't you the perfect, dainty little wife-to-be!' Tanya stated. We sat for a while with nervous laughs. I thought about how absurd I looked with tufts of tissues tucked into my armpits whilst in my engagement regalia and then looked at my friends. Before we knew it, we were laughing out loud.

'Are you ready to go?' Taj stopped, looked at me and shook his head. 'Please, for one evening, can you act like a normal woman?'

'I'll try,' I announced, throwing the tissues away before stepping out after Sakina. I straightened the sultry *sari* around me and ensured that it covered my hair before turning to my friends.

'What do you think?' I asked, feeling my nerves return.

'You're better than them, that's all you need to tell yourself.'

Nodding at Tanya's words, I took Taj's arm and walked to the entrance. My sisters and cousins waited to lead me into the restaurant. Passer-bys stopped and watched, and I felt like a star. At the entrance we stopped.

'You look good, sis,' Taj whispered in my ear before giving me a quick peck on the cheek. As the girls started to walk in, I turned to Taj and stepped into his ready hug. 'Be happy.'

I nodded and then we walked in. We had family and friends from the community standing, and as we passed them we *salaamed* them. I saw Jhanghir's family at the main table and froze when I spotted Jhanghir standing by his mother. He was dressed in a smart charcoal-grey suit, with open shirt and I thought that he had never looked as good as he did in that moment. I couldn't move. I looked round at my family who all smiled and chuckled at my reaction. Suddenly the whole restaurant came to life with applause when Jhanghir left the main table to step forward towards me.

'Maya,' Jhanghir greeted, taking my hand to put on his arm.

'Jhanghir,' I returned, bursting into a brilliant smile. 'How long are you here for?' I asked as we started walking towards the main table.

'Long enough,' he answered. 'Greet your guests,' he advised, nodding and *salaaming* those we passed. I tried to do likewise, but I couldn't stop looking back at Jhanghir, unable to believe that he had made the journey to be with me.

'Stop staring, Maya.' Hearing the caustic voice of Seema, I turned to smile at the uber-skinny, stunning sister-in-law who waited by the head table. 'Why don't you sit here?'

Jhanghir encouraged me to go with her and I agreed. I didn't hesitate when she placed me between Zain and Jhanghir. I kept smiling between the two men as everyone crowded in front of the table to take pictures of the new member of the Khan family. I caught Jhanghir talking quietly with his mother and watched as she stepped between us. I embraced her when she drew me into a hug and then stepped back. Jhanghir winked at me when his mother drew out a mint-green ring box.

'Oh my God! It's a Tiffany ring!' Leila breathed out loud enough for most of the guests to hear. The gasps of my sisters and friends confirmed Leila's suspicions. Mrs Khan took my hand and I tried to stop it from shaking, but I couldn't. She smiled sweetly before sliding on the Tiffany legacy diamond engagement ring. Everyone clapped, and I looked up at Jhanghir. There was no way we could be alone, but I wished we could have frozen this moment and just been alone. Jhanghir turned away and traded jokes being made about losing his bacherlorhood.

'Welcome to the family,' Mrs Khan said as she hugged me again. 'Be good for my son,' she whispered and I nodded, tearing up at the sincere request. And then, before I could breathe, my mother grasped me into her arms.

'My baby's getting married!' she cried, smothering me, as Chachijhi joined in on the hug. I could hardly breathe, but I managed to tug Hanna's *sari*.

'Mum's lost it,' I muttered as Amma sobbed as if she had lost me to another solar system. 'Do something,' I told my sister who took my mother into her arms. Jhanghir came to stand beside me when our families and friends came up to the main table to congratulate us. He placed a hand on my back, his first gesture of public affection, and I felt like we belonged together.

'How dare she!' Chachijhi cried out and I jerked around to see her crumble into Ayesha's arm. Frowning I looked forward and spotted Meena standing by her fiancé at the entrance. Instantly, I turned to Tariq, who followed our sobbing aunt as she raced away from the celebrations.

'Everything OK?' Jhanghir asked as Seema mocked the drama my family had created.

'Yes.' I smiled, trying my hardest to ignore the patronising comments to return to greeting our well-wishers.

The evening sped by so quickly that Jhanghir and I barely got a moment to talk. When the meal was served, the women sat around me whilst he ate with the men. When we cut the large cream cake to celebrate the formal engagement, we posed for so many pictures that my face hurt with the amount of smiling that was needed. And then, before we knew it, everyone was heading out, marking the end of the evening. The elders made small talk and I waited for my parents to collect me.

'You happy?' Turning at Zain's comment, I faltered as I found him standing behind me. I looked back at Jhanghir and wished he hadn't left my side.

'Very much so,' I replied. He was wearing a neat-fitted black suit over a grey V-neck.

'You nervous around me?'

'I have no reason to be,' I told him, finally meeting his steely eyes and instantly regretting the impact of making full eye contact.

'Really?' Nodding at his question, I smiled and couldn't draw my eyes away. 'Good.'

'Everything OK?' Both of us jumped at Jhanghir's appearance.

'Yeah, Zain was just telling me how gorgeous I look,' I told Jhanghir who paused at my comment, before looking at me closely.

'Gorgeous is kinda stretching the truth; I'd say passable . . .'

'Passable!' I cried out, whacking his arm and making him chuckle.

'Look at this trio,' Seema stated as she joined us at the table. I tensed instantly, looking to Zain who pulled her into a warm hug in spite of her protests.

'Don't feel left out, Bhabhi,' he told her with more than a tone of sarcasm.

'Oh I don't. I've no intention of ever being on the outside,' she laughed, before reaching out to pull Jhanghir into a hug. 'We're family.' I met her look. In less than a minute, she had isolated me. I smiled, giving her credit for sheer bolshiness. But this was my night. So I reached out and took Jhanghir's arm.

'And *we*'re set to get married, so, if you don't mind, I want some time alone with my husband-to-be.' Both Seema and Zain stopped smiling. But the grin on Jhanghir's face gave me the courage to lead him away.

'Nicely done. You'll fit right in,' Jhanghir said with a chuckle as we walked towards our parents. I refused to smile, but the twinkle in my eye told the world that no one was going to ruin my day.

Old rivalries, old fears and old cracks will appear

When I opened my eyes the following morning, I stopped a small smile and hugged the duvet to me. The sleepy groans of Mana and Pana, who had crashed out next to me, made me release the duvet. Slowly, I eased myself up and reached out for my iPhone.

'Maya, you're going to see Jhanghir *bhai* later, so don't be so desperate.' Leila's irritated mutter made me look under the cover to find my cousin. Putting my phone down, I eased back beneath the duvet and smiled when Leila hugged me. I stared up at the ceiling, cherishing the memories of my engagement day. Everyone had left the restaurant after the engagement and headed back to our house. It didn't matter that we ran out of space or that we were running around serving up several rounds of tea dressed in our finest; everyone was together and there was not the faintest hint of snobbery by Jhanghir's family to ruin anything. Seema stayed under control, Zain kept a decent distance. It felt like old rivalries and old fears disappeared when Jhanghir was around. Throughout the evening, Jhanghir and I had grabbed mere seconds together, but with the entire *kandaan* keeping a steady eye on the protocols of interaction, mere seconds was all we had. Either Chachijhi or Amma would pop up with some pointless excuse to drag one of us away and we would go, willingly, chuckling at the obvious unapologetic act. And when Jhanghir departed with all the members of his family, it took everything I had not to leave with him. I didn't hear anything further from him that evening as we all crashed out, talking about the day's events. But I didn't need to. Surprising me on the day of my engagement was more than I could have asked for. Holding my hand up, I stared at the diamond ring that now adorned my hand. I was engaged. Yes, I was.

'You happy?' Looking down at my old nemesis, Leila, I smiled and nodded. 'Good.' She smiled. I huddled back down and closed my eyes, but the smile never left my lips.

The smile didn't last very long when I woke up to find that I had slept through a call from Jhanghir telling me that he was flying out that afternoon. He finished by telling me that he was waiting in Carluccio's at Heathrow's Terminal Five. In a blind panic, I pulled on a black polo neck and cream pedal pushers and grabbed my tan hobo bag to race out of the house in black ballerina pumps.

'Where are you going?' Amma called out, running after me.

'Jhanghir's flying out; I've got to catch him at the airport,' I shouted over my shoulder as I raced towards the underground station. It felt like I was caught in a time warp that made everything feel slower. On the tube, I pulled my hair into a ponytail and regretted trying to apply eyeliner when a sudden stop caused a black streak of liquid liner to appear across my forehead. Cursing, I ignored the watching eyes of fellow commuters as I wiped the streak off. When we pulled up at Terminal Five, I decided against any make-up, keeping it to simple lip balm, and raced through the terminal until I stood before Carluccio's. Rushing into the renowned Italian restaurant, I stopped in the middle and swirled around, unable to spot Jhanghir. A deep fear bubbled within me that I had missed him. Shaking my head, I dug deep into my bag to fish out my iPhone.

'Hey.' Stopping at the calm call, I looked behind me to the far corner. Jhanghir looked as surprised to see me as I was to find him flanked by Seema and Zain. 'You came,' he said, walking towards me. Jhanghir was dressed casually in loose joggers, blue shirt with the sleeves pushed up and sandals, and he still looked every bit as gorgeous as those Adonises that grace Armani's catwalk shows in Milan. In comparison, I just felt rough.

'How come you're leaving already?' I asked as Jhanghir stopped before me. We didn't hug, there were no sweet nothings, we just stood there and I knew something was wrong. He looked worried and I darted a look across to where he had been sitting and noticed the papers on the table.

'I've got to get back to my duties at the hospital; there've been emergencies and I can't delay heading back any longer,' Jhanghir told me, leading me to the table. 'We've got to talk about the wedding.' The fear of being dumped post-engagement paralysed the smile on my face.

'Why? What's wrong?' Jhanghir shook his head and indicated for me to sit next to Zain. I greeted Zain and Seema briefly but Jhanghir had my full attention.

'What's all this?' he asked me, pushing the papers towards me. Frowning, I looked down at the invoices for our wedding, wondering if he had asked a trick question. 'Maya?'

'Well, they're . . . they're invoices for our wedding,' I told him, feeling daft for stating the obvious. Ignoring Seema's muted laugh, I looked up at Jhanghir. He shook his head and rubbed his face with both his hands.

'Maya, it's grand, I mean, it's like, a massive Bollywood production. Seriously, do we need Mogul statues and carvings? I mean, is it necessary?'

'I . . . uh, I thought the wedding should be uh, unique,' I told him nervously, looking to Seema and wondering if she had put Jhanghir up to this. 'Those are just projected costs . . .'

'What's with the wall tapestries at seven hundred pounds a pop and we apparently need ten?' Jhanghir continued, leaning forward to shift through the documents. 'Do we really need five ice sculptures around the hall?' I sat back and listened as Jhanghir questioned the tenets that underpinned my Mogul-inspired wedding until there really was very little left to call it Mogul-inspired. By the time he finished, I looked at Jhanghir with different eyes. He had left all the hard work, all the details and arrangements to me, and now he was breaking up my dream bit by bit.

'Maya?' Lifting my eyes to meet his, I raised an eye-brow in query, wondering why he hadn't been involved, why he had stayed hands off and, more importantly, why now, in front of the diva and Zain, he felt it was OK to make me justify my wedding dreams. 'Did you register anything I said?' The angry question was the last straw.

'What is the problem?' Jhanghir frowned and sat back at my reply. Yes, OK, when replayed back to me, the plans sounded a little over the top, maybe even too indulgent, but my pride refused to let me admit to the fact that I had got carried away.

'You don't see the problem here?' I shook my head

tentatively at his question. 'You really don't see it?' he asked again, pushing the pages across to me.

'I see the basis of our wedding, I, uh . . . I need you to tell me what the problem is.'

'Jeez, Maya, open your eyes! What is the point of having all this nonsense at our wedding?' Jhanghir shouted as he slammed his hand down on the table.

I jumped, startled by his anger and we sat in silence staring at each other, unsure of what to do to move forward.

'Nonsense?' I whispered, frowning at his attitude towards my hard work.

'Yes nonsense!' Jhanghir insisted, listing item after item that he considered unnecessary for the wedding.

'Those items you call nonsense, that's what makes a Mogul wedding.'

'What's the deal with having a Mogul wedding?' Jhanghir threw back.

'You don't want a Mogul wedding?' I asked, trying very hard to stay in control. At that moment an over-head announcement asked for passengers on Jhanghir's flight to start boarding. Taking a deep breath, I imagined the wedding, our start, our breathtaking beginning, and looked at him. 'Jhanghir, I've also wanted an ornate, traditional wedding, you know, to celebrate the best of where we're from, the richness and beauty of our culture with some hope that we'll have a blessed start . . .'

'Why does it have to be a Mogul-themed wedding?'

'Because that was an era of accomplishment, achievement, grandeur in our Asian history.'

'I don't want a fancy-dress wedding parading as some regal, royal wedding.'

'It is not a fancy-dress wedding.' There was no doubt in my words but Seema's smirk undermined my determination. 'So each time I emailed you for advice, for guidance, why didn't—'

'I didn't know I had to hand-hold you into making sensible, logical, practical decisions.'

'Sensible?' I breathed out, trying very, very hard to keep my temper and tears in check. 'This is our wedding—'

'This is nonsense!' Jhanghir shouted, then rubbed his forehead.

'Jhanghir, it's not nonsense. Maya likes dreaming and this is her way of getting a fairytale wedding—'

'I don't need you to defend my wedding,' I told Seema a little too sharply.

'Don't talk to Bhabhi that way,' Jhanghir warned and I baulked at his defence of her.

'She vetoed every single decision I made for our wedding because she's wanted to control—'

'Maybe if you had listened to Bhabhi, we wouldn't be in this mess.'

'I should leave before things get said and can't be taken back and tempers get out of control,' Seema stated, collecting her purse to leave.

'Bhabhi, don't go like this,' Jhanghir said, holding Seema's arm.

'No, Jhanghir, you need to sort things out with her.'

'*Her* is me and I have a name.' I told her.

'Would you show some respect!' Jhanghir's bellow silenced me.

'Jhanghir,' Zain stepped in, warning him to watch his tone. Jhanghir stared at his cousin, until he controlled his anger and then looked back to Seema. Somehow she had managed to turn my broken wedding plans into an issue about her. Somehow she was now on centre stage, attracting all attention and all concern.

'Call me when you get in; we'll sort this mess out,' Seema told Jhanghir before she smiled at me with accomplishment. 'Take care, Maya,' she said before strutting away.

'The mess being our wedding?' I asked, wondering when I had walked into a parallel universe where my perfect Jhanghir had been transformed into a mega mean, arrogant, cold Jhanghir. He picked up the papers, neatened them and handed them across to me.

'You think because my father's wealthy, you can throw good money after stupid ideas.'

'I've never wanted your father's money.'

'You think he's suddenly going to change his mind and pick up the tab you're running up fast without a second's thought.'

'No, this is our wedding—' I stopped when he stood up, threw his canvas barrel bag around him and grabbed his passport. 'Jhanghir?' He refused to meet my eyes, but I could tell by the way he gritted his jaw that he was fighting with himself. Something was seriously wrong and I needed to know what it was. 'Jhanghir?'

'I can't afford to pay for all this.' The admission was reluctant and loathed.

'What do you mean?'

'Maya, I don't have a penny to my name.' And without another word, he walked away. Frowning, I stared down at the papers he had left behind. Jerking around I watched him until he had disappeared from sight. Shaking my head, I raced after him and pulled him to a stop.

'You're just going to walk away?'

'I've got a flight to catch,' he stated as passengers filed past around us to get to the passport checkpoint.

'You can't just walk away. We got engaged last night and you tell me this now?'

'You can change your mind now that you know that I'm tapped out of money,' he chuckled as I narrowed my eyes, wondering what had got into him.

'No . . .'

'Really? I'm not the wealthy, connected Jhanghir Khan you fell in love with, Maya. If having a Mogul-inspired royal wedding or living a lavish life is important to you, I'm not the man for you.' I knew it hurt his pride to speak so honestly. I wanted to tell him that just having him alone was enough, that everything else was a bonus, but I hesitated. I couldn't believe he thought I was just interested in his money, after all the years we had known each other. Shocked by his judgement, I fought back tears and stared at him, wondering when he had got to this point. This point, where he judged me as if I was a money-hungry, deprived gold-digger, and not the fiercely independent accomplished woman with humble roots. In that moment, I knew that no matter what I said, he wouldn't believe me. He smiled, shook his head and walked away. I stood there hoping he would turn back, praying he would take back those words, believing that he wouldn't leave it like this between us. Not once did he look back. And yet I waited until he had disappeared through the passport checkpoint.

'Let's go and grab you some lunch.'

Turning, I found Zain by my side. I was lost for words, bewildered by the old cracks that were reopening. I nodded with half a smile, but before I could move. I burst into tears and stepped into his open arms.

Zain drove us through London and parked by Regent's Park. The serene park was full of Londoners and tourists making the most of the sunny weather. And yet, we walked silently through the park until we found the Garden Café and took a table.

'You OK?'

Looking at Zain, I nodded. The truth was that with red eyes, a red nose and all the fear of losing Jhanghir on the horizon, I felt exhausted.

'What's going on, Zain?' I asked, trying not to tear up. 'One day, I'm on cloud nine getting engaged to the man of my dreams, the next, he's walking out on me because I have some extravagant ideas for our wedding?'

'He's in debt, Maya.' The statement surprised me and it took me a little while to understand what he had revealed.

'What do you mean?'

'He's in debt, since Kaku froze Jhanghir's access to his trust funds, he doesn't have a penny to—'

'What are you talking about?' I breathed in disbelief, leaning forward to talk in hushed whispers. 'Jhanghir's a paediatric surgeon heading up his department . . . he's on a good salary—' I stopped when Zain shook his head and looked away. I watched him, reading the closed body language. The waiter appeared and we ordered a light salad lunch.

'What are you not telling me, Zain?'

He shook his head again.

'Jhanghir will tell you when he's ready, it's not my place—'

'Right now, the only thing Jhanghir and I are talking about is calling everything off,' I pointed out. 'Help me out here.'

'Maya, you deserve better than this.' Frowning at his reluctant comment, I stared in confusion at Zain. I shook my head at his words. 'He took everything in life for granted and now, well, now Jhanghir has to grow up . . .'

'Don't say that . . .'

'You want to know everything, Maya? Well, why don't we start with Jhanghir . . .'

'Zain—'

'Listen, I grew up with him. As the mixed-race cousin, I was the outsider, I saw the wealth and the privileges that

Jhanghir and his brother grew up with and he wanted for nothing.'

'He paid his way through uni . . .'

'Really? With a Saturday job on a student's salary?' Zain asked with a wry laugh. 'Do you know what the fees and living costs are for a foreign student, Maya? Do you think six pounds fifty an hour pays for those costs?'

'I was with him at uni, I saw him working,' I insisted, refusing to allow Zain to compromise my memories of Jhanghir.

'Were you ever with him when his father visited him with his open chequebook?'

'But Jhanghir's father never approved of him studying medicine; he refused to pay for any of Jhanghir's tuition fees . . .'

'Really? How do you explain the apartment his father bought for him in Russell Square?' I shook my head at the question. 'Or the swanky Mercedes SL class roadster?' Suddenly, flashbacks of Jhanghir arriving in his sports car, talking about frequenting another exclusive restaurant and jetting off to some ski resort started to reappear. The waiter arrived with our lunch, but I had lost my appetite. Memories that I had long forgotten now flooded back.

'It doesn't add up, does it?' The gentle question caught my attention, and slowly I looked up, met Zain's glance and shook my head.

'I . . . I thought he worked his way—' I stopped and breathed out, unnerved by the revelations. Biting my lip, I questioned how much I really knew about the man I was to marry.

'Maya . . .'

'And now?' I didn't want to hear the pity in Zain's voice; I wanted to know everything.

'Ask him . . .'

'I'm asking you,' I told Zain. 'Come on, why stop now that you've started?' I knew that I was being unfair but I was beyond polite niceties. 'Zain?'

'Under Preeya's influence, Jhanghir recently bought a one-point-five-million-dollar pad, thinking Kaku would come to accept his decision to marry you,' Zain explained. 'Only Jhanghir underestimated the depth of Kaku's disapproval; he didn't anticipate Kaku freezing his trust fund and family assets and—'

'. . . now for the first time in his life, Jhanghir has to survive knowing Daddy won't bail him out if it all goes belly-up,' I finished, now understanding why he had been silent in the past few weeks and why the cost of the wedding was such an issue. I felt guilty at my indulgent plans and over-the-top expectations. 'Why didn't he tell me?'

'He's been working every hour trying to meet his mortgage payments . . .'

'. . . or struggling about deciding whether he really wants a life without Daddy dearest and his fat wallet,' I suggested, meeting Zain's eyes. He put his fork down and leaned forward.

'Whatever the case, Jhanghir cares for you. He just needs a little time to figure that out.'

I stared at Zain, noting how dark his grey eyes were and how thickly lashed they were.

'Really, why didn't he tell me? You know, before . . . we . . . we talked about everything. He was – is – my best friend. We talked about everything, so why is he shutting me out now?' I pleaded, needing answers. Zain shook his head and placed a hand over mine. 'Zain, I don't need that wedding, I don't need a single penny from him, I just need Jhanghir to act like he wants this, that this isn't a burden, that I'm not making him sacrifice life as he knows it . . .'

'Ssshh . . . this isn't your fault,' Zain whispered as I teared up. He wiped away the tears that fell down my cheeks.

'What if he decides I'm not worth the sacrifice—' Before I could finish, I felt his warm lips against mine. I shut my eyes, blocked out everything and wanted this moment to be everything that I had wanted with Jhanghir. But it wasn't. A discreet cough behind us separated us. I stared at Zain and held my fingers to my lips, shocked by what had happened. I looked at the waiter standing beside us and then looked back at Zain with wide, scared eyes. Without another word, I grabbed my bag and rushed out of the Garden Café.

'Maya!'

'Sir, the bill!' The waiter called out, stopping Zain. In that moment, I got away, racing through the park. I didn't stop until I got to Baker Street station and fell into a seat on the tube. I rubbed my eyes and paused when my diamond ring caught my attention. Looking down at my hand, I touched the ring, recalling how breathlessly wonderful Jhanghir had made me feel yesterday. It was only yesterday, and it felt like a lifetime ago. Thoughts of our past moments, laughing, teasing, enjoying each other, ran through my mind. Then guilt arrived, tears stung my eyes and, leaning my head back on the seat, I questioned if my happy-ever-after was just a fantasy in my head.

'Here comes the bride, here comes the bride!' my cousins belted out from the kitchen as I walked in. They were all still in their pyjamas and nighties and looked as if they were in no rush to do anything but have a lazy day.

'So how is our Indian hero?' Jana asked as I wondered if she could tell that I had just cheated on Jhanghir. 'Oh my, look at how sad she looks! Don't worry, he'll be back to marry you!' she teased as the girls all laughed along.

'He's fine, thank you,' I stated, taking my shoes off in the hall before taking the stairs.

'Where are you going? We have lots to talk about!' Ayesha called out, stopping me mid-step. Closing my eyes, I struggled to find the energy to pretend that everything was OK. 'Maya!' Taking a deep breath, I turned around and walked down to the kitchen.

'Jhanghir catch his flight OK?' Amma asked as she put a pile of pancakes smothered in honey and jam in front of me. 'Eat, you're wasting away,' she instructed.

'Yeah,' I answered, tucking into the pancake. The normally delicious treat failed to extinguish the guilt I felt.

'Did you see Zain?'

'No!' My instant denial caught the attention of my family. 'Why would I want to see him?' I asked in a more measured tone.

'Because he called to make sure you got home OK.' Amma explained with a searching look that saw things that only mothers could pick up. 'Everything OK with the wedding plans?'

I avoided her eyes and smiled at my cousins who debated which tracks to use at my *henna*.

'Um-hmm,' I mumbled, taking a big, unwanted mouthful of pancake. I didn't have the strength to lie to my mother. Not after what I had done. So I kept eating to avoid the questions that followed until the conversation took off around me. For a while, I sat and listened, ignoring the rumbling fear inside me. The knowledge of what I had done plagued my every thought. And when I couldn't take any more, I excused myself so I could go for a jog. I changed quickly and declined Leila's offer of company.

Stepping outside the house I stared ahead before starting what would be a marathon session. Old rivalries, old cracks and old fears had resurfaced. I thought we had bridged the differences in our background, between his wealthy family and my humble roots, between his elitist circles and my modest, simple lifestyle. But we hadn't. We had merely convinced ourselves these issues no longer mattered; only they did, and the implications of this ran much much deeper. And yet, I had played into every one of Jhanghir's insecurities with my over-the-top wedding plans and my extravagant expectations, as if I had an unlimited budget. But how was I to know? How was I to know that he was struggling when he had stopped confiding in me, stopped turning to me with life's curve balls like he had in the past? Somehow, through all the pomp and ceremony involved with arranging an Asian wedding, we had lost sight of each other.

My confidence in Jhanghir's ability to be honest, candid and true with me was shattered; my ideal wedding was reduced to a fairytale fantasy; and worst of all, I had lost all confidence in myself. I had allowed myself to be kissed by another man when the man I loved, truly loved, had left thinking the worst of me, and I couldn't forgive myself. If Jhanghir was to think anything of it, it shouldn't be that I was a money-hungry social climber, but that I was lost with where we were going, what we meant to each other, and wondering whether there was a future for us at all. Yes, indeed, the old doubts were back. Only this time my doubts were so much bigger and deeper. There was an explosion of truth looming on the horizon. What I didn't know was whether or not we would make it through the fall-out.

Planning, practising and preparing for the perfect day

I spent the night tossing and turning at the day's events. By now, Jhanghir would have landed in New York and, like myself, be wondering where we were going with this marriage. When sleep evaded me, I slipped out from under my duvet, crept downstairs and into the garage. Wrapping my arms around me, I stared at various canvasses, smiling at those that were special. Stopping at my unfinished calligraphies, I perched on the stool and held my head in my hands.

'Maya?' Turning at Jana's quiet call, I found her at the entrance of the garage tying the belt of her pink dressing gown around her. 'Amma's worried about you.' Accepting the statement, I looked back at my work.

'You should be in bed sleeping.' Jana didn't heed my words and instead stepped further into the garage until she stood beside me.

'What happened with Jhanghir?' Turning at the question, I saw my sister raise a brow. 'When are you going to learn that we don't miss much in this family!'

Closing my eyes, I smiled and nodded.

'He's broke,' I announced.

'No, seriously, what happened?' Jana asked as she pulled up a stool.

'Seriously, he's broke,' I repeated, until the smile disappeared from Jana's face.

'He's broke?' Nodding at Jana's question, I shook my head and bit my lip. 'How broke is broke?'

'He's proper broke. He's so broke and so naïve about money that I don't think he knows what he's doing . . .'

'Wow . . . hold up a minute, can you just back up and tell me what's going on?'

'He's gone and bought us a one-point-five-million-dollar apartment not realising that Daddy dearest was going to cut off his trust fund so now he's dealing with a mortgage and bills and costs that he's never had to deal with in his life and—'

'. . . and what does that mean for your wedding?' Jana asked quietly.

'I don't know,' I told her honestly. 'He lost it about the cost of my Mogul-inspired wedding . . .'

'It was turning into a bit of a farcical-themed wedding.' Jana stopped at my glare. 'It's too contrived to pull off in a country home in Berkshire,' she explained, reaching out to hold my hand.

'Why didn't you tell me?' I asked as she smiled softly.

'Would you have listened?' I shook my head, Jana laughed along with me. 'So what are you going to do?' For a while, we sat in silence. It was a comfortable silence, one where there was no need for small talk. Jana patted my hand until I looked at her.

'You need to get a job.' She spoke my thoughts. 'If Jhanghir doesn't know how to manage his income and outgoings, you have to guide him. You have to show him you can cut back and manage the finances for him.'

'I'm getting married in two months, Jana, who's going to give me a job?'

'You can temp; there's good money in temping—'
Jana stopped at the expression on my face. 'Oh,
temping's not good enough for you?'

'That's not what I'm saying . . .'

'Then why aren't you supporting Jhanghir?' she asked
in annoyance.

'. . . I just expected him to be more independent . . .'
I stopped as I heard my own words, realising how
disloyal I sounded. 'I never expected to live off his
father's money, but I expected Jhanghir to be able to deal
with financial reality . . .'

'Well, isn't this the perfect way to show them that you
have no need for their wealth?'

'But I have a need for a man who has some basic
financial common sense.'

'So you're going to bail on him because he had a
privileged upbringing?'

'No . . .'

'How different are you from his family?' My outraged
look didn't stop Jana from continuing. 'They won't
welcome you into their life because you come from a
working-class family, you don't know the social graces of
their jet-setting elitist lifestyle, how would you feel if
Jhanghir abandoned you because of that?'

'He may do just that if he realises Daddy's money
makes life very comfortable.'

'Unless you show him how to manage his finances so
that he doesn't need to depend on Daddy.' The wisdom
of Jana's words began to sink in. I looked at my paintings
with a deep longing. It was time to get plugged back into
the real world again, away from pipe dreams of Mogul-
inspired weddings and showing my work off in art
galleries. Suddenly, I realised how blinkered I had been.

'Maya, you're talented and your paintings will always
be with you because it's in your blood. But right now you

need to focus on saving your future with Jhanghir.' Nodding at her words, I smiled and looked at my sister.

'Will you help me rearrange my wedding?'

She smiled in a way that lit up her entire face.

'I thought you'd never ask, Maya.' I patted her hand, realising how important it was for my sisters to feel involved in my wedding. 'I'm glad you did, lil sis.' I smiled at her quiet words, and looked back at my unfinished work. The guilt hadn't disappeared, but for now I had some direction. For now, that was enough for me to put my wedding and marriage back on track.

The following morning, I made appointments to visit three recruitment agencies, had breakfast, and then looked inside my cupboard. It had been some time since I had put a suit on, so I pulled out my black fitted one and put it on over a crisp white shirt. The girl staring back at me in the mirror told me that I had some way to go to get back to my slim, blubber-free self. So I opted for some cream slacks, a crisp white long-line shirt with capped sleeves and finished with a large brown leather watch. With my hair pulled back into a low neat bun, complete with bare illuminescent make-up, I headed out with my Mulberry leather Piccadilly bag. It was time to step up to the challenge of being Ms In Control again. So en route, I revised my CV, memorised my selling points and prepared myself for questions. Once I got to Holborn, I entered the first agency and waited for the agent to call me in for a meeting. When a spotty post-pubescent boy in an oversized unironed shirt and creased suit came to stand before me, I waved him away and declined any refreshments.

'Maya Malik, I'm Mark Jones. We spoke this morning.' I forced a smile and stood up to shake the agent's hand. 'Follow me.' The curt instruction told me he wasn't impressed with my dismissal, so I followed him quietly and stepped into the small glass-fronted meeting room.

'Thanks for coming in. As you know, I manage the placements of analysts. Why don't you fill in this experience form while I go and make a photocopy of your passport?' I froze at his request.

'I didn't bring my passport . . .'

'It's a standard procedure required for any placements,' the annoyed young man pointed out, reflecting how out-of-the-loop I was with the job market.

'I'm happy to email you a copy,' I offered, trying to build a bridge.

'It'll have to do.' The boy's unconvinced reply grated on my nerves, so I looked down at the form and proceeded to fill in my details.

'So, why don't you start by talking me through your CV?' Mark said, taking a seat facing me. So I began, explaining my responsibilities at Chambers Scott Wilfred, fielding questions about whom I worked with and the client management responsibilities I overlooked.

'Why did you leave?'

I stopped mid-sentence and stared at Mark. 'Pardon?'

'You left Chambers Scott Wilfred eighteen months ago, why?' I paused and wondered how I could tell him that I got sick of working without increasing my chances of a promotion.

'I wanted a career break; it was the right time for me to try something different.'

'Career break?' His grimace told me that this was a big no no. 'What did you do?'

'I painted. I won a bursary to Browns University in New York.'

'So you're not interested in working long-term?' The post-pubescent recruitment agent was sharp.

'Actually, I'm moving to New York, I'm getting married and settling over there, and uh, that's why I'm interested in a temporary position,' I explained as he whistled, looked down at my CV and shook his head.

'You're shaking your head?' I asked, meeting his eyes when he looked up.

'To be honest, it's difficult to place people who can't guarantee some degree of certainty . . .'

'That's the nature of temping positions; they're for people like me who can commit to short-term positions.'

Mark smiled at me patronisingly and I wanted to slap this childlike man.

'Hmmm . . .' Mark mumbled, staring back down at my CV. His disapproving silence infuriated me.

'I've got strong analytical skills in the consumer facing and retail sector, but I'm confident that I can apply them to across industry—'

'I just don't think we have anything on our books for someone like you.'

'But on your website you say that you have several temporary positions for analysts—'

'Well, I'll be happy to forward those to you, but I'm sure that they want someone more . . . well, let's say, more on the ball,' he told me and then followed it with a smile. I couldn't believe that this cretin with the life experience and, more importantly, work experience, of a gnat on Ecstasy, was passing judgement on my professional experience.

'On the ball?' I asked, and watched him nod. 'I got a first from UCL, I've worked with blue chip consultancy developing financial models for the retail sector, before being promoted to the position of a strategic consultant. Don't tell me I am not on the ball. And if you have problems finding me a temp job with blue chip creden-tials, then your agency and you in particular shouldn't be in the recruitment business,' I told him pointedly. I knew I had said too much when he sat back, folded his arms and smiled.

Suffice it to say the meeting ended abruptly. And, much to my annoyance, the following two meetings were only marginally better. I sat through the patronising questions from aspirant bimbos defending my decision to pursue a career as a painter and fielding questions that were designed to make you feel like your work experience up to that point was as useful as a chocolate teapot. With insincere promises of being forwarded potential opportunities, I stepped out on to Charing Cross Road feeling worthless, useless and without a hope.

Five minutes later, I was in the National Portrait Gallery. Spotting an exhibition on Bollywood, I paid the entrance fee and walked around the quiet, white, airy section. It was mid-week and light on tourists so I browsed as slowly as possible. Faces from the yesteryear graced the first foyer, including everyone from the charming Dilip Kumar, the charismatic Raj Kapoor, the serene Meena Kumai to the effervescent Madhubala. Smiling, I made mental notes of the glamour, vibrant colours, and subtle changes in style. Slower than a sleepy snail, I moved through my childhood era of Amitabh Bachan, Rekha and Hema Malini. There were iconic movie images, vibrant posters and behind-the-scenes shots. I moved to the current era where smouldering images of Shah Rukh Khan and breathtakingly beautiful shots of Ashwariya Rai dominated. Stopping at the OmShantiOm poster, I realised how I would rearrange my wedding. A slow smile crept across my face. A Bollywood wedding was on the cards and I was ready to go home to start planning.

*

'I've got it,' I announced, as I searched out Jana and found her in the living room giving Amma a head massage. 'I've got it . . .'

'You got a job already?'

Shaking my head at Jana's question, I sat down in front of Amma and stared at them both

'I'm going to have a Bollywood-inspired wedding.'

'Hai Allah, why can't this child have a normal wedding?' Amma called out, hitting her forehead with the palm of her hand.

'It is a normal wedding,' I told Amma, not ready to be put off. 'Just with a little bit of glamour.'

Jana watched me and I couldn't help but smile. 'First of all, tell me how the agency interviews went.' My smile dropped and I shook my head.

'No one's touching me. I've been out of the market for eighteen months, the whole economy's gone to pot, and for every job going, there're twenty qualified candidates gunning for it . . .'

'Why are you looking for work?' Amma demanded before turning to Jana. 'Why is she looking for work? No more independent woman, no more Miss Independent, now it's time for you to settle down and have four or six children, OK?'

'Amma—'

'No, I don't want to listen to any more excuses. I wasted too many years letting you gallivant around the world for your job.'

'Amma—'

'Jana, warn your sister that if she finds another reason to put off settling down—'

'They need the money,' Jana said, stopping Amma mid-sentence. She looked to me for confirmation and then she pushed Jana's hands away to lean forward.

'Whatever your father has, he'll give you what you

need, if it means you will get married.' I looked to Jana, deadpan, knowing Amma's desire to see me settle down ran deep.

'We can manage . . .'

'We can release some of the equity on this house, we're going to sell it when we move, so we may as well get that out early for you . . .'

'I don't need the equity released . . .'

'How are you going to help Jhanghir pay for the wedding?' Jana asked and I smiled and brought out the notes I had been working on, on my way back home.

'I've cut the costs from six-five thousand pounds to thirty thousand pounds.

'Sixty-five thousand pounds? What world is your sister living on!' Amma demanded, falling back against Jana. 'For one day? Does she think Jhanghir's father will pay for all this?'

'I've got twelve thousand pounds of my redundancy money left over, and I've another seven thousand pounds in savings. So as long as Jhanghir can find ten to eleven thousand pounds . . .'

'We can all pool together and give that to you as your wedding present . . .'

'No, Jana . . .'

'Then your *baba* will give you the money . . .'

'Amma!' I chastised. 'That's your pension, and I'm not taking a penny from it.'

'So you're going to have a budget wedding? What will everyone say?'

'Quite the contrary!' I smiled handing out my images. 'I'm going to have a Bollywood-inspired wedding.'

'What are you talking about?' Jana asked, laughing at the pictures I handed her.

'I'm going to have a red-carpet cordoned-off entrance leading into the foyer of Iver House where I'm going to have the photographers waiting to take red-carpet pictures. All the tables are going to be given Bollywood star names so we can have a seating plan . . .'

'No seating plan, people get offended when they're put in the back.'

'Not when they're put on Mudubhala's table or Raj Kapoor's table!' I laughed, seeing Amma's eyes brighten at the mention of the heartthrob of her hey day. 'I'm going to get the decorator to set the stage with a lectern as if awards are going to be given . . .'

'Tell me we're not going to have to dress up in different Bollywood styles . . .'

'That's what I'm having for my *henna*; we're going to dress up in different Bollywood styles.'

'I want to go as Madhubhala like in *Mughal E Azaam*,' Amma announced, making us both stop to stare at her. 'Or maybe as Meena Kumari from *Pakeeza*. I wonder who your *chachijhi* will go as.' We continued watching Amma who stood up to leave the room saying, 'Let me check if I have anything suitable to wear, otherwise your *baba* owes me an outfit.'

We laughed as she left and then turned to each other. Jana's smile faded to concern. 'You haven't spoken to Jhanghir yet, have you?' I shook my head at Jana's question, uncertain whether he would appreciate what I was doing in comparison to what had passed between Zain and I. Yet, I was determined to do something, anything, to help us work through this hurdle, because that's what it was. Jhanghir and I were strong enough to get back to where we were. Or so I told myself. 'He'll appreciate what you're doing . . .'

'Hardly, getting Cousin Yasmin to bake my cake—'

'That's a thousand pounds saved, she did my wedding cake and she does amazing cakes.'

I nodded at Jana's encouragement. 'I've decided that

Taj can be the MC at the wedding; his mate can look after the music and those doing speeches will be called up as if they're about to receive an award,' I explained, noticing that Jana was staring at me quietly. 'And I'm going to hire a marquee for our garden for my *henna*.'

'Are you sure you don't want your royal Mogul wedding?' she asked.

'And bore people to death with *qawaali* and sitar playing in the background?' Jana giggled at my words. 'This is definitely going to be more fun!'

'Wait till Leila hears about your idea; she's going to be so jealous!' In that instant, Leila walked in flanked by the rest of my cousins.

'What's to be jealous of?' she asked, tossing back her poker-straight two-tone highlighted long hair. Jana and I looked at each other and burst out laughing.

Question perfection

Sometimes the only way to feel like everything was going to be OK was to tell yourself time and again that everything is and will be OK. I was forever too busy to see Zain because keeping space between us was a good thing. I informed Seema over email about all the changed plans and even managed to find a good make-up artist at late notice. I jogged every day, sometimes twice a day; I ate five small carb-free meals a day, and religiously ticked off wedding tasks on the master poster that took up most of the kitchen wall. That poster steered everyone in one direction without any room for going off on tangents. And with mind over matter, plans for the wedding were progressing seamlessly. Yet nothing stopped me jumping at the mention of Jhanghir. And nothing was missed by my best friends who sat and stared at me, smiling over a regular coffee catch-up.

'What's wrong?' Tanya asked as she helped herself to my portion of the devil's cake. 'You're not a Stepford wife yet, so please stop smiling; it's freaking me out.'

'I'm happy, I'm allowed to smile,' I said, looking to Sakina and feeling the guilt resurface. 'How are things?' Both Sakina and Tanya stopped at my awkward question.

'How are things?' Tanya repeated with disgust. 'Now I know there's something wrong.'

'Nothing's wrong,' I told them, sipping the hot water that now substituted my caffeine addiction. 'I went for a facial today and I'm on top of everything, so all is good.' I refused to be unnerved by their silence and piercing stares.

'Come on, tell me; have you met up with Javed?' Tanya smiled at my question and slowly nodded her head. 'The old art of deflection . . .'

'No! I want to know that he's come to his senses!' I explained, regretting it when I spotted the hurt in her eyes.

'We're talking,' Tanya confided. 'My family are furious that I'm talking to him, but I've got to try.'

'And?' I pursued, spotting a small smile play at her lips.

'We're talking.' When I glared at her she held her hands up. 'If we work things out, there's going to be no big splash. It'll be a small intimate do at the mosque . . .' Tanya finally laughed as we whooped with delight and fell on top of her to hug her. 'Hey, get off me! I'm a good Muslim girl, I don't want anyone to think I'm into public orgies!!!'

Laughing at Tanya's provocative line of thought, we sat beside her and stared at her with genuine happiness.

'That's good, Tanya,' I told her as she smiled and nodded.

'So we're working on your *henna* routine,' Sakina said, refusing to allow the conversation to move on to her status. 'Everything's under control, but be prepared . . .'

'Did Zain get in touch?' I asked, silencing the voice within me when she took a deep breath.

'He called a couple of times, we talked about your wedding mostly, but nothing more.' She tried to cover her disappointment with a shrug and a smile.

'Did . . . did he say anything?' The hesitation in my voice caught their attention.

'What do you mean?' Sakina asked as Tanya sipped her coffee.

'Just curious, that's all . . .'

'You mean did he ask me out?' Before I could shake my head, Sakina held her hand up, not interested in my answer. 'He didn't.'

'Sakina—' I stopped when she picked up her bag and stood up.

'I'm sorry, girls, I can't do this today. I'm overjoyed for you both, I really am, but it's . . . I'm sick of being the spinster everyone pities.' And with that we watched her stride out of the coffee house.

Turning to Tanya, I stared at her, stunned.

'She's really feeling lonely at the moment,' Tanya explained. 'I think she really wanted something to happen with Zain and when nothing came of that, she took it to heart.'

I didn't think I could feel any worse for my indiscretion, but I did. Closing my eyes, I shook my head and tried to find the serenity I had fought for in the past week.

'Are you going to tell me what happened?' Snapping open my eyes, I found Tanya watching me. I was too ashamed to speak but it was ruining my peace of mind. 'Maya, he's George Clooney's bloody twin; you'd have to be a lesbian not to be attracted to him.'

'But he's not George—'

'Interesting that you didn't deny that you're attracted to him.'

'I'm not attracted to him,' I stated without any hesitation. Only I couldn't hold Tanya's sardonic stare. 'We kissed!' I confessed and then covered my mouth with both hands. Tanya stared at me and, for the first time, we both realised, she was lost for words. So she shook her head. I nodded. She shook her head again. And with a sad frown, I nodded.

'But sweetie, he's not the icon you've lusted after to almost stalking levels,' Tanya pointed out as if I had missed that small but all-too-important fact.

'I know,' I whispered.

'We agreed, you could only cheat on Jhanghir if the real George Clooney propositioned you like Robert Redford did Demi Moore in *Indecent Proposal*.'

'But it wasn't the real George Clooney,' I added as tears stung my eyes.

'So why?' Tanya asked, handing me a tissue.

'Jhanghir and I haven't spoken in ages . . .'

'But your engagement was so beautiful, you both looked so happy . . .' The reminder made me burst into tears and I shook my head, consumed by the guilt.

'The wedding's driving us apart; he just disappears and I keep telling myself "be patient". And then, after the engagement, we fell out big time, and I haven't heard anything from him since last week, and Zain was there, he was just there and . . . and . . .'

'. . . you guys kissed,' Tanya finished. I put the tissue down and looked at my dearest friend.

'Yes, and I've felt like a slut ever since,' I told her, taking another tissue from her. 'I'm terrible, I'm just awful and I don't know what possessed me.'

'And Zain?'

'What about him?'

'Well, you know . . .'

'I haven't seen him since . . . it happened . . .' I trailed off, remembering the moment with so much regret that I felt ashamed of myself. 'It just happened out of the blue. One minute we were talking and then I cheated on Jhanghir.'

'Maya . . .'

'Don't say it, I've been praying for forgiveness at every opportunity, I've given money to charity and I'm doing everything to help anyone with anything . . .'

'Jhanghir needs to know.'

'No . . .'

'He deserves the truth.'

'No.'

'It's the right thing to do,' Tanya advised, but I shook my head.

'I'll never see him again, Tanya.'

'But that's his choice, Maya. You can't deceive him, that's no way of starting a marriage.'

'But I'm not lying to him.'

'You're deceiving him. You can put it right, Maya. Javed did.'

Tanya's advice played on my mind all the way home. I let myself in to find Amma and Chachijhi practising Meena Kumari's Indi Logon Ni dance routine from *Waukesha* in the hallway. Both stopped at my appearance, breathless and holding the banister for support. Amma held up her hand to stop me from saying anything. Instead she waved me past before instructing a bored Taj to replay the track from the beginning. He shook his head in distress and, with a small smile, I walked into the living room where my cousins froze at my appearance.

'You can't see our surprise!' Mana shouted, forcing me out of the room. I took the cordless house phone with me. Finding Baba in deep conversation with Meena in the kitchen, and *Bhabhi* changing Hamza in the lounge room, I headed for my room. Dropping my bag on the floor, I fell on to my bed and stared at the phone. It would be the early hours of the morning in New York, and it would be the one time Jhanghir couldn't avoid me.

So with a deep breath, I called him. With no idea what I would say to him, I nervously bit my lip as the dialling tone rang over and over again.

'Hello?' The one thing I didn't expect to hear was the voice of a young woman.

'Hi, is this Jhanghir Khan's residence?'

'Who is this?' I wanted to tell her it was his fiancée but, more importantly, I wanted to know who she was and what she was doing answering Jhanghir's mobile.

'Maya, I'm Maya Malik. Do you know where Jhanghir is?'

'He's sleeping right here. Do you have any idea what time it is right now?'

'Sure,' I mumbled, reeling from the woman's words. 'I'm sorry, I'll call back.' Ending the call, I lay on my bed so confused that I stopped trying to figure out what was going on. I stared up at the ceiling with images of Preeya or some other equally lithe, stunning woman, sleeping next to Jhanghir racing through my mind. Shaking my head, I turned on my side, determined to give him the benefit of the doubt. Biting my bottom lip, I tapped my fingers on the pillow, trying to stop myself from calling him again. I wouldn't do it, I wouldn't lower myself to demanding answers or needing explanations. Jhanghir wasn't like that and I wasn't going to do it.

'I'd like to speak to Jhanghir,' I stated, the phone in my hand once more and my determination as steadfast as an ice cube in the Sahara desert.

'He's sleeping . . .'

'Wake him up,' I told her, refusing to be put off.

'But he's sleeping—'

'And I'm his fiancée and I want you to wake—'

'I'm up.' Freezing at Jhanghir's deep, sleep-heavy voice, I lost my will. 'Maya?'

'Who is she?' I asked, holding my breath at the

silence that followed my question.

'You serious?' Jhanghir finally spoke. Frowning, I wondered why I had given in to my doubts and knew I looked like a green-eyed psychotic girlfriend.

'Why is some girl answering your phone in the middle of the night?' I continued, unable to backtrack.

'That girl happens to my cousin.' The dry, unamused answer left me none the wiser. I wanted to ask if she was a 'cousin cousin', as in the never-would-go-there-type of cousin, or the *'cousin cousin'*, aka the hot stunner whom every aunty in the family wanted for their son. But I daren't ask him that. 'Anything else, Maya?'

'Ummm, well . . .' There were a million things to talk about, stuff that didn't matter to anyone, which would help to bridge the gap that was ever increasing between us. Yet I couldn't think of a single thing to mention. 'No, there's nothing else, Jhanghir.' He held on for some time, also lost for words, and tears stung my eyes at how far we had come from what we once were. Unable to handle the silence any more, I cleared my throat. 'I'll let you get back to sleep.' Ending the call, I frowned as I stared out of the window. There was no girl to blame; no distraction or infidelity masked the fact that there was something amiss between us. It didn't matter that I didn't know this cousin, or had the answer as to why she was beside my sleeping fiancé. No, there was no denying that the only thing that would stop me from sleeping tonight would be the widening gap between Jhanghir and myself, and the fact that it was unlikely that we would ever be able to bridge it.

The following morning, I arranged to meet Zain at Costas in Kensington. In spite of myself, I made an effort. With my hair in a loose knot, I dressed in an aqua-blue maxi dress with faint but bold Paisley patterns, gladiator sandals and a short-sleeved, cropped cardigan. Spotting him by the window, I ignored the butterflies in my stomach, and went to sit facing him.

'You're looking great,' Zain said, offering to get me a cup of coffee. The compliment made me smile as any woman needing attention smiled. Shaking my head, I looked at the handsome man. 'What made you come out of hiding?' he asked.

'I haven't heard anything from Jhanghir, it's been ten days, and I guess I'm wondering whether he wants to even get married . . .'

'You haven't heard from him?' Zain's surprise made me laugh.

'You sound surprised!' I said, and my laugh turned into a sad smile. 'How have you been?' There, I asked that question, the one that made friends of strangers.

'Busy. I've been setting up my office in Dubai, we're getting more and more contracts out there and—'

'My family are doing that,' I told him. 'They're all doctors and dentists and they're investing in a practice out there . . . actually, it looks like everyone's moving out there.'

'Maya, we need to talk about what happened . . .'

'No, we don't.'

'Yes, we do.'

'It happened, it was a mistake and we should put it behind us.'

'A mistake?'

I stopped at Zain's question and realised the insensitivity of my words. 'I'm sorry.'

He accepted my apology with half a grin and we stared at each other, both knowing that the attraction was still there. 'I owe you an apology, it was wrong and I take full responsibility for it . . .'

'It stays between us, Maya.' Zain's words stopped me.

'He's my cousin, I'm not proud of us . . .'

'There is no us, Zain . . .'

'Really?' I refused to meet his eyes or entertain his line of query. 'And you're happy?' I nodded even though the answer was far from the truth. 'You're a bad liar.'

'I love Jhanghir.' This simple statement failed to convince either of us.

'Do you?'

'He's all I know, all I ever wanted,' I whispered, wondering why it seemed to be getting harder to recall my good memories of Jhanghir.

'Until now.' Meeting his grey eyes, I saw that there wasn't the faintest sign of humour about him. Picking up my bag, I slipped on my shades and stood up. 'You running away, Maya?' Dropping back into my seat, I leaned forward.

'I love Jhanghir. We're going through a stressful time, now you can choose to help us or hinder us.'

'You kissed me.'

'You flirted with me.'

'You flirted back.' Stopping at the statement, I looked at him straight and saw the twinkle in his eyes. Finally, I smiled and he chuckled and we both laughed.

'You should go before you ruin our moment,' Zain advised as I shook my head.

'This isn't a moment . . .'

'There you go, you're ruining it.'

I bit my lip, refusing to humour him. 'I'm going shopping.' He raised his brows as if to query my decision. 'I'm not running. I have nothing to run from, right?'

Zain contemplated the weight of my question and slowly he nodded. 'Go.' I did as he asked. I knew he watched my every step out of the coffee shop and when I got on to the high street, I stopped and took a deep breath. I hadn't felt wanted in a long while, and Zain, well, Zain made me smile from within.

Little did I realise that I was indeed shopping bound. Shopping in Dubai and Dhaka. As soon as I headed home, Jana and Hanna pounced on me, hyper happy. 'We've got it. They've found a site for our medical practice,' Jana said. 'We're going out to join our men in Dubai and then we're going on to Dhaka in Bangladesh to buy all our clothes for the wedding.'

'And you're coming with us,' Hanna announced as we found Baba putting down the receiver and taking his glasses off in the kitchen.

'So, that's five tickets confirmed,' he stated. Amma handed him a cup of tea and my twin sisters whooped excitedly. 'That's two nights in Dubai and three nights in Dhaka.' Excitedly I looked to Jana and Hanna who hesitated.

'Are Ayesha and Amma joining us?'

'Your mother is needed here to coordinate the wedding invitations to all six hundred guests, so I've my asked my sister—'

'Don't say it.'

'. . . my sister, your *chachijhi*, to accompany you in our absence,' Baba finished. In stunned silence I turned to my twin sisters.

'We don't need a babysitter,' I stated, sitting opposite my father.

'Your sisters will be working with their husbands to sort the site out for their practice . . .'

'No, please don't leave me alone with Chachijhi.'

'You should be happy she's offered to go with you!' Baba pointed out. I turned to my sisters and they smiled naughtily. 'She's had such a terrible time with Meena marrying that boy . . .'

'This isn't funny, she's . . . she's . . .'

'She's what?' Baba asked. I struggled to find the words without offending him. 'Maya Malik, you'd be best to remember that she's your aunty who wants the best for you.'

'But I don't need a guardian, I've travelled across the US and Europe alone . . .'

'But you weren't about to get married,' Amma pointed out, making me look at her in confusion. 'We have to give you to Jhanghir safe and sound, we can't risk anything happening to you.'

'What could possibly happen to me? I'll go shopping in Dubai when I'm alone.'

'We've heard strange things happen in Dubai, we can't risk it,' Amma continued.

'What things?'

'Why are you questioning our decision?' Baba asked as the twins mocked me silently from the far end of the kitchen. 'Your *chachijhi* is accompanying you and that is the end of the matter.' Turning around in frustration, I headed up to my room and grabbed my laptop.

To: JKhan@NYMedics.com
From: MayaM@Instantmail.com

Hey, Baba's decided that my sisters and I are better off shopping in Dubai and Dhaka for the wedding. We're heading out this weekend for a week, and while I've got a million and one things to do here, this is a good way to make each pound go further. I can go to town with wedding cards, traditional outfits, gifts for loved ones, and the best thing . . . accessories! I can get bangles of every colour and description for next to nothing. So tell me what you need and I'll add that on to the list. Oh, you

know they say every good thing has a price? Baba's sent
Chachijhi to be my *mahram*.

I didn't hear back from Jhanghir before I left for Dubai.
I didn't hear from Tanya or Sakina either. Zain had
disappeared and it appeared that Seema was the only
one happy to keep communicating. My job search was
going nowhere, and the worries about managing the
costs of the wedding remained an ever-present cloud
hanging over me. Yes, this trip would help make savings,
but I still had no source of income and I had stopped
painting. And there was so much to be done; there was
the dress fitting, the food tasting to determine our
wedding menu, the invitations and seating plans. Most of
all, I was exhausted by the increasing silences between
Jhanghir and myself. So, nothing made more sense then
getting some much needed time away. Time to clear my
head, time to refocus on what was important, time to
stop worrying. So as my sisters and I queued up three
hours early for the Virgin Atlantic flight out to Dubai, I
threw all my cares aside and joked about all the shopping
that waited for us.

And then we heard Chachijhi's shrill call. 'There you
are!' Turning round we stopped and stared deadpan as
Chachijhi arrived in her signature bright flowery *sari*,
flip-flops and trademark patterned heavy cardigan
topped off with a huge straw hat and small round
sunshades.

'Lord, helps us,' I muttered, watching Ayesha walk
over to Chachijhi to help with her heavy suitcase.

'That Meena, she drops me off outside, doesn't even
give her mother a hand—'

'You're here now.' Ayesha smiled, coming to stand
amongst us. Chachijhi peered over her shades to look at
each of us.

'Now listen, girls, your father, my brother, sent me to keep an eye on you, especially Maya, so no hanky panky naughtiness, OK?' We looked at each other confused by her use of language. 'I'm your guardian and I have your *baba* on speed dial and I'm not afraid to call him,' she told us, holding up her mobile phone to demonstrate how serious she was.

'There's going to be no hanky panky and no naughtiness,' Ayesha promised, glaring at us all to give similar reassurances. And we did, only the mumbles from the twins promised otherwise and it was entirely missed on Chachijhi.

'Good, good!' She laughed. 'Maybe you girls can help your *chachijhi* with my dance routine for Maya's *henna*, huh?'

I listened to my family talk excitedly about my upcoming nuptials and I stared down at my phone. Everyone was so caught up with making my wedding perfect that they did not stop to question perfection. Deep down I knew there were big cracks appearing between us, how deep we would allow them to get . . . well, that remained to be seen.

Rumours ruin reputations and ristas

Reputation is everything in our community. It's what honours the family name, underpins the family structure and acts as your calling card. Rumours have no place in good Bengali homes, and if a family's reputation is strong enough, rumours are dismissed without question. But then there are the likes of Chachijhi who, despite having a rebel daughter who had eloped with a Jamaican Muslim, was happy to dig for dirt on me. Every moment throughout my flight was carefully watched. She questioned the texts I exchanged with Zain pre-boarding, assuming I was communicating with Jhanghir, she watched every women's magazine I flicked through to see what *types* of articles I read, and then she followed me around duty free to see what I would buy. By the time we landed, I was ready to snap.

'This is for you!' she announced just when my patience was about to run out. Looking at the massive straw hat she had worn throughout the flight, I shook my head. 'Come wear it; your mother told me to stop you going in the sun and to protect your fair complexion. You know our men prize creamy fair skin . . .'

'Really, Chachijhi, I couldn't . . .' Before I could

finish, she jammed the hat on my head and then instructed me to carry her bags. The twins curbed a giggle as I followed irritably behind everyone pushing an overloaded trolley. Ayesha's husband, Samir *bhai* and the twins' husbands waited for us outside Dubai International Airport and we rushed through the sweltering Dubai heat to jump into their huge black Land Cruiser. I watched as my sisters spoke to their husbands beside the car. There was no physical contact, but there was no mistaking the warmth and care that was so obvious in their expressions. Ayesha spoke quietly with Samir *bhai*, whilst Hanna's husband asked questions nineteen to the dozen. And then there was Jana, who sparred verbally with her husband until they laughed together. I felt so alone and distant from Jhanghir that it hurt.

'Hello!' Everyone jumped at Chachijhi's loud call. 'Your *chachijhi* needs refreshments, can you hold back your hanky panky greetings before the Dubai police lock you all away for indecent behaviour!' The comment was unnecessary, but dramatic enough to have everyone in the Land Cruiser in moments.

My mood didn't improve when Samir *bhai* told me that I'd be sharing a room and, more to the point, a double bed, with Chachijhi. In short, true bud style, we were all sharing the suites and I had royally pulled the short straw. After a quick shower, with breakfast consumed, we all jumped back into the cruiser and headed through Dubai's towering skyscrapers to see the proposed site for the family practice.

'Ahh so much fun!' Chachijhi breathed out, before taking a swig of water from her one-and-a-half-litre water bottle. 'Take some pictures of the tall glass buildings, I can show your uncle what he's been denying me the last forty years of marriage.'

'We can take better pictures later, Chachijhi, when we'll show you around properly,' Samir *bhai* said, navigating along Jumeirah. 'Maya, how are the wedding plans coming along?' Turning at the question, I felt my mind go blank and frowned.

'Fine, thank you.' The short answer made everyone frown, but for once I didn't want to talk about the wedding. I looked back out of the window, ignoring the concerned looks of my sisters and the prying stare from Chachijhi.

'Fine?' Samir *bhai* laughed. 'Just fine? I thought you'd be a bridezilla needing status updates every few minutes!' Everyone, including myself, chuckled at the image. At one time, I thought I'd be doing the same, but my enthusiasm and energy for my wedding was at an all-time low, it was the last thing I wanted to talk about.

'And Jhanghir, how's he doing? Is he making the most of his bachelor days?'

That was why I wanted to avoid the topic, because, without a shadow of a doubt, it always came back to Jhanghir and, more to the point, my lack of contact with Jhanghir. Not long ago, the thought of a mystery cousin staying beside my fiancé would have brought the most vicious of green-eyed monster out. Now, well, with my indiscretion with Zain, the huge vacuum called my relationship with Jhanghir, and a wedding that seemed more and more unlikely as each day passed, well, what could I say.

'Maya?' Turning to Ayesha, I raised a brow. 'Your brother-in-law asked you a question.'

'I'm sorry, I feel spaced out from the flight,' I lied, avoiding Jana's concerned look. 'I think he's making the most of his single days.' They laughed at my comment and I looked back out of the window, admiring the beautiful sail of the Burj Al Arab. Everything seemed so new in Dubai, so without history.

'I hear you boys are stealing my sisters away from England,' I said, and they hooted in denial.

'More like your sisters are pushing us out here. Talk about power-driven women, they secured the funding, the contacts and the paperwork!' Samir *bhai* said as my sisters debated whose idea it had been first. I smiled, watching the interaction, realising that I was going to be that much more removed from my family. Tears stung my eyes, as they laughed and joked and made plans for the future. None of which I had any part in.

'Maya, you'll love this location, I think you'll want to be the interior decorator for it.'

'I could be, I need a job!' I laughed as my sisters noticed my tear-filled eyes. 'I'll postpone the wedding for it.' And, before I knew it, I'd burst into tears.

'Maya! Oh my God, what's wrong?'

'Pull up, stop the car.'

'Wait, wait, I've got to find a parking spot.'

'Stop the car . . .'

'What have you said?'

'I haven't said anything!'

As my family argued around me, I desperately tried to stop crying. It wasn't the discreet, becoming way of crying. No, not me. It was the snot-dripping, hiccupping, unattractive sobs that had come to rule my emotions right now. When Samir *bhai* parked, I looked up to find seven pairs of eyes watching me.

'It's too much, the wedding preparation, this heat, all this running around and look at how much weight she's lost, she's probably dehydrated . . .'

'Sssh!' Chachijhi frowned at Hanna's tone before holding her bottle of water to me. I took a long gulp and coughed as it went down the wrong tube. Spluttering and clearing my nose, they thumped my back until I cleared my throat and wiped away the last of my tears.

'What's wrong, Maya?' Ayesha asked with a soft smile.

I didn't know where to start, so I shook my head and stopped the tears from brimming over again.

'I'm so sorry,' I whispered, before biting my lip. 'You'll all be so far away . . .' I stopped, feeling close to tears again at which point Jana and Hanna teared up. '. . . and I'm going in the opposite direction.'

'Guess what, Maya?' I looked at Samir *bhai*, who handed me a pack of tissues. 'We'll have a spare office for Jhanghir to practise out of.'

'You will?' All my brothers-in-law and sisters nodded together. I wiped at the tears that fell down my cheeks. 'Well, that's OK, then,' I said, laughing tearfully. They laughed with me and we were back on track.

'*Pagul!*' Chachijhi muttered, wiping her tears in the back of the cruiser. 'Anyone would think she's still a child!' Nobody minded her comments because she followed them by a comforting pat on my shoulder.

The building for the medical practice was everything Samir *bhai* had promised it would be. Caught between Emirates Hill and Knowledge City, the location was perfect to build a private and commercial practice in. The two-storey building was spacious, modern and flooded with natural sunlight. We walked around, debating the practice layout, who got what section, how big or small it should be, and decoration style. Samir *bhai* and Ayesha left the twins and their husbands to sort out the paperwork with the estate agent, to take Chachijhi and I out to Gold City. Grabbing some fast food takeout en route to Deira, we continued talking about the practice site as Chachijhi made the most of her

Burger King Royal triple burger whopper.

The traffic around Deira was insane; by the time Samir *bhai* found a parking spot and the sun was at its highest, we raced to get into the sprawling jewellery stores. These stores were unlike anything in England and attracted tourists from around the world. The gold on display simply made you gasp. A whole corner of Dubai was dedicated to Gold City and you knew that leaving Dubai without a strand of gold would be as worthwhile as visiting the UK without trying fish and chips. Wide eyed, I browsed the countless display units of earrings, bangles, bracelets, rings and necklaces. I stopped at the breathtaking range of wedding sets that outshone anything available in the England.

'Choose a set,' Ayesha said, coming to stand beside me.

'Are you crazy? Jhanghir's already bought my wedding gold!' I reminded my sister.

'You need more than one set!' she told me with a slow smile. 'After you get married, you'll have so many invitations and you can't afford to turn up wearing the same set on every occasion . . .'

'Then I'll mix and match it up with stuff I have.'

'Maya, your *bhai* and I want to give you a set for your wedding gift,' Ayesha insisted as she beckoned an assistant over. 'We'd be honoured if you wore it at your *henna*, but you don't have to.' Tearing up, she smiled at me and pointed at the display. I nodded and smiled as Samir *bhai* joined us and started barking orders about which set to bring out. We spent the rest of the afternoon visiting countless jewellery shops, trying on umpteen sets, until I settled on a beautiful Arabian antique gold set that draped elegantly with Paisley pendants around my neck and at my ears. I also picked out two wide *karas* that looked like they were made of the lightest chainmail. And then we chose several sets of earrings to give to all my cousins who had helped tirelessly with my wedding. We included Amma, Chachijhi, Kala and my sisters and, before we knew it, we had one full jewellery set, seven pairs of earrings, and six elegant necklaces for everyone, with one bracelet that Samir *bhai* spoiled Ayesha with.

Tourists and other shoppers stopped to look at us as we stared at the number of items we had selected. There was enough there to make for a gold bar. In preparation for the haggling, the assistant called over a more senior assistant. And then the bartering began. He scribbled down the cost of each item, added labour charge, and then gave us a discounted figure. Samir *bhai* took his pen and broke down the cost further. The verbal battle went back and forth for what felt like ages before Chachijhi stepped forward. And then, in perfect Urdu, she took over the bartering process. At some point, she managed to persuade the man to get us all cold drinks after convincing the assistant that she knew his aunty. We stood back and watched her speak, coax, tease and wind him into such a state that the assistant begrudgingly met Samir *bhai*'s offer just to stop Chachijhi talking. I had underestimated Chachijhi; she had skills I had never seen, but it was safe to say, her negotiating spirit was impressive. None of us laughed or congratulated Chachijhi because the done thing was to act like it was the least the assistant could do, given the size of our purchase. As the junior assistant packaged each item in its own individual box, requested by Chachijhi, Samir *bhai* settled the tab. In London, you had to be careful what jewellery you wore in public, but here in Dubai walking around with several bags of gold didn't attract the attention of a fly. Street crime wasn't tolerated and walking about gold laden seemed the most natural, glamorous thing to do. It felt even better to know that we had got a brilliant deal with the gold. So with shades on, Chachijhi, Ayesha, Samir *bhai* and I headed back to the cruiser. Life here was good. Very good.

We spent the rest of the day in Deira and Bur Dubai buying countless shawls, *hijabs* and *jilbabs* that were a fraction of the price they were in London. In his bid to show us the best of Dubai, Samir *bhai* barely let us drop off all our shopping back at the Aajmaan Rotana and grab a quick shower before herding us back out into the cruiser. With the sun setting over Dubai, we grabbed dinner at Phai Thai in Jumeirah and then went for a quick stroll along the broad walk. The city came to life in the evening. Young things with flash, ultra-customised sports cars prowled up and down Jumeirah looking for the hottest spot to stop, families with children relaxed, and tourists strolled – all without the hustle and bustle of London. It felt like a million miles away from the demands back home. By the time we got back to the hotel, we were so relaxed we barely spoke. The twins were out with their respective husbands, making the most of their time together. Chachijhi went straight to bed without any comment or criticism, a first ever, and Ayesha and Samir *bhai* decided to head out again to relax at the one and only open-air *sheesha* café. Waving them out, I walked into the large living room and fell on to a couch. Staring at my phone, I smiled at the numerous texts from Zain. We exchanged a couple more but, in spite of his ability to make me smile, Jhanghir stayed at the forefront of my mind. Without another thought, I dialled the hospital.

'BelleVue Paeds, how can I help?' For the first time, I hesitated.

'Dr Khan, please, it's Dr Malik from Dubai General.'

'Dr Malik . . . the same Dr Malik from Wembley General?' I hung up at being busted by the long-term secretary. Refusing to give up, I called him on his mobile phone.

'Jhanghir speaking.' His instant answer threw me, so I composed myself and sat up.

'It's me.' My words were quiet and loaded with silent fear.

'Hello?' His impatience didn't help my nerves.

'Jhanghir, it's me, Maya.'

'Maya.' Jhanghir was surprised to hear from me. The silence that followed was so uncomfortable that I shut my eyes and waited.

'What's going on, Jhanghir?' I asked when he refused to speak.

'Now's not a good time, Maya . . .'

'You don't ever to seem have a good time . . .'

'Maya, let me call you . . .'

'Who's Maya?' a sleepy female voice close to Jhanghir asked.

'Who's that?' I breathed, recognising the 'cousin' from the call I'd made from England.

'Let me call you later, OK?' Without giving me a chance to speak, Jhanghir hung up on me. I stared at the phone, fuming at the thought that he was cheating on me. I tried to calm my temper, telling myself that what happened between Zain and I was equally bad . . . but it wasn't. It wasn't, because it happened to me and it's never happened since. But Jhanghir . . . that 'cousin' . . . this was the second time. There was no avoiding that 'they' had been together, *sleeping*, the past two times I had called Jhanghir. He was busted. Busted! Shaking my head, I stood up and started pacing. Thoughts of the wedding where I was singularly making the arrange-ments, the bookings and the invitations raced through my mind. Fears about being left stranded at the altar, dressed as the bejewelled, blushing, shy Asian bride, with six hundred guests staring at me with pity as my heart shattered into a million pieces pushed me too far. I screamed and started throwing cushions around the room in sheer frustration.

'What are you doing!' Chachijhi demanded as she rushed into the room. Coming to a sudden stop, I turned to her and blew my hair back from my face. Panting, I held put my hands on my hips and looked around at the mess I had made.

'What's happened?'

'Nothing. Let's go out.'

'Maya, we've already eaten out.'

'Let's go for a cool smoothie somewhere.'

'I'm tired, I want to go to sleep.'

'Fine, Chachijhi, you go to sleep, I'm going out.'

Thirty minutes later, dressed to the nines in killer heels, leg-lengthening fitted jeans and long silk halter top, I walked into Planet Burgers with a grumpy Chachijhi who refused to make a similar effort. Dressed in her signature patterned polyester cardigan over a yellow flowery *sari* and Jesus sandals, she refused to smile when we were shown to our table. It was only when we sat down that I realised the ratio of men to women was highly disproportionate. Ordering two mega smoothies, I noticed that there were no families or couples in the burger bar.

'Where have you brought me?' Chachijhi asked as she looked disapprovingly at the young scantily dressed Pilipino women who moved in small groups and approached male dinners with wide smiles. The waiter looked at us in confusion and I realised why. This was one of *those* places, the type where women met men specifically to service their needs. Avoiding Chachijhi's glare, I sipped on my smoothie, burning with the humiliation of where I had brought an elder.

'Have your drink, Chachijhi, it's really nice.' She didn't return my smile and I prayed that no one other than the waiter would approach us.

'You bring me here for a milkshake, why couldn't you have ordered from in-house catering?'

I shrugged apologetically and focused on finishing my smoothie as quickly as possible, regretting the impulse to head out after Jhanghir's call. 'Thank the lord they don't have club music here . . .' And, before she could finish, the lights dimmed and blaring sirens screeched through the diner. Before we could close our open mouths, young, sexy, barely covered women jumped on to tables to writhe provocatively.

'Get down, get down!' Chachijhi shouted, batting such a girl from getting on to our table. 'Hai Allah, where have you brought me!' she shouted.

'Chachijhi, let's go!' I said, throwing some money on the table before taking her arm to lead her out.

'Don't touch me, don't touch me!' she warned men she passed whilst holding her bag up like a weapon. 'I'm not one of those cheap hussies, don't touch me.' Why she would think any well-sighted man looking for thrills would confuse her rotund body with that of the sexy sirens on the tables bewildered me. So I pushed through the crowded diner to get to the entrance. It proved impossible as the lounging male patrons suddenly herded around the tables to get the best views possible. And then one sleazy-looking moustached man stepped in front of me with a suggestive smile. Chachijhi didn't think twice about pushing him out of the way with her bag to lead me out.

As soon as we got out, we jumped into a cab and

headed back to the hotel. I looked at Chachijhi who sat with her eyes closed, touching both her cheeks repeatedly whilst praying for forgiveness. The small giggle that escaped my lips caught her attention. So I stopped it and started praying. Peaking one eye open I saw her trying to stop a smile and, before we knew it, we burst out laughing at the eventful excursion.

The following day, Samir *bhai* arranged for everyone to go for a desert safari, but I opted out, choosing to stay with Jana who was struggling with her pregnancy in the heat. With everyone out of the way, we had a long, leisurely brunch at the hotel and then took a quick cab ride to Mercato Mall, an Italian-themed shopping mall built in the spirit of Leicester's St Martin's Square. We took our time browsing through one shop after another, often spending more time taking ever longer coffee breaks.

Mid-afternoon my mobile buzzed to life.

'Hello, Zain!' I answered with a smile.

'It's Jhanghir.' He was irritated and unimpressed.

'Sorry, who?' I returned, refusing to be accommodating.

'Funny, Maya. Very funny.' His tone was dry and not in the least bit amused. Jana mouthed Jhanghir's name and I nodded. She pointed to a shop she wanted to visit and I promised to stay put in the café.

'Sorry, no, still can't register the voice,' I pushed, equally unimpressed.

'All right, Maya, if you're going to mess around . . .'

'Oh, now I know! You would be Jhanghir, the guy who disappears on his fiancée and has strange women by his side every time he answers a call.'

'I've had a lot on my plate, Maya . . .'

'I don't want to hear it, Jhanghir, I'm out of sympathy.' With every cell in my body, I wanted him to understand my situation for a change. 'I'm planning our wedding on my own, with no guidance, no input and no communication with the man who's meant to be my fiancé . . .'

'My father—'

'I'm not interested, Jhanghir. You have chosen to keep me in the dark, you have chosen to cut communication, and you've chosen to ignore me. There are strange women answering your calls beside you in the early hours of the morning, you cut calls with me to go tend to them,' I pointed out, 'and, through it all, I have kept smiling, telling everyone that everything is fine. But it's not, is it?' The silence that followed my question made me want to scream, but I refrained.

'You have a temper on you, don't you?'

'This isn't funny,' I told Jhanghir, recognising his amused tone.

'Have you finished?' There it was again, making light of my concerns. 'You want to know who she is?'

'This isn't funny.'

'You spoiling for a fight?' Crying out in frustration at his refusal to be serious, I massaged my forehead. 'My cousin's staying with me while she recovers from surgery. Each time you call, one of us has crashed out on the couch and the other one takes the call. She's going back to Bangladesh in a few days.' The calm explanation failed to address the growing distance between us.

'I'm really tired, Jhanghir, I'm trying hard to be patient, but I'm getting close to not caring any more.' No smart comment followed my confession. 'I can't do this alone, I really can't.'

'Zain's waiting for you guys in Bangladesh, he's going to take you everywhere you need to go.'

'That's not the point . . .'

'You have an army of people to help you, Maya; there's your family, Zain, Seema *bhabhi* . . .'

'You don't get it, do you?' I whispered, fighting the tears back.

'What do you want me to do, Maya? I'm in such a financial mess, I can't think straight.'

'Talk to me about it; we used to talk about everything. Why can't you talk to me?'

'It's my problem, I need to sort it out.'

'Maybe I can help.'

'Maya, there're some things a man has to take care of.' I stopped at his words, realising that he wasn't going to change his mind. 'Listen, as long as we get married, I don't care if you have red roses or towering lily displays. I don't care if we have a sponge cake or a five-tier wedding cake . . .'

'But I care,' I told him. 'I care that we smile at our wedding because we can manage the costs by working together . . .'

'Make this easy for me, Maya.' The beseeching request hit a nerve and I nodded, even though tears slipped down my face.

'Sure,' I whispered, frowning at the quietness between us.

'I'll give you a call later.' He signed off and I put my phone away and wiped my tears.

'Hey, what's wrong?' Jana asked, returning to the table with several bags of shopping. I cleared my throat and smiled whilst shaking my head. 'Jhanghir?' Nodding at the question, Jana smiled and gave me a few moments by getting herself another drink.

'Your *bhai* and I, we split up three times before we got married and on the day before our wedding, we were going to call it a day,' Jana revealed when she returned to the table. She read the shock on my face and nodded. 'Of course, we didn't have the history you and Jhanghir had, but we were going to walk away from each other at the last minute.'

'But he's besotted with you . . .'

'Maya, it's taken years to get to this point. You think marriages just work? That relationships are easy?'

It felt stupid to nod, but I nodded. 'They're meant to be, aren't they? That's the point of having a companion.'

'Why do you think marriage makes up one half of our faith, Maya?' Jana's point caught my attention. 'All of us, Hanna, Ayesha, Tariq *bhai* – we've all had issues in our marriages.'

'Hanna too?' I asked in disbelief, wondering how I had missed all this.

'They were going to get a divorce a year into their marriage. She was too mouthy, too independent, wanting everything her way and he was equally stubborn. They were arguing all the time. Do you remember when she moved back home when Hamza was born?'

'I thought it was because she needed Mum's help with Hamza?'

'Trial separation.' Shocked, I shook my head, but Jana's expression told me she wasn't exaggerating. 'And Ayesha, she wanted to come home a week after she got married.'

'But she wouldn't be without Samir *bhai* for the world . . .'

'Now she wouldn't be, but back then they rushed into marriage and realised they were too young, just starting their medical careers and, one week in, she was on the phone begging Baba to collect her.'

I felt ashamed that I had been so self-absorbed with jet-setting around the world with my corporate job that I had missed the distress of those closest to me.

'What happened?' I asked, taking the cold ice juice she held out to me.

'Baba refused to collect her.'

'No!'

'Yep. He told her she had gone against his advice to wait eighteen months to get married, that she was an adult, and that she had to grow up and sort it out. I think she got a reality check and started focusing on what she wanted.'

'And Hanna?'

'She didn't wait for Baba to collect her, she just arrived and refused to go back to her husband. Baba got a marriage counsellor from the mosque to work with them; it took two years for them to learn to live together as a couple . . .'

'Two years?'

Jana nodded and smiled. 'It's hard work, Maya. No matter what people say about his wedding, or her dowry, or how magical it all is, nothing in marriage matters beyond being prepared to work hard to make it easy for each other.'

Jana continued talking but she had no idea how much I needed her advice. She had given me the support that I desperately needed to persevere with Jhanghir.

'I'm sorry I wasn't there for you,' I told her as she reached out for my hand.

'Don't be. You're feistiness always gave us spirit, Maya.'

The following day, Chachijhi, Samir *bhai*, Ayesha and I caught the short flight to Dhaka International Airport. The twins decided to stay back with their husbands to progress with the establishment of their practice. We had two and a half days in Dhaka to do all our shopping. Having heard news about our short visit to Bangladesh, Nani, along with Uncle Khan and Zain, waited for us there. Recalling Jana's advice, we got through the painfully slow customs and stepped out into the blistering dusty heat of Dhaka. The crowd of waiting family, chauffeurs and cabbies held behind a glass wall shouted out in a deafening call.

'There's Uncle Khan,' Samir *bhai* said as he led us towards the ramp and beyond the gated airport area. In an instant, poor children begging for money surrounded us. Chachijhi shooed them away and I chuckled as it was as effective as selling ice to the Eskimos. Spotting Nani, I raced into her open arms.

'Don't they have food in London?' She held my face and looked at me closely. I laughed and pulled her into my arms. It was good to be back in Bangladesh.

When the driver pulled up at Zain's family home, we all sat in silence. The sprawling mansion beyond the steel gates amidst the rolling lush green lawn took our breath away.

'*Salaams*, how are you all?' Zain said as he walked down to the car to shake hands with Uncle Khan and Samir *bhai*. He was dressed in a thin long Punjabi top over jeans and he looked perfectly at home. 'Leave the bags, Anwar will bring those in.'

Chachijhi took off her shades and smiled.

'Thanks for hosting us,' Samir *bhai* said as he led us in.

'Not at all, you're virtually family,' Zain brushed off as he helped Nani up the stairs.

Following everyone in, I smiled as Ayesha gawped at the lavish floodlit marble interiors. I looked at the creamy white walls, the ornate mahogany and chocolate leather furnishings in the wide open-plan house.

'It's a beautiful home, *bhetha*,' Nani told him, with a gentle pat on the cheek.

'*Nani*,' I mouthed with half a smile. Chachijhi caught

the instinctive interaction before walking on ahead. Zain caught the reaction, and winked.

'You need to find a wife, *bhetha*,' Nani said, seeing everything. 'The best ones go fast and are bad news.' With a small smile, she let him lead him forward but I knew it was a warning to us both.

Heeding Nani's warning, we spent the next two days emptying out Newmarket, Elephant Street and Bondho bazaar of every type of wedding accessory you could imagine. Zain left his house manager in charge of taking us wherever we needed to go whilst he took care of family business. With the chauffeur on hand, we made countless visits to these shopping venues ending in bags of *saris*, *punjabis*, bangles, *shalwaar kameezes*, wedding cards and wedding stationery. This was another side to Bangladesh that people didn't see. It was the dusty, hustling, bustling city that never slept. Roads were clogged with super jeeps imported from Japan by the uber rich, who fought along rickshaws that all clambered to get to the trendiest malls. With the commotion of an overcrowded city rising through the drawbacks of yesterday, the *azhaan* would throw a calm, serene presence of the warm city of Dhaka. So we hustled with the growing middle class, shopped with the uber rich and watched over the poor trying to make a living selling everything from hair grips to magazines. And we kept going until Chachijhi and I sat exhausted in the lavish living room late in the evening.

'I'm tired, Maya, but you made me happy this last week,' Chachijhi said quietly. Looking to my aunty I frowned at her comment. 'My daughters, all they see is an interfering, gossiping, fat old woman. But you, you tolerated me and I know I infuriate you and frustrate you, but, Maya, I enjoyed our time this week.'

Touched by her words, I smiled. 'Why do you always judge people?' I asked out of curiosity.

'I don't mean any harm . . .'

'But it does harm, Chachijhi, when false rumours are spread about someone who could be up to something with someone . . .'

Chachijhi looked sad and looked down. 'People think I don't see what my daughters get up to. I know my girls were not saints. Leila, she had many boyfriends before she got married. You think a mother doesn't understand secret phone calls, late meetings and these matters?'

'We never judged you . . .'

'And now, Meena, she's got her heart set on this non-Bengali. You think I don't hear what people say about me and my girls?' Chachijhi asked.

'But that doesn't mean you get in there first!' I teased her until she finally smiled.

'And what does it all matter, Chachijhi, if Meena's very happy?'

'It gives me a purpose, Maya,' she answered honestly. 'What else does a woman like me do to keep herself occupied?'

'You are the biggest gossip in London, Chachijhi,' I stated as she hid a smile behind her *dupatta*. 'And you do test the patience of a saint,' I added, seeing the twinkle in her eyes.

'Old women are designed to warn young women what they can become,' she told me and I stopped smiling at the fear of becoming Chachijhi number two.

'And young women are designed to remind old women what they still could be.'

Chachijhi smiled at my comment and then Nani walked in with Zain.

'Where're Samir and Ayesha?' Nani asked, sitting beside me.

'They're having dinner at the House of China in Dhanmondhi,' Chachijhi answered, looking at Zain. 'You have a beautiful home, Zain, when are you going to get married?' The random question surprised us all. And then Nani chuckled slowly. 'Remember, my Maya is no longer available.'

Chachijhi looked mortified at the answer but Zain laughed at Nani's words.

'I see where Maya gets her spirit from,' he said before looking to me. 'I'll marry when the right girl comes chasing after me.' We all guffawed at the answer but he stayed absolutely serious. 'It worked for Jhanghir, didn't it?'

I stopped laughing at that point and looked down at my ring. The sultry humid evening felt charged with high emotion. I looked up and caught Zain's eyes.

'Tell me about Jhanghir,' Nani said, breaking into our stare. I turned to my grandmother and looked at her warm, watching face.

'He's the most aggravating, stubborn, hard-headed, contrary man I've ever met.'

Nani laughed at my description and clapped her hands with joy. 'Then he's perfect for you!' Nani remarked as Chachijhi snorted.

'Sounds like my husband,' Chachijhi muttered before calling the housekeeper to bring cold refreshments.

'You must bring him to see us as soon as you marry, Maya,' Nani said, taking a cup of freshly squeezed lemon sherbet. 'I would dearly love to meet him.'

'He's quite the charmer,' Chachijhi said as she helped herself to the samosas and bhajhis put out on silver platters. 'And my, he is a handsome fellow and what a doctor, any woman would feel lucky to have him look after her and her family.' I looked at Chachijhi, watching her throw a cursory look at Zain, and knew exactly what she was doing. She was trying to make him feel inadequate.

'I was so happy to hear my Maya was getting married, Zain, that I say extra prayers in gratitude every day,' Nani said. 'We tried everything to get her to accept *alaaps*; we had *alaaps* from every person we know, but she was so stubborn. She didn't accept any and, well, it sounds like Allah gave her the man she deserves.'

'Talking about prayers, it's time for *Maghrib*,' Chachijhi announced, taking an extra samosa before pushing herself up and off the couch.

'I'll join you,' Nani said, following Chachijhi. Shaking my head at the invitation. I watched them take the marble stairs up to their rooms.

'You ready to fly back tomorrow?'

Turning back to Zain, I smiled and shrugged. 'I don't know where two and a half days have gone,' I told him. 'We're shopped out, so thank God, we've got our pampering session tomorrow.'

'Aaahh, pampering session!' He laughed, helping himself to some sliced mangoes and pineapples.

'Waxing, threading, cleansing and massaging – yes, the whole works!' I confirmed with a chuckle. He indicated towards the veranda and I pulled my chiffon *dupatta* around me and followed him to look out over the manicured gardens. The sun was setting and cast a beautiful orange hue over Dhaka.

'This is my favourite part of the day,' Zain said, leaning against a tall white pillar.

'It is beautiful,' I agreed, coming to stand beside him. I pulled the chiffon *dupatta* loosely over my head as was the custom and looked out at the breathtaking scene. I felt him pull me against him. Without protest, I leaned against him and held his arm close as we stood in silence, both perfectly aware of the other, and the need to get no closer than we were. The sun slowly crept lower, and I wished time would stand still.

'Thank you for being here,' I said, looking straight ahead.

'Jhanghir would have been here if he could.'

'Jhanghir would have found a reason not to make it,' I corrected, smiling sadly. 'Do you think he wants to get married?'

'You're asking the wrong guy.' He laughed and I muted a smile.

'Seriously, sometimes I ask myself if we're just doing this to see through some kiddish promise.'

'Are you?'

I thought about Zain's question and I shook my head. Jhanghir was right for me in every way, but I doubted he would say that about me.

'I think Jhanghir is.' Zain shook his head, but I continued. 'I think he thinks I'm a good mate who'll do.'

'That's insane, I don't need to tell you you're hot, Maya; you have that natural sexiness about you, why would you doubt—'

'That's why!' I burst out, looking up at him. I wished I hadn't. Hearing what he thought suddenly made a difference to me. 'Jhanghir's never said that to me. Even after we got engaged or agreed to get married, he's never tried it on, tried to take advantage . . .'

'Do you want him to?' Zain asked with a frown. I shouldn't have said anything, but I nodded. He held my eyes and I knew what he was thinking. I should look away, I told myself. I looked up at Zain and he met my eyes. A slow warm smile crept on to my lips when he slowly moved forward. I closed my eyes and froze when I saw Jhanghir's face. Snapping my eyes open, I shook my head. But it was too late, I felt the touch of Zain's lips.

'Maya!'

Zain held me close, but at the call I pushed him back with a sharp slap. Turning around, I found Chachijhi staring at us.

'Chachijhi,' I called out as she stormed inside. I raced after her and came to a stop when she turned on me.

'Not a word,' she told me, holding a finger up before me. 'I want to hear not one word about what I just saw.'

'You don't understand . . .'

'I understand too much, Maya. I have eyes, I have ears, and I have instinct. And I may be old, but they all help me understand what happened on that veranda.'

'No, please . . .'

'You have reputation for a reason. Do you understand that?'

'Chachijhi, please let me explain . . .'

'Not one word!' The sharp order startled me and I stood still as she stamped up the stairs just as the housekeeper showed Ayesha and Samir in.

'Maya, what happened?' Turning around I smiled and ignored Zain's returning form.

'We're squabbling as usual!' I laughed as I walked down to join them.

'I'm going to catch up with a cousin,' Zain muttered before taking his leave. Nothing was missed on Ayesha, but the presence of Samir stopped her from asking.

'It's been a long day and we've got a lot of packing to do tomorrow. I'm going to hit the sack,' I said, taking the stairs up to my room. I rushed across to the window and watched Zain drive away. Resting my head against the glass, I felt torn between feeling abandoned by Jhanghir and revered by Zain. This was all a matter of reputation, so I stepped back from the window and went to lie down. Looking up at the ceiling fan, I frowned at the weight on my heart caused by the thought of loosing Jhanghir. The weight felt heavier with the realisation of the damage done to my reputation if my *alaap* to Jhanghir fell through because of Zain. Holding my hand up, I looked at my engagement ring. Chachijhi knew. Now what damage she would inflict on my reputation and *ristai* would depend on her regard for me. At the moment, this was non-existent. I now faced a torrid waiting game to see if my reputation would in time become non-existent too.

Save shaadi to prevent slide back into singledom

Sometimes a moment of clarity hits you so hard that you realise you're about to lose the one thing that's right for you. My preoccupation with Zain was so reckless that it made for a one-way ticket back to singledom. Chachijhi hadn't spoken to me since she had walked in on us and assumed the very worst. I was in the wrong and I should have known better. We returned to London with three times as many cases as we had had on our way out, but none of it mattered beyond the realisation that the biggest gossipmonger in our community had the juiciest and most wedding-destroying bit of news filled me with terror. The silence between us on the flight back to London concerned my sisters and whilst Chachijhi put it down to being tired, I wondered how many different ways she was going to break this shocking piece of gossip. No matter how many times I tried to talk to her, she advised me to stay quiet and keep my distance. Leila was at hand to pick her up at Heathrow, but they rushed off leaving Baba and Amma to envelop us all. I watched her leave, knowing it was only a matter of time.

'Everything OK, Maya?' Turning back to my father, I nodded. 'You clean out Dhaka's wedding shops?' Smiling at his comment, I nodded and let my sisters fight each other to tell Baba about our marathon shopping sprees and comprehensive pampering session. My thoughts were elsewhere; I was preoccupied with how I could limit the damage to my reputation and save my *shaadi*.

Everyone and their extended family had arrived at our house to welcome us back and whilst it was lovely to see my brothers and cousins, I wanted to lock myself in my room and speak to Jhanghir before word got out.

'What did you get? Taj *bhai* said you shopped every day, all day long.'

'Yes, yes; now move out of the way, my bladder's about to give,' Jana grumbled as she ousted two teenagers from their seat to fall on to the sofa.

'How about we look at the wedding shopping later?' Ayesha suggested, as Baba and Tariq *bhai* piled the cases up high in the dining room.

'Let's get the guys their refreshments,' my cousin Kala said, causing Mana and Farah to follow her. 'Pana!' the sharp call caught my attention. I looked at my cousin who had been giggling with Taj and looked back at Kala, who was none too pleased. Quietly I made a mental note to have a word with my brother.

'Food, where's all the food?' Samir *bhai* asked as he fell down beside Jana and patted the space next to him for Ayesha to sit down. The considerate act made my decision for me.

'I'm just going to go change . . .'

'Maya, we've got to talk about what needs to happen when—'

'Sure, Pana, give me five minutes.'

'And Tanya has been calling about your hen night.'

Thanking Shireen *bhabhi*, I continued to back out of the room until I could race up to my room. The door-bell stopped me on the stairs and slowly I turned round to see Chachijhi arrive with Chacha and Leila. I was out of sight, so I crouched by the stairs and zoned in until I could hear her ask to speak with Baba privately. My eyes widened and I scooted up to my room. Grabbing my hair back, I wondered what the fall-out would be of Chachijhi telling them about what had passed between Zain and I, how Baba would tackle it, who would know and how fast the news would spread that I was dumped and back on to the singles planet. Unable to think clearly, I called Tanya to plead with her to come round but she wasn't picking up her calls. Sakina would never forgive me so there was no point in calling her. I did the only thing I could – I went downstairs to face the music like an adult.

Knocking on the closed dining-room door, I heard Baba's angry tone advising everyone to give them some privacy. Taking a deep breath, I stepped in and stood against the wall. Chachijhi was sobbing, Chacha held his head in his hands, and Leila tearfully sniffed into a tissue. I daren't look at Baba, not ready to deal with the disappointment he would have in his eyes. They all knew about the incident between Zain and I, but I was determined to give my perspective on the matter.

'Maya, I've asked everyone to give us some privacy . . .'

'I thought I could explain what happened . . .'

'What do you know about Meena eloping without her family's knowledge?' Shocked by Baba's question, I stood silent in disbelief that the drama wasn't about me. As selfish as it was, I thanked Meena for her spirit to stand by what she thought was right. Suddenly, I realised everyone was staring at me, waiting for an explanation. Quickly, I shook my head.

'You say you know something about Meena getting married?'

'No! No, I don't know anything about her tying the knot!' I breathed out in relief, and then reminded myself not to smile as everyone looked at me with confusion.

'We had hoped she would call off the engagement, come to her senses about her errant ways,' Chacha said quietly, shaking his head so very sadly.

'Maybe I can talk to Meena?' I offered, seeing the depths of his disappointment.

'No, thank you, I want the wisdom of the elders to deal with this catastrophe.'

Chachijhi's stern refusal told me with considerable certainty that she wanted nothing to do with me. Baba beckoned me away and I accommodated him all too happily. Taking my master wedding planner from the kitchen, I passed by the rowdy living room and refused calls to join them as I withdrew to my room. I had been given a short reprieve, and in that time I had to put things right. And the first place for me to start was with my fiancé.

'Jhanghir?'

'Maya, is everything OK?'

'Why wouldn't it be? What have you heard?' I asked, feeling my heart stop.

'You're calling me at a normal time; that's unlike you.' My heart started beating again and I laughed at his comment a little too quickly, and maybe a touch too forcefully. 'You OK?'

'Yeah, we just flew in and I wanted to see how you're doing,' I said, looking at the planner in front of me.

'Not talk about the wedding?' The tentative question made me smile.

'We can come to that later,' I said, enjoying the sound of his laughter. 'Are you managing?'

'I read your email about your family's medical practice in Dubai. It sounds like an awesome lifestyle change . . .'

'Awesome enough for you to consider joining them?' I asked, silently praying the answer would be yes. I had it all planned, I would put my art bursary on hold or get some kind of international transfer to a prestigious art school in Dubai and we would be with my family and . . .

'I've got too many commitments, here, Maya, and we're about to get married,' Jhanghir reminded me, bringing my dreaming to a halt.

'But what better time to make a lifestyle change.'

'Don't push me, Maya, it's a good option, maybe in a few years, but not right now.' I stopped at his comment and took a deep breath and reminded myself to make it easy for him. 'You have your art bursary to think of, why, after all the years of postponing your dreams of becoming a recognised artist, would you want to sacrifice that? It's time for you to cut the apron strings, Maya.'

I stayed quiet at his words, unhappy with the outcome of my suggestion.

'Are you managing?' It took all my of will power to drop the Dubai discussion but I had bigger wars to win. I sat on the floor and listened to Jhanghir. He talked about the apartment, the mortgage and getting the finances into shape and, for the first time, I realised how worried he was at losing everything, including me.

'I know you're going to find it hard leaving everyone back in London, I wanted to get everything set up right for you, and I didn't think my dad would drop me so fast.' Tears stung my eyes at the harsh judgement I had made

of him and his silences. I was lost for words about the
lengths he had gone for me and felt even worse about my
flirtation with Zain.

'I'm so sorry,' I whispered, wiping away my tears.

'Hey, I got us into this mess.'

'No, I'm sorry I haven't been there to help you.' My
admission was heartfelt.

'I wanted to give you the privileges and welcome
Seema *bhabhi* got . . .'

'I just need you,' I told him with no hesitation. 'Your
father's wealth, the privileges that all affords, none of it
ever mattered to me.'

'I've been such an ass about things . . .'

'Can I have that in writing?' I teased.

'How about I give it to you when I see you next
week?' I bit my lip at his comment. We continued talking
for what felt like ages. It had been a very long time since
we had spoken so openly or freely, and neither of us
wanted to stop. We sparred verbally, we talked about life
after marriage, and we talked about our wedding. I
ignored calls for me to free up the home phone line, and
calls to join the family as all the wedding outfits from our
shopping trips in Dhaka were being distributed, but I
had no intention of doing so.

'Promise me there'll be no more silences.' It was dark
and I was close to falling asleep. 'No more silences.'
Jhanghir gave me his word and I smiled. He continued
to tell me about the department he was running, and at
some point I fell asleep. I knew he wouldn't mind, I had
done that many times in our yesteryears and it felt like
everything was back on track.

Amma, Ayesha and I headed to Suraya's for the trying
on of my wedding dress. Amma and Ayesha seemed
unnaturally quiet and each time I asked, neither

divulged any information. Refusing to believe that Chachijhi had spoken, I dropped the matter as we descended into the boutique. Nervously, I gripped my hands together, praying that this time round they had got it right.

'The prices here are astronomical!' Amma whispered as she returned to the large couch in the centre of the boutique. 'I hope Jhanghir's able to manage this . . .'

'Here it is!' the designer announced, holding up the covered outfit to hang up outside the changing room. Watching him unzip the cover, I held my breath and then stared at the gem-encrusted wedding *lengha* of my dreams.

'Oh my goodness, that's beautiful,' Amma cried out as she pulled me into a hug.

Pulling myself free, I walked over to the outfit and touched it gently.

'It's beautiful,' I told the anxious designer, who broke out in the widest smile.

'Let's get you into it,' Amma said. And with that, I spent the next ten minutes slipping into the long *lengha*, and clipping on the wide-neck blouse. Although it felt a little loose, I stepped out in the supplied four-inch heels. Amma and Ayesha's silent reaction made me smile.

'Oh . . . oh . . . my baby's getting married!' Amma told the designer who frowned as she burst into tears. 'My baby is getting married,' she repeated as we rushed to her.

'Amma, you've been praying for it since I was born.'

'You look so beautiful,' Amma told me before pulling me down to her bosom.

'My dress . . . my dress!' I cried out, untangling myself from Amma's arms to stand up and compose myself.

'Amma, if you're going to cry every time you mention

Maya's wedding, you're going to jinx it,' Ayesha said, putting a warm arm around her.

'Oh no, no, no! I would never do that, you have to get married,' she said, drying up her tears instantly.

'It's a little loose in places,' I told the designer, who disappeared briefly to return with his notebook and a box of pins.

'You've dropped three dress sizes,' he estimated, holding up the loose material at my waist. 'You've got a great figure . . .' The designer trailed off at Amma's loud, disapproving cough. 'I wouldn't recommend you lose any more weight, the shape of the outfit needs your curves.' Feeling slim, toned and in good shape, I reassured him that I wouldn't lose any more weight.

'Can you take it in at the waist and at the capped sleeves so that the fit is perfect?' I asked, looking at every detail, line and curve in the mirror.

'I was just about to say the same,' he said, pinning the waist until I got the fit I wanted. We spent a while debating other minor changes as I swished and swirled in the outfit until I felt I never wanted to take it off.

'It's perfect!' I finally told the designer, turning see Amma hide her tears behind her tissue. Catching Ayesha's eyes, we put our arms around our mother and smiled at her sentimental reaction.

The three of us spent the rest of the afternoon visiting my florist to order the flower displays before shopping for accessories. Then we made our way to the wedding decorators and I knew they wouldn't be happy with the changes. Nevertheless, I was determined to make them. Sumi was waiting and she looked disappointed when I turned up without Zain.

'Three weeks to go and you're positively glowing!' she said, looking towards the entrance hopefully.

'Thanks, my mum and sister have come along to confirm the wedding decoration details,' I told her, putting her out of her misery. She cleared her throat and smiled.

'So where do we stand on the details?' Opening up my wedding book, I leafed through to the *henna* section.

'The Arabian nights theme complete with *sheeshas*, low tables, cushions and lanterns still stands. It just needs to get delivered to my parents' garden as we're hosting it in a garden marquee.'

'Uh, have you got adequate floor coverings and matting?' Nodding at the question Sumi smiled and confirmed the details item by item. 'And for the wedding?'

'There are a few changes I'd like to make . . .'

'Uh-oh!' Sumi laughed a little too nervously.

'We didn't approve of it,' Ayesha offered without a smile. 'We thought it was too contrived.' Sumi looked intimidated by Ayesha and smiled at me.

'Let's do away with the wall tapestries, no ice sculptures, and we have no use for the wall lanterns – oh and, the ceiling draperies, let's cut those too.'

'Wow, that's a lot of change, we booked those for your wedding . . .'

'I'm sure you have enough customers chasing these items,' Ayesha returned, leaving no room for discussion.

'Anything else?' Sumi asked, no longer smiling.

'The stage and colour theme of gold, cream and ruby-red is as is, but we'd like the crystallised waterfall of lights behind the backdrop on the stage, complete with a lectern. Also, we need to have a red carpet with the cordoned-off posts at the entrance leading into Iver House.' Sumi raised a brow and worked through my changes. She pushed back on some ideas but with Amma and Ayesha on board, the refusals melted away. By the time we finished, I had ordered the basis for my glamorous Bollywood wedding.

The days that followed were lost to writing out invitations using old school Italian calligraphy and a handy gold pen. My cousins teased me for scrutinising every detail but I shrugged it off, laughing with them. We finalised details for the wedding cake, the script for Taj as the MC and the buffet meal that Tariq was to deliver for the *henna*.

'Stop.' Looking up at Shireen *bhabhi*, I frowned. 'You have your hen night to get ready for. So put away your wedding book, your itineraries. and your master plan.'

'I just need twenty minutes . . .' I stopped as my sister-in-law took my folder and held it away from me.

'I've run you a bath, you need to pamper yourself to celebrate.'

'Ten minutes?' I pleaded, biting my lip at her glare. 'OK, OK! I'm going,' I laughed, before making my way up to my room. Stopping at the entrance I saw Hamza standing by my bed looking at the outfit that his mum had laid out for him.

'You're going to a party?' he asked as I touched the sheer blush-coloured chiffon halter-neck long top with a heavily beaded neckline. Beside it, Shireen had placed delicate glass bangles and long chandelier earrings from Swarovski.

'Yes, Hamza aunty's going to see her friends,' I said as Shireen came to stand next to me. 'You shouldn't have.' She hugged me from behind and gave me a kiss on the cheek.

'It's our pleasure, isn't it, Hamza?' Before I knew it, Hamza had raced across and hugged me too. My eyes filled with tears at the realisation that these were my last few weeks at home. Shireen teared up too, reading my thoughts and smiling.

'Crying tightens the eye bags,' I explained, knowing she didn't believe a word I said.

'You don't have bags underneath your eyes, bags are for shopping!' Hamza piped up, making us both burst into laughter.

At seven p.m., Hanna, Janna and Shireen *bhabhi* drove me to my hen night in Piccadilly. Everyone looked stunning in fashion-forward trends mixing tunics with skinny jeans and killer heels. I was uber excited and ultra cosmopolitan in the delicate halter dress worn over a skin-coloured three-quarter-length top for modesty, skinny jeans and four-inch strappy leather heels. Janna curled my hair until it fell in lush glistening waves over my shoulders, whilst I finished off the look by slipping on the bangles and earrings. With a little clutch bag, I felt like a diva ready to take the catwalk and, as we walked through Mayfair, I laughed when I spotted Bar Bollywood.

'No way!' I cried out, laughing when we walked arm in arm into the venue. Bollywood hits blasted out through the bar and we whooped as a good-looking waiter led us through to the sophisticated Bar to our table. Seeing my friends and cousins taking up the far corner, I cringed as they all bellowed at my arrival. Leila raced forward to put a 'Bride to Be' sash over me before leading me to the centre of the table.

'You look gorgeous!' Pana squealed, reaching over to hug me.

'Hey, Trouble,' Tanya said, laughing as I jived in front of her. 'OK, girls, tonight there are no limits!' All the girls cheered in support.

'Oh lord!' I whispered as a waiter arrived with a non-alcoholic cocktail.

'She's not even married and she's having Sex On the Beach!' At Tanya's announcement I sputtered out the juice I had sipped and shook my head as all the girls laughed at my reaction. Just at that moment, the anthem 'My Desi Girl' blared through the bar.

'Can we call Maya Malik to the dance floor.' Freezing at the DJ's announcement I looked around at Tanya and Sakina. They pointed to my sisters who pointed to my cousins. 'Is there a Maya Malik in the house?'

'She's here!' Leila shouted, grabbing my arm to drag me to the dance floor.

'Here she is, everyone give Maya Malik a whoop whoop!'

The bar whoop whooped as I bit my nail and looked towards my table with beseeching eyes.

The DJ went on to call up several other girls also on their hen night to the dance floor. Laughing amongst ourselves, we danced self-consciously and then froze when a group of waiters ran on to the dance floor to cosy up next to us. Before we knew it, they had started grinding and bumping against us. I looked at the hairy beast in front of me and frowned. The more I moved away, the closer he got. Then, at the sound of police sirens, they pulled off their outfits and pumped their tools, dressed only in itsy bitsy neon g-strings. Screaming out loud I closed my eyes and pushed him away. The laughter from the sidelines didn't put me off, and each time I tried to escape, the beast pulled me back and had me twirling until I stood frozen with my hands over my face. When the song came to an end, I peeked through my fingers as the beast gave me a quick peck before picking up his outfit to leave. The club anthem 'Chava Chava' came on and everyone raced on to the dance floor. With all my friends and family dancing around me I started laughing. The shock of the strippers slowly wore off and I hugged Tanya tightly as she apologised in good humour. We spent the evening dancing, joking and messing around. Moving around the table I spent time with each of my friends and family, enjoying the cheeky conversations.

'Maya.' Hearing Pana's call, I looked up with an amused but concerned look. 'How much do you know about your husband to be?'

'Enough to get married to him,' I returned as my friends raised a glass at my confidence.

'Good, we've got him online and we've got a few questions for you.' Frowning at her words, I watched Ayesha reach beneath the table to pull out an iPad. Everyone watched her log into Skype and, before we knew it, Jhanghir had accepted her invitation to a video call.

'No!' I screamed as Ayesha held the iPad up for everyone to see.

'Hi, Jhanghir!' They chimed together as I stared at Jhanghir. It felt like for ever since I had last seen him and he looked good.

'Hey, girls,' he replied before leaning close to the camera. 'I hope you treat my girl good tonight.' His quip made everyone laugh. 'Hi, Maya.'

'Hey,' I returned with a shy smile.

'So I told the girls you know everything about me,' Jhanghir told me. 'I have every confidence in you; otherwise, for every question you get wrong, I'm honour bound to buy each one of those of girls a present.' Laughing, I looked to Tanya, who distributed the question cards.

The first few questions I knocked off without hesitation, and then Ayesha asked, 'What does Jhanghir prefer, boxers or y-fronts?' I knew the answer because he was a boxers type of guy, but to get it right would make me the brunt of another round of teasing.

'You know this!' Jhanghir called out, making the girls ask me why.

'He's a boxers type of guy. I mean, he walks the wards all day, he needs to be comfortable!' I explained, laughing, when they all jumped on the opportunity for more ribbing. Jhanghir laughed along too.

'Is Jhanghir a butt or a boobs man?' I turned with wide eyes to look at a deadly serious Tanya. Some of the girls tittled with laughter and I shook my head at her.

'You definitely know this one,' Jhanghir threw in, adding to my humiliation on purpose. By the time we got to the end of the quiz, I was beyond mortified and Jhanghir owed no more than three gifts. All the girls *salaamed* Jhanghir farewell, but before they could end the video call, I reached out to Ayesha.

'Let me talk to him,' I asked, as everyone teased me. Standing up, I took the tablet and walked outside. Crouching down against the outside wall, I leaned back and looked at the iPad.

'You look gorgeous, Maya,' Jhanghir said as I smiled down at him. 'But right now I can see up your nostrils!' Holding the iPad in front of me I glared at him. 'Seriously, you look breathtaking and I wish I was with you.' I reached out and touched his cheek on the screen.

'I miss you,' I said. 'In less than three weeks, we're going to be married.'

'Well, that's if I survive my stag night tomorrow . . .'

'You're having a stag night?' I asked as passer-bys looked at me in confusion.

'Yeah, Zain's organised one with my buddies and colleagues and he's in charge of the plans for the guy *holud*, which we're going to try and have in London.'

'Zain's organising it?' I asked hesitantly.

'Yeah, you're good with Zain, right?' Nodding in

agreement, I smiled and flicked my hair back from my face.

'I should go back in,' I told him as he grinned and leaned forward.

'Be good.'

I laughed at his advice and closed my eyes when he logged out. I missed him so much it hurt and after a few moments I walked back in to join the party.

'There she is!' Janna shouted at the belly dancer. Ayesha grabbed her iPad back from me just as the voluptuous belly dancer pulled me beside her.

'You think I have any shame left after the male stripper?' I shouted at my table. Before they could reply, I joined the belly dancer, matching her move for move as everyone cheered me on. Beckoning Tanya and Sakina to join me, we outshone the belly dancer as we took over and performed an impromptu dance. Those in surrounding tables started clapping along, and when everyone applauded we laughed and bowed.

My hen night was amazing and went on for ever. I smiled so much my cheeks hurt and I laughed so hard my sides ached. We stayed until the Bar played its last song. My married friends rushed home, having stayed out later than expected and those who weren't ready to call it night, all headed back to my house. We tossed off our heels, loaded up on ice cream and chocolate cake and looked through our DVD collection. I stopped at my all-time favourite *Out of Sight* but, with one look at Tanya, I put it away and pulled out *How to Lose a Guy in Ten Days*. Huddled up in a massive group, we clutched cushions and ate freely until sleep took us away to dream-land one by one.

Tough talking intensifies tensions

For those who dream about getting married, let me advise you that there is nothing dreamy about arranging your wedding. You have to be tough, tenacious and totally on top of your timings, otherwise you'll end up with a day so disjointed you wished you had eloped. That's why, when all my cousins and family slept in after my exhausting hen night, I was up at the crack of dawn chasing up the decorator, florist and MC to confirm all the details and preparation times for my wedding day. Hearing hushed giggles emerge from the garden, I frowned and scrambled off my bed. Finding Taj and Pana talking intimately out of view of my sleeping family, I narrowed my eyes and watched enough to know that I had to have the big sister talk with my brother. Turning around, I stood two steps away from my window and started coughing. I knew they could see me, and, in an instant, Pana raced back into the house. Leaning out of the window, I saw Taj shake his head.

'We should talk,' I told Taj who put a finger to his lips to hush me. 'I'm happy to talk like this . . .'

'All right, all right, I'm coming up!' Taj breathed out before jogging back into the house. He was in my room before I could work out what to say as big sister, so I folded my arms and looked at him for an explanation.

'It's harmless . . .'

'She's your cousin.'

'Chill-ax sister, we're just messing!' Taj laughed, falling on to my bed to leaf through my wedding diary. 'Boy, you're in hyper-Bridezilla mode.'

'Taj.' I waited until he sat up and looked at me. 'She's our cousin, would you let some bloke mess around with her?'

'No, I'd proper smack them up,' he retorted angrily. 'Listen, Pana and I, we're just . . . we're just on a level, you know, having laughs.'

'So why the hushed, hidden conversations?'

'Listen, just cuz you're getting married it don't turn you into some big woman who can tell me what to do,' Taj said, getting up to leave.

'Maybe Kala should be the one telling you what to do.'

'Don't say anything to Kala!' Taj begged, suddenly on the back foot.

'She's a good girl, Taj, don't ruin her future by being selfish . . .'

'We're just joking.'

'You've never had hushed, hidden, joking chats with me . . .'

'Urrghh! You're my sister!' Taj threw back with a disgusted look.

'Well, she's certainly not your wife.'

'Hold on, I'm a free and single bachelor and I'm enjoying that, thank you very much!'

'Well, if she's not your sister and she's not your wife, then what is she?' I asked, watching Taj work out the dimensions in his head.

'A good friend,' he told me with a satisfied smile.

'Does Pana know that she's just a *friend*?'

His smile didn't last very long.

'She's innocent, Taj, don't play with her.'

'He won't have to.' Turning at the quiet comment, we froze as we found Pana standing at the entrance to my room. Her big brown eyes were filled with tears and before we could speak she dashed off.

'Pana!' Taj called out, racing after her. Cursing, I followed Taj to the bathroom where he quietly knocked on the door, asking Pana to open it.

'Leave her to me,' I told him, forcing him away from the door. I leaned against the door and heard muffled sobs. When she had quietend down, I knocked gently. 'Pana, it's Maya, let me in, sweetie.'

'Maya? What's going on?' Kala asked, emerging from the room she was sharing with Amma. Taj turned to me, eyes wide open and ready to faint. I waited until Taj silently pleaded with me to help. 'Maya?' When Taj looked like he was about to collapse, I turned to Kala and encouraged her back to bed.

'One of the girls ate something dodgy, Kala, I'm just sorting it out,' I explained before firmly closing the door behind her.

'I promise to stay away,' Taj promised and when I nodded he took the stairs down. Returning to the bathroom, I knocked again and waited until I heard the lock turn. Slipping into the bathroom, I locked the door behind me and looked at my red-eyed, tearful cousin. I sat on the edge of the bath next to her and put an arm around her shoulder.

'He's an idiot,' I said, as she wiped her nose on the back of her sleeve.

'I'm the idiot,' she mumbled, leaning against me. 'I'm such an idiot . . .'

'No, you're my pretty, innocent cousin and he wouldn't have been interested in you if you were an idiot,' I corrected as she looked up confused. I nodded but she didn't understand. 'Our men don't go after seconds, Pana. That's why you've got to stay one step ahead of them . . .'

'Is that what you did with Jhanghir *bhai*?' she asked, and I hesitated, remembering how I had raced after him and asked him to marry me.

'Kinda,' I lied, but felt it was merited in this instance. 'Listen, Pana, treat him like dirt for the next few weeks, actually treat him like he's invisible and find some other man to preoccupy yourself with.'

'Another man!' she breathed out, outraged by my immodest advice.

'Well, you can pretend that he doesn't exist. I tell you what, I'll send you random anonymous texts for you to giggle over, trust me, he won't know what's hit him.'

Slowly Pana smiled and then giggled at the plan.

'I didn't mean to mess around,' she guiltily, her smile gone.

'I know you didn't, sweetie,' I said with a sad smile at the pain she was feeling.

'I've got to toughen up,' Pana whispered.

I didn't believe a word and hugged her when she burst into tears.

Anyone who knows anything about Asian weddings will tell you that it's all about the food. Yup, it's not the bride, however lovely or not she may be, nor is it about the gorgeous décor that intrinsically tries to be different but ends up looking like every other wedding you've attended. No, with Asian weddings it's all about the food. We've moved on from the days of school hall weddings where irritated waiters hired from your uncle's restaurant would dish out oily lamb bhouna and vegetable curry on a paper plate like sloppy seconds, with no thought for sophisticated service. No, we as a community had moved on a long way.

Such was the importance of the food at weddings that we devoted an evening to putting together a 'menu' for the wedding courtesy of the in-house caterers at Iver House. Normally, the taster evening was designed for the prospective bride and groom along with two members of each respective family to try a combination of starters, mains, daals, rice, breads and chutneys, and, of course, not forgetting dessert, to decide on the final selection of fifteen odd dishes that would comprise any good wedding menu. Now I say normally, because in preparation for it, seven members of my family insisted on coming along to determine my all-important menu and appeared not in the slightest bit concerned about grabbing a free meal at the same time.

Inevitably we were running behind schedule and I waited in the hallway holding my wedding folder against me.

'We're going to miss the starters!' Taj muttered, pulling on his Adidas before going to his Audi A3. 'Tell them to get a move on, I'm hungry.'

'It's a food tasting evening, not a wedding!' I reminded him before calling up to my parents who insisted that they had to make an effort for their meal out. 'Taj is hungry!' I added, hoping the guilt mothers felt at hearing that their child was hungry would kick in.

'Hurry up! My *bhetha* is hungry, why must you take so much time getting ready!' Amma asked two minutes later, leading Baba down the stairs.

'I take time . . . me, I just put on a shirt and a tie . . .'

'. . . but you insist that the tie must match the colour of my *sari*, why still, after forty years of marriage? Everyone knows we're married. Now my baby child is hungry!'

At the front door, Amma picked out the shoes Baba

needed to wear, after which Baba held Amma's hand to steady her as she slipped on her kitten heels. They had been married for forty years, and during much of that time they struggled to make ends meet, but they were truly devoted to each other. My eyes blurred with tears at the thought that my marriage would take me far from their love. 'Maya, everyone's waiting, why are you dithering?'

Normally, I'd have protested like a petulant child that it wasn't my fault and that in fact they had kept us waiting, but I couldn't. Instead, I smiled. Amma read my expression in a millisecond and teared up too, before turning away.

'Always late, my whole life we've never been on time for anything. I'll be surprised if there's any food left by the time we arrive,' she said. Following my parents out to Taj's car, we jumped in and followed Samir *bhai*'s bullet-grey Mercedes CLS for the forty-minute drive to Iver House.

'Yeah?' Samir *bhai* answered as I called him and put him on speaker phone.

'So, I've got a provisional menu ready for . . .' Realising that I couldn't compete against Dad's favourite Lata Mangeshkar on Taj's music system, I patted his shoulder and indicated for him to turn the volume down. 'I've got a provisional menu . . .'

'Provisional, hah! Don't make me laugh! That's why we're going to decide the menu tonight!' Chachijhi piped in on the call.

'But there're over thirty starters and fifty main dishes to choose from . . .'

'That's what I call a free meal!' Taj joked as Samir *bhai* happily agreed. 'Fifty dishes for free.'

'We're not going for a free meal!' I reminded him, knowing that I had long lost that debate with the men of my family. 'OK, so I was thinking we go for something different . . .'

'Different?' Taj threw back as if it was the most offensive word in the English dictionary.

'Why different?' Amma asked in confusion.

'Different isn't good,' Samir *bhai* added.

'It's Maya, innit?' Taj continued. 'She has to be different.'

'I don't want the same line-up, you know, I want something a little distinct, more sophisticated . . .'

'Sophisticated?' Taj repeated, making everything I said sound reprehensible. 'We're talking food here, proper food.'

'What's wrong with having a menu that's distinctive and different?'

'We're talking about a man's belly here and filling it with proper food,' Taj pointed out. 'If something works, like chicken tikka or a succulent lamb bhouna, then why mess with a formula that works?'

'Because everyone has chicken tikka and lamb bhouna!' retorted with a frown.

'Listen, Maya, if you serve the Asian guests with haute cuisine Bengali food—'

'It's not about having a Michelin-starred menu . . .'

'Who's Michelin? Why is Michelin coming to Maya's wedding to cook?' Amma asked Baba, who turned the volume up further to lose himself in the world of Lata Mangheskar's sweet voice.

'Michelin isn't coming the wedding,' I muttered, leaning between the front seats to turn the volume down.

'People will talk, if the food cooked by this Michelin man is Western, they'll be saying my daughter doesn't know the difference between a chicken tikka and a chicken nugget, do something!' Amma told Baba as I fell back into my seat in frustration.

'We can get a good proper Bengali *bhaisaab* to cook some good food,' Chachijhi suggested.

'At least hear my menu out,' I insisted. When I got the silence I wanted, I looked down at my menu to read out the items.

'Starters will include Hariyali chicken, reshmi kebab, malai tikka with aloo tikki and papri chaat aloo.' The silence that followed my suggestion made me frown. 'Mains will consist of Butter Chicken, Keema Kofta, bhindhi Masaala, and saag paneer.'

'Nah, don't know any of those, and don't like them,' Taj declared.

'What's Hariyali chicken?' Pana piped up on Samir *bhai*'s phone.

'Pana's coming?' Taj breathed, looking back at me in shock.

'Focus on the road!' Amma called out as we swerved to avoid a car in the next lane.

'You all right?' Samir *bhai* asked as Amma prayed in relief. Assuring him we were all OK, I asked them what they thought about my menu.

'It's different,' Samir *bhai* confirmed, although his lack of enthusiasm told me everything I needed to know.

'Baba?' Turning to the man who made everything right, I looked to him for support.

'I like what I know, Maya. You may look down on chicken tikka, lamb chops—'

'Lamb chops, yeah, that sounds good!' Taj shouted in appreciation.

'. . . there's nothing wrong with old traditions, that's why they last the test of time,' Baba finished as I snapped my folder shut and stared out of the window.

'Uh-oh . . . she's going to get into a mood because she's not getting what she wants.'

'I'm not in a mood.'

'I like the sound of Hariyali chicken,' Pana said in a weak sign of support.

'You don't even know what it is,' Taj threw back with a laugh as we drove along the long tree-lined pebbled drive to Iver House.

'At least I'm cultured enough to try something new, something different.'

'What's that supposed to mean?' Taj demanded, reading the subtle inference that was lost on everyone but me. Despite myself, I smiled as Taj parked next to Samir *bhai*. We left the car and headed for the manor house.

'It means she's bored with the typical and ready to try something new,' I explained to Taj, who looked at Pana, who had obviously spent all day turning herself into a stunning version of her usual dowdy self. 'I'm going to have to keep an eye on this one,' Chachijhi told Amma, pointing to the stunning Pana. 'Otherwise your sister will never forgive us if, God forbid, some wayward ill-intentioned young buck tried to charm her away from us.' Taj was silenced and I bit my bottom lip. With a quick wink at Pana, we followed Baba and Samir *bhai* into the luxurious venue.

'Maya!' Spotting Seema at a large round table with her father, aka Rugman, and Zain, I froze. My family turned to me for an explanation but I was stunned at having to face Zain for the first time since Bangladesh. 'Jhanghir asked us to help you this evening. He feels ever so bad about leaving you to make all the decisions.'

'Isn't Jhanghir the most considerate man?' Chachijhi reminded everyone, with a disapproving glare in my direction to bring me to my senses. I watched as everyone rushed to join them and I stood frozen by Zain.

'Maya, you OK?' Nodding, I couldn't meet Baba's

concerned look, so I walked around large tables filled with couples-to-be and their families making equally important decisions about their wedding menu.

'Maya!' Unclejhi called out, patting my back excitedly. 'Isn't she a beauty?' he asked everyone before patting the seat next to him. I looked to Baba who quickly took a seat next to Amma, and then to Taj, who tried to sit next to Pana, who instead sat in between Zain and Chachijhi. Realising that no one was prepared to build bridges with Seema's father, who had turned Jhanghir's father against us, I took the seat reluctantly. My family's reaction was missed on Seema and she chose her expression very carefully.

'How are you, Uncle and Aunty?' She asked my parents, who looked at her and mirrored her exact expression.

'Fine, we're so busy with the preparations for the wedding, but one mustn't complain,' Amma returned in her posh Bengali accent. 'The *henna* is next week . . .'

'And look at the radiant bride-to-be!' Unclejhi chimed in, having lost none of his effeminate qualities since Hamza had tried to rip his hairpiece from his head. 'You must have lost what . . . two stone since then?' My smile dropped at his comment. Turning to Unclejhi, I wondered how fat he thought I had been. 'Not that it matters, she's positively glowing, isn't she? Isn't she?' he asked, making everyone nod at his insistence.

'She gets it from her mother,' Baba said, without thinking. We all stopped at the compliment, including Amma, and he looked embarrassed. Though they were devoted to each other, it was a rare moment for Baba to compliment Amma and I wondered if Amma's renewed interest in dancing had anything to do with it.

'If I look half as good as my mum, I've got a good future ahead of me,' I covered for Baba, who coughed uncomfortably.

'Wonderful! Just wonderful!' Unclejhi muttered with muted enthusiasm, looking at my plump, lovely mother before looking back at me. And then he went on to talk about Jhanghir's family. My parents and family maintained a respectful silence as Unclejhi updated everyone as to how well Jhanghir's father's business was doing, explaining that it was due to his good family friends in Abu Dhabi and fostering relations with people who mattered. No one commented on the obvious fact that Jhanghir's father was absent, but then my family were too considerate to point out that it was insulting to be 'deemed' not important enough to 'foster' relations with. As Unclejhi and Seema dominated the conversation, I caught Pana's attempts to strike up conversation with Zain whilst ignoring Taj. Zain accommodated her and then he looked at me. Something had changed; he looked almost apologetic and I narrowed my eyes when he looked away. It didn't matter that Chachijhi had tensed up at our interaction; my instincts told me something deeper, darker was brewing.

'The starters are here!' Samir *bhai* declared with a loud clap of his hands, happy to have some distraction from Unclejhi's diatribe about the importance of ambition and accomplishments. At Samir *bhai's* announcement, smartly dressed waiters arrived with huge platters of chicken, meat and vegetables starters. The assortment was so vast and colourful, that no one knew where to start.

'Bhai?' Baba offered Unclejhi in the true spirit of hospitality and the first sign of fostering relations. And with that, we started. All too happily, we sampled small bites of as much as we could manage, and debated what worked and what didn't. I made notes of the dishes that everyone devoured and added to the list as everyone had their fill. Well, everyone except Taj and Samir *bhai* who appeared to have bottomless bellies. I smiled uncomfortably as Seema and Unclejhi watched them eat until dishes sat empty on the vast table.

'So, the spicy lamb chops were—'

'. . . out of this world,' Taj finished as he cleaned up his plate, sat back and patted his belly. 'That was good,' he said with the smile of a satisfied man.

'Which one exactly?' Seema asked in a barbed dig at his appetite. 'My, it looks like you haven't eaten Indian food for a long time.'

'My brother owns a restaurant and a takeaway,' Taj reminded her without a smile.

'Yes, precisely,' she finished, clearing her throat. Her dig was understood by all, but to rise to it, would give her the ammunition to stir Jhanghir's father's wrath even further. Yet the insult dealt to my family was unbearable. 'Excuse me, I must go and wash the smell of spices from my hands. I find it reminds me of villagers who can't move on with the times.'

Unclejhi chuckled at Seema's comment, watching her leave the table.

'She has such a way with words!' he chuckled with such pride. The waiters appeared to take away the dishes and plates before the host announced a ten-minute break until the mains were to be served. 'So, Maya, have you packed for your new life in Amreeka?'

'Why should she pack now? She has many weeks to go before she needs to think about that,' Amma reminded him as if thinking about it was unbearable.

'But, the wedding's is a mere—'

'Yes, yes, and there's too much to do right now. She can pack any time, right, Maya?' She looked at me for support, and I read the pain in her eyes, the pain of a mother losing another daughter to marriage.

'It takes five minutes; I'm not even thinking about it,'

I said, seeing the relief in her eyes before she turned back to Unclejhi with a triumphant smile. Yes, for now she still had her daughter.

Excusing myself, I headed to the ladies to seek out Seema. Entering, the ornate mahogany and marble washroom with huge mirrors and armchairs, I found Seema washing her hands.

'When are you going to stop belittling my family?' I asked when she stopped to look at me in the mirror.

'Not until it stops amusing me,' she returned with half a smile.

'Why are you such a bitch?'

Seema slowly dried her hands with a small hand towel, before turning to face me with narrowed eyes.

'Jhanghir deserves better,' she told me. I watched her long enough to smile.

'You're jealous,' I realised. My suspicions were confirmed when her smiled disappeared. 'You're jealous of what we have, that Jhanghir's willing to turn his back on everything to marry me.'

'Don't be so ridiculous!' And yet with every word I spoke, I knew it to be true.

'You are, aren't you?' Seema looked like she was about to explode at my words and headed for the door. 'But why would you be jealous? His family adore you, you're rich, a successful businesswoman, you're stunning, and your husband must—' And then I stopped. In all the time I had known and seen Seema, she had always been without her husband.

'You know nothing about my husband and our marriage,' Seema defended too quickly. She corrected her *dupatta* over her shoulder and then turned around to leave.

'Are you happy?'

The question made her stop at the door. Slowly, she

turned around and walked back to me.

'Very,' she returned without hesitation and yet confirming the contrary.

'You're not, are you?' My question made her laugh.

'You villagers are so quaint!' The insult meant nothing because I knew she was lashing out. 'You think marriage is all about *love*, and *being happy*, like some silly Indian movie where there's a happy ever after. Well, it's not, it's about making sacrifices for a better life, to get to a better status . . .'

'Status? You married Jhanghir's brother for status?'

'My in-laws are one of the wealthiest families in South Asia, one of the most well-connected and influential families in the region; it wasn't a hard choice to make.'

'Choice?' The comment piqued my curiosity.

'Stop digging, Maya, you don't want to go there.'

I met her square on and smiled. 'Choice?' I pushed.

'Fine,' Seema returned, taking a seat in one of the armchairs, crossing her legs and smiling. We watched each other, both aware we were on unchartered territory and that there'd be no going back from this point. And yet, I had to know.

'Choice, Seema? Who was the lamb you sacrificed to marry Jhanghir's brother?'

'Zain.' It was then that I realised that she had always had the upper hand.

'Zain,' I whispered, steadying myself against the marble counter. It made sense; they were never without each other. Only when Jhanghir instructed Zain did he venture out without her. And then the memory of our closeness flashed by and slowly I looked up to meet Seema's stare. 'You know,' I whispered. She smiled.

'What are you guys doing!' Pana asked, bursting into the ladies. 'The mains are being served,' she announced, beckoning us to follow her.

'Why don't you run along and tell Maya's brothers to save us some?' Seema instructed. Pana glared at her and only when I nodded did she leave reluctantly. I looked back at Seema who stood up and corrected her designer *shalwaar kameez*.

'I know, Maya,' Seema confirmed, coming to stand very close in front of me. 'Who do you think put him up to it?'

'You put him up to it, the flirting, the teasing . . .' I stopped at her soft chuckle. Seema caught my wrist before my hand could connect to her cheek.

'Be very careful, Maya. How do you think Jhanghir would feel if, say, I ran back to him, beside myself with the knowledge that his fiancée had been caught cheating on him with his beloved cousin?'

'You wouldn't?' I breathed, wrenching my arm away.

'After all this, you doubt what I'm capable of?' Seema laughed slowly. 'How humiliated would your family be if they knew . . .'

'Leave them out of this . . . they've done nothing to deserve this.'

'Oh, I know,' she agreed. 'But you have.'

I stared at her and frowned. 'Why?'

'Because you don't belong in the Khan family . . .'

'That's not your choice.'

'Oh yes it is,' she corrected without the slightest bit of humour. 'You haven't sacrificed anything to get here, you haven't had to give up the one thing most important to you for a life—'

'Don't punish me for the decision you made . . .'

'I'm not, I'm punishing you for yours. Jhanghir deserves better,' Seema told me. 'I want you to walk away from Jhanghir, on your wedding day, put it down to a change of mind, and I give you my word, the truth about your little, how should I say it, "dalliance", won't ever come out.'

'No,' I whispered, shaking my head, feeling as if my world was falling apart around me.

'No . . . as in you don't want to protect your family's reputation, or no, as in you won't walk away?' Seema had me at my weakest with a choice between losing my family and losing Jhanghir. 'Why don't you let me know what you decide?' I didn't see Seema leave, or notice the women who used the washroom around me. The choice reverberated in my mind until I lost track of how long I stood there.

'Maya?' Looking up at Amma's call, I stared at her as if I had seen her for the first time in a very long time. 'Maya, did Seema say something to you?' she asked, walking into the ladies. Shaking my head, I did everything I could to stop the tears from appearing. 'What were you talking about?'

'We were talking about the food, what she liked and, as usual, she wants everything as English as possible!' I laughed, seeing her face relax with a soft smile.

'*Hauhah*, let's go see how she convinces your *baba* of this.'

I returned to the table, filled with umpteen bowls of curries, bhajis, bhounas of every style, colour and flavour.

'You're missing out, sis!' Taj muttered in between bites as Pana ladled more bhouna on his plate. The gesture didn't go unnoticed, but I looked at Zain, who turned to the smiling Seema.

'Isn't this oh so . . . traditional!' Seema derided, tearing up tiny bits of roti to eat.

'At Seema's wedding, we imported three chefs from India – you know, the ones who run Al Raja's in Dubai . . .'

'Yes, know it well!' Samir *bhai* replied in between bites. 'I didn't rate the restaurant or the food very well.'

'We're talking about Al Raja's on Jumeirah Road, Dubai . . .'

'Yes, I know exactly the one you're talking about,' Samir *bhai* told Seema. 'We're setting up a medical practice out there, we know Dubai very well.'

'You're expanding to Dubai?' Suddenly, Unclejhi and Seema appeared to have more time for my family beyond making small talk. I looked to Zain, more disappointed by him than angry. He had lost his love to Jhanghir's brother and yet he had never found the strength to cut ties, instead opting to live through Seema as and when she dictated.

'Maya, try the dishes.'

Turning to Chachijhi, I smiled as she piled my plate with several dishes. She was doing her best to protect me and I loved her the more for it, yet I knew she couldn't protect me from Seema's intentions. I watched Pana flirt with Zain until he looked at me. It was the first time I recognised sheer sadness in this most handsome of men, a deep-seated sadness. One that drove him to do anything that was asked of him by the woman he couldn't have.

'Maya,' Baba's call made me close my eyes.

'Yes, Baba?' I returned, unable to meet his look.

'I like this lamb bhouna dish.' His plate, piled high with the dishes I had suggested in the car had a small serving of lamb bhouna in the middle. He had accommodated my every wish.

'Then we'll have it,' I stated, as the fear of never making it to my wedding made me tear up. 'Taj, what are your favourites?' I asked, looking away, but never meeting anyone's eyes directly.

'Ah, sis, you've got to go with the lamb chops, and chilli paneer for the starters,' he said, beaming at being given the chance to contribute to the decision.

'The chicken tikka is awesome here, seriously; they do it tender and the spices are mouth-watering,' Samir *bhai* suggested, ending his conversation with Unclejhi who was probing the idea of investing in the family medical practice. 'And don't forget to include your papri aloo chaat . . . you wanted that, and it is different to have in a Bengali wedding but, more importantly, it is really, really good.'

I noted down the ideas suggested, along with the choice of spicy chicken jalfrezi, Baba's lamb bhouna, saag paneer, and aloo muttar. I selected jasmine rice, naan, and roti, with kheer and mango kulfi as the dessert. By the time we had finished, I had myself a perfect traditional and very popular menu for my wedding.

'Our girlie chat was delightful!' Seema chimed as we stood at the exit ready to make our respective journeys home. 'I look forward to the next one, maybe at your *henna*?' She gave me an awkward hug before doing the same to Amma, Chachijhi and Pana.

'We should talk more,' Unclejhi said to Samir *bhai* as they shook hands. 'Really, I think you have a brilliant business plan. I think we should talk about giving you financial backing to really make it world class,' he said, patting his hairpiece to ensure that it was in place. He shook hands with Baba and Taj and then looked at me.

'Bhetha, make your parents happy, soon you'll be leaving them,' he reminded me, patting my cheek before taking his leave. We headed for our cars. Everyone was pleased with the choices made. They talked and laughed about which item worked and which didn't, and I left them to it. My mind was filled with the anger, fear, shock and a million other emotions caused by Seema's ultimatum. She was asking me to walk out on my wedding day, to protect Jhanghir and my family from the knowledge of my indiscretion. To continue with my wedding, would ruin both my marriage and my family's reputation and would leave me with a divorce a few moments into my marriage.

'Maya.' Amma reached out to take my hand as everyone continued debating the menu. 'Whatever she said, it doesn't mean a thing. We're a good family, a decent family, with not one jot of scandal, so don't let her try and make you believe we're inferior in any way.' I nodded, but Amma's words served only to make the decision harder. My attempt at tough talking had failed. The tension I felt, well, it was as unbearable as one could imagine.

Unmasking the truth unravels everything

In the days that followed, I felt like a person possessed. The realisation of the inevitable made me bend over backwards to accommodate Jhanghir's every request and my family's every wish. Sleep evaded me, so I had more than enough time to do as asked. Everyone's happiness was my only desire because I knew it would be short lived. I obsessed over every wedding detail and every minutia of the upcoming events until I expected nothing but total perfection from anyone involved. I snapped at Ayesha for forgetting the timing for my *henna* arrival, I shouted at Pana for confusing the dance routine sequence and I criticised Amma for her choice of wedding gold, comparing her to the villagers who thought that big was best. The pain in her eyes only made me focus harder, if only to forget why I wanted the best for everyone around me.

'Maya.' Turning at Amma's call, I stopped scrubbing the kitchen floor. 'What are you doing?' Pushing my hair back from my face, I looked at her frowning.

'I'm cleaning. The mop doesn't get the grime off the floor . . .'

'It's three o'clock in the morning, why are you cleaning at this time of night?'

'I can't sleep, and we've got so many people coming for the *henna* tomorrow.'

'Stop.' Amma came to sit on the floor beside me.

'Amma, please go back to bed, I can't sleep, I just need to—'

'To what, exhaust yourself until you collapse?' Amma took the scrubber out of my hands and put it down before taking my hands.

'Amma . . .' I tried to pull my hands away, but she held firm.

'Humour me,' she said. Amma had never been good at mother-daughter talks, preferring to take on the role of admonishing mother. 'You're letting the wedding stresses take you over.'

'No, I'm not . . .'

'I asked you to humour me.' Stopping at her request, I crossed my legs and looked at her square on.

'If you carry on the way you are doing, you will look back and regret not enjoying the last few days with us.'

I snorted at the comment.

'If I don't stay on top of things, who is going to do them? Like today, I needed Yasmin to confirm that the cake will get to the hall before everyone arrives and she tells me she was going to get changed and arrive with the family . . . I had to point out to her that the cake had to be set up before we got to the hall.'

'Did you have to make her feel stupid?'

'But surely she wouldn't want someone to assemble her wedding cake in front of six hundred guests at her wedding!' I pointed out as Amma shook her head.

'Listen, none of us are professionals and we're all doing the best we can.' When I shook my head, she waited until I looked back at her. 'You're worse than

Leila was when she was getting married . . .'

'She was a bridezilla, I'm nowhere near as bad as her . . .'

'You're the prototype bridezilla; how many times did you get Pana and her sisters to practise their dance routine? How many times did you get Ayesha to work through the itinerary of the wedding and the *henna*? And poor Tanya, how many more times are you going to get her to go over the seating plans?' With each example, I had less to argue with. 'Everyone's walking on egg-shells around you, thinking that you're stressed with all this change and that it's your last few weeks, and they don't want to upset you, but they're not enjoying it, Maya.' Tears stung my eyes. Realising how horrid and temperamental I had been, I looked down. 'You're not eating, you're not sleeping, you hardly talk to anyone. All you do is work and you're wasting away,' Amma whispered before looking down at my hands, which she was clasping.

'I remember these very hands when they were teeny tiny, clenched tightly shut from the moment you were born. You didn't cry until the doctor smacked your bottom and then you screamed to high heaven.'

'All babies do that, Amma . . .'

'No they don't; most cry the moment cold air touches them, but not you. You waited for the first blow and then you cried.' Amma nodded at the memory, before looking me straight in the eye. 'Nothing's changed since, Maya. You keep things locked inside of you, you hold on to them so tightly that no one knows how to get you to open up. Which blow are you waiting for to make you open up?' Amma and I rarely talked about things that mattered, but her levels of perception were scarily accurate. I looked at her and wondered if, for the first in my life, I could open up and confide in her. She wanted me to, but I thought of her happiness at my upcoming marriage, her refound joy of old Indian classics with Baba and, above all, her precious pride in having a scandal-free family. Lowering my gaze, I couldn't bring myself to open up and ruin her happiness.

'Try and give us good memories of this time.' I nodded at Amma's request. She patted my hand and I knew she was disappointed with my decision to stay quiet. Amma took a deep breath and stood up.

'There's not an inch of this house that hasn't been cleaned, is there?' I shook my head at her question and looked at the hand she held out. 'Come, lay down with your old mother.' Holding back tears, I took my mother's hand and followed her to my room. Amma cuddled up and promptly fell asleep. I, on the other hand, knew time was running out. Sleep evaded me like the peace of mind I had once had, so I lay in bed staring up at the ceiling, counting down to the inevitable.

I was up with the early birds, making breakfast for everyone. A pile of pancakes smothered in honey and cream, croissants and toast greeted my family who, one by one, walked into the kitchen. Each stopped, looking at me wearily before nervously taking a seat at the breakfast table.

'Relax, I know I've been a psycho,' I said, holding a big mug of coffee, despite knowing it was the last thing I needed after having my teeth whitened. 'This is my way of saying I'm sorry and I'd really, really like everyone to have a good time tonight.' Jana started the whooping and, before I knew it, everyone started chanting: 'I gotta a feeling.'

Taj led all my cousins dancing and prancing around the kitchen. I laughed and clapped along, bumping hips with Jana as we swayed arm in arm.

'What is going on?' Baba asked, walking into the kitchen stern faced with Amma following behind.

'N . . . nothing,' Pana stuttered, sitting down quickly with all of her sisters.

'Bhai, show them how it's done,' Kala said as she started singing with Amma whilst Baba copied Amithab's famous dance moves in the middle of the dance floor. After the initial shock, we all burst out laughing and whooped and clapped. Baba pulled a reluctant Amma to the centre and danced around her. Jana pushed me amongst my cousins and, without any encouragement, they all danced around me.

'What an earth is going on today? Elders, children, are there no boundaries left these days?' Chachijhi asked, walking into the kitchen whilst taking her jacket off. Before she could finish Taj dragged her amongst us. In spite of her protests, he hugged her close until she couldn't protest any more. There wasn't an inch to spare in the kitchen but it didn't matter, for that moment it was our arena and we danced to our hearts' content.

Mid-afternoon our house officially turned into a mad-house. Still in my pyjamas, I coordinated the marquee suppliers, the decorators and my cousins, who helped with the layout of cushions, lanterns and my golden swing chair with two seats on either side. I instructed a semicircle be cleared in front of the swing chair and then showed Taj where his friend was to set up the sound system in the back corner of the marquee. Tariq was shown where the buffet-style large silver serving platters were to go for the evening meal and then I outlined to Ayesha the itinerary with strict instructions that after nine-thirty p.m. she was responsible for getting all the men into the house so that the women could party freely.

'What are you doing?' Amma asked, finding me in the

kitchen helping Kala to make two bucket-sized bowls of
salad. Mana raced in, dressed only in a petticoat and
blouse and without a *sari* to grab a bottle of water before
racing out again.

'I'm helping . . .'

'I can see you're helping, but why aren't you getting
ready?' she demanded, taking the knife from me.

'It's too busy, have you been upstairs? It's like the
back stage scenes of a beauty contest.'

'Get yourself ready, Maya Malik!' she ordered. With
no room to argue, I looked outside and then was
frogmarched out of the kitchen. 'Upstairs,' she ordered
before closing the kitchen door firmly behind me.

'What are you doing?' Finding Hamza in the living
room watching football with Baba, I walked in and
flopped down beside him.

'Maya,' Baba muttered, unable to tear his gaze away
from the match. 'Aren't you getting ready?'

'There's loads of time,' I returned, hugging Hamza to
me. 'What are you wearing?'

'Foopi, are you leaving us?' Stopping at my nephew's
question I looked down at him. 'Who told you that?' I
asked as he held my hands.

'Mummy said you're getting married and that means
you're going to go and live with your friend for ever and
ever.'

Shaking my head, I swallowed the lump in my throat
and smiled.

'Don't be silly,' I whispered. 'I'm not leaving you.'
Pulling him into a hug, I felt my heart shatter all over
again.

'Maya.' Looking up over Hamza, I found Amma with
her hands on her hips.

'I was going upstairs . . .'

'Now!' Without another thought, I took the stairs up,

walked through the cloud of hairspray that hovered in the hallway, and passed my cousins who rushed around in different states of readiness to enter my room. Hanna was turning Jana's hair into a 1960s Audrey Hepburn *Breakfast at Tiffany's* hairdo whilst Pana finished off Zara's make-up. Spotting the iPad hanging out of Ayesha's bag, I picked it up and stepped into the toilet. Logging in, I turned in to Skype and dialled up Jhanghir.

'Jhanghir,' I greeted when he accepted my video call.

'Maya, are you in the toilet?' Smiling at the screen, I screwed my nose up and nodded.

'We're not married yet and you're losing all your mystique already . . .'

'I'm not doing anything, it's just the only place in the house that doesn't have half a billion people in it,' I told him, touching his cheek on the screen. 'It's my *henna* tonight.'

'I know, and I wish I could be there.' I nodded at his comment and wondered if I should tell him about Zain. 'You look sad, Maya, everything OK over there?' Nodding at his question, I looked at him. He felt so close and yet, yet he wasn't.

'You sure this is the right thing?' I asked with a nervous laugh.

'You sound like you're having second thoughts,' Jhanghir said without a smile.

'Second, third and maybe even fourth thoughts,' I teased, but he refused to smile.

'Maya?' I stopped messing with him and closed my eyes.

'I'm so tired, Jhanghir, I just . . .' I didn't know what to say to him. All this small talk meant nothing when I knew he deserved to know the truth. 'I'm tired.'

'Today's your *henna*, the pre-wedding party for the wedding you've spent years craving for and all you can say is that you're tired.' I know it sounded pathetic, but it was the truth and I felt terrible for telling Jhanghir.

'I'm sorry, I just needed to see you, you know, make it feel real . . .'

'You're tired, you're arranging everything, but it doesn't feel real, Maya; you want to tell me what's wrong?' Shaking my head, I smiled.

'Maya! What are you doing in there?' Jana demanded, knocking on the toilet door noisily. 'I know it's your *henna* tonight, but don't tell me it's given you diarrhoea.'

'Do you have diarrhoea?' Jhanghir asked in confusion.

'Is Jhanghir in the toilet with you?' Jana asked, loud enough for all the girls to rush to the toilet.

'Maya?' Jhanghir asked at the same time as Jana.

'No, I don't and no, Jhanghir isn't in here,' I returned loudly, pushing the flush as I ended the Skype call. Slipping the iPad under my pyjama top, I opened the door to find a gaggle of girls waiting for me. They all looked behind me, half expecting to find Jhanghir in there with me. Without a word, they parted to let me pass. I took the stairs down with half a smile. As the world went *henna* crazy, I found Baba watching the football alone. I snuggled up on the couch next to him. My head hurt, my body ached and that dark, anxious feeling left me drained. When it was half time, Baba looked down at me.

'Just five minutes,' I begged, relaxing when he put an arm around me. Sometime later I heard Amma's piercing call, but with one comment from Baba I was left alone. With half a smile, I closed my eyes and let sleep take me over.

'Maya, Maya.' At Ayesha's quiet call, I mumbled for her to leave me alone. 'Maya, wake up. Your guests are arriving.' Snapping my eyes open, I looked at Ayesha. 'What time is it?'

'It's six . . .'

'Six p.m.!' I shouted, sitting upright. 'Why didn't anyone wake me?'

'No one dared tell Baba it was time for you to wake up,' she whispered, looking over her shoulder to see if Baba had entered the room. 'This is the first time he's left you to go to the bathroom, so if he walks back in—'

'Ayesha, did you wake my Maya up?' Finding Baba at the door, I stood up and walked over to hug him.

'I have to get ready.' He cupped my cheeks and rubbed his nose against mine until I giggled like a girl. 'Thank you, Baba,' I whispered as Ayesha sneaked out behind us. Without a word, I raced upstairs and found Jana, Leila, and Pana waiting for me. In an instant, I was pushed into the shower, dragged out of it, creamed, clothed and then put in front of the mirror. Pana slipped on my sunset-gold antique *choories*, as Jana deftly applied my make-up and Leila blow-dried my hair into a beehive with a mass of drooping ringlets.

'We're ready,' Jana announced, sitting on the bed to massage her tummy.

'You're not ready.' Turning at Amma's call, I frowned and stopped when I saw her hold my sun-kissed orange chiffon veil. She stepped forward and kissed me on my cheek before pinning it into place so that it covered most of my face. 'Now you're ready,' she announced. Before she could well up, I hugged her tightly. Jana joined in, followed by Leila and Pana.

'You're squashing my baby!' Jana announced, making us all laugh tearfully.

'We're ready,' I breathed, causing Jana to lean out of my bedroom window to yell down to Taj that I was about to make my entrance. It wasn't quite the refined entrance I wanted to make, but I didn't have time to direct her so, with a quick prayer, we headed for the marquee one by one.

'The marquee looks amazing! It's like something out of Arabian nights,' Hanna told me as we waited in the kitchen with all my sisters and cousins. Everyone wore the same green *sari* with a red border, and had the same beehive hairstyle with sixties make-up. *Chooris* clinked delightfully, trays decorated with carved fruits and Indian sweets piled high were nervously balanced, and cameras clicked away as we waited for Taj's indication to enter the marquee.

'The speakers have jammed, we need five minutes,' Taj shouted back to Samir *bhai*, who yelled the message back to Ayesha.

'It's packed full of your friends and family, waiting to see you. They're just getting seated,' she interpreted as if I didn't hear the chain of commands coming from the garden.

'Typical! Something had to go wrong, and it had to be the stereo,' I muttered, looking around until it dawned on me. 'We can hook it up to Taj's iPlayer speakers,' I said quickly, putting down my posy bouquet of yellow and red roses embellished with pearl pins.

'What are you doing?' Amma asked, stepping in front of me.

'I'm getting the speakers, so that we can get started . . .'

'No, you're not.'

'Amma, there's a problem . . .'

'And your brothers are dealing with it. Shut up and stand still,' she instructed.

I picked up my posy and did just as she said.

'Does she think she can waltz in there, hoick her *sari* up to her pants and rig the stereo system together?'

Leila's mother-in-law asked, looking at me with disapproval.

'I'd strip off the *sari* first,' I told her with a wide smile that earned me a smack to the back of my head, which made my cousins titter behind their hands.

'Your in-laws are here; I wouldn't be such a smart arse now,' Chachijhi reported as she stepped into the kitchen. 'Seema is here with her parents and several women in full *burqas*. They must be extra-strict Muslims from Jhanghir's mother's side because we can only see their eyes; just their eyes!' she emphasised, tightening her scarf around her head as if it would make her a more observant Muslim.

'They're here! Why?' I demanded, having told Jhanghir that I preferred to have a small, private relaxed *henna* without his family and their dramas if he wasn't going to be attending.

'What kind of girl doesn't want her in-laws at her *henna*?' Leila's mother-in-law asked, nudging Leila, who rolled her eyes at the interference. Amma glared at me to stop me from replying.

'How long are they going to stay?' I asked, tutting when Amma smacked the back of my head again. 'They disapprove of me, so why have they turned up?'

'Be respectful, they'll probably get bored in fifteen minutes and go,' Jana said as she corrected my veil and forced a smile on my face. 'Smile, you promised us all a good night.'

Heeding her words, I took a deep breath and forced a smile. 'I'm going to act like they're not here . . .'

'Oh lord, does she show no respect for her in-laws?'

'Will someone get this women out of my kitchen!' I demanded, pointing to Leila's mother-in-law when the last of my patience had disappeared.

'Maya, she's my mother-in-law!' Leila defended as

the elder covered her mouth in shock.

'Then tell her to say something nice or shut up!' I threw back.

'Shut up?' The offended mother-in-law gasped as Chachijhi and Amma covered their faces in embarrassment.

'Why are you in here?' I continued before turning to Leila. 'Can you ask her to sit in the marquee and find someone else to criticise . . .'

'She's family!' Leila bit out, chasing after the departing woman who made a very big commotion about being the insulted, aggrieved relative.

'Your family, not mine!' I called out behind my cousin. 'While you're out there, can you find out if I need to hoick my *sari* up to fix the stereos?'

'What is wrong with you!' Ayesha asked in despair. 'Everyone can hear you.'

'Well, if someone sorted out the stereos, then maybe we'd all be able to hear something else!' The impatient, inconsiderate streak in my retort shocked me and I covered my mouth, reaching out for a seat.

'She's going to faint!' Chachijhi declared. 'Quick, help her sit down.' Perching on a stool, I let everyone fuss and fan around me.

'I'm a bridezilla,' I whispered, holding Ayesha's hand. 'I'm so sorry. Will you go and apologise to Leila's mother-in-law for me?'

'You won't do a thing,' Chachijhi bit out, grabbing Ayesha's arm. 'That dragon makes my daughter's life a living nightmare; she needed to be brought down a couple of pegs!'

'Will someone sort out the stereo, please?' I asked as Hamza raced into the kitchen.

'It's working, the music is playing!' he announced, eyes wide open with excitement.

'It's working!' everyone announced to me.

'Thank you.' I smiled.

'Well, come on, then!' Amma laughed as everyone lined up two by two to walk me into the marquee. Suddenly, it was my time. Taking a deep breath, I picked up my bouquet and walked to the front of the queue to stand in between Amma and Chachijhi. Hearing my walk-in song 'Laal *Dupatta*' play, I smiled and we started walking. Stepping out of the kitchen and into the garden, we strolled into the marquee. The Arabian nights atmosphere stunned me. The marquee was highlighted with lanterns, low tables, and cushions sprawled everywhere. Our guests were grouped around the low tables, and we greeted those we passed with a smile. Cameras flashed simultaneously around the marquee as we walked to my swinging chaise, where I sat down and looked at the sea of faces beside me. Amma and Baba sat either side of me and my sisters and cousins lined up behind us. Once again, we smiled as guests rushed forward to take pictures.

'Wait for me!' Hamza yelled, racing down the middle of the marquee to jump on to my lap. 'Let's swing, Foopi, this is cool!' he piped up, making everyone laugh. Amma took Hamza from my lap as, one by one, my sisters and cousins put the carved fruit trays and platters of Indian sweets on the table before me. And then, as protocol dictated, one by one each of my guests came to sit beside me to feed me a piece of the sweet or fruit. It felt like it would go on for ever, so when the thirtieth person came up, I asked them to give me a sip of juice instead. When Tariq and Taj came to sit beside me, I stopped them from feeding me and fed them instead. Tariq leaned forward and hugged me. No words were spoken but he held me so tightly, I knew he was beginning to feel the effects of my upcoming departure.

'Tariq,' Amma said quietly. I continued smiling when

I saw him turn away to wipe his eyes. The run-up to weddings did this to the strongest of men and women. It reminded them that change was coming and nobody knew if it would be for the better. I hugged Taj, who laughed and kissed my cheek before standing up to announce the beginning of the entertainment.

With that, Pana, Mana and Zarah raced forward in 1950s sweater tops and full skirts and Mary-Jane shoes. On cue, Dusty Springfield's 'Wishin' and Hopin'' chimed through the marquee to which they danced and play-acted until everyone laughed at their cheesy antics. I blushed at the lyrics and chuckled when Chachijhi winked at me. When the song phased into K3G's 'Yai Ladka Hai Allah', I burst out laughing when Taj, Samir *bhai* and Tariq *bhai* raced on to the dance area to copy Shah Rukh Khan's infamous moves. But it only got better when Leila, Hanna and Yasmin joined them and they competed with the guys to get the better routine. The whole marquee came to life, clapping and cheering them on until the final climax when everyone whooped at the fast, complicated Indian dance. Then P-Diddy's Bad Boys blasted through the speakers and everyone looked confused when the group of four tall, large, completely covered *hijabis* walked to the centre of the dance area. Turning to Ayesha, I indicated for her to stop them from hijacking the evening to turn it into a night of sermons about the wrongs of music and dance. But then they started dancing, cutting some moves that would get respect in RnB clubs in major cities. I covered my mouth when they turned towards me, walked close and then pulled off their *nikabs*. I screamed when I spotted Jhanghir amongst Zain, Ed and Mo. Everyone gasped in shock when they pulled off their *jilbabs*. They were dressed in Punjabi tops over jeans. In an instant everyone jumped to their feet, cheering as they dragged me to the centre of the dance area and moved around me. I laughed and clapped along, cringing with embarrassment, yet loving every moment. I locked eyes with Jhanghir and I'd never felt so happy. When the song came to an end, everyone clapped for what seemed like ages. My family surrounded Jhanghir to shake hands with him and hug him, and I gripped my hands, overjoyed at his arrival. My fiancé was here and I couldn't stop grinning.

'Sit down, Maya,' Amma said before turning to Jhanghir to encourage him to sit next to me.

'Maya.' I stood up for Mrs Khan and hugged her. 'You look stunning, my daughter,' she said calmly before kissing me on my cheeks. I noted the absence of Jhanghir's father, and accepted that he still disapproved of our marriage. I accepted that his approval would take much longer to gain, if at all. In fact, in that moment, it was enough that I had Jhanghir and members of his family who were supporting our upcoming marriage. For now, that was more than enough.

'Thank you.' Jhanghir's mother was as serene and graceful as ever, and I indicated for her to sit next to me.

'That's for you and my son.' Mrs Khan smiled before feeding me a small piece of pistachio barfi. 'Be happy, I'll speak to you both later,' she told us as she fed Jhanghir too. He kissed her on her cheek and hugged her before retaking his seat.

'Maya, Jhanghir, don't you make a beautiful couple?' Seema said with a wide smile. She hugged Jhanghir and air-kissed me on each cheek. I avoided meeting her eyes and forced myself to continue smiling. 'Anything I can do, tell me,' she told Jhanghir before her parents took over and made a show of fussing over the two of us.

'Hey, gorgeous.' This was Jhanghir's greeting when the two of us were finally given a moment. I refused to smile or lift my veil to look at him. 'I see you made it out of the toilet.'

'If your dancing is anything to judge by, I'll be returning to it very soon.'

Jhanghir laughed at my reply and then turned to my sisters who arrived with a platter. Setting it before him, they handed him a mirror. Jhanghir took it and angled it so that he could see my reflection. I refused to smile, even though he winked.

'I don't know, she looks like she's put on weight,' he told everyone. Outraged, I pulled back my veil and looked at him, only to realise he was riling me. Everyone laughed and I quickly pulled the veil down and gave in to smile at his antics. Ayesha handed us both small Egyptian glasses of rose-flavoured milk, which we in turn gave to each other to mark the beginning of a fresh, new, happy beginning. When a round of applause filled the marquee, the music was cranked up and we smiled happily for our blessings.

Before long, the men were herded out of the marquee and back into the house to allow the women complete freedom to dance into the early hours without the need for their *hijabs*. As soon as the marquee shutters were closed, *hijabis* and *jilbabis* got out of their shrouds to appear as modern, stunning, cosmopolitan women. Tanya, Shireen and I hid behind the stereos to disrobe down to our belly-dancing costumes. At my nod, Pana dimmed the lights and put on Beyonce and Shakira's 'Beautiful Liars'. We walked on to the stage and then began the provocative dance. Some gasped at our shocking moves, others touched their cheeks in total disapproval, but before we got to the end of the song we had every woman, young and old, trying to shake their booties and jiggle their bosoms. Throughout it, we took happy picture after happy picture. Laughing and clapping, we danced well into the night as if it would never end.

'Maya, you're wanted outside by the shed,' Ayesha told me, pointing towards the house. Smiling at the thought of seeing Jhanghir, I pulled on a *jilbab*, wrapped it around me over the belly-dancing outfit, and walked out barefoot. Passing by friends and family, I walked over to the shed and stopped when I spotted Zain. Turning around, I started walking back to the marquee.

'Maya . . .'

'Not now.' When Zain grabbed my arm and pulled me around, I gritted my jaw.

Taking his arm I led him to the side of the house where it was dimly lit and without any guests. 'This is my night, stay away from me.'

'I've put it right,' Zain told me. 'Seema, I've put her right.'

'What are you talking about . . .?'

'I talked to her about telling Jhanghir. She's not going to do it.'

'Because she loves you?' I laughed, hating myself for hurting him. 'Stay away from me and my family, I want nothing to do with you or Seema.'

'I understand.'

'No, you don't. We kissed, Zain, and I have to lie to Jhanghir about it for the rest of my life.'

'He doesn't need to find out, we can put this behind us,' Zain assured me.

'Really?' I asked with disbelief. 'Seema won't tell him?' Zain shook his head without hesitation.

'She gave me her word,' he said, as I closed my eyes in relief.

'She needn't have done that.' The rich baritone of

Jhanghir's voice pierced through my heart. 'Seema *bhabhi* knows where her loyalties are.'

'Jhanghir,' I whispered.

'Jhanghir, you've misunderstood . . .' Before Zain could finish, Jhanghir knocked him to the ground, then gingerly touched his fist. Screaming, I crouched by Zain, whilst Jhanghir turned around and walked away. 'Jhanghir!' I shouted, racing after him.

'Pana!' Stopping at Kala's scream, I turned to look at the back of the marquee. We all raced there and stopped when we bumped into Kala to stare at Taj and Pana in a compromising position. The scream Kala let out was blood curdling, one that caused Taj and Pana to scramble around, rearranging their clothes.

'What's happened? Who's fainted?' Chachijhi cried out, racing behind everyone.

Seeing Jhanghir storm away, I pushed past the crowds and ran after him.

'Maya, what's going on?' Amma called, seeing Jhanghir storm away.

'Nothing!' I shouted.

'Whom do I help? Where do I go?' Chachijhi cried out, running in circles, unsure of where to go.

'Ayesha! Tariq! Go after Maya!' Amma called out behind me.

'Jhanghir, wait!' I shouted, grabbing his arm to pull him to a stop in front of the house where Seema was getting into her BMW X6.

'Get your hand off me. We're done.'

'No, we're not,' I defended, refusing to let go of his arm.

'Let go . . .'

'What's going on here?' Tariq demanded, seeing Jhanghir's anger. 'Maya?'

'Bhai, go back inside . . .'

'Tell them, Maya.'

'Let's sort this out between us,' I pleaded as Jhanghir laughed at me.

'What happened?' Tariq insisted, pulling me round to him.

'She made out with Zain, my cousin,' Jhanghir filled in with a hateful smile.

'Maya?' Tariq *bhai* asked in disbelief.

'Tell him!' Jhanghir shouted, making Ayesha and I jump. Nodding slowly, I felt tears slip down my cheeks as Tariq *bhai* let go of me and walked back to the house.

'Bhai!' I called out, but it fell on deaf ears. Ayesha backed away, shaking her head, and I turned to Jhanghir.

'You're dead to me.' His tone was devoid of any emotion. 'Cover yourself, you look like a street walker.'

Realising that my *jilbab* had come loose, I pulled it tight around me over my belly-dancing outfit. Jhanghir jumped into the four-by-four beside Seema and, without a passing look in my direction, they drove off.

Numbly I returned to the back garden where Kala's screams, Pana's sobs and Baba's raised voice ruined a most beautiful celebration. With the night over, Hanna and Jana herded guests out of the marquee. Through the commotion, I slipped into the house, cleared the make-up from my face and changed into my pyjamas. Then I waited, cross legged and silent in the sitting room for the news to spread. The commotion over Taj and Pana went on for some time. The shouting, crying and sobbing came in waves and culminated in Kala slamming out of the house with her daughters in the late hours of the morning to return to Hove. Still, I sat and waited. When I heard Amma's cries, I knew that Tariq had spoken with Baba and Amma.

'This is the blow you've been saving!' Amma yelled as

she burst into the living room. The short, sharp slap left me numb compared to the pain I felt at losing Jhanghir.

'Shame!' she cried. 'You've brought shame on this house. You and your brother!' She slammed out of the room crying.

'Dry your tears up . . .'

'Baba . . .'

'I don't want to hear you, see you or think about you,' he stated, turning his back to me.

'Baba, please . . .'

'When your mother and I are ready to face you, we'll call you.'

'Baba, it was a mistake . . .'

'Get out.' It wasn't a shouted yell. The quiet instruction was powerful enough to have me in my room packing to go and stay with Jana for a few days. I spotted Taj's digital camera on my desk and scanned through the pictures on the screen. I stopped at the ones of Jhanghir and I smiling into the camera. I started crying. No words or thoughts came to mind beyond the fact that I had lost Jhanghir. Falling to the floor, I leaned against my bed and sobbed.

Value veils over vanities

The screams from the living room jerked me away. Rubbing my eyes, I winched against the light realising that I had fallen asleep crying. Then the scream pierced through the house again. It was Jana, and I raced downstairs to find her in a heap on the floor. Blood and water surrounded her.

'Jana!' I cried out as everyone surrounded her.

'The ambulance is here,' Tariq shouted, racing into the house.

'What's happening? Is she having the baby?' I shouted, grabbing Jamal *bhai* who looked lost at his wife's pain. The paramedics rushed in, gently eased her on to the trolley bed, raised the trolley and whisked her away to Hammersmith Hospital. Leaving Shireen *bhabhi* with Hamza, everyone jumped into one of the family cars and raced off after the ambulance. Taj and I sat together in his car, both lost in our own personal hell and with worry for Jana.

'She just started screaming, out of the blue, doubling over.'

Tears stung my eyes at the thought that the tension from our night had caused this. 'If anything happens . . .'

'Stop it, Maya.' Clearing my throat, I shook my head of the worst thought. 'She's having a baby; pray to God, they're both in good health.' The advice left us without any further conversation. Eleven of us raced through Hammersmith Hospital to Queen Charlotte's Hospital to find a shell-shocked Jamal *bhai*.

'There're complications, they're taking her into surgery straight away.' Amma fell on to the seat crying, Chachijhi comforted her and Baba sat down quietly.

'She's going to be OK, isn't she?' Hanna asked after her twin, brushing her tears away angrily. Jamal *bhai* shrugged.

'It could be Jana, it could be one of the babies,' he muttered, dragging his hand through his hair.

'She's going to be OK, isn't she?' Hanna demanded again, pushing her husband from her. 'She's my twin, I'm going to find out what the complication is, why are we all sitting here? There're five doctors here, we can help her, we can . . .' She lost steam and fell to the ground sobbing. I slipped out of the hospital unnoticed. I called Jhanghir on his mobile and left a message. I called Zain and left a message. I finally called Mrs Khan. 'I'm sorry, please don't hang up on me,' I begged. 'Jana, my sister, she's in hospital, it's bad, really bad . . . could you ask, please, I'm begging you, could you ask Jhanghir to come down?'

'Maya, tell me which hospital and ward Jana's at.' Through tears I gave Mrs Khan the details and then wiped away my tears before heading indoors to the waiting area. No one spoke. No one dared break the silence. Amma and Chachijhi recited prayers, Baba just sat ever so still. My sisters leaned against each other, numb with worry whilst my brothers and brothers-in-law paced the waiting room.

'Any news?' When Jhanghir strode into the waiting room, everyone stood up. 'Where is she?' Immediately

Jamal *bhai* went to him to update him and lead him through to the area we were forbidden from.

'Maya, he's a good doctor, isn't he?' Amma asked as fresh tears stung her eyes. I couldn't speak, so I nodded. 'He's going to make things OK, isn't he?' Again I nodded. She smiled at me through her tears, but I looked away ashamed of myself.

The following day, in the late afternoon we were told that Jana was in post-Caesarean recovery but that her twins were in intensive care under the care of Dr Shaw and counsel of Jhanghir. Every two hours Jhanghir appeared to give Jamal *bhai* an update, even if it was to tell him that there was little change. He was courteous to my parents and respectful to everyone else, but to him I was invisible.

'Maya, Taj, you both should go home,' Baba said. We looked at each other surprised. 'Jhanghir is helping us in spite of you. Don't embarrass us any further . . .'

'She's my sister and my nieces are in intensive care . . .'

'Ayesha will keep you posted. Taj, take your sister home.' Taj didn't try to argue with Baba, he looked like he had aged in one night. We didn't speak another word. Instead, we left quietly.

'Why did you do it?' Taj asked when we stepped into his car.

'It doesn't matter why, the fact is I did it,' I told him, staring ahead of me. 'I have to face the consequences of my actions. So do you.'

'I'm worried about Pana,' he confided as we cut through the A40. 'What if they take her back to Bangladesh to have a forced marriage? They could do that. I've heard that parents take their daughters back once their reputations have been tarnished . . . I've ruined her life.' Taj sounded so broken, I didn't have it in me to remind him that he once thought Bengali girls in Britain all had reputational issues. Not when he was the cause behind it.

'We screwed up,' I told him. Neither of us laughed, instead we stared ahead. 'What are you going to do?'

'Shit!' Taj muttered, speeding past Dad's house. 'That's Pana's dad's car. Kalu and Kala are here for answers.'

'Where are we going?' I asked as he raced away from the consequences of his actions.

'Starvin Marvin's!' Taj stated. 'It's an American diner on the A40; they have bottomless coffee which is a good thing because I'm not leaving until I know they're gone.' So, that's where we ended up. For most of the day, we sat in our booth, with two cups of coffee. Normally, getting endless top-ups for the price of one coffee would leave me smiling. But not today, today it left me as unimpressed as the waitress who topped up our large mugs. Today we didn't care. The only thing that mattered was receiving that call to tell us that our family would be fine.

Neither Taj nor I could hide from our actions for much longer. Early in the evening we received a call from Ayesha. She told us that the twins were out of danger, but still in intensive care, making slow but steady progress. Then she told us to return home to face the music. The ten-minute drive home did nothing to ease the tension when we found Kalu's car still parked outside our house.

'Taj, Maya.' Hearing Baba's call, we walked into the living room, to find our parents along with Tariq *bhai* and Ayesha sitting with Pana and her parents. Everyone looked exhausted and devastated. Pana looked like she hadn't stopped crying since being discovered and I wanted to hug her and tell her everything would be OK.

But I couldn't, not because I didn't have the courage, but because I didn't know that it would be. 'Sit down.'

'Kalu and Kala want answers,' Ayesha informed us. 'They want us to explain why this happened when Kalu sent his daughters to stay under the care and protection of Baba.'

The question hit Taj to the core. He knew that, as the man, his reputation in the medium term wouldn't be tarnished. But within the family, no one would trust my parents again with the care of their children.

'Taj,' Baba prompted but he shook his head and stayed silent.

'Maya, apparently you knew this was going on?' Ayesha prompted, surprising me with the knowledge.

'It's not Maya's fault, she warned both of us to behave,' Taj defended instantly. 'She told me off, and then said that if it didn't stop, the elders would be informed. This isn't my sister's fault.'

'It's somebody's fault, because half the Bengali community saw you compromising my daughter,' Kalu's words humiliated Pana, and she covered her face and started crying again.

'Bhaisaab, these things happen in today's generation. We must guide our children when they err.' Chachijhi, the mother of the once notoriously Loose Leila, advised, entering the room to sit next to me.

'Bhenjhi, I must ask you to stay quiet. My standards and my expectations of my sister and her husband appear to be higher than yours.' Chachijhi smarted at the return, but stayed quiet. 'Pana's at the age where she's getting *alaaps*, but who's going to want her now for their son after last night?' When no one spoke, I looked to Baba but he refused to justify what had happened. 'I'll have to take her back to Bangladesh to find her someone there, but word carries and it will get to Bangladesh

about this . . . this . . . sordid mess.' Pana's sobs inten-
sified at the prospects being laid before her.

'Say something!' Kala demanded of Baba and Amma.
They shook their heads with shame and looked at both of
us.

'You want me to defend the indefensible, Appal,'
Baba said, taking a deep breath.

'I'll marry Pana.' Taj's comment silenced the room.

'You must teach your boy when to speak, because this
is not the time for jokes.'

'I'm not joking; I'll marry Pana.'

I stared at my brother in shock and slowly shook my
head.

'Marriage is no light matter, Taj, it's a matter for
parents to talk about, for us to consult each other . . .'

'Listen, I screwed up last night. This isn't Pana's fault
and it's my responsibility to do the right thing.'

'You don't know what you're talking about,' Amma
said with disapproval. 'He's tired, we're all tired, none of
us, we're not thinking straight . . .'

'Why won't you listen to me?' Taj asked, leaning
forward. 'I'm a child in your eyes, but I won't let you take
Pana back to marry some stranger. I can't have that on my
conscience. I'm responsible for her reputation now, let
me honour that—' Before he could finish, Kalu stood up
and gathered Kala and Pana together.

'We're taking our leave, but my daughter's future is in
your hands . . .'

'I haven't finished . . .'

'Taj,' Baba warned as Taj stood up to stop them from
leaving.

'Don't take her back to Bangladesh,' he told Kalu,
who pushed past him. 'Baba, don't let them take Pana
back to Bangladesh,' Taj pleaded, but Baba sat silently on
the sofa as my cousin and her parents put their shoes on

to take their leave. 'Tariq *bhai*, do something, they can't take her back. I don't want to lose her, she's the girl I want to marry, I'll put things right.' Taj's words fell on deaf ears, and the sounds of Pana's sobs could be heard all the way to the car.

'Why won't anyone help me? They could take her back, I could lose her for ever . . .'

'Why are you begging now?' Amma asked with half a smile. 'We have protocols, we have traditions for a reason, and now you want to do the right thing?' The question silenced Taj.

'Taj's prepared to stand up to his error and do the right thing . . .'

'And you know all about doing the right thing?' Amma threw back at me. Shaking my head, I looked down as she laughed sarcastically.

'This can all be put right if you stand by Taj.' Without a word, Baba stood up and left the room. The snub silenced me.

'All this nonsense and drama!' Amma breathed out, gathering all the cups and saucers.

'All you had to do was tell us and we would've managed everything, everything, but you know better, huh? You all know better?'

'I didn't know I wanted to marry her . . .'

'So you thought you would try before you buy? Like your sister?' The question was aimed to shame and it hit the mark. 'For all of Jhanghir's family's snobbiness, they had no real criticism of Maya, and now, now can you imagine what they must be thinking? That's she's no better than a street girl . . .'

'Amma, leave Maya out of this,' Taj guided. 'Pana is—'

'You don't value our ways, we do not take what is not ours before the eyes of Allah. Now you face the consequences of your actions, and realise why the old ways are sometimes the best ways.' One by one everyone left the room, until Taj and I sat alone and in silence.

I spent the next few days at Ayesha's house. Most of the time I was alone. Samir *bhai* and Ayesha were both back at work, and then headed straight to the hospital to see Jana before spending the rest of the evening with our distraught parents. So I spent my days praying for forgiveness and asking Allah to give me the strength to face whatever he deemed was best for me. One mindless, pointless act had cost me my fiancé, family and friends – the dearest things to me. The only thing I clung to now was my faith. I spent a lot of time reading the Qur'an and Hadith, taking guidance on becoming a stronger, better person. My wedding was now less than three days away and I refused to cry about it. Everything connected to my wedding was back at my parents' house. My phone rang constantly with calls from family and friends asking about whether or not there was still a wedding, to which I simply answered yes. It wasn't a vain response, nor was it a hoped-for response. Only when Baba confirmed to our guests that the wedding was off, could I start relaying the message; until then the answer would simply remain *yes*. I had appointments for facial, waxing, threading, manicures and pedicures. All of which I attended. Being outside the Bengali community meant that my Indian beautician hadn't heard the news so we talked and laughed as if it were still happening. Each time I left the session, I would review the monies I had spent on the wedding minus all the deposits I would lose for late cancellation. With the remainder I began looking to put together a small deposit for a one-bedroom flat. It was time to get realistic about my future. I was numb about Jhanghir, indifferent about my wedding and accepting of the fact that my life was destined to be spent as a single, lonely, ageing Asian girl. Vanities were great for the outside persona, but once you peaked inside, your virtues were all you had. So I valued those. I put aside every dream, every hope and every plan. It was time for new dreams, new hopes and new plans. Ones that didn't centre around finding a man, having a wedding and wanting to get married.

Weddings are for life, not for one day

When I gathered enough courage, I visited the hospital. Loaded with baby boxes filled with Mama's & Papa's finest, I sought out Jana's private room. Peeking through the glass window, I breathed in relief to find her alone with Jamal *bhai*.

'You clean out the entire store?' Jana asked as I carted the bags into the room. Jamal *bhai* took the bags and boxes from me, and then left the room to give us time alone. I reached down to hug my Jana. She held me, crying and refusing to let me go, so I sat on the bed beside her and held her.

'Where've you been?' she asked, leaning back to look at me.

'Hiding out at Ayesha's,' I laughed. Jana gingerly lay back against her pillows, but held my hands. 'How are my nieces?' At my question, she fought to hold back her tears.

'They're coming on, but it's going to be a slow and steady process,' she stated. I listened as Jana explained what the complications were and how the team had worked through the night to save them. I wiped at my tears, as she told me how hard it was not to be able to hold them or touch them.

'They're fighters,' I told her, making her laugh through her tears. 'OK, seriously, look at the girls in our family; we totally rule things. They will be out of here before you know it and poor Jamal *bhai*! Can you imagine him being outnumbered by three women?' It was good to see Jana smile and I kept her laughing until she sat up. I stopped when she reached up to cup my face as tears spilled down her cheeks and she shook her head.

'Look at you! When was the last time you ate?' The truth was I didn't know, but I chuckled at her question. She touched my hair that fell out of the untidy knot, and I felt self-conscious in my black-rimmed glasses, dressed in jeans and knitted hoodie that had seen better days. 'Who's looking after you? . . .'

'Like I'm a kid that needs looking after?' I returned, but she didn't smile.

'Maya, what've you done?' Jana asked, pulling away from me to look down. 'Why now, after your dramatic proposal, dealing with all his family drama, after winning Jhanghir over in spite of all the odds, why now?' I met Jana's large tear-filled eyes and shook my head.

'I don't know . . .'

'What were you thinking? This was your big wedding to Jhanghir, you know, the great gorgeous, not forgetting *surgeon*, Jhanghir . . .'

'I've heard his name a couple of times . . .'

'Maya, this isn't funny. Weddings aren't for one day, Maya, even though it may feel like it before you get married. They're for life, weddings mark the start of your ever after, they're for life, and that's why we celebrate it . . .'

'I know, and I don't have any answers, that's the most

ridiculous thing. It happened, I wish it hadn't, but I . . . I messed up big time.' Jana read the confusion on my face and pulled me into a hug.

'I'm sorry,' she whispered, and I frowned at the first sign of affection since my life had unravelled. 'We'll work through it, I promise.' Clearing my throat, I pulled away and smiled.

'Jana?' Turning at the call from the door, we froze as we spotted Jhanghir's mother.

'Please come in,' Jana invited, and when Mrs Khan hesitated at my presence. I stood up and picked up my bag.

'I'll go and see the babies,' I told Jana with half a smile.

'They won't let you get into the ward of incubators, but you can see them through the glass wall. Jamal will show you, OK?' Nodding at Jana's instructions, I passed by Mrs Khan with a quick *salaam*. She returned in kind before going to sit next to Jana. Stepping outside the room, I leaned against the wall and took deep, long breaths. My heart was racing at the encounter with Jhanghir's mother, and I fought with myself as to what to do. Refusing to be cautious, I leaned back into the room.

'Can I have a quiet word?' I asked of her. When she looked embarrassed, I continued. 'Please.' When she nodded, I stepped back out and scrambled around to find the right thing to say. Mrs Khan joined me, looking regal in her cream headscarf and elegant *jilbab*.

'I owe you an apology . . .'

'No, you don't.' The crisp return told me she wasn't interested in apologies.

'Please hear me out. I'm not apologising to make things better or to get things back on track, but because I disappointed you. You've always been kind and honest with me and it's the least I can do, given the mess I've caused.'

Mrs Khan smiled and nodded. 'I appreciate your candidness, Maya, but if one per cent of what Seema has told us is true, then I'm afraid you've made grave mistakes and I'm not sure if there's a way back from those mistakes.' I riled at the mention of her daughter-in-law, but I kept my calm.

'I'm not looking for a way back. I can't forgive myself, so I'm not looking for forgiveness from others,' I explained as she frowned.

Jamal *bhai* arrived with coned ice creams, and started to back away. But we both caught him and Mrs Khan smiled and held the door open for him. I looked back at Mrs Khan, because it would be the last time I would see her.

'Thank you for always treating me like an individual, I'm sorry for all of this.' Before she could say anything, I *salaamed* her and walked away with tears in my eyes. Taking a deep breath, I asked the nurse to direct me to the babies, and I made my way to the section. Spraying my hands with sterile wash twice in the ultra-hygienic, ultra-secure zone, I smiled as I finally stood outside the glass partition and looked at the incubators where my nieces slept. I recited a number of prayers for them and then leaned my head against the glass, wishing I could hold them and protect them from the pains of life. I promised myself I would stay for a short while, but time slipped by unnoticed. I envied their new start, the fight they shared to beat all the challenges to get to life and living. Smiling, I felt like I had lost my spirit with my transgression and somehow had forgotten that I was still the old me, still the feisty, fortuitous girl who made the most of life. Shaking my head, that girl, that naïve, emotionally untouched innocent girl, no longer felt like me. I felt bruised by life, short changed by fate and exhausted with a life going nowhere. Taking a deep breath, I blew a kiss to each of my niece, and turned around to leave.

'Excuse me . . .'

Stopping, I stared at Jhanghir. He looked rough, pale, stubbled and angry.

'Excuse me,' he muttered, brushing past me. And suddenly, everything I was going to lose became real, felt achingly, painfully real.

'Jhanghir,' I whispered, wanting to double over with the sharp loss of us. 'Jhanghir,' I called making him stop to face me. He walked up to me and leaned in close.

'We're done . . .'

'Please let me explain . . .'

'I'm not interested. I'm here to check on the twins.'

'I'll wait,' I told him, wincing when he gripped my arm and marched me out of the secure unit, through the double doors and past the reception to leave me at the lifts. He opened up his wallet, grabbed all his notes and threw them at me.

'Now go away.' The sharp slap shocked us both and left us glaring at each other. His cheek reddened instantly and he touched it. A passing nurse picked up the money and handed it back to Jhanghir before stepping into the intensive care unit.

'How dare you make this about money . . .'

'It was always about the money . . .'

'It was never about the money,' I corrected. When the doors pinged open, he shoved me in. 'It was never about the money.'

'Oh yes, my mistake, it was about how you were living the high life with Zain while I slaved away like a mug in New York trying to build a home for us . . .'

'Enjoying the high life?' I asked in confusion.

'You've forgotten already?' Jhanghir threw back with a snort. 'You don't think I've seen the pictures from your nights in Mayfair clubs, on table tops, making out with strangers?'

'What?' I demanded, outraged at the image he painted.

'I'm not a frickin idiot, Maya, once I may have bought the innocent, good girl act, but not any more.' The doors pinged open and he took my arm again and led me out of the hospital. Slowly, it dawned on me where he would have got this; Seema and her pictures from the night out with her friends. I tried to wrench my arm free, but he gripped even harder and he stormed down to the car park.

'Let go of me!' I yelled, jerking my arm free. 'You believe that bitch Seema over me . . .'

'Be very careful how you talk about my family,' Jhanghir warned.

'You believe *her*? She's the one who ruined everything!' I shouted at him. 'No, don't touch me!' I shouted when he went to take my arm again. Jhanghir narrowed his eyes as I paced before him, trying to contain the fury within me. Unable to speak, I strode away in the opposite direction to him.

'It's easy to blame someone else, isn't it, Maya?' His words stopped me in my tracks. Turning around, I walked back to him frowning.

'What did you say?' I asked quietly as he folded his arms before him.

'You, blaming Seema *bhabhi*; it's an easy way not to face your mistakes . . .'

'Have you asked yourself what your beloved Seema *bhabhi* was doing at the club where she so readily took those pictures and why she waited until now to tell you?'

'Because I demanded she tell me everything after I caught your little tête-à-tête with Zain . . .'

'Otherwise she would have knowingly let you get married to a cavorting, loose, immoral woman?' My point hit home and Jhanghir massaged his stubble, lost for an answer.

'Why isn't Zain married, Jhanghir?' I stopped at his snort of derision.

'Well, by all means, get him to show up tomorrow and you can have your happy ever after . . .'

'Why hasn't he settled down?' I persisted, watching him narrow his eyes. 'Your father met Seema at a barbecue that Zain's parents threw. She and Zain were high school sweethearts, totally devoted to each other through university and first jobs. Then your dad rocks up, arranges a marriage for your brother for a cash-rich designer life, and it's goodbye, Zain . . .'

'You really should avoid getting your information from the Bengali grapevine . . .'

'I got this all from the horse's mouth, Jhanghir. You see, your sister-in-law can't stand to see anyone in love, she can't tolerate it . . .'

'She is not the wicked witch of the Khan family, Maya.'

'She's still in love with Zain and he's besotted with her. Why do you think they're always at the same places, Jhanghir?' He looked so uncomfortable but I was determined to make him face the truth. 'She asked Zain to flush me out, so that she could prove to everyone in your family that I wasn't the "good girl" you presented me to be.'

'She wouldn't do that.' Even to both our ears, his words lacked conviction.

'She did,' I stated, as he searched my eyes, struggling to make sense of everything.

'You kissed him, Maya. I was your fiancé, and I've barely touched you . . .'

'He kissed me after you pretty much walked away from me at the airport. Do you know many times I've asked myself why you're not interested in being intimate with me, why you never compliment me or get close to me? I feel so unattractive to you . . .'

'That's why you kissed my cousin . . .'

'He just kissed me, it just happened, and there's no excusing it. It lasted for—'

'I don't need details,' Jhanghir muttered through clenched jaw.

'You need to know the truth. It lasted for seconds, because it was wrong,' I told him.

'And the truth is, I knew it was going to happen.' I should have stayed quiet, but with nothing more to lose, this was the moment to get everything out in the open. 'I had a fiancé who called me a gold-digger and then literally disappeared on me before my wedding, and I desperately needed to feel attractive, to feel wanted . . .'

'So you got lonely?' he mocked with a dry laugh.

'I have earned my way through life and now suddenly the man, the only man, who's ever seen the kind of sacrifices I've made for my family to live comfortably tells me I'm marrying him because I'm nothing but a two-bit gold-digger. I didn't know who I was marrying any more; you had become a different man . . .'

'And the next time I'm knee-deep sorting out a financial black hole, are you going to cheat on me then too?' Jhanghir asked with a raised brow and an indifferent shrug.

'There won't be a next time, will there, Jhanghir?' I pointed out. He stopped and I smiled, not meaning to catch him out. 'It's OK, Jhanghir, I know we're done.'

'So why are you telling me all this?' he asked after a long silence.

'Because we should break up over the truth,' I told him. 'I've been so fixated with arranging this perfect Bollywood wedding with the man meant for me, that I haven't thought about the rest of our married life. And now that I think about it, I don't like the thought of forever feeling invisible, never being wanted or complimented or being included in life decisions that make our lives together better, even happier.' Jhanghir looked away at my words, frowning.

'Maybe we're just meant to be a maybe.' I nodded at his words as tears stung my eyes. I wanted him to reach out to me and pull me into a long hug and tell me that everything would be OK, but it didn't happen. We were stuck in that limbo, that place where people in love get stuck, which feels so hard to get out of that you doubt whether you have the energy to keep trying. 'I should get back to the twins.'

Nodding at his comment, I stepped back to let him pass. There were no back glances; with hands dug deep in his pockets, he headed back to the hospital. When you had nothing left to say, silence said it all. So much for amazing, heart-wrenching goodbyes.

I returned home to pick up my wedding folder. It contained all the numbers for my wedding organisers, decorators and suppliers as well as all the invited guests. It was midday, the time of day when Baba went for *jumah* at the mosque and Amma shopped with Shireen *bhabhi* in Ealing Road. Sitting on the stairs, I leafed through all the pages and looked at my scribbles, the cut-out images of styles, fashions and decorations. I swiped the tears that slid down my face and bit my lip until I was overcome by the loss. Covering my face, I sobbed into my hand, unable to stop at the realisation that everything had to be cancelled and the road to Jhanghir would be closed off for ever. I didn't hear the door open, but when Amma called me I looked up at her. She had tears in her eyes too, but she couldn't speak. Unable to bear the pain, I grabbed my folder and raced past her.

'Maya.' I didn't stop at her call, I kept running until I sat on the tube going into London. Staring out of the tube, I stopped myself thinking about all the times Jhanghir and I had had together. I didn't think about the fun we had had at university, the long line of *ristais* that led me to proposing to him, I didn't think about how we had danced together at my *mendhi*. Closing my eyes, I touched the diamond ring that Jhanghir had given me at our *paancini*. Looking at it, tears streamed down my face and I felt the futility of our loss. I found myself at Regent's Park mosque. I promised myself I'd make all the cancellations tomorrow when I was more composed. Making ablution in the women's section, I dried up before heading up to the women-only balcony. I spent the day in prayers. At *jumah*, I joined the congregation, otherwise I sat with my back against the wall reading the Qur'an. Late that evening, Tanya came and joined me. She didn't talk, so I leaned my head against her shoulder as we listened to a sermon.

I returned home later after performing evening prayers at the mosque. Letting myself in, I stopped when I faced my entire family.

'Is Jana OK?' I stopped when Zain stepped forward. 'Why is he here?'

'Maya, where have you been? We've been worried sick,' Amma cried as she wiped her eyes with her *asol*. 'We thought you were going to do something stupid . . .'

'Why is he here?' I repeated, looking to Tariq and

Ayesha. 'Get out, get out of here!' I shouted at him, opening the door to show him out.

'Maya, we know.' Stopping at Tariq's comment, I leaned my head against the door, exhausted. 'We know what happened . . .'

'Maya, I'm so sorry,' Zain said, stepping forward. 'I told them everything . . .'

'I don't care,' I whispered to myself.

'This is my fault, I should have put a stop to this a long time ago . . .'

'It doesn't matter,' I told him, pushing past everyone to walk into the living room. Dropping my bag on the floor, I switched on the TV and sat down to watch the latest developments in the celebratory world on the E! channel.

'Maya, everyone is here for you . . .'

'Please, I just . . . I can't deal with this . . .'

'What your sister is trying to tell you is that we can put things right, with Jhanghir, his mother, with the family,' Amma said, walking in to sit in front of me. I stared at her and then looked at everyone. Baba followed behind Shireen *bhabhi*, Zain and Tariq. 'I think we can go and speak with Jhanghir and his mother tonight. Zain will come with us and we can have the wedding the day after tomorrow.'

I listened to everyone trying to work out the best way to make things right again, the enthusiasm was palpable. Looking around, I tried to find Taj, but he wasn't there.

'Where's Taj?' I asked, bringing everyone to a stop.

'Don't worry about that boy, he's staying at Jana's house, rueing over what he did . . .'

'He should be here,' I said, causing everyone to frown at my request.

'Maya, we know you weren't at fault . . .'

'And that makes it OK to stop punishing me?' The

question made Amma gasp. 'We all make mistakes, we can't stop being a family because of that.'

'Maya, this is about you, your wedding and your future . . .'

'Jhanghir knows.' Amma quietened at my admission. 'I saw him at the hospital today, I told him what happened . . .'

'And so everything is fine, we have a wedding to prepare for.' Amma stopped when I shook my head. 'But it wasn't your fault, his sister-in-law set this up . . .'

'He's still blaming you. I'll go round and knock some sense into him,' Tariq muttered between gritted teeth.

'*Bhai*.' He stopped at my call, I looked at him. 'We're finished.'

'They didn't even have the decency to speak to us?' Baba mentioned, breaking his silence to look at me. 'He knows the truth, and yet he leaves you stranded with a wedding?'

'He may need time . . .'

'Time?' Baba bellowed, making everyone jump in fear. 'The wedding's the day after tomorrow, guests are calling on the hour, asking if there's a wedding to attend!'

'I'll call everyone tomorrow. I'll make the necessary cancellations . . .'

'You'll do no such thing. We have a wedding to attend and we will not hide from it.'

'Are you insane?' Amma demanded, looking at Baba as if he was insane. 'We can't turn up at a wedding without knowing if the groom's family will turn up . . .'

'We will not hide from the community. No, Maya will prove to the community that she's not the one in the wrong, that she has nothing to hide from . . .'

'He's gone mad, we can't do that, and everyone will be watching her . . .'

'Then everyone will see that she's not the one at

fault.' The debate took off around me, and I sat quietly indifferent to it all. Everyone fought to shout over the others to prove that they had the solution. Everyone was still intent on making it to the wedding day, but nobody got it that Jhanghir had decided that he didn't want to spend the rest of his tomorrows with me.

Cross the marriage line

The following morning the Malik family moved into strategy mode. Baba pulled together a delegation team including Tariq, Zain and Samir *bhai* to ambush Jhanghir at the hospital, after which they would go to speak to Mrs Khan. Images of Baba sitting on Jhanghir until he agreed to turn up at the wedding or Tariq forcing him to turn up ran through my mind but I shook my head at them. Amma, along with Chachijhi and Hanna, started working through the list of six hundred guests to confirm the details for the wedding and attendance levels. Shireen *bhabhi* spent the morning organising everyone's outfit for the wedding, along with accessories, shoes and bags so that there would be no last-minute panic searches for missing accessories. Hanna and Ayesha took the day off to get me prepared. After my shower, when I was dressed only in a short towel, they massaged olive oil on to my arms and legs before applying it to my hair. Yasmin arrived with the cake in sections to finish off the icing at my parents' house. And when Leila and Meena arrived, they rang the vendors and decorators to ensure that everything was as outlined in my wedding plans. Everyone was taking care of everything, leaving me with nothing to do. Closing my eyes, I listened to the sweet, soothing melodies of AR Rahman that filtered through the house, leaving my sisters to pamper me into a place halfway between slumber and sleep. When Baba and my brothers failed to return at lunch, everyone continued to work solidly, refusing to allow doubts to set in. Taj drove me down to Iver House with Leila and Ayesha. The venue manager met us and took meticulous notes at my instruction. I pointed out where the red carpet should go, where the camera man should stand, along with my main photographers, as well as the student photographers whom I had hired from the local photography school, to ensure that they acted like the sea of photographers at any Bollywood event. Then I moved on to explain the Bollywood stars seating plans.

'Bollywood stars?' he asked in confusion as I pulled out my map.

'Guests of the Khan family will sit on tables marked with Shah Rukh Khan faces and guests from the Malik family will sit on the Amitabh Bachan tables. The tables that surround the stage are for immediate family only; in essence, they are the VIP tables. Close friends will sit on Ashwariya Rai tables and everyone else can choose whether they want to sit on Amir Khan's table, Kajol's table or Priyanka Chopra's table.'

'Oh lord, she's making this work!' Leila laughed as she looked at the seating plan.

'This is a list of guests matching the table plan. Please pin it up on a board in the first-floor entrance balcony,' I said, handing him a laminated A2 plan. Walking down to the main hall, we discussed the position of the stage, the video interview corner where guests could leave messages against the backdrop of a film set, the photo corner for shining stars, and then the chocolate fountain fruit corner to keep the kids entertained. By the time we finished, it was time for us to head back and we returned to find that Baba had come back with the boys, downcast.

'Maya, you have a guest.' Turning towards the dining room, I looked at Shireen *bhabhi*, wondering if Jhanghir was in our home too. Seema stepped forward out of Shireen's shadow, looking pale and drawn. Dressed in a simple *shalwaar kameez*, with her hair dragged back from her face, she looked like she was ready to collapse. Nodding to Shireen, I watched my sister-in-law leave the room before walking into the dining room.

'He's left me,' she announced, when I sat down facing her.

'Jhanghir's brother?' I asked, not the slightest bit surprised.

'Zain,' Seema threw at me. 'You did it, you made him.'

'For your information, he made that decision when he realised what a scheming two-timing little—'

'Where do you get off spreading rumours about me to Jhanghir and his family?'

Stopping at her audacious question, I smiled at her.

'That's your style, Seema. I don't get the kicks you do from ruining people's lives, although it does give me some satisfaction to know that finally you've been dumped . . .'

'Dumped!' she mocked with a brittle laughter. 'Dumped! You think Jhanghir's brother is going to believe any of this?'

'I don't really care what he thinks . . .'

'I thought I should tell you that I'm moving back to New York to be closer to my husband and the family business,' she said with half a smile.

'You should've saved yourself the trouble . . .'

'Zain didn't choose you, you know,' Seema pointed out, raising her jaw defensively. I nodded and smiled sadly at her.

'You didn't choose Zain, Seema,' I reminded her as she fought between anger and tears.

'He doesn't love you; when I click my fingers he comes running. He wouldn't choose you over me. How could he? Look at you, look at what you come from . . .'

'Get out.'

Jumping at Baba's words, I shook my head at him before turning to Seema. 'I feel very sorry for you. You make out like you are some independent business-woman who's made it on her own, when that's so far from the truth. You sold out for money, but you did it by mistreating the only person who truly loves you. Instead of fighting for that, you sit here lecturing me about how you're better than me?' I told her, totally in control. 'If nothing else, I still have my integrity and you will forever live your life knowing that you sold yourself for money . . .'

'How dare you . . .'

'Not under my roof,' Baba pointed out, catching Seema's hand before she slapped me. 'It's time for you to get back under the rock you slithered out from,' he said, escorting her out of the room.

'How dare you manhandle me! I'm going to press charges against you, I'm going to file a lawsuit of harassment . . .'

'Tell someone who gives a crap,' Baba told her as he threw her purse and shoes out after her before slamming the door shut. He turned to find me watching him and dropped the grin on his face that told me how much satisfaction he had got from throwing Seema out of our house.

'Jhanghir didn't commit to tomorrow, did he?' I asked quietly. Baba shook his head and indicated for me to follow him into the living room. I followed him and watched him sit down and struggle to find the right words to speak. So, patiently, I waited.

'This week has changed my world upside down. Hearing what happened, it broke my heart to think my baby girl could do wrong. By my heart, Maya, I couldn't even look at you,' he confessed, so emotional that he had to clear his throat, but he looked up at me with determination. 'We're going to go to the wedding tomorrow . . .'

'No, Baba . . .'

'Maya, you have to trust me in this matter. For your future, you must go tomorrow.'

'They're meant to bring me my wedding dress, gold and—'

'We have everything you need. You'll wear your *bhabhi's* wedding sari and your own gold, if need be . . .'

'I'll be humiliated in front of six hundred people when Jhanghir fails to show up . . .'

'Six hundred people will see that you have nothing to hide and you were left stranded on your wedding day, only one person will come off badly from that and it won't be you . . .'

'I don't want people's pity.' Baba was preparing me for the worst, but I didn't know if I was strong enough to face it.

'You need to settle one day, you need to walk away from this untarnished.' Closing my eyes at Baba's words, I realised that in fact everyone was preparing themselves for the worst. 'You must be strong, you must act with your head, because your heart will hurt for a long time, my daughter.'

Tears streamed down my face at what was being asked of me. I shook my head and looked at Baba.

'I can't,' I whispered. 'I can't sit there, praying for Jhanghir to turn up, all the while knowing that he won't.'

'My daughter, you have strength in you that you have

no idea about,' Baba told me, taking my hand. 'Trust me, this is the right thing for your future.'

'What is all this gop shop? Maya has to pack, get her *mendhi* applied!' Chachijhi determined, storming into the living room. Wiping my tears away, I looked at Baba and Chachijhi, wondering how long they thought this charade would last. 'Come, no more wasting time,' she insisted.

'Maya.' Stopping at Baba's call, I turned to him. I felt as if my heart was breaking. Tears blurred my vision, but I took a deep breath and looked at him. 'If your courage fails you, trust me.'

I nodded. Chachijhi wiped away my tears and cupped my face to look straight at me. Her eyes were red with unshed tears.

'You must cross the line into marriage, Maya, even if marriage is not meant for you tomorrow.' Against my will, I nodded and smiled whilst wiping at my tears. It was the right thing to do.

Yesterday's girl is now a woman

Everyone turned up for my last night at home. Jana insisted Hanna had her permanently logged into Skype, Baba cooked up a storm, and my brothers prepared their cars with ribbons for the morning of the wedding. When Taj turned up with Kala, Kalu, Pana and the girls, I smiled with pride. My brother had grown up and he announced that another Malik wedding was to be planned. Leila turned up with her husband and mother-in-law, but also led in Meena and her husband Karim Jones. When silence descended at their arrival, I took Chachijhi's hand and led her forward. She looked at me with tears in her eyes and I nodded.

'Welcome,' she said, unconfidently in English. Meena broke into tears and fell into her mother's arms. There wasn't a dry eye in the house as mother and daughter were reunited. Seeing the gratitude in Karim's eyes, I nodded and laughed when Baba pulled him into a bear hug and led him into the kitchen to pile his plate high with royal chicken korma and pilau. I felt different, this was my home, my life and my family as I knew it. But I was no longer the girl desperately seeking the end of her singledom; that was yesterday's girl. Now, I felt like a woman with a future untold. I was calm where I had been flighty, I was composed, where I had been hyper, and I was more thoughtful of those around me.

'Maya.' Turning at Amma's call, I knew it was time. 'You have to pack.' Every set of eyes turned to me and I nodded with a small smile. My sisters were already in my room, emptying out my cupboards and drawers whilst Shireen *bhabhi* folded the items neatly. I sat on the floor where two large Samsonite cases lay empty and open. My cousins took to packing away my cosmetics, photo albums, books and all those things that made me me. Amma sat on the edge of the bed, every so often wiping at the tears that fell. One by one, I packed the items away, brushing away my tears as I made the transition from being a daughter into a woman who was about to become a wife. When Amma could no longer bear it, she ran out of the room.

'I'll go,' Ayesha said, stopping me as she fought back tears. Chachijhi smiled tearfully and indicated for me to continue. Every so often, we would stop and talk and there seemed to be no end to the supply of refreshments. Then we would go silent at the thought of finishing packing, and then, inevitably, one of us would start crying.

'Why is everyone so quiet? We're not mourning!' Jana shouted through Skype, making us all laugh through our tears. 'Can someone put some music on at least, if only to hide the sound of snorting snot and tears?'

Mana did as she asked and filled the house with old Indian classics that had us laughing, dancing and, more often than not, crying through the evening.

When we finished, we looked at my life packed up in four large cases. I had more than anyone had expected, but it now looked so very little.

'Your hands?!' Holding my hands up at Leila's scream, I stared at them and frowned.

'Oh my God, has she cut her wrists?' Amma cried out, running in from her room, having heard Leila's scream. 'Where is it?' she demanded, taking my hands and looking them all over slowly.

'No I haven't!' I retorted, wondering when all this high emotion would come to an end.

'Who's slit their wrists?' Jana demanded, making Zara hold the iPad so that she could see everything.

'No one,' I said, only to be drowned out by the thumping arrival of my father and brothers, who burst into the room.

'Where is she?' Baba came to a stop as everyone stared at me in confusion. Then everyone turned to look at Leila who laughed nervously.

'No *mendhi* . . . she hasn't got her wedding *mendhi* on.'

As a result, Amma thought it best if all the girls congregated in the floodlit garden where she laid out a large white sheet. 'It's the stress,' she explained. 'It makes girls do strange things,' she finished. It also allowed her to keep an eye on me from the kitchen and make sure that I was safely away from anything that could harm me, as if I would pre-empt my death like some heroines in a tragic Bollywood love story. Taj set up his stereo system, every so often the men would race out to the garden for some impromptu *bhangra*, whilst the girls applied *mendhi* in the lovely summer evening.

Sitting on a stool in a simple nude-coloured cotton shift *shalwaar kameez*, I held my left arm out as Leila started the long and intricate art of applying *mendhi* to my arm and hands. Tanya and Sakina turned up after work and whilst I couldn't move, they teased me endlessly about my big day, unaware of the uncertainty surrounding it. The conversation was as free-flowing as the food and when either stopped, the music and play-acting made up for it. We teased Pana about her up-coming *mendhi* and laughed when Taj came to her defence. Every so often Amma came out, finding some reason to feed me, kiss me or touch the top of my head. Each time she did, tears were shed. The next time she came out to feed me, Taj joined her and pretended to cry into her *sari*. We all laughed until Amma chased him around the garden with a *chapel*.

'They're here,' Hamza announced, coming to sit on my lap.

'Who's here?' Shireen *bhabhi* asked as Jana laughed through the iPad. Everyone turned to look at Jana.

'You guys are so slow, who do you think is left to turn up?' The unanimous silence was shattered when the elders and men scrambled to get to the front of the house. My heart raced. It was Jhanghir's family. Gripping Amma's hands with my free hand, I looked at her, terrified at what this latest event would bring. She wiped at my tears and smiled, barely able to contain her own worries. Ayesha leaned forward to pull my chiffon *dupatta* over my head when Baba walked back out into the garden. Mr Khan and Jhanghir both followed him, carrying huge, beautifully wrapped gift boxes. Mrs Khan stepped out, followed by Zain and several young women I failed to recognise. Taj and Tariq moved the garden table and, in an instant, it was covered with boxes of every shape, colour and size. Tears stung my eyes when I spotted Jhanghir. He smiled and nodded as I wiped them away. Amma, Chachijhi and Kala left me to embrace Mrs Khan.

'Don't move, Maya, let them come to you,' Jana advised before telling Mana to angle the iPad better so that she could see everything. Mr Khan took off his shoes at the edge of the white sheet and approached me with Mrs Khan by his side. I daren't speak for fear of saying the wrong thing or ruining the moment. Looking down modestly, Mrs Khan leaned down and lifted my chin.

'We will all be ready to receive you and welcome you into our family tomorrow,' she said tenderly, wiping away the tears that fell over my lashes, before leaning down to hug me.

'You're a brave woman, Maya,' Mr Khan stated, looking to Jhanghir with a proud smile. 'Jhanghir chose well.' Amma burst out crying and leaned into Baba's open arms as Mr Khan finally gave his blessing. 'Don't let your courage fail you tomorrow. You must be strong for your parents.' With a soft touch of my cheek, he turned to Baba and they walked into the house to talk elders' talk. Amma escorted Mrs Khan in, and was quickly followed by Kala and Chachijhi. Hanna and Pana tended to Jhanghir's female cousins. Tariq *bhai* kept Jhanghir busy, whilst Zain made his way to me.

'Keep it brief, keep it brief. We're almost at the last hurdle,' Jana whispered.

'I'm sorry . . .'

'Zain, thank you.'

He, along with everyone around me, stared at me open mouthed. 'You're welcome,' Zain replied in confusion. 'But why are you thanking me?'

'It takes a lot of backbone to face up to reality to make it better for everyone.' He stopped at my words and I knew he was still hurting from the end of his devotion to Seema. 'It gets better,' I said, nodding towards Sakina, who chided me for being so obvious.

Zain laughed and nodded.

'Keep me in your prayers,' he asked, and I nodded, patting him on the back when he reached out to hug me.

'How many times do I have to tell you to stay away from my wife!' Everyone gasped at Jhanghir's comment.

'She's not your wife yet!' Another round of gasps filled the garden.

'Here we go again,' Jana muttered. 'This girl never learns.'

'No, no, no! No hugging, not with that man!' Chachijhi cried out, *sari* hoicked up to her knees as she came running into the garden. I looked at Zain and then at Jhanghir and we burst out laughing. Sure enough, everyone followed, stopping Chachijhi dead in her tracks. Feeling silly, she laughed and straightened her sari.

'Chachijhi, take this man away. Keep him locked in doors, he's not safe to keep around unmarried women,' Jhanghir told her, making her giggle with laughter when Zain pulled her into a hug. With everyone watching Zain's antics, I looked to Jhanghir and found him watching me.

'No grand gestures OK? I'm doing her *mendhi*,' Leila muttered dryly when he crouched down before me and took the *mendhi* tube from Leila. 'What are you?'

'I'm writing my name . . .'

'You don't know how to . . .'

'I have to write my name into her palm in a way no one but fate can see,' he finished, never once dropping his gaze.

'This newly married besotted thing, it'll pass,' Leila pointed out, unimpressed. When she realised neither of us were paying her any attention, she left. Jhanghir looked down at my arm and I enjoyed the soft touch of his hands.

'I never compliment you because you are nothing less than beautiful to me,' he told me, concentrating on applying the *mendhi* with the slightest of movements. 'I don't sweet talk you, because it diminishes what we have to trivialities. Your spirit, your feistiness is what attracts me; I don't want an airheaded bimbo who's easily impressed with easy words.' I took in every detail of his face, his gorgeous, heavily lashed grey eyes, the soft tan complexion. 'I don't touch you or speak of touching you because I want all of God's blessing for our marriage, not his anger, not his wrath. I want a blessed life with you, Maya, and nothing less than that; no sneaky make-out session or back-seat grope is worth the blessings of waiting until marriage.'

'That is a man!' Jana announced loudly, breaking my moment with Jhanghir. He smiled at the interruption, but continued.

'I've written myself into your fate; whether you can see it or not, I'll always be here.' Looking down at my palm, I frowned, unable to see where amongst the intricate henna he had drawn in his name.

'You haven't—'

'Look closely.' Holding my hand up, I searched for his name but shook my head. I showed my palm to Hanna, Ayesha and Pana, yet no one could spot it.

'You're joking!' Pana stated, as Jhanghir shook his head. With the nozzle of the *mendhi* tube, he pointed to his name that was interwoven along my fate line.

'Even when you doubt me, I'm here,' he told me. I stared at him with half a smile, not happy, not ecstatic, something more than that, which left me so fully complete.

'Someone get the hose pipe out,' Hanna announced, making us all laugh. When he leaned up to hug me, everyone gasped.

'What, I can't hug my wife?' he asked, stopping mid-way.

'She's not your wife yet,' Tariq *bhai* pointed out,

causing a family 'ooh' to ripple around the garden. Jhanghir looked at me with a cocked brow, but I shook my head.

'Strangers can hug my wife—'

'Fiancée,' everyone corrected.

'. . . fiancée, but I can't touch her,' he muttered, stepping back with a wide grin. 'OK, OK, you guys have her for one more night, and then we'll see who tells who what they can do.'

Leila returned to take the *mendhi* tube from him as Mrs Khan returned with Amma and Chachijhi in tow. Mrs Khan got her nieces to bring all the gifts forward to place on the ground. With Jhanghir beside her, she opened up one box at a time, displaying many jewellery sets containing diamonds, rubies and pearls. One box was filled to the brim with the best of Decleor, Clinique and Bobbi Brown. There were several sheer chiffon *saris* and silk *shalwaar kameezes* with accessories to match. Boxes of *choories* in every possible colour were displayed.

'We thought this was more becoming for your wedding,' Mrs Khan said as she opened a large velvet box containing a gold set that would drown me. Turning to Jhanghir, I frowned.

'The set you chose, where is it?' I asked.

'But that's such a modest set, Maya; it was the best that Jhanghir could afford at the time . . .' Mrs Khan stopped when I shook my head and insisted on the original set Jhanghir had first picked out.

'That was good enough for me. Please, if you don't mind, I'd like to wear it.' Seeing Jhanghir smile, I met Mrs Khan's eyes and noted her approval.

'Very well,' she accepted as Chachijhi and Kala muttered how crazy I was at turning down a massive gold set.

'Jhanghir *bhetha*, why don't you go inside for this?' At his mother's encouragement, Jhanghir disappeared and Mrs Khan opened the last of the big boxes. A veritable sigh of awe emerged as she held up my wedding outfit. 'We liked it very much,' she said as everyone reached out to touch the ruby-red *lengha* set that was heavily embroidered in antique gold.

'Thank you, this is so much,' Amma said as everyone helped to pack the boxes away. Mrs Khan smiled at me before returning to the house again.

'Have I taught you nothing?' Jana asked from the iPad. 'If it's anything to do with gold, you always go BIG!' she shouted, making everyone collapse with laughter.

Jhanghir and his family stayed until the late hours of the night. When it was time to go, they came out into the floodlit garden to take their leave. In front of everyone, Jhanghir walked towards me, confirmed that it was past midnight, and then pulled me into a warm, loving embrace.

'It's our wedding day, and she's my wife,' he declared. No one protested. When the laughs turned into chuckles, Jhanghir leaned back and cupped my cheeks.

'Thank you for not giving up on me,' he said. I nodded at his words, and he partly smiled, forcing me to hold on to his look. 'I'll see you tomorrow, Mrs Khan.' I watched him leave, ignoring the winks and smiles of my friends and sisters around me.

'Mrs Khan, is it?' Refusing to rise to the teasing, I smiled. It was the first day of the rest of my life. Yesterday's single, lonely, ageing Asian girl was indeed gone. It was time to become a wife.

Zindaghi

There was no sleep that night. When it got too chilly
in the garden, everyone moved camp and set up
base in the dining room. Samir *bhai* and Taj had cleared
the room of furniture, and we sat around talking and
laughing through the night. With *mendhi* up to my mid-
arms and on top of my both my feet, I could barely move.
So I lay down on Amma's lap and listened to the conversation around me. Amma talked about her wedding day,
which set off every married woman to share her wedding
story. There were happy stories, sad stories and funny
stories. When some dropped off, others continued and
just when another tired lull in conversation emerged
someone would start up another line of conversation.
Several times Baba, Amma and Chachijhi encouraged
me to go up to my room to sleep, even telling me that I
would look sleep deprived on my wedding day, but
nothing would make me spend my last night alone
without my family. At one point, I gathered the gold gifts
I had bought for everyone in Dubai. To each of my
cousins, I gave a pair of gold earrings, and my sisters and
elders received gold necklaces each. I cried out when
they all surrounded me to give me a group hug. The

truth was that I was too excited to sleep. Jhanghir's words reverberated in my mind. I couldn't wait to see him and yet I wanted this night to go on for ever. When the first bird began to sing at sunrise, Baba called the *ikama*, rousing everyone awake to start the day with morning prayers. Those who didn't join in moved to the kitchen to start making breakfast. One by one those who wanted to pray performed ablution and then joined together to follow Baba in prayer. As we all made *duaa*, Baba asked for the day and our marriage to be blessed. Baba's emotional prayer moved many to tears. So when he finished, I waited as he came over to me.

'Are you ready, my daughter?' I nodded, looking at Baba through tear-filled eyes. 'Every new thing you do without your parents around, you must start with a prayer.' When he finished, I hugged him and held him. 'It's time for you to get ready.'

Then began the crazy day otherwise known as my wedding day. Waiting for the bathroom, I watched everyone run around in different stages of ready, rushing and hurrying as if time was racing away. My make-up artist arrived the minute I stepped out of the shower. I put on my wedding lingerie and then pulled on my robe around it. For the next two and half hours I sat still whilst I was moisturised, powdered and painted. I daren't look in the mirror and smiled when she gently applied the false eyelashes. Mana brought up refreshments and stopped for a moment to chat about the day ahead. My sisters, cousins and elders checked in between getting ready as the anticipation for my big moment was palpable and growing. The make-up artist started on my hair and took a further hour and a half to sweep it into an elegant Jennifer Lopez-inspired high bun wrapped around the base with two single braids. When she stepped aside, I stared at my reflection and gasped at the woman starring back. An ultra sleek, stunning model with wide kohled eyes, and stunning red pout stared back.

'Oh my goodness, what have you done?' I asked, turning my face in every angle, shocked by the transformation from being cute to being a stunner worthy of double takes.

'You don't like it?' the make-up artist asked, worried, and I broke out laughing.

'I love it, it looks stunning . . .'

'You make a beautiful bride,' she said, putting all her tools and brushes away. 'Wait.' She used industrial-strength hairspray until there was a literal cloud surrounding me. 'It sets hair and make-up.' She smiled. Coughing through the mist, I gave her the thumbs-up. She helped me slip on the red *chooris* until they reached midarm and then screwed on the wide *kara* bangles.

'You ready to put on your *lengha*?' At the question, I made a quick dash to the loo and then raced around the house making sure everyone was getting on OK. During my journey, I helped Amma neaten the pleats of her matt gold and cream *sari*, finished off Hanna's subtle eye make-up and pinned Pana into her Tiffany green *sari*,

'We've not finished you!' the make-up artist said, taking my arm to lead me back to my room. With a smile, I slipped on the four-inch Swarovski-encrusted single-strap heels before taking my robe off. 'I hope Mr Groom appreciates that body.'

'He'd better do; this is the result of four months of work-out and bad-food denial!' I returned.

'Oh, trust me, if your body doesn't do it for him, he's marrying the wrong sex!' Laughing at her comment, I stepped into the skirt and slipped it on over my hips. Zipping it into place, I held my arms out as she put the blouse on and hooked it into place. 'Bend over and hock your boobs up.' Doing as instructed, I smiled as the blouse fitted perfectly. 'You look stunning!' she breathed before leaning out of the room to call Amma and my sisters. Taking a deep breath I looked into the full-length mirror and stopped. Staring back at me was a bride-to-be, elegant, stunning and very, very ready.

'Oh!' Amma breathed out as Ayesha, Hanna and Shireen *bhabhi* piled into the room. 'Oh! Look at my baby,' Amma said through tearful eyes. Without a word, the make-up artist handed Amma my wedding necklace. Amma slipped the chainmail gold necklace around my neck and set it into place at the base of my neck. She then took the heavy oval earrings and put them into place before hooking the chain around my ear and into my hair. Sitting on the chair, I waited as she hooked the five-strand gold *bandi* chain along the centre of my head and then two strands along my hairline. The make-up artist then opened up the long and heavy chiffon *dupatta* that was embellished with heavy gems and intricate antique gold embroidery along the edge. Folding a section over my shoulder in front of me, she clipped and pinned it into place, and then, with Amma's help, she placed the other end of the *dupatta* ever so gently over my head to give me the modesty required of Asian brides. The make-up artist pinned the *dupatta* into place at the bun, whilst Amma neatened it so that the front of my hair and the gold *bandi* could be seen. Then they both stood back. I looked at Amma and saw her proud, tearful smile.

'You're ready,' she announced.

I don't know where the time went, but as soon as I was ready, my photographer arrived to take 'behind-the-scenes' family shots of the bride's final moments as a singleton. My cousins, all dressed in shades of green and gold *saris*, left early with my friends to receive the groom's party who, traditionally, arrived before the bride. Baba left with my brothers-in-law, leaving Amma, Chachijhi, Ayesha and Hanna behind to keep me company. When the house stood quiet for the first time in months, we sat looking at each other.

'No grand gestures,' Chachijhi advised as she massaged my arms. 'Just be the quiet, shy bride and don't smile too much; we don't want people to think you're forward . . .' and where she trailed off, Amma continued.

'No talking, OK? I know you can't stop bak-bakking, but today you're a different woman, you have to understand that talking and smiling is not good for a bride.'

'You enjoy your day,' Ayesha corrected them as she crouched before me to cup my cheeks with wide eyes brimming with tears.

'Make-up!' I reminded her quickly with a smile as I felt my eyes well up.

'My baby sister,' she whispered. 'Look at you, you're no longer my baby sister . . .'

'Make-up! Make-up!' I reminded her again as I fanned my hands before my eyes to dry them up. Laughing along with my family, we froze when the tooting of my wedding car blared from the street. Taking a deep breath, we stared at each other.

'It's time, it's time!' Hanna cried out, jumping up and then remembering to carry her iPad everywhere as Jana wanted to see everything. Amma and Chachijhi went into a tizzy about making sure all the doors and windows were locked and Ayesha and Hanna remembered to take the trays of rose petals and tea lights. The photographer snapped away like an annoying fly but I kept smiling.

With everything checked, I picked up my cascading bouquet of red and white roses and waited at the door. Amma whispered a quick prayer before indicating for me to step out with my right foot. Taj held down the horn of Jana's BMW X5 and his friends, in a troop of six to eight cars, followed suit, making our neighbours step outside to clap and congratulate me on the big day.

'We got two grand from Jhanghir *bhai*'s grand entrance!' he shouted from the car.

'And look at these!' he shouted, holding up a pair of *chapaals*.

'You stole Jhanghir's *chapaals*?' Amma cried as she smacked her forehead.

'He's barefoot and waiting for you, so get a move on!' Taj laughed, continuing to bleat his horn.

'I tell my children to stay traditional and they take it too far!' Amma muttered, tutting.

'But imagine, if Jhanghir has last-minute doubts, he can't run away!' Chachijhi said as we all chuckled at the thought of Jhanghir in his wedding finest waiting for his *chapaals*.

'Come on, Foopi, we've got a party to go to!' Hamza called from the car. Laughing, I sniffed back tears as Amma and my sisters led me towards the car and the rest of my life.

There was a receiving party waiting at Iver House when we arrived. To mark our arrival, the *dholkis* started playing their large Indian drums and my cousins lined up with trays of rose petals and tea lights to walk me in. My videographer and photographer positioned themselves and when they were ready, Baba arrived to help me out of the X5.

'You ready, my daughter?' Looking at the man who had raised me and loved me, I saw him smile. I copied his smile but I wanted to jump back into the car and drive home to the girl I was. When I nodded, a cheer went up and slowly my wedding group parted to let Baba and Amma lead me forward. Hamza led the way, beckoning us as if he only knew the way. Taking my steps along the red carpet, my brothers and sisters fell behind us along with my cousins. When we reached the photography sector, we stopped and smiled at the myriad of flashing lights, feeling like stars arriving for the Oscars. Baba spoke to the interviewer at the interview section, and then the *dholkis* ramped up as we found a ribbon blocking us from entering the reception area.

'Reverse gate,' Zain and Ed stated as the groom's wedding party danced around waiting for us to pay to get into the wedding, normally a long-standing tradition for the groom.

'No money, no partee!' Zain sang as the chaotic bartering began between both families. Putting my thumb and forefinger between my lips, I blew an ear-piercing whistle, bringing everyone to a freezing stop.

'So elegant,' Chachijhi muttered, shaking her head.

'Let's go home, everyone,' I suggested, turning around to lead my family out. The groom's party looked stunned when everyone turned around to leave, and with a quick turn I ripped the ribbon free and raised it above me as everyone cheered.

'So, so demure,' Chachijhi added, not the least bit surprised.

'That's the way to do it!' Taj bellowed as family members from all sides hugged and greeted each other. Baba left me with Amma and Mrs Khan, who looked gorgeous in a custom-made *jilbab* in cream Japanese raw silk with gold embroidery at the edges. They walked alongside me as we passed the reception area where our guests waited whilst being entertained by a classical

Indian singer who filled the venue with some of the old classic favourites. Spotting family and friends from every stage of my life, I smiled as we were bathed by flashing lights and calls to look in different directions. The hall looked amazing, lit up moodily with starlights and huge flower displays everywhere. Slowly we descended the stairs to the dining area. Don't trip, don't trip, I told myself when everyone followed, rushing to get to the stage where Jhanghir was waiting to receive me into his family. When we got to the base, our guests rushed past us to get the best vantage points. I spotted the stage beneath a canopy of gold and cream chiffon swags, and stopped at the breathtaking five-tiered wedding cake covered with white Belgian chocolate cigarillos and decorated with the reddest roses that stole your breath away. Taking a deep breath, I caught the winks of Yasmin and smiled whilst shaking my head. The soft dulcet song of 'Salaam' by Umrao Jaan filtered through and when a path was made for me to get to the stage, we stepped forward slowly. My heart raced and I was too scared to look at Jhanghir. Keeping my eyes lowered I smiled, realising I was acting like the perfect demure bride. Spotting his bare feet, I hid a smile behind my hand and stopped when he reached out to take my hand. Slowly I looked up, noticing how becoming he looked in his ivory cream *sharwaani*. Then, finally, I met his grey eyes and stopped. He smiled and cocked a brow. Refusing to smile back I lowered my gaze again, feeling my heart race at how gorgeous my husband-to-be looked. And yet I hesitated to take that step forward.

'Maya.'

Hearing Amma's encouragement, I took the first step and then joined him on the stage. Hamza rushed forward to give Jhanghir his *chapaals*.

'I stole them back for you!' he told everyone as he

helped Jhanghir to put them on. 'I got it, I did!'

Jhanghir lifted him up high as Hamza held a fist up like Pele had when he scored the winning goal in the world cup. Everyone laughed at Hamza's antics before he wriggled free to go and find his next adventure. Jhanghir looked round at me and as we stared at each other, the myriad flashlights took over.

'You ready, Mrs Khan?' he asked as we both turned side by side to smile at the cameras.

'I was born ready,' I returned.

'For tonight?' My smile dropped at his comment and I looked back at him, shocked. When I saw the light in his eyes, I burst out laughing. 'Look at Chachijhi,' he instructed, and in the sea of faces, I spotted Chachijhi making faces to get me to stop smiling. Instead, I gave her a wide smile and waved in her direction. Everyone looked at her and she stopped to wave back self-consciously. Jhanghir chuckled and led me to the golden chaise from where we would watch the evening unfold. Slowly everyone returned to their designated tables and pointed to the projected screens around the room that showed images of the guests arriving on the red carpet. And then Baba and Mr Khan arrived with the Imaam who sat beside Jhanghir. Taj handed the Imaam the mike and he proceeded to lead a prayer before giving a short talk on the virtues of marriage. I didn't dare look at Jhanghir when the Imaam turned to us. Our parents and brothers and sisters lined the stage to witness our vows.

'Jhanghir Khan, do you accept Maya Malik as your wife?' the Imaam asked as silence descended throughout the hall.

'I do,' Jhanghir accepted. And when the Imaam asked him twice more, as required, he accepted on both occasions.

'Maya Malik, do you accept Jhanghir Khan to be your

husband?' I looked up at Jhanghir, and every emotion, memory and event leading to this moment flashed through my mind. From the moment we met to the proposal, to the fear of losing him. And here he was, about to make my *alaap* absolute.

'Maya?' Seeing Jhanghir frown at my hesitation, I turned to my parents, who wiped away their tears, and then to my friends, who had supported me through every high and low moment.

'Maya?' Hearing Jhanghir's prompt, I looked at all our guests who would witness that I, Maya Malik, was officially about to leave singledom.

'Maya, say yes to the question!' Chachijhi whispered, loud enough for everyone to hear, but that didn't stop her from continuing. 'Say yes, this is the time to say yes . . .'

'You mustn't pressure the bride to agree,' the Imaam chided Chachijhi, who nodded at the Imaam, before vigorously and silently indicating for me to say yes.

'Maya Malik, do you accept Jhanghir Khan as your husband?' Turning back to the Imaam, I nodded. 'You have to speak,' he advised as if I was slow. 'So that your guests and witnesses can hear.'

'Now she's forgotten how to talk!' Kala muttered to Chachijhi, who quietened at the Imaam's stern stare like two naughty schoolgirls being told off.

'Maya Malik, do you accept Jhanghir Khan as your husband?'

'I do.' He didn't hear my whisper so he held the mike closer to me. 'I do.'

'*Mashallah!*' Chachijhi cried out, clasping her chest as if a burden had been lifted.

'Maya Malik, do you accept Jhanghir Khan as your husband?'

'I do.' I looked at Jhanghir and smiled slowly.

'Maya Malik, do you accept Jhanghir Khan as your husband?'

I looked to Jhanghir and smiled. 'Yes, yes, I do.' He grinned at my answer as our families congratulated each other at our union.

'The rings,' the Imaam guided. Tariq *bhai* and Zain stepped forward with the respective boxes as the videographer and cameramen rushed behind us to capture the moment. I took Jhanghir's platinum milgrain wedding band and slid it on to his wedding finger. Jhanghir pulled out the Tiffany legacy band and slowly edged it up to sit next to my engagement ring.

'I'm married,' I breathed, holding my hand up before me.

'Yes, in the eyes of Allah, and your witnesses and guests, it is my honour to declare you husband and wife!'

'I'm married!' I repeated loudly, making Jhanghir laugh at my announcement whilst Amma and Chachijhi shook their heads with muted smiles.

'*AllahuAkbar!*' Taj bellowed, rousing the guests to follow the cheer three times before everyone clapped. Our families hugged each other again, wiping away happy tears whilst clapping each other on the backs. The sweet song of 'Kabhi Kush Kabi Ghaam' filled the hall above the claps and cheers. And then, out of the blue, my cousins and brothers raced to the front of the stage to dance to a medley of the great Indian songs. They used Indian folk sticks, mixed *bhangra* with R'n'B, and stirred the guests with so much excitement in the hall that the cheers shook the walls. With everyone distracted, Baba oversaw us singing our Islamic wedding certificates, and Taj acted the brilliant MC, making everyone laugh and clap as he introduced speakers. As the five-course dinner began to get served, the guests were kept entertained by the funny speeches from our respective best friends and then the emotional speeches from family. And then, Jhanghir led me to the head table where we sat with our best friends to share our first meal as husband and wife.

'Hold back, Maya; we know it's food, but the cameras are on you!' Ed pointed out with a grin.

'Well, someone has to show the Neanderthal husband the etiquettes of fine dining.' Tanya threw back, coming to my defence like the best friend she was.

'Come now, everyone be on your best behaviour. Maya is now my wife and I won't have this mindless banter,' Jhanghir said as everyone frowned at him. 'Now, woman, serve me food and make sure it's big portions.' His friends burst out laughing, clapping him on the back as I calmed my friends and smiled eagerly like the dutiful wife. Taking his plate, I put it aside and put a whole tandoori roast chicken platter in front of him. Their smiles dropped and I stayed smiling with wide-eyed innocence.

'Is that a big enough portion for you, husband?' I asked, laughing when he nodded and chuckled along with his friends. My girls laughed loudly and in that moment, I caught a fleeting glance pass between Sakina and Zain. With terminator-style narrowed eyes, I looked between the two.

'You've only just got married, don't turn into an aunty just yet!' Sakina defended as I raised an innocent brow. Before I could continue, our guests started arriving at the table to congratulate us. Jhanghir and I stood to receive every well-wisher, feeling like stars shining bright with happiness.

'Shall we?' Jhanghir asked, holding his hand out.

'Shall we what?' I asked, frowning when he pointed towards the dance floor. Shocked and wide eyed at the idea that he was suggesting a first dance amongst a largely conservative crowd, I breathed out, 'Are you insane?'

'I meant shall we go and greet our guests?'

'Sure you did,' I threw back when he grinned at my reaction. I took his hand and we wandered between the tables, thanking everyone for their well wishes whilst smiling at their surprise at our 'forward' inter-active behaviour. Brides only moved from the stage to eat and use the loo, and once in a while they would crack a smile. So it felt wonderful that Jhanghir was leading me to a life that teased the boundaries. We walked to the photography corner where secret couples posed as the latest Bollywood stars, and then on to the interview section where family and friends left us messages for the future. Pushing past the queue of guests waiting to have their turn, Jhanghir pulled me in front of the camera, despite my protests.

'Mrs Khan, how are you doing?' he asked, mimicking Joey Tribbiani's infamous line. I shook my head, unsure of what to say and he leaned in close.

'No!' I breathed as the videographer stood back from the camera, shocked at Jhanghir's antics.

'She's got chicken in her teeth!'

Realising he was joking, I pushed him back and stormed off just as Taj called us back to the stage. Laughing, we returned to the stage where the regal family photos were to be taken. First we sat with Jhanghir's parents, then with his brother and a very quiet, subdued Seema, before having pictures taken with the extended family, including Rugman, Jhanghir's friends rushed the stage and posed in various styles of crazy whilst I laughed. Then my parents came to the stage. It was the first time I recognised the grief in my mother's eyes, and I hugged her close, telling her to be happy until Jhanghir pulled me away. We smiled through photos with my sisters, my brothers and then my extended family before my friends came on to the stage.

'Cake! Cake! Cake!' the guests chanted, tired of waiting for the photos to end, and so, encircled by family, we walked to the far corner of the stage to the cake. I hugged Yasmin who stood proudly with her fiancé Zachary and thanked her for the cake. And then, with Jhanghir, I picked up the cake cutter and we cut our first slice. He picked up a section to feed me, but when I opened my mouth, he pulled it back, making everyone laugh. When I turned away, he pulled me back to feed him and I reciprocated. Various members of the family stepped forward to feed us, a symbol of their blessing as well as for good fortune.

'Is he the One?' Claire, my ex-work colleague asked as we sliced up the cake to be distributed around.

'He'll do!' I said with a shrug. 'I waited and waited and, well, got bored of waiting and thought he'd do . . .'

'What is she saying?' Chachijhi whispered in disbelief to Kala. 'The girl, she's . . . she's . . . she's . . .'

'Maya, I'm Maya,' I said, holding up my hand to flash my brilliant ring at them. 'And I'm married,' I told them as I fed them a portion of the cake with a wide smile. I saw Ed murmur something into Jhanghir's ear before they checked their watches.

'OK, Mrs Khan, we're got to leave.' My smile dropped at Jhanghir's comment.

'What do you mean?' I asked, shaking my head.

'I took care of the honeymoon; we're going to the Maldives . . .'

'Maldives? We're going to the Maldives!' I cried out, clapping my hands with delight. 'We're going to the Maldives!' I told my friends, swirling around so that the skirt of my *lengha* swooshed around me.

'. . . but we've got to leave now to catch the flight.'

'But we can't leave our wedding . . .'

'It's time, Maya,' Jhanghir said before he turned to tell his family. Shaking my head, I continued cutting the cake and handing it out.

'Maya, it's time,' Baba said as he took the cake cutter from me. I'd been to more than a hundred Asian weddings, and I never understood why there were emotional breakdowns and rivers of tears shed when it came to the time for the bride to leave. Now it dawned on me. This was the moment when the rest of for ever started. Slowly, I shook my head and teared up.

'Baba . . .'

'Maya, I asked you to be strong.'

I threw my arms around him as tears streamed down my eyes. 'Go to your new life, my daughter.'

Jhanghir gently pulled me back, and I spotted Amma sitting down, crying into Chachijhi's arms. Jhanghir nodded and released my arm. Walking over to Amma, I crouched down and eased her round to face me.

'Are you going to let me go without saying goodbye . . .' Before I could finish, Amma threw her arms around me and sobbed.

'Goodbye!' Chachijhi threw out in disgust whilst wiping at her eyes. 'Goodbye? For ten years we've been trying to get rid of her and now we cry, now we—' Before she could finish Chachijhi burst into tears and fell into Kala's arms. Feeling Jhanghir's arms on my shoulders, I stood up, handing Amma over to Shireen *bhabhi* who hugged me briefly. I felt like my heart was shattering into a million pieces as, one by one, I kissed and hugged each member of my family. By the time I got to Ayesha, I was crying. Everywhere around me there were faces who had loved me, cared for me and harassed me in some way, and I was leaving them all behind to start a new life with Jhanghir in New York. The banter stopped as everyone turned towards the entrance. Turning around I saw Jana in a simple chiffon *shalwaar kameez* holding a tiny bundle. Running towards her, I stopped and stared down at my precious niece. 'This is Suraya,' Jana said through tears. 'We couldn't miss your wedding.' Wiping away my tears, I looked at Jamal *bhai* for my second niece.

'She's not strong enough yet.'

I nodded and looked back at my niece and then back at Jana. 'I have to go,' I whispered as she nodded and put her arm around me. 'I don't have to if you need me . . .'

'It's your time, Maya, you have to go.'

'We have to go.'

Hearing Jhanghir behind me, I shook my head and spun around so quickly that I fell against him. Jhanghir scooped me up into his arms. I burst into tears as he carried me out to our waiting car. Our families and friends rushed to escort us out.

'Call every day and make sure you don't go out without Jhanghir; New York is a dangerous place!' Kala cried.

'Have a baby quickly, Maya; you can come back to stay with us for three months!' Leila shouted out.

'Why are you talking about babies when it was that rumour that started all this wedding talk!' Chachijhi chided her with a clip to the back of the head.

'Make sure you keep a fire hydrant close by when you cook,' Leila's mother-in-law added. Through it all, I sobbed in Jhanghir's arms as he carried me to my future. A stream of cars followed us halfway to Heathrow until my family slowly and surely allowed me to start my new life with Jhanghir.

That's how my Bollywood wedding ended. The happiest of times was also the most poignant and saddest of times.

The transition from being somebody's daughter to becoming somebody's wife was celebrated and cried over in equal measure. The journey was one I craved for and doubted that I'd ever achieve. And now that I was married, I felt the loss of being just a daughter. I had stepped out of the *saya* of my parents towards a new life that waited ahead of me. One that I would build with Jhanghir, through good times and bad. I would have to learn the role of being a wife, and I knew that, before long, there would be talk about the virtues of being a mother too. There's be talk of babies, planning a family, and advice about the problems of delaying children until your mid-thirties. And that was all to come. For now, I held on to Jhanghir; he was all that I had. He had taken this single, lonely ageing Asian girl and turned her into a sophisticated married woman. Jhanghir Khan did indeed make my *alaap* absolute to give me my Bollywood wedding.